# ARMS AROUND
# FRANK
# RICHARDSON

# ARMS AROUND FRANK RICHARDSON

## Sylvia Colley

MUSWELL
PRESS

First published by Muswell Press in 2022

Typeset in Bembo by M Rules
Copyright © Sylvia Colley 2022

Sylvia Colley has asserted her right to be
identified as the author of this work in accordance
with the Copyright, Designs and Patents Act, 1988

A CIP catalogue record for this book is
available from the British Library

Printed and bound by
CPI Group (UK) Ltd, Croydon CR0 4YY.

ISBN: 9781739966096
eISBN: 9781739966072

Muswell Press
London N6 5HQ
www.muswell-press.co.uk

*To my grandchildren Harrison and Juliet*

# Prologue

In the evening he came to her with the pebbles in a jar. She was so pleased to see him.

'Look,' he said, and shook the pebbles into her hand and she laughed. 'Wonderful, aren't they? They were mine when I was little. I found them by the sea. And when you lick them! Look!' She put out her tongue to wet a pebble and it gleamed like liquid in the light.

'They're jewels,' he said, 'for my box.'

'Do you want a swing now?' she asked, but he didn't, and disappeared somewhere out of sight. She wandered through the garden to the tree where Henry had hung the swing and limply sat and swung, enjoying the warmth, before returning to the side of the house, where she found him lying on the grass with the pebble stuck in his throat.

Now, in the same wicker chair, she was leaning forward clasping around her middle, holding in the shock, imprisoned by the memories of the dream.

Then she heard Frank calling, 'Alice! What are you doing? Supper's ready.'

Heard his footsteps slow and long, crunching the path behind her. 'Everyone's waiting.'

And there he was, holding out his hand, lifting up her stick, which was balanced on the table.

'What's wrong? Are you not well? Is it your leg again?'

1

She took his hand as she licked tears from her lips and shook her head. 'It's just . . . that dream. Suddenly, out of nowhere.'

'Come on now, Alice.'

'But why, Frank? Why now?'

She took his arm; he carried her stick and they walked back up the path together.

1965–1969

# Frank

It was a thin, straggly Christmas tree, crooked in its plastic bucket. There were lights, small and flashing, and silver foil and baubles he had put on the tree with the help of Kitty, who could only reach the lower branches: she was four; he was seven and tall for his age.

There were presents: badly wrapped – but the red paper was enticing. The parcels crinkled and crackled irresistibly. Mum and Dad were drinking in the kitchen. Shouting. Kitty was in bed already. It was late and Frank was forgotten.

He sat fingering a parcel with his name scribbled across it: fingered at a corner, rubbed the thin paper into a hole, worried the edges wider and wider. He was absorbed with excitement, with curiosity. That was when his father opened the door; saw him and swore. That was when he picked him up by one arm and one leg and threw him across the room and his head caught the edge of the open door. He heard Mum screaming. 'Stop it, Pete. It's Christmas, for Christ's sake.' That's when his father swung his arm and sent Mum falling into the passageway; that was when he hit him over the head, kicked him, pulled him up by his school jumper and hurled him into the parcels. Frank hit the tree: it crashed over. Mum had run upstairs. He heard her shout to Kitty. Dad ran after her. Frank heard him kicking the bathroom door. 'Come out here, you bitch.' That was when his Dad fetched the kitchen

5

knife and waited with it in his hands: waited, sitting at the bottom of the stairs.

Frank was rigid, like stone. His head was bleeding, the blood running into his eyes. He shut his eyes, disappearing into himself, seeing the flashing lights behind his eyeballs: on-off, on-off. Then he heard Dad groaning, that horrible animal noise, and knew he was asleep. He felt the fear sickness creeping into his stomach. Then Mum came with Kitty and they went, all three, creeping and shaking to Aunty Phil's house. That was when they called the police who came, their blue lights flashing, and found his Dad asleep at the bottom of the stairs: the knife still in his hands.

A layer of dirty water sprawled across the middle of the play-ground. Two dinner ladies dragged out a small boy who had been kicking and splashing as if at the seaside and then put some red cones either side of the puddle to keep the children away. It had stopped raining, but it was grey, and the air was heavy with cold moisture. Frank watched water dripping off a gutter at one end of the school building He was standing on the edge of the playground, his arms tightly folded and his fists clenched under his armpits.

From where he stood, he could see into the infant-school playground and watched Kitty as she played skipping with a group of girls. He could hear her shrieks. How could she so happy? It was all so strange. They had only moved to a new house and come to this new school two weeks ago. Yet Kitty seemed quite settled. For him it was the constant pain in his stomach, the heavy ache, like a lump which wouldn't go away, however tightly he folded his arms. And then there was this horrible stinging all over his body and his tongue felt stiff and leathery, like a cat's. All he could do was to hold himself together and keep very still. Try to disappear; didn't want to be noticed: if they looked at him, they would know that Dad was in prison.

Mum had said he'd gone so that Dad could get over his drink problem, but when the social worker took him to visit that time, it seemed like a prison with the clinking of keys and all those gates and thick metal doors locking behind them, banging and echoing off the stone floors one after the other. But nobody actually said, and he was too frightened to ask. Never asked, 'Is Dad in prison?'

He was the only one who seemed to understand that really all this was his fault, Dad being in prison; he shouldn't have opened that parcel because he knew what Dad was like when he'd been drinking.

He hadn't wanted to visit, but they said Dad missed him and wanted to see him, so he should go and cheer him up. He asked, 'Can Kitty come too?' But Mum said she was too young. Mum kept saying things like, 'And I'll tell you one thing, he's never coming back here. Never, Frankie, not setting a foot. The police won't let him anyway, so that's that. So not to worry, Frankie.' But he wanted Dad to come home. He wanted him back. But he couldn't say.

He was nervous and he wet the bed the night before the visit and they had had to stop the coach so he could go to the toilet, but his pants were already damp, and he could smell himself.

He didn't recognise Dad straight away: he'd shaved off his moustache; his fair hair was shorter, and he looked young. He looked nice, like when he was happy. But Frank was shy and couldn't look at him. Not really look. He wanted Kitty there, not this social worker.

In the prison they had to sit the other side of the table and keep their hands on the top all the time. There were other people visiting and men in uniforms, who Dad called scouts, standing at either end of the lines, watching, making sure they didn't touch each other.

Dad seemed to be having a good time there. Seemed to be enjoying himself. He was doing carpentry – a doll's house

7

for Kitty, a table for home. He had wanted a multi-storey car park for his cars. But, beyond anything he could think, dream of, Dad had sent him a bike for his birthday. He treasured that bike above everything; it showed Dad loved him after all. Dad thought about him. The bike and Dad seemed to go together . . . in a good way.

Now Dad was leaning towards the social worker, smiling that smile. She was grinning, too. Sonia! He hated Sonia, always interfering in their lives. And he could tell she didn't really care about them; it was just a job. He didn't want to look at Dad and Sonia and so he watched the other visitors, the other men behind the tables, the woman further down who was crying.

'I'll be home soon, son.'

Standing now in the dripping, unfamiliar playground, Frank wished he could have said something to Dad. Tell him that he still got top marks in maths, that he was trying hard. But there never seemed to be the right moment to say anything. And there'd not been the right moment then to say he was sorry about the parcel. That he loved him.

He dreamed how he would make everything all right again when Dad did come home. He thought how Dad would get a good job and they could all live together and Mum would laugh. That's what he had dreamed, as they sat in the bus on their way home from the prison.

But it had all gone wrong, because when Dad did get out, he started drinking again and one night he came to the house, their old house, when he wasn't supposed to, and Mum wouldn't open the door to him, so he broke the downstairs windows. Mum ran upstairs with Kitty and Frank had just stood rigid in the front room among the shattered glass. Someone must have called the police because they came again and took Dad away. He clenched his fists under his arms. Mum should have let Dad in; she should have.

And now there was some court order and the social worker

had made them move here, to a different house and different school where Dad couldn't find them. But he couldn't bear the thought of Dad being all by himself.

Now, instead of Aunty Phil, they had Mr and Mrs Griffiths for neighbours. She smiled a lot and called everyone 'love'. She made Mum cups of tea and gave Kitty orangeade and biscuits.

Her name was Ruby. She said to Mum, 'Call me Ruby, Lynn.'

Mr Griffiths was a postman, so he was off early every morning on his bike. But he was home before they got back from school and always in his shed. Frank walked slowly past their gate so he could look and see into the shed when the door was open. Mr Griffiths was like Dad, in the way of doing carpentry. He wore an old, leather-looking apron and a cap on his head. Frank wanted to go into the shed, to look at the tools, to watch him working. He wondered what sort of things he made. He wanted to be like Dad. He wanted to do carpentry too.

Just yesterday, after school, he stopped by the gate and watched as Mr Griffiths seemed to be turning a chunk of wood on a machine that spun round. He was holding something like a knife to shape the wood as it turned. Frank opened the gate and walked up the path to the shed door and stood there, watching the wood chippings spin onto the floor at Mr Griffiths' feet. Then Mr Griffiths turned off a switch and the machine slowly came to a stop, and Mr Griffiths twisted round to see him standing there, adjusting the cap on his head as he took off his goggles. 'My pride and joy, this lathe,' he said, and patted the machine. 'I got it second-hand some years ago and look what it can do. How old are you, lad?'

'Nearly eleven.'

'Never too young to start learning. You'll do. Come round on Saturday and I'll show you how it works. OK, lad? '

'I'd like to do carpentry,' he remembered saying.

He was looking forward to that. And Mum was happy in

9

the new house. She painted her nails red and wore her skirts short. She'd taken up with an old boyfriend, Carl, who was spooky. Scary. And it was a shock to see Mum with someone else. It wasn't nice and he'd started wetting the bed again.

A teacher whose name he didn't know came out into the middle of the playground and lifted her arm up and down as she rang a brass bell. Everyone stood still and waited until she called each class to line up. But he was already standing still. When his class was called, he moved into the line and followed as they walked back into the school. He noticed the water was still dripping off the gutter.

He didn't want to stare. He didn't want to look. But the design of the entwined snakes, which twisted around the back of Carl's neck and down his arms until the fangs shot along the top of his hands like blue veins, haunted him: the inky blue snakes slithering down his thin white arms.

He was always there. Carl. And his battered blue Ford Cortina straddled their path and patch of grass in the front. Sometimes Carl went off in it but never said where he was going. He was on benefits, that's all Frank knew. Like Mum. She was on benefits and kids' allowance. She collected it from the post office every Friday. Then she bought loads of fags, a bottle of vodka and cans of beer. She even bought them sweets and they had sausages and chips from the fish and chip shop. Fridays were usually good days, but other days . . . Sometimes Mum stayed in bed with a headache and depression and then Frank would fetch her pills and make her tea. Carl hated it if she was in bed when he came in. 'Get up, you lazy cow,' he'd shout and then they'd fool around on the bed and Mum would laugh and they'd start drinking.

Carl touched Mum a lot. He saw. Saw his hands and dirty nails and the snake's fangs near to Mum, touching her, feeling her like an animal and he crunched inside. If Carl caught Frank's disgust, he'd get up from the kitchen table and thump him one. 'What you looking at then? Cunt.' And then go back to Mum and make her giggle. He had this crooked smile that hovered between a twitch and a grin. But when he was angry his narrow eyes became slits and the mouth spat out dirty things. Fists clenched, shoulders rounded, hunched, neck strained forward with veins pulsing. You could see the veins. Then Mum would leave the house and go out if she could. If she could get away. Then Frank would get the punch and the kick instead. But Mum always came home and Carl might slap her face, but mostly they would laugh and drink and pop pills and go all sleepy and soft and lie back on the bed or the sofa with their eyes closed.

Frank knew it was drugs. Carl got the drugs. Somehow.

Carl was small and thin with hair tied back in a ponytail He wore tight jeans that made him feel his crotch all the time and had this swaggering walk. Cool like a cowboy. He wants to be like a cowboy, Frank thought. And then, stupid, Carl put on a woolly hat, which he pulled over his ears when he went out. It was green with black dots all over and long tassels that hung down each side. Stupid. Dad would never wear anything so stupid. Sometimes Frank wanted to laugh out loud.

But it was Kitty that was worse. So much worse, you couldn't say how much worse. You couldn't say to anyone because you wouldn't know what to say exactly. Just that Carl was creepy with Kitty. Gave her sweets and sat her on his knee even though she'd try to pull away. Sat her on his knee and ran his hands up and down her legs. Kitty would try to laugh, try to make it into a joke, make some excuse, before pulling away if she could, and Carl would laugh and hang onto her just long enough. Just long enough to let her know he could do it anytime he wanted.

Then Carl wanted to be part of her bath time. He shut out Frank, shouting he was too old to bath with Kitty now. He pulled the bolt across the door. One evening Frank banged on the door. It wasn't right, something not right. It was whispery

11

and quiet with just the odd splash of water. It didn't sound like a proper bath time.

Afterwards Kitty always ran out of the bathroom with a funny kind of laugh. It was the laugh of playing tag when you are afraid of being caught. Just a game, but a bit of a scary game. Frank would watch her closely, but she ignored him, seemed silly and distant at first, and then she would sit on the sofa close to him sucking her thumb. And he was too frightened to ask her anything. But inside he was sickening, shaking. Perhaps he could be like Dad and take the kitchen knife. If Carl touched him with his horrible white hands and dirty nails. If Carl had secrets with Kitty. When he was especially anxious that there was something wicked happening, a grown-up thing, dirty, that you couldn't control, that might capture you too, he'd take out his bike, his precious bike that Dad had given him, and he'd cycle all around on the pavements because, 'Keep to the pavement, son,' Dad had said. Up streets he didn't really know. On and on. The air cleansing. He was away, away, from everything. Faster and faster. On his bike.

The only time he felt really safe, felt Kitty was safe, was when they were at school and even then sometimes Carl would try to keep Kitty at home, pretending she had a cold. But Mum didn't want that. Mum wanted them away at school. She wanted Carl to herself. Mum loved Carl the best. Even though Frank was the one who made her tea and fetched her pills and ran to the shops for her fags when she'd run out. She seemed bewitched. That was the word. Bewitched. But couldn't she see what was happening? Couldn't she know? At night, he bit his pillow to smother his groaning sobs of helplessness. Everything was wrong and he wanted Dad, no matter what he'd done. Wanted his own Dad. Dad would soon sort out Carl. Carl was a weedy thing compared with Dad. And he screamed into his pillow.

*

He stood rigid, squeezing himself into the corner of Mr Griffiths' shed, listening, as Carl brought down the iron crowbar onto his bike. The metallic thuds echoed in his head, electrocuting raw nerve endings; he felt the twisting of the spokes and the buckling of the wheels, the cracking and splintering of the frame. Blow after blow and the bike folding in on itself, broken, smashed, finished, and his body heaved with rage and terror. Kitty felt his body throb. She was kneeling among the powdery sawdust and clinging to one of his legs and he stood there, stiff in the shadows, breathing the smooth, sweet scent of Mr Griffiths' linseed oil.

It was dusk outside the shed, and the light from the broken street lamp flickered through the window, mottled with sawdust and flakes of woodchips. The creamy flakes and dust clung to their clothes and hair. Kitty was shaking; she was only wearing her cotton pyjamas. Frank knelt down beside her and put his arms round her. Listening. Mum's voice. Calling for them. Then speaking to Carl. His voice, shouting, laughing. He swore and the door banged shut. And then opened again and Mum crying again and muttering voices and footsteps and then the door shut. Mum shouting, 'Carl, Carl.' She was crying. Then nothing. Silence.

They'd been watching *Animal Magic* sitting on the sofa together, when they heard the back door open and his voice. Kitty had fled upstairs but Frank remained fixed and still, concentrating on the screen. Mum had gone out to get some fags.

'Where is she?' He came into the room, a can of lager already in his hand. Frank shrugged.

'Answer me, you little cunt.'

'Gone to get fags.'

'Gone to get fags,' Carl minced his voice in imitation. And then shouting, repeated. 'Gone to get fags, has she?' Then landed one on the side of his head, knocking him sideways, but he recovered his stillness, stubbornly refusing to show his fear. It angered Carl. 'Turn that bloody thing off.'

He hesitated. Carl was not his father to tell him what to do, to come into their lives, their family and tell them what to do. *Dad*, he prayed, *please come home*.

'Where's that little Kit?' Then, 'Gone upstairs, has she?' His Adam's apple bulged as he swallowed down the last of his beer. 'Right then! Time to pay that Kit a visit. I'll read her another story.' And he laughed, that laugh.

It was the way he said it, the look. Something you couldn't explain, but something was terribly wrong. Something was not right, not nice. It was the same feeling as he'd had before, but this evening the revulsion, the panic was strong enough to drive him upstairs to Kitty. Now he didn't want to remember Carl on her bed, hand under the covers, her lying unnatural, stiff, like at the doctor's. He didn't know, couldn't stop to think. Just hurled himself at Carl. And Kitty ran. Carl swore, knocked him down. Called him 'little cunt' and then went out for his bike. Frank found Kitty hiding behind the bathroom door and they had run here, through the gap in the fence, into Mr Griffiths' shed. And he knew they could never go back.

'I'll knock on the door in a minute.' He stood up in the shadows. He was twelve, old enough. Old enough to look after Kitty. Ever since Dad had gone and Mum had taken up with Carl, he'd looked after Kitty, protecting her, as far as he could, from the drunken blows, which came without warning, from Mum's mood swings, which were just as violent and unexpected. It was almost as if nothing had changed, yet it was worse, dark and hopeless. One thing only had changed. He, Frank, who had driven his father away, knew he was not to blame for Carl.

Suddenly the shed filled with a moving beam, a searchlight, and they heard the familiar cough and choke of Carl's car. The light moved away with the car.

'I'm going now,' he said. 'Come on, Kitty. Stand up.'

She had stopped crying and was just shaking. Frank put his nose against the grubby window. Their driveway was

14

empty. 'He's gone.' He opened the shed door and pushed Kitty out. Then, with his arm around her shoulders, they ran to the Griffiths' back door. The light was on in the kitchen, but the blind was down and they couldn't see if they were there. Frank banged on the door with the flat of his hand. Kitty's teeth were chattering now. He banged again and tried the handle. The door was locked. Then they heard Mr Griffiths' voice shouting, 'Coming, coming.' They saw his shadow behind the blind and heard the scrape of the bolt. The door opened. Mr Griffiths stood there, Mrs Griffiths behind, holding two dinner plates. She was in her dressing gown and slippers.

'Now what? Now what? Where the hell you been? In my shed. You're covered.'

Mrs Griffiths came closer. She was shaking her head.

Mr Griffiths stood away from the door. Frank pushed Kitty in first. And shut the door behind him. He pushed the bolt across. Terrified.

Specks of wood shaving and dust spotted their patched lino and he bent to pick it up, the flecks of dust, sweeping them into his hand.

'Leave that. Leave that now, forget it. I'll get the pan. Leave it and come here.' Mrs Griffiths put down the plates in the sink and sat down at the table, weary for them, weary eyes for all their trouble. She sighed. 'You're frozen. They're frozen, Stan. I'll get a cardie for her.'

Mr Griffiths moved them away from the door and checked the lock. 'What you young buggers up to, then? In trouble again?'

'Can we stay?'

'Stay? Stay where?'

'Stay here.'

'You can't do that.'

'But we can't go back.' He watched an ant running along a crack in the lino.

15

'Why ever not? You have to. It's where you live Why ever not?'

Frank tried to think. What could he say that they'd not heard a dozen times before? No one would believe him. They would think it must be his fault. It must be his fault. He couldn't say about Carl. He couldn't say what he thought he knew. What could he say exactly? After all, it was just this horrible feeling he had, which he couldn't put into words. It would sound silly. They would laugh at him, think him dirty. He couldn't look at Mr Griffiths, couldn't meet his eyes. He was ashamed.

Kitty had stopped crying and was sitting on Mrs Griffiths' lap, digging her hand into the biscuit tin, picking out a broken piece of chocolate biscuit. Mrs Griffiths laughed. 'Guess who eats all the chocolate ones?' she said, but she was looking at Mr Griffiths and her eyes were worried although she was laughing. Frank saw that her eyes said things.

'Let them stay a bit,' she said. 'Go and see what's up, Stan. They can watch some telly for a bit.'

Frank followed her into the front room. She had Kitty by the hand and moved a paper off the sofa so they could both sit down. It was cosy there and safe and Frank wanted to cry, but he fixed his eyes on the telly. He wanted so much for everything to be all right.

There was a draught when the kitchen door opened. Frank wondered about the ant, if Mr Griffiths had trodden on it by mistake. He got up and went into the kitchen. No one seemed to notice. The ant had gone. He stood, stupidly doing nothing, just standing, staring at the blind hanging across the back door. He lifted it up and tried to see around the corner to his front door. What would Mr Griffiths be saying to Mum? She had been drinking, he was sure of that. She was probably lying on the bed, her hand over her eyes. That's what she did when she had a headache. So often he had fetched a glass of water and the tablets for her. She had so many tablets for her headaches.

16

That's what she said. He was trying to picture her smiling and happy, when the door opened with a bang and Mr Griffiths pushed past him as if he were very angry.

'Get the ambulance, Ruby. Dial nine-nine-nine. Something's wrong.'

Frank ran through the open door and squeezed himself back through the hole in the fence. It was damp with night dew and his shoes let in the wet from the long grass. Their front door was open and he could see the light through gaps in the curtains.

'Mum,' he called. 'Mum!'

She was splayed out on the sofa. Legs apart and one arm hanging down the side. Her mouth was open and there was spit in the corners. He could smell the vomit, the nicotine and the gin. The smells whirled around his head and eyes. The bottle of pills he'd brought for her was on her lap, open, empty. He picked up a round, pink pill from the floor and put it carefully in the bottle. 'Aren't you well, Mum? Mum?' He pushed her hair out of her eyes. 'Sorry, Mum. I didn't mean to upset you.'

It was the same social worker who had taken him to see Dad in prison, the one who had moved them to this new house, the one who visited after Mum died, Sonia Marsh, but they always called her 'miss', like at school. Only Mum had called her Sonny, which was her nickname. Mum had been quite friendly with her and then called her a silly bitch when she had gone. He looked at her now and thought, Silly bitch. Silly bitch. She wore a short skirt above her knees and white pop socks. She had fat legs with a large brown mole on her thigh, which showed whenever she twisted in her chair. Silly bitch. Silly bitch. She looked tired and seemed to pick up on his feelings of anger and despair. She sat at Mr and Mrs Griffiths' kitchen table. Kitty was sitting on Mrs Griffiths' lap, head on her shoulder and sucking her thumb as usual. Too old to still be doing that. Mr Griffiths stood with his back to the sink his arms folded. Frank sat on the other chair at the table. It creaked when he moved and so he tried to keep still, but it was difficult because his legs felt all tingly and he had to keep wiggling his foot up and down, up and down.

'Your nan moved to Scotland, what – seven years ago?' she was saying.

There were some papers on the table, which she kept going through, as if looking for something she couldn't find. Time and again she riffled through them. Then there were moments of silence and his chair creaked.

She looked up. 'There isn't anyone else.' She seemed to be talking to her herself. She looked at Mrs Griffiths. 'I'll be contacting their grandmother,' she hesitated and turned again to one of the papers. 'Mrs Kincaid. I don't know if this is her current address. Is your Nan still living at 60 Dryden Road, do you know, Frank?' He didn't know. He hadn't seen Nan for years, could barely remember what she looked like, but she'd quarrelled with Mum. Over the drinking. He shook his head.

The woman sighed. 'Well, I'll do my best. She's the obvious person to have you now – if she will.'

He heard the words down a long tunnel. Kitty was asleep, still with her thumb in her mouth. Mr Griffiths shifted his position. Frank's foot rocked up, down, up, down, faster and faster.

'I'm sorry, Frank,' she was saying, 'you won't be able to be together. But it won't be long if your nan will have you. Otherwise we'll find you both a nice family. Don't worry,' she added, rather feebly.

But something swished up and through Frank: he was becoming his father – angry, violent. He jumped up from the table and ran to Kitty. 'No!' he was shouting. 'No. I won't. I won't. You can't make us. We want to stay here.'

Mr Griffiths had come across to him, put his arm round him, but Frank shook it off. Then seeing the faces, still and

18

staring around, seeing the hopelessness, he returned to the table, put his head into his arms, closed his eyes and held his breath. He wanted to die.

It was Kitty screaming that made him draw breath. Suddenly everything seemed to be moving, everyone talking. He couldn't hear the words, or focus clearly on the faces, just the turmoil. Sonia was getting up, picking up the papers, a frightened, helpless look on her face. Her short skirt was creased across her stomach. Then Mrs Griffiths was speaking. He heard her, not at once but suddenly, a little later: 'Can't they stay here until things are settled?'

Frank's yearning was too great, his control gone. He knelt by Mrs Griffiths, his head in her lap and sobbed. 'Please can we stay?'

# Alice

She was an erratic red dot: up, down, up and down across the expanse of wet sand. She skipped awkwardly, lopsidedly, the canvas shoe leaving a faint print, the heavy leather boot a deeper, darker hole; and all the time her voice piping and trilling; all the time, shouting against the wind, against the air-spitting rain; against the heavy breathing of the sea as it swelled and retreated. At times like this, when she was so happy, she never allowed her thin little legs, now frosted with goose bumps, nor her limp to deter her; the shortened leg was nothing more than an inconvenience. At this very moment she didn't care. She wanted to take armfuls of the bruised, swollen clouds, wanted to eat the granulated seed-heads of sand that squelched under her feet: somehow take it into herself. For her, the beach was bathed in magical purple lights and there was a life of endless breathing and movement. She couldn't explain. She had a thirst – a thirst that couldn't be quenched by drinks, just the inexplicable need to be part of everything, to do something with it; to say something about it, to share it, whatever it was.

And then at the edge of the jetty, where the foam fingered onto the sand, she saw the pebbles, shiny like syrup and rolling like liquid: shifting, jostling, reflecting the moving sky. She wanted to drink the liquid pebbles and she shrieked as she tumbled them into her plastic bucket. She had already dropped her spade.

'Be careful, Alice. Don't get wet. Don't get wet. Go and get her, Lawrence.'

But she had turned, shouting something they couldn't hear and, hopping, skipping, cantered back to them, holding high the bucket, her red plastic mac luminous in the cold. 'I'm thirsty. Look at these pebbles. I want to eat them.'

'Let me see.' Her da took the bucket.

'Show me too,' Ma said. 'Very nice. Look at all the colours.'

They were sitting among the long, tough grasses. Alice watched them move like water: like waves, darkening, lightening, first one way and then the other. It was cold but the windbreak helped.

'Please can we buy a house here. Please. So I can find pebbles every day. And look, there are boats. Da! You could have a boat. Not just motorbikes.'

'Are you cold, pet?' Ma asked. 'Pity about the weather.'

'But the kids are enjoying themselves. Look at Alistair. Look at him, Dot.'

Alistair was nine and concentrating on a complicated structure, always the same: a helter-skelter for ping-pong balls. He was quiet and absorbed as he patted the sand, as he forged a series of 'rabbit holes' for the balls. When he returned for his tea, he walked, solemnly, thoughtfully; he was a sturdy, dark-haired boy.

Although they had many days out to the seaside, it was this outing she always remembered.

When they got home to the bungalow, small and cream-coloured, two lattice windows either side of the front door; inside, brown and smelling of plants and dust and stale tobacco, she put her pebbles in a saucer of water to keep them shiny and placed them on the windowsill in the sitting room because it was sunnier there; she wanted to watch them change colour with the day, with the light, with the sky.

'Did you hear what she said about the clouds? Said they looked like big bruises. Did you hear that, Lawrence? I don't know how she could have thought of that, do you? For a child of six. What made you think of that, Alice?' And Alice had dissolved into rivers of giggles, looking up and exposing a missing tooth that the fairies had given her sixpence for.

For days she had struggled with her crayons: trying to get to the heart of the sea and clouds that day. What surprised them was her unexpected and unusual seriousness, her quiet hours of struggle. But her pictures were never right. One day she sobbed with frustration and disappointment. Had they been right, had they satisfied the thirst, she may never have become a painter, never have gone to art school; never met Henry.

'You've got more clouds than sea, Alice. Very purple and dark. Would you like a paint box if we go to the shops? Anything to keep you quiet!'

It was the beginning.


The three of them sat round the kitchen table, Da with his two allotment friends, Reg and Dennis; thick winter jackets, hats still on, scarves loosened and gloves stuffed into the tops of boots ,which leaned awkwardly against each other, like drunken friends, on the mat inside the kitchen door. The air was foggy with the steam from the kettle and the smoke from Reg's pipe. Drops made rivers down the clouded window. It was warm and muggy and the men clasped the blue-and-white mugs in red, cold hands.

The allotments ran along the back of the bungalows and all three had been out this Saturday to dig up leeks from the frozen ground and pick sprouts for the Christmas lunch. They sat round the kitchen table in silence, sucking up the tea and grunting. Through the open kitchen door Alice squealed and coughed in turn. Giggles turned into rasping wheezes and breathless coughs.

Reg scowled. 'She's got that asthma again, then?'

Lawrence pushed a strand of damp dark hair out of his eyes.

22

'It's that kitten. Makes her cough, man, but nothing will stop her. She loves that thing better than anything.'

Dennis moved his stockinged feet under the table and shook his head.

'We should probably have been stronger, but what could you do? Comes home from school, late of course, so Dot is worried sick again, and there she stands with that Jo, the Wilkinson girl, and the kitten wrapped up like a baby. Alice just decided on her own. Went back to their place after school and said we wouldn't mind. Said she knew for sure we really wouldn't' mind. What could you do? Dot gave her a ticking-off, but she's hopeless over that child.'

Reg was still frowning. 'Won't do her any harm, surely.'

There was another shriek from the hallway and then the thumps of unbalanced, breathless running, followed by another bout of coughing.

'Alice!'

She appeared in the doorway, the kitten jumping at a conker on a piece of string, her face scarlet with the coughing, but even before the choking had subsided, her face had broken into a wide and impish smile. Her green eyes gleamed with naughtiness and her lips turned up at the corners into such a smile it made them smile with her.

Reg stretched out his arm. 'Come here, Pixie, show me this kitten, then. What's its name? Come on, then.'

She bent to pick up the kitten; held it out towards him. 'Pebbles. She's naughty little Pebbles, aren't you?'

Reg pulled Alice towards him and put his arm round her. 'Pebbles, aye?'

'Like my pebbles. She's like them with all these patches. Like my ones in the saucer. Didn't we, Da. Didn't we think so?'

She looked at Lawrence and then burst out laughing, doubling her body into Reg's lap. Then the coughing began, and he patted her back as she lifted a scarlet face towards him. The kitten had escaped into the hall.

She pulled away and limped after her. 'I'll show you.'

'You should put that blasted pipe out, Reg. When she's around.' Dennis leaned towards him with a whisper. He pulled off the woollen hat he only wore on the allotments and rubbed the bobbles between his swollen fingers. His thin, sandy hair stood up in spikes, caught by the hat as he took it off, opened the back door and knocked out his pipe against the wall. He fingered the tips of the fir tree propped up against the window. 'That tree's grown a bit since last year, Lawrence. How much more digging up will it take?' He shut the door against the bitter air.

The sun had fallen low behind the allotments and threw long shadows across the gardens. The sky was reddening and gave the frost a strange pinkish glow in the dusk.

Lawrence turned towards the window. Outside the branches scratched against the glass.

Then they heard the shout of anguish and Alice sobbing loudly outside the door.

'What now?' Lawrence widened the door to see her and she stood there whining into the kitten's fur.

'What is it, Alice, for heaven's sake, what is it now?'

Her head hung low and she shook with the sobs.

'Where are my pebbles? My pebbles have gone. They're not there anymore. Ma's thrown them away.' She wailed even more loudly, and the men stared helplessly.

'Don't be silly, Alice. Ma wouldn't have at all, you know that. Come here. Don't be silly. She only put them away for now, for Christmas with all the cards and things. Stop crying and look in that drawer.' Alice looked up. Silent. Watched as Da fished the bag of pebbles from the kitchen drawer. He held them up.

Dennis sighed and slumped back in his chair. 'There now, you see. What a fuss.'

She took the bag and, opening it, held it out for them all to see.

'See! Look! I told you. Browny, white and blackish. Yellowy, just like Pebbles is.' She stared at their faces and burst out laughing.

'Reet now! And we've got summet to show you now. Look there.' Reg pointed to the window and the branches of the Christmas tree.

'The Christmas tree!'

'Yes.' The men grinned.

'Is it last year's? I liked it last year, Da.'

He nodded.

'Can we put it up now? Can I put the fairy on the top? You promised.

1972–1974

# Alice

M a had said, 'Come on now, Alice, don't be silly. You know you need it.'

But it was too late, for she had flung her stick across the hallway and it landed with a crack against Alistair's bedroom door. She watched it fall onto the carpet and then threw herself against the front door, half sobbing, half laughing. Muffled words. 'I don't want to be a barometer.'

Now she sat on the playground seat and watched girls from her class looking at her sideways, nudging, giving a laugh and then moving off; boys kicking a ball around. Younger girls lined up to jump over a rope. 'My mother said that I never should play with a gypsy in the wood. If I did, she'd sure to say . . .' She added to herself, '. . . naughty little girl to disobey. One, two, three, OUT.' Then the next one had a go and it started all over again. She sat and watched. Jason, who had left his group of boys, was shouting, grinning and coming towards her. 'Give us your stick, Alice. Go on.'

She held on as hard as she could but he ripped it out of her hands with, 'You're a cripple,' fading into the playground noise. She watched him hold up the stick, swing it round as the others, whooping with excitement, ran to it like a magnet. She watched as Jason and Martin each held an end, while the others clung on behind, like a tug of war. There were more on Martin's end because he had more friends than Jason. With hands around waists, they held on and spun faster and faster, screaming until one let go and they all fell in heaps to the ground and the stick struck and bounced and rolled to a stop. Alice laughed then. The stick was always a source of fun; it had their names scratched and scrawled all over the wooden surface, as if it were a leg plaster. She watched Jason strolling away from trouble rather deceitfully as Miss Jennings appeared from nowhere. I thought he liked me, she thought.

Miss Jennings was not amused. She picked up Isabel, who was now crying with a graze, so Alice stopped laughing as Miss Jennings approached with Isabel in one hand and the stick in the other.

'Alice. I think we've had this conversation before, haven't we? This is not a toy.' She handed her the stick. As they moved off, Isabel spat in a whisper, 'Spastic.'

'Go to hell.'

Isabel whined. 'Miss Jennings, Alice said go to hell.'

They stopped abruptly. 'Did you, Alice – tell Isabel to go to hell?'

'She said spastic to me first.'

'Did you, Isabel? Did you say that to Alice?'

'No'

'You did, Isabel.'

'I didn't.'

'She did.'

'Right!' said Miss Jennings. 'I think we'll have a little talk about this. Both go in and wait in the classroom.'

Alice sat at her table, waiting. Isabel stood by Miss Jennings's desk, eyeing Alice with spite and then every so often turning her back.

It was Alistair who had told her to say, 'Go to hell.' 'If any of the kids tease you about your limp,' he said, 'don't let them see you upset, just tell them to go to hell.'

Alice loved that; it sounded so strong, so sort of 'I don't care', so, sort of 'You don't bother me-ish'. But it was difficult

30

to explain to Miss Jennings, especially as 'Go to hell, Isabel' sounded like a rhyme made up especially for her, which it wasn't; the rhyme was an accident. But Alice thought it was good and wanted to remember to tell it when she got home. 'Go to hell, Isabel.' She could say it to Jason, even, leaving off the Isabel bit. Just, 'Go to hell, Jason,' next time he snatched her stick away. Jason had asked her to his party; she thought they were friends. Probably because I'm a cripple, she thought, she didn't very often get invited to parties and things, and had been so happy taking the invitation home and putting it on the mantelpiece. Now he was saying things and playing with the others. Alice couldn't understand at all.

Miss Jennings didn't seem to understand either. She was cross with both of them and Isabel still gave Alice that smug look, with a toss of the head, and walked a bossy sort of walk when Miss Jennings wasn't looking.

But her real best friend, Jo, said later, 'They don't mean it, Alice. Jason really likes you a lot. Pity about the wax in his ears, though.' And they both hid their laughter behind their hands.

Jason Bodimead was a big boy, awkward and scruffy, and it was true, he had sticky-out ears with wax. In some ways Alice was sorry for him. Mostly he was kind to her.

Although she was only ten like Alice, Jo seemed so much older, perhaps because she lived on a farm, which Alice passed back and forth on the school bus.

At lunchtime Jo asked, 'Hey Al. Do you want to come home after school? We can catch the ponies; you can ride Little Polo again.'

She would have liked to very much. She was just the same as everyone else when she was on Little Polo. You couldn't' tell any difference when she walked and trotted on him.

She learned to groom and clean hooves, to clean the tack and to put on the halter and saddle – with some help. The stables were full of straw and smelled of dung, and loose bits were trapped in the gullies that ran along each side of the barn. There were rope bags of hay in the stalls but Little Polo and Toffee were usually in the fields behind the house and had to be caught. She would stand by the stone wall and watch Jo catch the ponies and lead them back to the barn. She was big and strong for her age. Short-cropped dark hair, a round, cheerful face, large legs, sturdy. Alice begged Da for a pony like Polo.

'I can't today,' she said. 'I think I couldn't do it – today.'

'We'll get out the steps. Mam can put you on like before.'

'Can I come when my hip is better? When the weather changes, I expect it'll be all right. Da says I'm like a barometer. When the weather is damp or cold my hip is worse. Tomorrow, perhaps.

# Frank

He watched Stan Griffiths pushing his bike up the path and heard the squeak of the gate. It was dark, frost on the ground, but Stan was doing some relief work, as it was extra busy at Christmas time. He cycled to the sorting office and then picked up a proper post office bike. 'Don't know what's wrong with mine,' he used to grumble.

Now he was awake properly, he realised he was damp again and the bottom sheet soiled, even though he'd started wearing pants under his pyjamas. He was ashamed; it was just another thing to feel anxious about. Everything worried him and especially Kitty. She wasn't easy nowadays. Moody, rude and no matter how often he warned her they could be sent away if they were any trouble, she didn't seem to care.

He removed his soiled clothes and rammed then into the plastic bag that he normally put his football kit in and then shoved it into the bottom of his school bag. He had done this before. And then after school he would go to the launderette. He had pocket money and enough for a wash and dry. He would have to spend the extra on a dry because he couldn't hang the things out on the line for everyone to see.

His bedroom was a small box room. They'd been kind and turned out all their rubbish to make room for his bed from the other house, the chest of drawers and the stool. There wasn't room for anything else, but Stan had put up a rail across the corner for hanging space as well as some shelves above his bed for books. They had even bought some cheap carpet, red with black flecks. Nearly five years it had been his room, and all that time he kept it immaculately tidy; was obsessive about it. And Kitty, who had the bigger room, the room they had slept in that first night, was so untidy. He often went in and tidied up after her and made her bed.

'Kitty,' he had said, 'they're not young anymore. Don't be a trouble to them,' and the thought of it all, the dread, being sent away somewhere else, made him put his face in his hands. This was home now. But Kitty would just shrug and shout, 'So what?'

She liked Ruby Griffiths and often cuddled up to her on the sofa with her thumb in her mouth, calling her Aunty Ruby, and they would both giggle. She acted like a baby at times, although she was nearly thirteen and wearing mini-skirts and wedged shoes whenever she could get away with it. Another family had moved into his real home, next door, not long after ... a fat woman and three children and her husband, who was a car mechanic. He ignored them, blanking them out so he could cut himself off from the memories, the image of Mum in the doorway, the front room with the sofa. Everything. He tried blanking out his ongoing nightmare. Carl. It helped to imagine Dad in the garden, tousled blond hair, brown and strong, kicking a ball about.

Once he saw Kitty in the garden rocking the baby in its pram and talking to the boy. He hated that. And no one to tell. Even Andy at school didn't know that much about them; he never spoke about any of it.

At school they all had their own lockers with a key, because there had been stealing and so lockers were provided. He arrived early that morning, anxious about his soiled clothes. He shoved the plastic bag far back in his locker, behind his football boots and some books. It was all done before the others began pouring in and then Andy, last as usual.

Andy was easy and talkative; Frank didn't have to think what to say. All he had to do was listen. Unlike him, whose best effort to look 'cool' were his flared jeans and tightly fitting top, Andy was really trendy with his large round glasses and hippy-style hair; long to the back of his collar with what he described as 'flower-power bangs but short enough not to get in my eyes'. Strands of his hair flopped up and down if he ever ran, which was seldom, for Andy only ambled in a casual, relaxed way, which Frank found annoying at times. Andy didn't believe in sports and constantly quoted Oscar Wilde's quip, *If I feel I should exercise, I lie down until the feeling has gone away!* It was quite funny the first time.

The one thing he was definitely better at than Andy was football, and he was popular with the team because being tall and strong and with an obsessive determination not to be beaten by the ball made him a good goalie. Andy, on the other hand, was highly respected as an *ACADEMIC*, something whispered just loud enough behind his back and Frank therefore always questioned why Andy picked him for a friend. It helped a lot, though. Gave him some street cred, which he reckoned he could do with. Yet they were opposites, he and Andy; Andy never stopped talking for one thing, while Frank tried to be to be chatty. He did try, but it was a struggle, that's all he knew. Yep! They were different all right.

'I fancy being a political commentator,' Andy had announced that afternoon as they walked out through the school gates. 'Picking the bones out of politicians. Rhetoric here, rhetoric there. You should listen to Robin Day on the radio. He gets listeners to ask questions of politicians. He doesn't half give them a hard time. He's actually rude sometimes. Not sure how he gets away with it. But it's very popular, that programme. Do you ever listen to stuff like that? Verbal games! Just up my street.'

'We don't have on much radio. Just Ruby won't miss *The Archers*.'

'Oh yeah! Story of country folk.'

'She thinks it's real life! Stan spoils it for her sometimes by telling her it's all acted. I wish he wouldn't do that. I don't know why he does.'

'I shall vote Labour first chance I get. Can't stand ...' and Andy proceeded to lift his shoulders up and down with a, 'Ho, ho, ho!'

'What's all that about?'

Andy was laughing. 'Heath. Edward Heath. Can't stand the man. His laugh! When laughs he always lifts his shoulders up and down with his ho-ho-hos. Should've stuck to conducting. Not that I think he's 'specially good at that either. Anyway, HO, HO, HO!' And again, he lifted his shoulders in time. 'Look out for his laugh next time he's on telly. I'm definitely voting Labour when I get the chance. What about you? '

Frank shrugged. 'Don't know much about it.'

'You must vote. Women died to get the vote.'

'Oh yeah! Well, there's not a lot you can do if you're dead.'

'Oh, very droll!'

Andy loved the word 'droll' and that made Frank smile. 'All I know is that you'll do something that involves talking A LOT, that's for sure.'

'And you? You never say.'

'Me?' He didn't want to say, but Andy was staring at him through his huge round glasses.

'Look, I'll do carpentry. Try and make some good stuff.'

'But you should go to university. Do maths. You could do.'

'Yeah!' He shuffled his school bag onto the other shoulder. 'Thing is, I have to work. Get a job and earn money. Can't depend on ...'

'Now I think of it, you could become a master carpenter. A member of the guild. You know, the guilds in London. Bloody hell! I mean, that could be *formidable*.'

'Yeah well ... it's just Stan has got me interested. And my dad, he was clever at making things.'

'Your dad? You've never mentioned him before.'

'No, well. Anyway, Stan's keen for me to do an apprentice-ship at Tallinn's Architectural Joinery over at Eastheath and they give you a fortnight off every so often to go to college to do City and Guilds. Which I shall do, if I can. Stan says it's the best. So I don't think it'll be university for me. Need to earn money.'

'Shame, Franko. I can't wait to go. Not least to get away from home and *les parents*, who drive me up the proverbial.'

'I don't know if I'll get there. It's oversubscribed. Have to show samples of my work and my drawings. Dutton's helping too. Dutton's good. He's going to recommend me I think.'

'Buggery, hell, dude! That's the most you've said for at least six months. You'll be an artisan, Franko. Lot to be said for that. Arts and Crafts movement, cathedral carvings and chancel screens. I'll come to your first exhibition.' Andy swung his school bag at Frank's shoulder and in return Frank swung his bag with some force, hitting Andy in the back and making him skip quick steps forward to keep his balance.

And they both laughed.

'You know, I'd ask you home. I've thought about it. But things are a bit on the tricky side at the moment. Between the parents. Atmosphere not that great for visitors. That's why I haven't invited you. I'd really like to though, Franko. Ask you over.'

'That's OK. I never even thought of it,' he said, and remembered that one time he'd been 'asked over' he'd hated every minute. All the other boys, and it was just boys then, larking around, noisy butting and boxing, private jokes everyone else seemed to get but him and eating so much. He was completely out of it. In fact, they didn't seem to know he was there at all. Kitty had been to a few 'parties', though and come back with a goody bag of sweets and a piece of birth-day cake. She was happy enough. She made friends easily, it seemed to him. Ruby always made sure she looked neat, brushed her hair and when she was in junior school took her and collected her. Now, when she was 'asked over', she went on her own.

After school, Kitty was supposed to wait for him outside the gates but sometimes she wandered off with a gang of friends. All the wrong sort, he thought. Once he caught her smoking and went mad at her, but she just laughed and went off without him. Christ! She was only thirteen. What the hell was going on? Please God not drugs. Not drugs again. And her school skirt was too short. Showing off those long legs, which she was now kicking up and down as she sat on the wall, waiting for him.

Andy had pointed towards her. 'You'll have to watch her, methinks.'

'I fucking well know.'

Andy elbowed him. 'Cheer up, Franko. The sky's not falling in yet, is it, boyo?'

It was the Welsh accent this time, just marginally better than his Scottish effort, which would go something like, 'It's allreet, mae laddie. The burrrns and brrrrays are still there.' Great rolling of the Rs. 'Och ay and away with ee.' Oh! It was terrible! He might become a political commentator but he'd never make it as a mimic!

He lobbed an empty bottle along with his toe and there was a moment's silence. He wanted to tell Andy. But it was awkward. He mumbled, 'It's just . . .'

'Go on, dude.'

'Well.' He turned to see if Andy was listening. 'Well, the thing is . . . well, Ruby and Stan are getting on, you know. Stan's about to retire. It could be difficult for them . . . for them – you know – to keep us on. Moneywise. I have to get a job, so we're no trouble. But Kitty, she doesn't think.' He gave the bottle a hard kick into the gutter.

'Don't worry! They'll not let you go, Franko Not what I

hear. You're family now. Don't worry, boyo.'And then out of the blue punched Frank in the ribs with, 'Life can really fuck things up, if you ask me.'

They'd reached the crossroads and Andy turned left now. 'See you!' He raised a hand before crossing the road. 'See you tomorrow.'

Kitty was there, sitting on the wall, swinging her legs and smoking. He pulled her off the wall. 'Where did you get that?'

She pursed her lips, blowing smoke towards him. 'Mind your own bloody business. For Christ's sake, Frankie.'

Without a word Frank knocked the fag out of her mouth and stamped on it.

She yelled, 'Fuck you!' and, clenching her fist, raised her hand to hit him, but he caught her by the wrist.

She struggled, but his hold was tight. Tears filled her eyes. 'You're hurting me, Frankie! You're hurting me.'

He let her go and, in one movement, swept her into his arms, where she stood shaking and sobbing. He wanted to say, 'I love you, Kitty.'

But she was saying, 'Don't keep saying that all the time, Frank. I'm so sick of it.'

'What?'

'What you're always saying, always going on about, always telling me all the time.'

'What? Keep on what?'

'About being bloody lucky, bloody grateful and being bloody tidy and bloody no trouble and saying thank you all the time and bloody not eating too much and not eating Stan's bloody chocolate biscuits and all stuff like that all the bloody time.' She began to run down the road.

He called after her.' I've got to go to the launderette.'

She stopped running and turned. 'So what?'

'Will you go straight back, then? Kitty, don't mess about. I won't be long.'

*

39

He sat hypnotised as the washing swirled round in the machine. Watched the soap's frothy bubbles explode against the glass. The Carpenters' 'Yesterday Once More' was playing from somewhere. A young woman had picked an *Intro* magazine from the pile in the corner. Large black letters on the cover read: *Free Instant Eyeliner.* One thing Kitty really didn't need with her thick black lashes and blue eyes, but which of course she would love. She was dark like Mum, but with Dad's blue eyes. Frank's eyes were brown like Mum's.

It was usually quiet at this time of day. He fiddled with some lose change in his pocket and wondered whether to go next door and pinch a Mars bar. His normal pattern was to buy one and then to put another in his pocket. He didn't know why he did it. Why he stole things. Not from friends or from locker rooms, but from shops. Small things: a packet of screws, a little red torch and then the batteries, spare bulbs. He stole bags of Turkish delight and took it back to Ruby. Turkish delight was her very favourite. He couldn't do it often. Just sometimes. In Smiths he took a book off the bestseller table. Had no idea what it was, never read it, just dumped it in one of the street bins on his way home.

Mr Griffiths would be home by now and Frank knew he would be in his shed working on the table he was making for their sitting room. Made from maple, the top was oval and he'd carved a piecrust pattern round the edge. He would expect Frank to go and see him, to continue working on the box he was making. Frank was relaxed and easy handling the tools, making something useful – even special – out of plain, rough pieces of wood. It took his mind off everything else.

Last week Stan had taught him to French polish, practising on an odd piece of wood. First, he had to put a wodge of cotton wool into the middle of a piece of cotton sheet about the size of a handkerchief. Then he had to gather up all the edges and twist them round and round until the cotton wool formed a ball inside. He watched as Stan poured French polish into an old cup, adding a couple of drops of linseed oil and mixing it round before soaking the cotton-wool ball in the liquid. When it had soaked up enough and was not dripping, Stan showed him how to quickly run the cotton-wool ball across the unfinished wood, going round in circles, and Frank watched the pale mat of the wood darken into a rich glossy finish, its true colour and grain revealed. He found that really exciting.

'Now you do it.' And Stan watched as he, copying Stan, laid on several coats before leaving it to finally soak in and dry.

'You're a natural,' Stan said. 'Do that apprenticeship. Get really good at a trade, like carpentry and you'll never go short, and what's more, you can be your own boss. Not like me, tied to the PO for God knows how many years. Too many, that's all I know. No! You aim to be your own boss, Frank, lad.'

When they were working together, he often imagined Stan was his dad. It was strange that Dad did carpentry in prison. He could have been just as good as Stan, but Frank didn't even know where he was now. Out of prison, but disappeared. They'd never even had a birthday card. But the presence of Stan's back, small and solid, his warm breath from his puffing comforted him and, sometimes, if he closed his eyes, he could imagine Dad working beside him among the wood chippings and the linseed oil.

The young woman reading the magazine pulled a blue plastic basket off the pile in the corner and put it in front of her machine, which was spinning violently. She smiled at Frank and stood, her arms folded, waiting. 'Takes for ever when you're in a hurry,' she said and laughed. Frank wasn't sure if he had answered her or nodded or shown any sign that he had heard her. He wasn't sure. Sometimes it was only in his head. He looked away and stared at his pants and pyjamas twisting and turning. She was pretty; he couldn't imagine her swearing, screaming, crying so terribly. Always having headaches, like Mum. Drugs and stuff.

Her voice had a laugh in it. 'Yours is done.'

'Yes, thanks.'

'Want a basket, then? You can have this.'

'It's OK.'

He waited until her back was turned before he pulled his washing out of the machine and stuffed it back into the plastic bag. There was a lot he had to keep secret, had to hide. That's why he couldn't say too much to anyone.

# Henry

The library smelled of wax and linseed oil, and the floors, mellow and worn by ages of feet, reflected the moving shapes from outside the windows. The edges of the bookshelves shone with polish, highlighting the dust motes, which showered in clouds as books were replaced or removed by the keen, the studious, the academic. Henry glanced at them with self-pitying spite, telling himself that this serious attention to work was pathetic. If he yawned it would show his indifference.

In front of him on the library table where he had been sent to do his revision were his history books. Opened on the pages about the Thirty Years War, the Treaty of Utrecht. He ignored them and allowed the tip of his pencil to shape the outline of a grey gelding, shading the muscular haunches and highlighted the gleaming body. He had the horse exactly in his mind, could remember the long head, the classically arched neck, the tapered legs. Ever since Aunt Lola had taken him to the Cheltenham races he had been struck by the beauty of horses, the shapes and colours. He wasn't so interested in the racing world, the crowds, the noise, the gesticulating bookies, but he was excited by the horses and their riders. For once he actually experienced some kind of enthusiasm and, with it, unexpected energy. Even some, well ... could you call it happiness?

He had always doodled, sketched and painted in a casual,

disinterested sort of way; art was the only thing he got good marks for at school, which he expected and took entirely for granted and was depressed by how he was, in his mind, misjudged and underestimated in everything else.

Now, instead of revising his history, he recaptured the gelding. His pencil lifted the legs into the gallop, the head forward, the tail flying out behind, the jockey leaning across the straining neck.

'That's bloody good, Bancroft.'

Henry barely lifted his head but raised a hand in what appeared to be dismissive thanks. Yet secretly he thrived on praise. It was the one thing he needed. Now he'd started on the bay mare. This time the horse looked at him, head slightly sideways, ears forward, questioning, proud.

Suddenly, the library door opened and Mr Radcliffe stood in the doorway, black gown billowing. He held Henry with a withering look as he put his hand over his drawing, furtively pulling over his history book to hide it.

'Get on, Bancroft. You're nor here for the good of your health. You know the situation.' He slammed the heavy door shut.

The situation. Henry gazed out of the window. At Stowe no one left with just one A level. And the only A level he was sure to get was art. Since going to the races, he had decided to do art and, to please his parents, had agreed to go to Newcastle University, which ran a course that seemed vaguely reasonable. But no one at Stow school left with only one A level. Even two were considered a 'pretty poor show indeed'. But one? The only subject that made sense, went quite well with art, was history – he could see that – but this sort of history was absolute rubbish. The Thirty Years War he couldn't care less about. But he had to do it and get at least a B grade. Not a chance! He was not like brother Robert, who fulfilled everything the school and the parents could possibly want. He was studying for his O levels and taking about a thousand – all with predicted A grades, of course. He told himself he must be fond of Rob because he was his brother, but they had nothing in common and, frankly, despite Robert's obvious gifts, Henry always felt superior, that although he was mis-understood and undervalued, he knew inside himself that he was special. Just needed the odd dose of praise to keep the depression at bay. Luckily, Mother and Father were relatively indifferent to their sons' work at school; so long as neither was expelled and they 'kept their noses clean', they were content.

Everyone thought Father was a charming man – loving company, fair-minded and generous – and he was a bit of a media personality, who spoke on the radio and from time to time was interviewed on television. The family listened and watched, sometimes only out of duty. Henry never did. And he was amazed at his mother's generosity towards this man who always stole the limelight. She was shy and liked her own company, which she had most of the time, as she shut the door to her study and wrote her stories for teenage girls. She got them published too, but often nobody in the family thought it that special. It was a bit like baking a nice cake – well done, but nothing to go overboard about. She was a writer and that was that. Her sons had always been somewhat distracting. He couldn't remember her ever hugging him.

He knew he would have to cheat. To get the right grade. As he had been gazing out of the window it had become clear to him: he would have to cheat and really it was in a very fair cause. The school would not be disgraced, his parents would not have to raise an eyebrow and he would set off on his paint-ing career. It was morally justified in his case. He turned back to his history book. Gregson was on the other table writing something or other, and Smithy, short for Corbett-Smith, was leaning against a bookshelf, a huge red book in his hands; he was immersed. Henry began to practise, writing names, dates and facts randomly on a spare piece of paper just to see how much he could get on. They were always given pieces of rough paper in exams. If he had the same paper folded very small in his pencil case – no, perhaps inside a handkerchief. He could blow his nose – perfectly permissible – slip his piece of paper onto the other rough papers and hey presto! It would be easy to muddle them all up; in any case, who could say that he hadn't scribbled down the notes during the exam? The masters, who invigilated, more often than not were engrossed in marking their own class's exam papers, grateful for the time and quiet the invigilation afforded them. They only glanced up now and again and even more occasionally walked the length of the desks. All he needed was practice. Even now he put a folded piece of paper inside his handkerchief and then into his pocket. Keeping his eyes fixed on Gregson and Smithy, he withdrew the handkerchief, leaned over his papers as he blew his nose, and tried shaking the paper loose onto the table. It was not as easy as he had envisaged. God, he would need to practise this.

# Fiona

Even with the windows open, it was hot in her study. Barns had turned on the hose and she listened to the rhythm as he gushed the water to and fro across the car. It made her thirsty. She leaned back in the chair and pushed her hair behind her ears. Had been typing all morning, stopping for nothing, and even the coffee Lilly had brought her stood cold and curdled in the mug. It must be nearly lunchtime. She got up and went to the window. There was Barns, his shirtsleeves rolled up, holding the green, snake-like hose while the car stood obediently as the drops ran down its body like sweat. In this bright sunlight the gravel was as yellow as sand, she thought. Lilly appeared, her blonde curls almost white in the sun, and gesticulated until she caught Barns' eye. Fiona watched her careful, voiceless words, mouth opened wide, hands speaking with her mouth. Then he nodded and waved her back into the house. He had been warned that lunch was nearly ready. Fiona still felt guilty having Barns and Lilly. Living in the Cotswolds like this, the house and grounds, Lilly and Barns; it made them privileged and she was uncomfortable about that. Yet she had come to believe that Max was right. They were happy. Loved it there and the cottage. 'Don't be silly, Fee,' he said. 'What would they do if they didn't have us to boss around? And to be honest, not many people would employ a deaf and dumb woman. And what a star she is. We're lucky; they're lucky.'

It was true, they were equally dependent on each other. She looked around the mess of her study: books and papers everywhere. No order. She could never keep house. Everything would be wrong. Cooking! Housework. Time. But just the shopping. She insisted on that, made her feel she was contributing something, at least. She knew she was lucky: able to escape to this room and write her books. Nobody seemed to mind her self-centeredness. The boys didn't know any different. She had managed to bring them up somehow, with a great deal of help from Lilly and Barns. And Max. When he was home with them, he took trouble. Spent time and talked. Never seemed to want to escape them like she did. And now they were coming back for the summer holidays, but first she had to endure another speech day. Endless speeches. Prizes galore in the lofty hall: oak panelled, stained-glass windows, crested boards carved with golden names and singing 'Jerusalem'. Oh, and the hats, the one-upmanship. She endured it for the boys; she could, at least, do that for them and was quietly hopeful. Rob would probably do well again. Everyone would clap. But Henry? Lazy, stubborn, sulky. Surely they could find something to praise now he was leaving. But being good at painting did not count at this school. As long as he got the grades. Pray God. Then, at least, he could be away at university. She definitely did not want him hanging around here, at a loose end.

Mindlessly, she picked up some papers from the floor and dumped them onto a chair. She certainly should make a supreme effort today. It was easy for Max: he loved all the ceremony and the talking. Had such an easy manner. Talked so naturally, as if he were interested in whoever it was. Not like her. And he had never once asked her to wear a hat or to try to look smart. Never once. And never once in all their twenty years had he made her feel plain. No dress sense, mousy hair, hooded eyes, teeth just slightly protruding. Shush. She'd stopped looking in a mirror years ago, when she was eighteen or so. She was plain and that was all there was to it.

Max said she had a dazzling smile. Perhaps it was true. She had heard it before. Father used to say her face lit up when she smiled. But she couldn't spend all day going about with a grin on her face. She thought the only romance she would find was in her stories, but Max arrived. He used to say that it was her offhand manner that attracted him. Her honesty. And her sudden, inexpressible, irrepressible, redeeming smile. If she was a disappointment, he never showed it.

Today she would make a special effort. Try to be chatty. But most certainly, she had now decided, she would not wear a hat. In any case, the boys would not recognise her if she did. Secretly she thought they were proud she didn't dress up for the show. She could not, would not compete with the fashion show; some of the women seemed to treat speech day like a catwalk. Tripping across the cricket pitches in ridiculous winkle-pickers. Holding their hats, their bosoms exposed. And the dowdy ones too. But they were all bluestockings and arrogant in their dowdiness. Max was much more generous. Liked crowds and people and talking. Most barristers did. Yet he was not loud-mouthed or opinionated, like some she'd met.

She left the window because Lilly had rung the bell. It had been arranged years ago that the bell would be rung fifteen minutes before whatever it was, as she was never ready on time. She must hurry now, for Barns had gone to fetch Max from the station and she was supposed to be ready. She felt so hot.

# Henry

They'd only been home an hour or so and Henry was already bored and dissatisfied. He had been expecting something, some recognition that he'd left school, that he was about to begin a new phase. He's thought today would be about him. Robert, wasting no time, was out with friends, but Henry lay slumped in the chair, legs like long, lean shadows, aimlessly stroking the cat. It had wandered over from the cottage, as if to welcome him home. Seemed only the cat was pleased to have him back. 'I think I'll just go and – if that's all right with you – and put the cat among the chickens.'

'What? Oh, very funny, Henry. Well, why don't you? Go for a walk or something.' Fiona was anxious about his lethargy. 'Go and see Lilly and Barns. You haven't really seen them to talk to. Properly.'

'They're out, Fee. I said they could take the car.'

Max was celebrating the holidays with a brandy. Nothing he enjoyed more than sitting outside on a summer's evening like this, at the end of the week, weekend to come. It called for a brandy. The shadows were long across the lawn and the cedar cast dark spiky flecks onto the grass. 'So, on the whole you think they went all right, then. The history as well?'

'It was OK, I think.' Henry didn't want to talk about it. Wanted to forget it. Cheating had been too easy. He should get the right grades. And all he wanted now was to get away, go to Lola's and paint. Lola made him feel good about himself.

'Did you have a word with Lola, Mum? I'd really like to go as soon as poss.'

The cat leapt off his lap as he leaned towards his mother. All he could think about was going to the races again —and the horses.

'Ring her tomorrow, Henry.' He knew she would be pleased to see him go for a week; his hanging around disturbed her routine.

'Are the kittens still here? Did we keep any? He enjoyed drawing the kittens. He got up and retrieved the cat from where it lay on the edge of the lawn, in a last bit of evening sun.

Fiona shook her head. 'Don't you ever listen? I told you the last one went two weeks ago, down the road to the Turners.

'Oh. Pity.' He started to walk towards the cottage and the side of the house. 'I'm going to put this cat among the chickens then.'

Max put down his brandy and got up. 'Hang on! I'll come. Come and tell me your opinion of the hen coops. You haven't seen them yet, have you? We might find some eggs. You are coming, Fee?'

But she waved them on, staying alone as the sun went down.


One of the good things about being an artist, Henry thought, was you could do a lot of sitting about. You could sit about in a relaxed kind of way and just look at things. It was true that, sometimes, once you started something, you had to really concentrate and work quickly, sharpen up, as they would say at school, trying to catch a certain position, turn of head, look of eye, before the horse moved, flicked the flies away with its tail, shook its head, shuffled a foot. Even the flecks of sunlight on the back of a horse could disappear in a second when it shifted its position. Then he had to get on with it, work fast, concentrate and, unnoticed, time passed. It was marvellous to get rid of a boring day, a dull moment in life, for with that sort of concentration time vanished most gloriously and it was suddenly lunchtime or supper time, and he could stop and sit about again and be lazy with impunity, quite satisfied that he had not been wasting time. It was the only way that he didn't waste time when he was concentrating like this. Perhaps if he used his camera more; the still image, a reference point that he could adapt at will with his pencil and paints. It was probably the only way in the end to capture what he saw and felt. On the whole, though, he preferred not to think too deeply about motives and reasons. Never think about anything that might make him feel inadequate.

Now he sat back in the canvas chair he had carried out from the house and placed just inside the meadow gates. The two mares, one bay, the other white, had forgotten him and were alternately pulling at the grass, flashing their tails and moving dreamily from place to place. They had to shake their heads to keep away the insects that swarmed around their eyes, as well as the heaps of warm dung. The acidic smell of manure mixed with the dying sweetness of baked grass wafted past him in puffs.

He studied the horses with an intenseness that in everything else was entirely uncharacteristic of him, and sketched the heads in every position, upright with ears pointing forwards, then downwards, with smooth, arched necks as they nosed into the grasses. He outlined a leg, shaded a round, smooth, muscular flank, and whisked his pencil as they whipped the flies off their backs.

He was an unlikely country boy, but since his first visit as a three-year-old, he had loved to come here, to stay with Lola. Always the familiar bedroom, with the thin blue cotton curtains that moved easily, lightly, making liquid shadows on the whitewashed walls. There was the blue cotton bedspread, marked in places and frayed along the edges, and the worn mats on the floorboards. Lola, he thought, had better things to do with her time than worry about what the house looked like. But he still loved to wake early, as he had as a little boy, and listen to the sounds: the cockerel, the snort of a horse, the rustling of unidentified movements, a secret life that hid itself once you were out and about. He would watch the curtains move inside the open widow. Outside the broken concrete path led down to the hen coops and a straggly copse, behind which, in the spring, you could find clumps of white anemones. He still enjoyed collecting the eggs. There was something about that. Then there was the pigsty. Lola always had a sow and raised piglets before selling them on. He never ceased to be taken aback by the sharp, prickly skin, the solidness of a struggling piglet, its round tummy as hard as a man's shoulder.

Lola called him from the house. 'Phone, Henry. Fee's on the phone. It's Mum,' she repeated. 'Quick! She might have some news.'

He didn't hurry, pretended not to care about the results. Lola stood there, large bosom, bright lipstick, mass of greying curls tied back untidily with a blue scarf, her wide hips poured into faded riding trousers. She passed him the phone and raised her eyebrows. 'I'll be in the paddock,' she whispered.

He waited until she had gone then slumped down into a sunken armchair. 'Yes, Mother?' He was sure he sounded perfectly laid-back.

He heard her draw a breath, the habit all the family knew well when she wanted to take time before saying something. Today it made him nervous. 'I'm afraid Dad's opened the envelope. He said he couldn't wait; he opened it before leaving. Well, I'm just ringing because he should have waited. Anyway Henry, you've passed. I mean you got an A for art and, don't faint, a B for history. God knows how you did that! I should think old Radcliffe is lying in a darkened room with a cold towel on his head. Anyway darling, well done. Dad's thrilled. Good, isn't it? So now you can go off to Newcastle . . .' Mum only gabbled occasionally, when something extraordinary had happened, which was rare.

She's so relieved, he thought, not least that she can be rid of me, in a nice kind of way, with no guilt involved, but she can be rid of me, her eldest yet least loved son, out of her way, out of his hanging around and stopping her from getting on with her precious routine. It hurt and angered him at the same time. He was worth more than that.

He kicked his legs over the side of the chair, remembering the day in the library when he had begun to practise his sleight of hand. It had worked, then. He should be delighted. He was, of course. Why shouldn't he be? He had achieved what he wanted. The means justified the end – or was it the other way around?

'Thanks for ringing, Mum. I don't blame Dad at all. That's OK. Does Rob know?' At least, he thought, he wouldn't be a complete loser in his brother's eyes. Rob the Brain, as he called him. At least whatever brilliant results Rob got, he, Henry, had not failed. He was not looking forward to university, but he had to do something while he worked things out for himself. In the meantime, everyone was relieved and happy.

'What are you going to do for the rest of the day?' she was asking. 'You ought to come home so we can celebrate. Dad will want to do that.'

He told her that Lola was taking him to the races later. He didn't want to miss that. But he would come home tomorrow.

After taking the remaining biscuit out of a tin open on the kitchen table, he walked across the drive to the stable block to find Lola. It was a long, high building housing rows of individual stables on each side. The flypapers, which hung from the rafters and turned in the breeze, catching the sunlight, were studded with the small black bodies and the transparent wings of flies and moths. At one end stood a steaming, acrid-smelling pile of dung, punctured with lengths of straw, and as he walked through the heavy wooden doorway out of the sunlight and into the mottled shadows, he saw Debbie upturning a barrow-load of dung onto the pile. She had her back to him and he noted her buttocks, firm and rounded as she bent over. Her jeans were rolled up to her calves, her crinkled white cotton blouse was hanging out untidily, and her breasts rolled like well-set jelly as she moved. He had noticed them before. He noticed a lot about her, but he was nervous about chatting her up in case she was unresponsive, unimpressed. A negative response, as he saw it, left him depressed, sometimes for days. Why was it he so much preferred this rather ordinary, unselfconscious girl to the smart, public-school girls from the tennis club, who showed little interest in him. They were, in his opinion, over-made-up, pushy, loud and vain. Sexual predators. God! How he loathed them.

Debbie showed no interest either, but her indifference was a challenge. And she would notice him in his new flared jeans and yellow polo neck. If he did something nice for her, she would notice him and he'd feel rather good about that.

Now she disappeared inside a stable and he heard the clack as her hand slapped the haunch of a leggy bay. 'Move over,' he heard her command and again, 'move yourself.' And then the ring of the horse's shoes on the stone floor as she pushed him into position. He saw her duck under the horse's head and then emerge from the stable, shutting the door behind her. The bay tossed his head over the door and she patted his nose before picking up the yard brush.

'Let me help,' he said. Then she noticed him standing there and, laughing, waved the top of the broom. 'OK! If you like.'

Nervous and unsure, he watched as she swept the surface water into the gullies from where the stinking brown liquid trickled into the drains, which were partly blocked by scraps of straw and muck. A green twisted hose lay along the wet concrete, reminding him of the time when she had flicked cold water at him and how he had dodged the spray and how they had laughed.

'I'll come back and help you later.' Knowing he wouldn't, but her smile of thanks was enough.

Lola was cantering round the worn, circular ring in the paddock. He stood by the gate listening to the rhythm, the pounding on the dry ground, studying the movement of the horse's feet. Lola saw him and turned the horse towards the gate as he called, 'All's well. I'm off to Newcastle, apparently.'

'My darling man. That's wonderful. Congrats.' Nobody else would ever call him 'my darling man'. She made him feel good about himself. He thought he loved her for that. She slid off the horse as he opened the gate. 'We'll crack a bottle, shan't we? I'm very proud of you.'

'We are going to the races, though?' He had visions of them drinking champagne all afternoon.

'Of course. We'll take a table in the restaurant afterwards and crack a few bottles there.'

Lola always behaved as if she were a millionaire, Max said, but Henry enjoyed her extravagant behaviour and thought of his stained bedspread, the thin, faded curtains and the threadbare mat; she didn't spend money on housey things. But 'crack a few bottles' because her nephew has got his A levels? Nothing would stop her. It was the Italian in her, he decided. They all had Italian blood in them from somewhere in the past. Not Mum, of course: she was very English. Very English indeed!

He knew, with Lola, they would be tight for time and as usual tried desperately to look cool, but his feet were tapping anxiously beside her in the jeep. She knew all the shortcuts but, as they approached the racecourse, the road was jammed.

'Bugger! I didn't realise we were late. Bugger it.'

He raised a silent eyebrow and swallowed his irritation.

'I'm parking here.' And she rammed the vehicle up on the tyre-marked grass verge. 'It'll be quicker to walk, anyway.'

Already out and striding towards the cacophony of noise, he

heard the ritualistic babble of the touts and felt the drumming of hooves. Oh! Lola, he thought, please don't keep stopping to talk to people. He hesitated, but she shouted at him to go on and so he went on without her.

The stands were packed, but they found spaces by the fence and watched as the jockeys mounted, the horses champing and turning in circles, one bucking, impatient to be off. The colours of the jockeys were like bright patches of thick paint against the sky. Trainers adjusted stirrups, patted their beasts and said last words to the riders, short-legged, holding crops and leaning forward, caps shading their eyes. But, despite the noise, the anticipation, the jockeying, the champing, the hot breath, the shouting, the anxiety, Henry only heard silence and saw the wildness, the empty expanse of plains, the primae-val grasslands, and the horse, untamed, dominant. His mind encompassed that ancient world where the horse roamed, holding within itself secrets from the beginning of time. He was obsessed with the idea of the horse's genetic memory, its private world. And that's what he wanted to capture with his paints. Something secret within the horse. All animals had their inner worlds and genetic memories. That's what fasci-nated him. Now he wished he could take out his paints but, in the meantime, he clicked endlessly, for he had remembered to bring his camera.

It took him some time to reconnect with the world around him, and they were halfway through the meal before he could concentrate on the conversations. Lola had booked a table in the best restaurant and, as she had promised, they had con-sumed any number of bottles and everyone was full of chat and laughter. Lola had boasted about his results and they had toasted him with generous smiles, but he couldn't help being suspicious at their apparent pleasure in his success. Did they really like him, think him worth knowing? Strange, but not unpleasant. It was not like this at home. Lola's friend Clive

Stockman, who owned several racehorses, was there. Henry had met him on many occasions and wondered if there was something going on between him and Lola. Now she was on about his paintings and how wonderful they were and how Clive should get him to paint one of his horses.

Two of his horses had run: Credential had come nowhere, but Domino, a black gelding with a white nose, had just missed third place in the Cleveland Cup.

'Bring him over,' he was saying, and then to Henry, 'Would you like to have a go at one of mine? Paint one. Hang it in pride of place if you're as good as Lola says.' They looked at each other; she smiled just faintly.

'Come over tomorrow. A nice portrait of her standing in the paddock, aye?'

He was referring to his bay mare, Sugar Candy. What a ridiculous name, Henry thought, and was overcome by nerves and the prospect of—

'I'll be the first person to commission you,' Clive was saying. 'I'm sure it will be a good investment. I can see fame all over your face.' He was laughing though, so he probably didn't mean it.

# Frank

As Frank approached the gate, he saw Stan with his apron on standing outside the shed in a patch of late-afternoon sunlight and knew he was waiting for him, and before Stan could say anything, he called over, 'Right-o. Be right out.'

'Don't let her detain you. We're going to use the lathe. Got some wood specially.'

Stan had bought the lathe second-hand some years before, gradually collecting all the necessary tools to use with it, which he proudly explained to Frank: the roughing-out gouge, parting tool and screw chisel. He'd taught himself, with hours of practice, to turn and shape table and chair legs and to make bowls. They had a walnut fruit bowl on the windowsill in the front room he had turned. His first success after many failures. Now Stan wanted Frank to learn how to use a lathe. 'Can't be a proper carpenter without a lathe, lad.'

'Put these on, then.' And he handed Frank a blue-striped apron that had hung on the nail inside the shed door, a pair of cheap goggles and an old pair of leather gloves.

'Got this today,' he said, holding up a chunk of rough, pale-coloured wood. 'It's Mexican walnut. Got it from the yard. It's the best for learning on. OK?'

He turned to the lathe with the wood in his hand. 'Now lad, put this in place between the headstock and the tailstock. You've seen me do it.'

Frank took the wood, marked the centre at both ends, and screwed in the turning screws and then fixed these between the headstock and tailstock, adjusting the tailstock so that the piece of wood fitted exactly in between.

'Right, lad, that was good and careful. So, OK, what do we do first?'

'Roughing out?'

'Right. So, take the roughing-out gouge and watch me. Now this is the tricky bit You must keep the tool on the resting plate all the time and have the chisel turned slightly to the right. Not flat on.'

Frank held the gouge on the resting plate and placed the sharp edge of the chisel onto the rough wood. Stan took his arm, as if to reassure him. 'OK now, it won't go too fast to begin with, but keep the tool steady and let the lathe do the turning. Try to run the tool smoothly along as it turns. When you come to the end of the wood, come off cleanly and go back to the beginning. I'll clean up and smooth out the piece ready for turning, nicely. You'll see.'

Frank felt a rare sense of pleasure as he waited. Stan switched on the motor and the wood began to spin. He held the roughing gouge firmly and moved it evenly along and the wood peeled off like orange rind and fell to the floor in curls. Three times he ran the tool along the wood, by which time it was rounded and smooth.

Stan switched off the lathe

'Bloody chipper! Very well done, lad. You didn't jump off once. That's because you kept the tool slightly tilted. Now for the parting. This parting tool will make your grooves and beads like on banisters, so now we need to mark out on the wood where we want the grooves and beads to be. On that piece we can only get two, but it's just practice.'

Frank was just releasing the wood from the lathe, absorbed in this new skill, when they both head Ruby call from the back door that tea was ready.

'Did we hear that Frank, or was I dreaming!?'

'I think we heard it, Stan, sorry to say!' He touched the old man on the shoulder as if to guide him out of the shed, but first they hung up their aprons and put down the goggles and gloves on the bench ready for tomorrow.

'Thanks, Stan, I really enjoyed that.'

'You're going to do well, lad. Very well. No worries there. How's those exams going, anyhow? Has that teacher gone through that application with you yet? Can't hang about.'

1976–1979

# Alice

S he stared at the poster, which hung in its brown wooden
frame on the back wall of the shed; an old poster advertising a motorbike. It read, 'Thrilling sport and thrilling
transportation. The Harley Davidson Hydro-glide.' She
wished she was like the pretty, happy-looking girl sitting on
the bike behind her smiling boyfriend. They were out for a
ride in the country, heads forward, hair blowing behind them.
The girl in the poster was blonde like her.

She was fed-up, depressed. She'd never have a boyfriend
like that. She couldn't even play netball properly.

She'd come out to be with Da. Ma always fretted and got
upset if she wasn't happy. Da was different, so it was easier
to be near him when she was feeling miserable. Now she sat
in the bright turquoise sidecar with Pebbles on her lap. She
watched Da fiddle with bits of motorbike. He had his back
to her, his brown overall tied in a bow, looking so funny she
wanted to laugh. It was the bow made her laugh; it kinda
looked ridiculous. And his hands were black with grease.

She stroked the cat that had followed her from the house.
'Pebbles is almost nine, Da. How old is that in cat years?'

He half turned and nodded at her. She sighed. Everyone
was busy and all she wanted to do was talk.

'We lost at netball. Basically, I'm useless. I can't jump and
leap properly. They only put me in to be kind. My stupid

leg.' She burst into tears. 'I'm sick of it, Da. I'll never get a boyfriend either.'

The cat made to leap off her lap but she clung to it, while urging tears to drop onto her cheeks so Da would feel sorry for her. Lawrence turned and studied her. He had that look she knew so well as he stared quietly at her over his goggles, and her tears turned into a cough and as her cheeks puffed out, her mouth widened into a grin, her lips turned up at the corners and she burst out laughing.

'Now look here, Pixie. You know what the consultant said. It'll all be fixed once you've stopped growing. And that won't be too long now. Look at you! You'll surely not grow much taller. You're up to me already. And as for boyfriends! Well! You've got Jason Bodimead. He's always wanting to be with you. He sends you notes, doesn't he?'

She grinned. 'Da! Really! He's got wax in his ears.'

'Alice!' He frowned. 'That's not very kind.'

She doubled over the cat to smother her giggles. 'Can we go out for a ride soon? This bike goes all right, doesn't it?'

Lawrence patted the great shiny handlebars of his vintage, Harley-Davidson 45 c.i., which was leaning against his workbench. His favourite bike, the 74 c.i Knucklehead with its sidecar was the one he used for family outings, but the 1942 45 was only his. He rode it at weekends in the winter mostly, when there wasn't so much to do on the allotment and, occasionally, he rode it to work.

Alice's had forgotten her miseries and watched the movement of shapes on the walls made by the flickering sunlight as it caught the edges of the tools. They wove in and out of each other, darkening, fading, a mixture of soft edges, melting tools, dancing, it seemed to her. She screwed up her eyes to focus more sharply, to squeeze colour out of the shadowy shapes, already imagining her painting. But Ma would not be pleased. She had already told her off for spending too much time painting and not enough time on her school subjects. Her end-of-term report was full of, 'could do better's and 'does not concentrate's. 'It says I'm a pleasant member of the class, though,' she had argued. 'It says I'm always cheerful. That's good, isn't it?'

'They should see you at home,' Alistair had quipped. Rather unkindly, she thought.

Lawrence turned off the blowlamp and pushed the goggles to the top of his head. 'How about a nice cup of tea, Alice. Make us a cup, aye? And a piece of Ma's fruit cake.'

She slid, bent knees, out of the sidecar, the cat running ahead of her. Once standing still, she straightened and practised her steady walk across the driveway towards the front door, which she had left slightly ajar. In fact, she had very nice-shaped legs, just the right shorter than the other, and longed to be normal but dreading the operation. Sometimes she even thought it would be better to stay as she was.

She liked the bungalow when it was dark and shadowy: the walls, the furry carpets, the glow from the Rayburn in the front room. It was silent and warm. Ma had gone shopping and Alistair had taken time off from his endless A-level studies to go to his model shop to get some bits for his model making. The kitchen was flooded with mellow autumn light from the falling leaves; the ground at the back was bright in the gloomy afternoon with carpets of yellow.

She put on the kettle and cut two pieces of fruit cake and put them on a plate, knowing, that really, she should be in her room doing schoolwork, but being with Da was more fun, making tea and eating cake and well, just being. It wasn't that she didn't enjoy school; it was that her mind was always somewhere else. She made up stories in her head and took herself off to other places. 'Stop dreaming,' Ma was always saying, 'and get on with it, Alice, for goodness' sake. Concentrate.'

She was already eating her cake when the phone rang. It made her jump. It was Ma sounding worried. 'Alice, I know this is silly, pet—' She stopped and then, 'Get Da, will you?

I know it's silly, Alice but— I'm ringing from Carter's. The thing is, I've forgotten where I've parked the car; I can't find the car, Alice.' Her voice cracked a bit and Alice knew she was nearly crying. 'Get Da, will you?'

She hurried, running unevenly and calling all at the same time. 'Da! Ma's forgotten where the car is. Da. Oh Da.' Now she was crying again. 'What's wrong with her, Da? I hate it when things go wrong.'

When he turned to look at her, she saw that same mixture of anger and worry that she had seen before. She watched as he smeared his hands with the green jelly before rubbing them hard on the dirty cloth. Then he removed his overall and hung it on the peg. But all the time he eyed her with that look.

'What are you going to do, Da? Go on the bike? Can I come?"

She was standing by the sidecar, her hand resting on the roof, when she heard the skid of wheels, the spitting and splitting of the gravel, and turned to see Alistair braking towards her up the path. He was wearing the old leather cycling helmet with the yellow scarf twisted round his neck and looked like one of the motorcyclists in Da's magazine. Alice liked him when he dressed like that. Alistair propped up his bike and took a plastic bag off the handlebars. He looked at then with a shy grin and, holding the bag in the air, said, 'I got the model, Da.'

'Ma's forgotten where she parked the car, Alistair. She sitting in Mr Carter's. Waiting.' Alistair dropped his arm and shook his head. His hat was a bit crooked and Alice gave a nervous giggle. 'Are we going on the bike? I'd like to. I want to go.'

Alistair ignored her. 'I'll go. It won't take a minute to cycle there. I'll go. I bet she's just left in at the Co-op.'

Lawrence pulled on the old jacket that had been flung on the back of a broken chair. 'Get your coat, Alice. We'll go, Alistair. I promised her a ride, in any case.'

*

He had to put on the headlights, and the November leaves, copper and gold fairy lights, flashed by. The road sped away beneath them, a winding dark river. Alice sat back in the sidecar, snugly wrapping her arms around her long woollen cardigan. Speeding made her excited; the light beams breaking the darkness like flashes of lightning.

Lawrence stopped outside the chemist's and clicked the bike onto its stand before opening the sidecar door and helping her out. The lights of the shops and street lamps glowed comfortingly, and she noticed that there were even Christmas lights around Mrs Arnold's. Nearly Christmas, she thought.

Ma was sitting on the chair by the counter, watching as Mr Carter stuffed tablets into a bag for the elderly Mrs Barton. She went straight to Ma, putting her arms round her shoulders. 'We're here, Ma. How could you forget where the car is? You always park in the Co-op.'

Ma laughed and looked at Mr Carter. 'You must think I'm mad.' She laughed again.

'Not at all, Dot, not at all.' But Mr Carter's face had the same look as Da. He was a tall, thin man and had thick folds, like channels, that ran from his nose to his mouth, small eyes, like a bird's, behind round glasses through which he looked, smiling at Ma as if she were a child.

Then Da came in. 'Have you got the keys, pet? Come on! Give me the keys.' He eyed Mr Carter, whom he called Ivor, shaking his head. Ma pulled a bunch of keys from her coat pocket. 'I'm sorry, Laurie. But I panicked. Sorry.'

He looked at the Co-op bags piled round her. 'You'll have parked in the Co-op, pet. For sure.' He winked at Ivor. 'What have you got for a silly missus who panics and then can't find the car?'

Alice knew he was trying to be funny, trying to make Ma feel OK so they all laughed.

'It is! It's in the Co-op. Sorry, I've just remembered. Sorry.'

'Wait here, then,' Da said. 'I'll find it and bring it round.

Won't be a tick.' But she knew because she had overheard him say to Alistair that he was going to get her to the doctor's.

'Just short of fifty. She's too young to have anything that serious.'

She wanted to be extra-helpful. She didn't know how exactly, so she began by putting the bags into the boot of the car and knew she must go back with Ma. Not in the sidecar.

On the way home she talked about her afternoon, exaggerating the time she had spent on her history homework, for Ma snapped alive when Alice mentioned schoolwork. 'Is it finished, then? And what about the English? What was it you had to do?'

Alice forced herself to sound cheerful and enthusiastic. 'Just about friendship. You know, Ma, I told you last night. Who was the best friend to Romeo and why, et cetera, et cetera. The usual stuff. It's obvious, anyway. Benvolio.' Alice shrugged. 'Boring but sensible. I shall just write Benvolio was the best friend to Romeo because, although he was dull and boring, like Jason Bodimead, he was sensible and reliable like my brother Alistair.'

'Don't be silly, Alice. You're nearly fifteen years old. Not a baby. It's not funny.' Ma took her eyes off the road. 'You won't be laughing if you don't get your exams next year. And you haven't got that long. I thought you wanted to go to art college. You have to pass your exams for that. Cranfield College has a good reputation. It doesn't just take anyone, you know.'

Alice looked at Ma's seriousness and burst out laughing. 'But I'm not anyone, Ma.'

# Alice

*Three years later*

The mop head swept rhythmically across the lino, leaving bright, wet pathways. The long sodden strands reminded her of the hair on a rag doll. She was calmed by the rhythmic sploshing. A cleaner in a green overall was mopping backwards and forwards: into the corners, around the cupboards, under the beds. The bed opposite had been empty since she'd come in. It lay there, flat and still, with green curtains pulled back either side, the bedside cupboard bare and waiting. On every cupboard a jug of water and a glass. There were eight beds, four either side and each with a clipboard hanging at the end, just like in the TV series *Emergency Ward 10*, which she'd watched when she was younger. If she was feeling particularly nervous, she tried to pretend it was just an episode of *Emergency Ward 10*.

Now she sat in the armchair beside her bed with the magazine unopened on her lap. The woman, in the next bed, Margery, had been knitting something blue but now she was making up her face, squinting into a small mirror as she put on her mascara. The nurses had been round and propped her up against a mound of pillows. The bed table was pulled across in front of her. The ball of wool had twisted off the table and rolled onto the floor. She tutted and looked at Alice.

'I'm knitting this for a friend,' she said, and held up a knitting pattern with the photo of a smiling woman wearing a bed jacket like the one she had on. 'She liked this,' she said and pulled at the edge of her jacket, 'so I thought I might as well while I'm here. I've had my gallbladder out. Should be going home in a couple of days, all things being equal.'

'Oh! That's good.' Alice had pulled her dressing gown across to hide the white-cotton hospital gown she had had to put on that morning before going down for blood tests and final X-rays. The gown made her nervous and so, as a distraction, she picked up the ball of wool and put it back on Margery's bed table

'What you doing in this ward, anyway? You don't look old enough.'

'They said I'm too old for the children's ward. I'm seventeen, so I suppose that's right.'

'You do look a bit pale. What you here for?'

She explained about her hip. Dysplasia.

'Putting in a metal one?' The woman put down her knitting 'Old people have that. Hip replacement, it's called. Well, I hope all goes well.'

Margery had a loud voice; everyone in the ward would hear her, and Alice, embarrassed but not wishing to appear rude, decided to escape. 'I think I'll just go for a little walk,' she said.

'Don't get lost!' And Margery shrieked a laugh.

Alice went towards the nurses' station; she had to pass the woman who had been admitted late last night. She had a plastic bag hanging beside the bed; it was half full of blood and urine. There was drip machine by the bed and a tube attached to her hand. She was quiet now, her eyes closed.

They had turned off the main lights at ten, just before the last medicine round, and put on instead blue-coloured night lights. Two nurses had pushed round the trolley, and she had listened to their feet on the lino and their chatter as they doled out the pills. She heard curtains drawn, the rings clanging,

72

and the secretive voices of patients. A little later the woman was brought in on a trolley. Then the curtains had been pulled round her and several doctors came and went, speaking quietly, urgently. Giving instructions. She heard the moans amidst the whispering and pulled the bedclothes up over her ears. Now the woman was silent and asleep.

'Alice!' The staff nurse looked up from the desk. 'Don't be long. Mr Rigby is coming to see you any minute.'

There was an old man called Jonathan Rigby. He went to market to sell his ... Pigby. Diddle diddle digby. I'm going quite mad, she thought.

But it wasn't just Mr Rigby; Mr Johnson came as well, the anaesthetist.

Both very smart in suits and polished shoes. Longish hair, and Mr Johnson had sideburns. Trying to look trendy, she thought. Mr Rigby was very handsome; he was taller and straighter, but Mr Johnson did have a nice smile.

They stood by her chair looking down and then Mr Johnson sat on the bed beside her.

Trying to be kind, she thought. Trying to make me feel OK, not so scared.

Mr Johnson said, 'I'm going to look after you tomorrow. I thought we should say hello because I shall be in a gown with a mask when you come in to surgery. But it'll be me,' he said in a jolly kind of voice. 'There's nothing to worry about.' And immediately she began to worry.

'After supper nothing more to eat and just a few sips of water. OK? The nurses will remind you and tomorrow before your operation we'll give you something to make you feel sleepy and relaxed. The next thing you know it'll all be over.' He patted her hand. 'Don't look so worried. You know Mr Rigby. He'll be there to look after you, too'

Mr Rigby looked serious, she thought. Was he afraid something might go wrong? To reassure her he said, 'You'll be fine. The new hip will take a little time to settle in but,

73

after a month or two, at the most, hopefully, no more limping and no more raised shoes.' He stared, waiting for her to look as happy. 'Cheer up!' But it was too much for her. No matter how hard she tried, she couldn't stop from crying.

'Come on, now. The nurses will be here.'

Mr Johnson stood up. 'See you tomorrow, then.' He patted her hand again.


By the time the family, including Alistair, came to visit, she was feeling better because staff nurse had been to talk to her, saying, 'Honestly, pet, Mr Rigby is absolutely fantastic.' She shook her head. 'Such a good surgeon. I would trust him with my life.'

Alistair, although he had brought some work to do, tried to cheer her up. 'I brought you these, Fatty,' he said, and dropped a box of liquorice allsorts on the bed, and Da said that when she came home, he was going to take few days off, and Ma brought her more magazines, some orange squash and grapes. Ma gazed around a lot and asked several times if she was having her operation in the morning, but otherwise she seemed to be having one of her better spells. Alice wanted them to stay with her, didn't want them to leave her alone, for behind his smiles she imagined she could see a worried look in Da's eyes, so she tried to cheer him by telling them what the staff nurse had said about Mr Rigby. 'It's good that, isn't it?'

Later that night she heard some noise in the corridor; someone had been put into one of the small side rooms. There was a bit of rushing about and then the groaning screams began. She could never have imagined such sounds; they became throatily primaeval screams, bubbling, choking from the throat, hysterical loss of control. It was beyond hell and she had to put her fingers in her ears and pull her pillow over her head to deaden the noise. Shaking with terror beyond terror; it was like someone being burned alive.

And then the silence, like death itself, unfathomable

darkness and, even when she heard the cries of the baby, she was not comforted, but shook with disgust that it had been human noises and knew then that she would never allow herself to be like that; to go through that; to be an animal. She could never have a baby.

She hated these grey, nothing sorts of days, everything still and lifeless. From her table she could see across to Mrs Howles's bungalow. The windows were blank and private-looking. She hated that. Sometimes when the sun shone from behind their bungalow onto Mrs Howles's and she waved across, her movements were reflected like in a dusty mirror. She should have been working but instead she was fiddling with the long strand of hair that constantly fell across her right eye, squinting to see the varying flecks of blonde and corn. They said it was the colour of barley. She fiddled and gazed out at their own dismal front. Da kept it neat, but it was unimaginative, to say the least. 'Just keep it simple,' he said to Ma. 'Gravel keeps off the weeds and the concrete the same.'

The front was divided from the pavement by a low red-brick wall, which matched their bungalow. There was a round bed in the middle with a Japanese maple, the red leaves already falling. She might go and sweep them away for Da. To the left was the tarmac drive where the Fiat was parked. Da kept the garage for his motorbikes. Suddenly she longed to go out in the green sidecar again and feel the air whizzing past.

They had given up all idea of her going to university, like Alistair, who was doing his maths and physics degree at York University and there was talk of him going on to do a master's at Durham. Alistair was always working. She wasn't clever like Alistair.

She looked down at her notes. *Othello is an idealistic man but easily corrupted. Discuss.* She was only doing art and English; it shouldn't be so difficult to get the grades. The art college was more interested in her portfolio, in any case.

She wrote: 'Othello thought everyone was good and could be trusted.'

The thread of hair dangled across her words and now she rather more determinedly shoved it back behind her ear. She really must get on, but there wasn't much more to say except that was why he believed Iago. But she could hardly hand in the essay with the lines: 'Othello was an idealistic and trusting man and thought everyone was good and truthful, and he was easily corrupted because he believed everything that Iago told him or suggested to him.' She couldn't help laughing. How she would love to hand in that answer, but realised she was being exceedingly childish.

'Al!' she called, and crossed the passage to his door, which she opened without knocking. 'Listen to this, Al. Al, listen to my essay.'

She sat on the bed, which did not please him. 'Alistair, you're not listening.' She read out the question. And waited. Alistair stopped writing without moving his head. There was a pause and then slowly he turned towards her, his back still bent over his work

'Yes, and?'

She burst out laughing, doubled up on his red candlewick bedspread. 'That's it,' she gasped. 'That's it, my essay. My award-winning, Nobel Prize-winning essay '

Alistair turned back to his books, which made her laugh even more, her knees doubled into her stomach.

'It is! It's a scream. You should see your face!'

'Don't be silly, Alice. You can't make any more excuses now with all that "I'm in pain. My hip aches" stuff.' He imitated her whining voice. 'No more excuses now. Look at you! You're so much better. The operation went very well, you know that; hardly notice your limp most days.' He turned, looking at her in a heap on his bed. 'It's up to you, Alice, but they'll be pretty upset and worried if you can't get into college.'

'I'm no good at anything, Al.' The laughter had evaporated.

'Oh, for God's sake, Alice. Tell you what! You're right good at self-pity. Pull yourself together and get on with it. You're being really feeble and it doesn't suit you.'

'It's all right for you. You weren't born with dysplasia. You weren't strapped up half your childhood like in a cage,' she added to get his attention. 'You weren't put in a short-leg hip Spica cast,' she enunciated heavily.

'Oh, for goodness' sake! Go and write your essay and let me get on. If we finish in time, I'll take you out on Davey, OK?'

She cheered up immediately. 'That's the sort of thing I like most, Al. Which reminds me. I must just tell you this, then I'll go and write my bloody essay. Yesterday I went down to the stream, to the pool part, and the sun was just coming through those trees, like torchlight, on to the pool, and the water was picking up the blue of the sky and those browny stones, you know, Al, they were this brilliant green. Honestly, Al, they were so green beneath a sort of blue glass, green stones in a fluted glass cabinet. Do you see? It was amazing what the light did. I just stood and looked and looked. That's the sort of thing I think about; that's why I don't get on with my work.' She didn't mention the other thing; the thing she wanted not to think about. She heaved herself off the bed, exhausted.

As she reached the door, he said, 'If only you realised you have a gift and what an excellent teacher you could be, Alice. Think how kids would love to hear that stuff. All you have to do is get into the art college and be a teacher. You'd like that. Settled?' He stared at her. 'See you when you've finished.'

Standing in front of the long mirror that hung inside the wardrobe door, she pulled at her rather baggy grey woollen trousers and pulled down the grey and blue striped jumper, then, pushing back her hair, she adjusted her weight so that she was standing perfectly straight. It was all much better than it had been; she should be happy; but she didn't see a pretty young woman in the mirror. She thought if Desdemona had been an ugly cripple the tragedy would never have occurred, because Othello would have known that nobody else would want her; he wouldn't have been so insecure about his marriage and there would have been nothing Iago could do about that. But what if it was all turned round and Iago made the ugly Desdemona jealous of Othello; that might have been even more interesting, because she would already be feeling angry about her disability, already hating herself, and she could never really, truly believe that anyone, leave alone Othello, could love her for ever, for herself.

Perhaps Ma felt insecure sometimes. She sat down; it was a shocking thought; it was a sad thought. Da was so cheeky and smiley, with his dark hair always falling over his eyes and his crooked smile, which creased the furrows from his nose and made him look craggy and strong. Perhaps Ma felt lumpy, dumpy and frumpy beside him, especially now she was more forgetful and dreamy, not all there sometimes. Dear Ma, with her books and her reading and her worrying over them all.

Perhaps if her pebbles from the beach had not been so amazingly beautiful, she would not have spent so much time painting and then possibly she would be clever like Alistair.

She put her head in her hands. When she was depressed, she couldn't get that screaming out of her head.

# Frank

The hall light seeped through the doorway, casting shadows. The tiled fireplace stood cold and empty; he had turned off the electric fire when they'd gone to bed. Lights from passing cars lit up the curtains, disappeared into the far corner of the room and then in a wide beam arched along the ceiling. Frank watched and waited, waited for the lights to halt and a car to stop outside. He was slumped in the dark, twisting round and round, the loose, frayed thread hanging from the arm of the sofa. He didn't want Kitty to know he was there. Spying. He hunched back into the sofa, into the shadows.

He had nearly finished his five-year apprenticeship at Tanner's and was well on his way to getting his City & Guilds when Kitty left school and started at Gossip, the local hairdresser, which she said was a just-right name, because they did gossip all the time. She washed hair and swept the floors and messed about making the other girls laugh. That was the trouble with Kitty; she was too attractive, with her long legs and dark hair like Mum's and her high spirits. She could get away with murder. But she did go to night school twice a week and worked hard, because she enjoyed that. She was fond of repeating in forcible tones, 'They all say I'll be fantastic when I'm trained.'

Now she was eighteen and her dark hair was cut short, dyed blonde and permed into masses of curls. He thought it was cheap-looking. And she smoked quite openly, although, surprisingly, had the sense not to smoke in the house, but she stood outside the back door. Stan had warned her about stubs lying around and for once she looked genuinely shame-faced.

When she turned up early last Friday evening on the pretext of waiting for him to finish work, wearing her mini skirt and black knee-high boots, the workshop came to a standstill; all twelve workstations suddenly silent as the men turned to see her hanging around outside again. Somebody whistled and Frank snapped down his slide rule.

'That's OK! Leave it to me, mate.' It was Steve. Twenty-four years old, a muscular, beefy bloke, fair-haired and tanned and the boss in the workshop. Frank watched as he and Kitty talked and laughed and smoked together. She hadn't come for him at all; she'd come for Steve.

Frank had first worked with him in the windows-and-doors unit, where Steve was manager. That's when Kitty first met him. She'd come after the hairdresser's, stand there in the yard, long-legged, dyed-blonde hair, too much lipstick and treading out a fag before he could see. 'Sixteen going on twenty-five,' someone joked. That's when Steve first caught sight of her; left what he was doing; walked towards her. But Frank didn't like it. He didn't like his sister acting like a tart. The men yowling like animals. He went cold with anger. Sometimes he wanted to strike her down.

Now he listened. Watched for the lights. Still. Except for a foot rotating in time with the twisting of the cotton.

Suddenly he heard an approaching car slow to a stop outside. He leapt up and went to the window, waiting with his back to the curtains. Listening, watching the beam of lights halt across the ceiling. It reminded him of the night in the shed; waiting in the dark and seeing the lights of Carl's car as he drove away and Mum's voice calling. He heard the car doors open and Kitty laugh; she laughed again and then a low murmur, a man's voice with a throb of a laugh in it. Frank pulled back just an inch of curtain. He didn't want to look, but he saw them standing close, face to face; saw Steve's hand rub up the back of her thigh under her short skirt and he twisted away with his eyes closed, hands clenched and waited for the panic to pass. Then the gate squeaked, the car revved, the lights lit up the room and he, like a criminal, flung himself back onto the sofa. He heard the key in the lock, her steps in the hall. He whispered, 'Kitty,' but she didn't hear him. She went up the stairs, her shadow moving inside the door. At the top she turned off the light and left him sitting in the dark.

The hairdresser's was on the corner of the parade and opposite the bus stop. Kitty'd been there two years and worked later on Fridays now, because she was doing her final training sessions: cutting, perming, colouring, working on the other girls and some clients who were happy to pay less for a trainee.

He could leave earlier on a Friday now he'd been moved to the furniture workshop; Mac, who really rated his skills, always let them go at five. He was getting on fine there. Loved the work: making tables, chairs, cupboards. He was good at it and the other men seemed to respect him, even asked for his advice sometimes. And when he was concentrating on the joining and shaping, the grains and veneers, he could forget about everything else. He was just about to complete his final fortnight away at college in Southampton, where he had been studying for his City & Guilds. Once he'd been accepted onto the course, Mac had given him time off to study, which was a fortnight every three months. 'It'll be worth it,' Mac had said. 'Job opportunities and all that. Wish I'd done it myself.'

He got off the bus. It was raining and the windows of the salon were misted up and running with droplets. He could see the figures moving like a silent film behind the plate glass and women under the pink hairdryers. He'd gone in once when Kitty was late out, stood by the open door and waited until she saw him, but he was a distraction, it seemed; the other girls called out and made funny remarks, and Carol had flirted and offered to do his hair, touching the top of his head, ruffling it with a wink, turning back to Kitty, who was sweeping the floor.' You should bring 'im inside, Kit,' and laughed. He wouldn't go in again.

But now it was raining and so he stayed in the bus shelter and waited, and thought what he could say to Kitty. What he had failed to say to her last night; what he had wanted to say to her and then hadn't the courage. But it was probably for the best; they would only have had a row and woken Stan and Ruby up. Now he was earning, he planned to look for a small flat. Not far away – he would still want to be some help to Stan and Ruby. They never complained they were short of money but Frank knew that the money he could now give them each week was very welcome, although they never said. Stan had sniffed and said he'd have no part in taking money, but Ruby had nodded behind his back and said, 'Thank you, Frankie. Every little helps.' She pointed towards Stan. 'He knows that but would never say.'

Frank was more than fond of them. They were good through and through and he and Stan enjoyed their times in the shed together. Ruby had always tried to be a mother to Kitty from the moment that she offered her the treasured chocolate biscuits. Perhaps because they had no children of their own. Frank sometimes dared to contemplate that they might even think of him and Kitty as theirs. Even love them a little.

He watched the blurred figures move like a dance behind the condensation. At least Kitty was back to her own dark hair; the blonde phase was over for the moment.

What could he say? How should he put it? That he wanted everything to be all right for her. They were family. Even two makes a family. He thought of Mum, the drugs the drink, Dad's violence: the smell of abuse. The little pink pills spilled on the carpet. He stood under the dripping shelter; shoulders hunched. But what could he do? He lived with the dread that one day at breakfast or tea Stan would say, 'Sorry but we can't manage any more. We're too old now, and with Ruby's swollen legs. Rheumatism all over.'

A woman laden with shopping and grumbling pushed up beside him on the seat and he got up to make more room, pulling her shopping trolley out of the rain. She nodded thanks, too puffed to speak. He looked at his watch; she should be out by now. Perhaps he could go over. He stood at the side of the road while cars splashed past and then he saw them, heard their voices, shrill and happy. Kitty opened up a fawn-coloured umbrella and, linking arms with her friend, pulled her under it. The girl had on a tight, shiny red mac that reflected in the puddles, and white boots with leather tassels. Kitty called over her shoulder to Frank. 'Come over here, Frankie. This is Sandy.' The girls whispered, heads together.

After Sandy had turned off down Hurley Way, he took the umbrella from Kitty and held it high for them both. His blue gabardine had kept the worst of the wet off him, but his hair was plastered and dripping into his eyes. He wiped his arm across his face. Kitty was dry enough; she was wearing the three-quarters camel coat he had bought her for Christmas; she had the wide collar pulled up to her ears. They got it from Hembreys, the large general store that sold everything from kitchen pots and pans to carpets and clothes. The store ran a never-never scheme and you could pay things off a little each week, but he would never do that. He saved until he had the money, though Kitty often tried to persuade him to buy something. 'Get now, pay later,' she would sing 'Go on! You're really stuffy sometimes.'

Luckily there wasn't a queue at the fish and chip shop; they always took back fish and chips on Fridays and Ruby would be waiting with the table laid so Frank didn't have much time to say what he wanted to say. The rain had stopped; he carried the two fish and chip bags and Kitty swung the umbrella.

'Where did that come from?' he asked.

'Someone left it. We have hundreds out the back – that people have left.'

'Do you have to take it back?'

Kitty shrugged. 'Don't know – didn't ask. She just said, "Take a brolly, it's pouring out there." We all took one.'

Cars splashed past on their way home for the weekend; pedestrians weaved and elbowed, avoiding the puddles and Kitty ran the point of the umbrella along the garden walls. He listened to the scraping.

'How did you get home last night, Kit?'

She stopped. 'Like always, for Christ's sake. On the bloody bus with Sandy. How many more times?'

He held his voice in tight. 'With Sandy?'

She didn't answer, just scraped the brolly more viciously, leaving powdery marks along the wall. He leaned across to take the umbrella away from her, but she snatched it out of his reach. 'Are you quite sure, Kitty?'

'Why are you asking,' she shouted, 'when you bloody well know already, don't you? Because you were spying – as normal. For Christ's sake, Frankie. Leave me. I can't stand no more of this. On and on and bloody on.' She banged the brolly repeatedly down on the ground, again and again, until her coat was splattered with muddy water. 'Now look. Look!' she screamed, and then, thumping down the umbrella, ran off up the road.

As she reached the corner she turned and shouted, through gushing tears. 'I'm leaving anyway. Me and Steve. We're going.'

Then just as he thought there was no more to be said, she sank down on a wall, head on chest.

Holding himself stiffly inside, he concentrated on picking up the umbrella before slowly walking up to her. He waited until she looked up, wiped her nose on the arm of her coat, repeating quietly, 'I'm going away with him, Frankie. He's

84

getting a job with a builder somewhere near Doncaster We're getting a flat. I'm going, Frankie.' She stretched out her arm to touch his coat. 'Don't be anti. I love you. Please, Frankie.' Her eyes were red; her nose dripped. 'It will be all right if we get married first, won't it, Frankie? In the registry? You'll be happy then, won't you, if we're properly married, Frankie?

'But you're only eighteen, Kit. It's—'

'Can't you think how much I want my own place?' she was gabbling. 'They've been good, I know that, but it's not home, not like ours. Like before ...' She turned away, mumbling, hesitating, 'Things went a bit wrong, I know, Frankie, but it was at least our place, wasn't it? Our place. Be honest, Frankie.'

They'd never spoken about 'things going wrong'. Nothing had ever been said.

Now, almost whispering, he explained, 'I was going to get us a place – that's what I wanted to say. Move out when you've trained. Get a flat not too far away. Make our own home. You could still see—'

But she wasn't listening. 'I shouldn't say, I know, because they have been good, like you say, and I won't ever not see them. I love them. Oh! And you know I love you, too. But Frankie how can you not think things? I don't want to think things. I don't want to see that house no more.'

He nodded because he knew there was nothing else to do.

1980–1984

# Frank

Saturday had been their day, but Kitty had gone and there was no point now to the shopping, the wandering, the mooching about; going into Hembreys to sit on chairs and sofas; try out the beds. No more buying her things out of his pay packet; he'd bought her winter coat and the large black handbag with the gold chains that she loved so much. He used to take her to Paphos Café for bacon and sausage, strawberry milkshake, or hot chocolate piled high with artificial cream and chocolate chips. And then to the local 'flea pit', as it was known. The last film they'd seen was the comedy 'Carry on Nurse' with Kenneth Williams and the usual crew. She'd laughed a lot; seemed happy to be with him. But she wasn't here any more, and so to fill the long space of the day he'd gone early to the launderette.

It was deserted and tidy; the plastic baskets piled high and the washing machines' doors open ready. Still some recorded music. David Bowie's 'Suffragette City'. He emptied the clothes into a machine, poured washing powder into a slot and then pushed in the coins and waited for the hum of the motor and the jerk as the water gushed in. But he couldn't sit and wait. Not this Saturday. He couldn't sit and watch the washing, the endless swirling and swishing.

The park was just across the road. It was a tired place, just neat and functional with patchy grass criss-crossed by concrete paths. In the middle stood a green wrought-iron bandstand, now littered with fallen autumn leaves, and over on the far side was a children's area with two swings, one damaged and hanging crookedly, and a shiny slide. Across the park and opposite the shops and launderette was the gloomy Victorian church set back behind railings, and on either side the big houses stood, three storeys high, red-brick with turrets and castellated balconies.

There was no one around and he sat on a bench, straight-backed, arms folded and legs outstretched, listening to the Saturday traffic and the ebb and flow of footsteps. It was a pale day on the edge of winter, a weak sun appearing through shuffling poplars, which showered mottled leaves onto the grass and paths.

He'd seen her before in the launderette on Saturday mornings. Normally she stayed inside with the boy, who played around with odd cars and bits she brought for him, but this morning, for some reason, she had followed him across the road to the park seat.

She dropped a bag of jelly beans between them on the bench. The kid flashed yellow in his plastic coat as he rode past on his two-wheeler, every so often stopping by them to dig into the bag.

'Kevin! Kev! Give the man one,' she said this time. The kid looked up at her and she nodded.

'Go on.' He rummaged in the bag, looking closely for a colour he didn't like. 'Come on!' She held up the bag and the kid fished out a red bean, which he automatically lifted toward his open mouth. 'No!' she shouted, and so he opened out his hand and pushed the sticky bean towards Frank.

He shook his head. 'No thanks.'

'Go on' she persisted. 'He'll never learn otherwise.'

'OK, thanks.'

The boy took another for himself and then made off on another circle around them.

She was a plump girl. The purplish mottling of her cleavage and breasts that dolloped soft and fat over her tight V-necked jumper aroused him: a mixture of tingling excitement and fear, and he had to lean forward over his knees to hide his erection. Fuck! he thought.

She had a flabby, pallid face, with spots speckling her chin and around the corners of her full lips. He noticed the dimple when she smiled. He didn't know why she had to wear such large round glasses and that pink colour. She needed to wash her hair too, straggling down to her shoulders.

'You come every Saturday, don't you? I've seen you often.'

He nodded without looking at her.

'I bring some of Mum's as well,' adding, 'I live with Mum now.' She laughed. 'How funny's that!'

'Yeah.' He tried to smile

The kid managed to ring his bell as he passed.

Frank nodded towards him. 'How old?'

'Nearly four.' She sounded surprised. 'I can't really think he'll be going to school soon. God! Doesn't seem possible.' She pushed the bag of sweets towards him. 'Have another if you want.' And then went on speaking quickly. 'No – he'll be four the eighteenth of December.' She laughed again. 'Shame, really, having that and then Christmas so soon – it's better if it's spread out, don't you think? Mine's in May – the third. When's yours, then?'

He bent down to scrape a rotten leaf from the sole of his boot. 'November.' He nodded again towards the boy. 'He rides that bike well.'

She nodded and pulled her thick blue cardigan around her, covering her breasts for a minute. 'How old will you be then, this November? It's not Fireworks Day, is it? That would be good, a big bonfire and fireworks on your birthday.'

Now as he looked at her, he noticed the dimple because she was smiling.

'It's the twenty-seventh.'

'And?' She stared at him. 'And – how old? I'd say about thirty-ish.'

'I'll be twenty-two.'

'God!' she tossed her head. 'I thought you were older; you look older, I think. It's because you're dark and . . . well, you know, strong, sort of muscly, not fat and not . . . anyway. Don't you think? I think dark people always look older; the fair ones look younger, kinda more babyish. Baby-faced. Anyway, I was just wondering – I'm Julie, by the way – I was wondering, why don't you come with me and my friends to the Cavendish tonight? You know – have a beer. Cheer yourself up. You look a bit fed up. I said to Kevin, that man looks fed up this morning. I said to him let's go over the park and you can give him a sweet. So, look, we go about eight. Mum doesn't mind; it's my night out, Saturdays. We don't do any harm. Have a beer and a laugh and that's it. Why don't you come?' She touched him lightly, but he tightened, jerked his arm away like an electric shock and he knew she'd noticed; looked surprised, a bit hurt.

But she went on. 'That's if you've not already doing something. You know, got another date. This isn't a date, by the way.' She spoke quickly and gave a little laugh. 'I'm just asking, that's all.'

But he was thinking of Ruby saying, 'Come here and let's give you a hug.' And then, as he froze, 'It's not that bad, is it, Frankie? Never mind. It doesn't matter. One day someone will come along, and you will love a hug,' but he knew that wasn't true. He could take a hug from Kitty, but that was all. But . . . seeing his mother on the sofa with her legs wide open and pants round her ankles and her breasts showing and Carl on top, naked from the waist down, making animal noises. 'Stop it, Carl!' his mum had shouted. She did try to push him off. She did try. He was sure of it. And she called out to him, 'Frankie!' And Carl had laughed and pushed her down and said, 'You want to watch this, you little fucker. You might learn something,' and started going up and down and laughing and groaning, and he had fled outside, gone to the shed for his bike, and although it was dark and he had no lights, he cycled away, away, down the road and then another road; on the pavements, like Dad had told him. 'Keep to the pavement, son, then you'll be safe. Not on the roads yet, lad.' The bike was his father; it was being with his father, being near him. Wanting him. And Carl had smashed it.

Julie was waiting for him to say something and suddenly he felt rather sorry for her. 'I'll see, OK?'

He stood up. 'It should be done by now.' And he nodded towards the launderette. 'Thanks for the sweet,' he called as the kid cycled past again.

'Kev!' she called. 'Come on. We're going now.'

Frank picked up the bike and carried it across the road for her.


He thought it was all so brown and cheap-looking: imitation wood, plastic tops stained and scratched, huge glass ashtrays bulging with fag ends. Nicotine hung in the air, clung to the curtains and stained the walls yellowish. He looked at the old-fashioned black-and-white photos in their thin frames; the Co-op in 1922, with staff outside in long overalls and caps, and another of the gas works. The third was taken in the park; a woman in a tailored coat and cloche hat pushing a huge pram with the hood up and beside her a neatly dressed girl in an overcoat and hat rather like the woman's; it must be her mother. She was smiling down at the child, who was pointing at something. A good mother, probably. The band-stand was there in the background. He would have liked to change this place: make tables from solid oak with turned legs; straight-backed chairs with curling arms and stretchers; solid wooden floors, polished and grainy. And seafaring pictures, galleons, rolling waves and sea birds on the walls. Away from here. Far away.

The anxiety had gone, the nervousness. Julie was gabbling

with the other two He'd bought her a Dubonnet; the others wanted vodka and orange. She had make-up on this evening, thick to cover up her spots. They were all heavily made-up: thick lashes, dark lines around the eyes, bright lips. Julie had her hair held up in a blue hair clip. They're quite relaxed here, he thought. Easy. It's normal for them; like at work, the men always joking. He needn't have been so agitated, waiting outside across the road like that, half hidden in the bus shelter, pretending to read the evening paper. But Julie had spotted him and called him over. She'd been OK; she hadn't flirted or touched him.

Frank relaxed against the wall, his beer on the bar. He couldn't not have a beer; he'd make it last the evening, though. And then for one mad moment he thought he saw Kitty, this dark-haired girl, standing alone. The same height, the same flicking curls, the same long legs. And she was smoking in that awkward way, holding the cigarette away from her face. She was half turned from him. Not Kitty, but lovely all the same. The girls let him pass without noticing him as he moved around them and towards her. She saw him and smiled, her glass empty.

'Can I get you a drink?'

She stared at him for a moment and, swivelling round, called to a group playing darts beyond the fruit machine, her voice horribly shrill. 'Hey, Johnnie. He wants to buy me a drink.' She jerked her thumb toward Frank, threw back her head. He heard the laughter and a wave of shame engulfed him like a hot flush. He turned, unseeing, deaf, and then felt the thud in his back, which sent him lurching into the arms of a man carrying two glasses of beer.

'What the hell!' the man shouted. 'Fucking idiot.'

He tried to brace himself against the second blow to his back and the hand that grabbed his shoulder. It was a mechanical reaction that he picked up the bar stool. It was not heavy; he swung it around him and it crashed on the bar top, one leg spinning away. He held the broken stool up, high above his head. Ready this time. Ready.

It was Julie who pulled away the stool, who took his arm, who led him away, out of the pub and across the road to the park,

'What happened, Frank? she asked. 'What was all that about?'

He shook his head. 'It's OK,' he choked. 'You go back. Go on, please.' She didn't touch him as he walked away from her into the darkness.

# Henry

He was wearing the frock coat Phoebe had found in Carnaby Street and bought for him. She had been very pleased with herself. 'The caption is going to be: "Artist at Work."' And raised her eyebrows as she dumped the bag onto his workbench. 'Under the photo, I mean. Go on. Stop frowning and have a look. It'll just make a really good promotional photo. Go on.' She sounded impatient as he, reacting slowly as always, had lifted the bag, eyed her with suspicion and then, with a sigh of irritation, pulled it out, unfolded it and hung it out to look.

'Isn't it great? Put it on. Oh, go on, Henry, for God's sake,' she had persisted.

And she was right: the black frock coat, which he had later deliberately daubed with bright oils, made a perfect painting overall. Buttoned up to the neck, it fell from his shoulders and swung about gracefully as he moved. Made him look taller, slimmer. Secretly he enjoyed wearing it, although he would never admit it to Phoebe; she always thought she was right about everything anyway. But he was wearing now, in his studio.

The converted garage, now his studio, was bright and clean, and the vivid colours of his paintings showed up well against the whitewashed walls. Now he lifted the easel to the far end of the garage and then, with his back to the windows, stood, arms folded, and studied the painting. Wasn't sure what Phoebe would think of chickens. These were the chickens from home. Golden-speckled and chestnut-brown hens scratching in the soil for grubs, their thin creamy legs hard with scales, lifting delicately; long claws, heads down, bright red combs, the texture of rubber overshadowing small, curved beaks, black beaded eyes with raspberry-pink centres. Searching. The evening light tipped the edge of the feathers. There were daisies among tufts of grass, and long evening shadows. He had been absorbed, watching them and making the sketches, hoping, but pretending indifference that Phoebe would select it for the exhibition. It was a change from the horses and racing scenes for which, in his small way, he was beginning to be known. His painting *Mounting Jockeys* was now hanging in the Cheltenham Club dining room, thanks to Lola and her friend, who had commissioned the painting of his racehorse, Dalliance. And there had been a review of his work in the *Horse & Hound*, with his photo wearing the frock coat and with Phoebe's caption, 'Artist at work.' And underneath, 'Naturalist painter, talented Henry Bancroft, who studied in Milan under Gabriel Ufino, is our new Stubbs.' The magazine was somewhere among all his stuff. He'd been pleased with himself.

For *Mounting Jockeys* he had worked from a series of sketches and photographs taken the last time he went with Lola to the races. Had stood by the fence of the mounting paddock and watched stable boys, in their overalls and boots, walk in the horses, fiddle with girths and stirrups ready for the jockeys – in vivid red shirts, blue caps, white breeches – to mount. The jockeys pushed down hard with rounded backs, knees level with the horses' necks. He had to work quickly, capturing a toss of the head, a dark eye, ears pricked or flattened, fine legs and polished hooves glinting in the light, necks and rumps, glass-radiant like shifting streaks of lightning. He decided to include some trees and hills beyond the white railings and a sky rolling with purple clouds. He was rather chuffed with this imaginary addition. He turned away from the very different painting of chickens and, pulling the canvas chair from his drawing table, collapsed into its sagging seat.

This garage had once housed Edmundo Ross's Rolls-Royce. It must have been a huge car! Max had paid for the back wall to be replaced with plate-glass windows. The flat was above. Max had bought it years ago, but now that he so seldom came to London he'd given it over to Henry when he returned from Milan, 'to get started on the London scene'. Meanwhile, Max, who had become hopelessly enamoured with Italy after his frequent visits to Henry while he was in Milan, was now in the process of buying a house in a small village on the edge of Lake Garda. He chose Garda because it was the nearest to the city of Verona. It had been a toss-up between Milan and Verona, but on balance Max declared Verona the winner.

He was exhausted by his father's enthusiasms and energy; he was beaten by it, could not compete: it made him tired and depressed. Because of his dreamy, withdrawn demeanour they had nicknamed him 'the poet' at school. They didn't know he was a cheat. Still, that was then, and this is now. And now he was allowing Phoebe to organise him. Anyway, as an agent, it was her job to put on exhibitions, to promote new artists. She was older than him, knew her way around the art scene better than him. Knew all the right people. Great networker, someone said. They had met on the plane coming back from Italy; that's how it all started.

Now he was aware of the blur of traffic. He looked past the painting to the yard outside, pebbled and with a couple of terracotta pots Mother had contributed. Beyond were the gardens and further back still the brown bricks of terraced houses, which overlooked the park. There was never any direct sunlight, only shadows that crossed the yard morning and evening.

He looked at his watch. He was going to be late for the cinema.

None of the others wanted to come back for coffee, just Phoebe, of course. They had had a drink at the pub around the corner and he'd sat and listened to the talk of the City, and banks, retailing and business, and had nothing to say. Nothing. These others had to go because of 'work tomorrow' and laughed. Phoebe didn't have to open up the gallery until 10 a.m. and in any case she had parked her car in the mews.

Phoebe was easy because she never stopped talking, so he was able to drift along without having to do much. Although he found it tiresome at times. The constant bright chatter.

She wanted first to go into the studio. 'Have you finished the jockey painting yet?' She was straight in, pushing, pushing.

'I have. And I've started something a bit different.'

'Let's see, then. We haven't got a bundle of time, you know. It's only a couple of weeks.'

He said nothing, simply pointed out the chickens as she went on. Almost too busy talking to look, really look.

'I'm keen to put this exhibition on. Your first. Personally, I think it'll go down well. There are still buyers, collectors who like the realistic school. Not everyone wants pseudo-Picasso or French impressionist-type stuff. I've sent out over a hundred invites to the previewers and we have adverts in most of the mags. I'm really hopeful that Duncan will bring those Moroccans. Anyway, I told you they're looking for some sort of holiday advertising. You know, camels in the desert kind of thing. God, Henry if you got that it'd really bring in the money. We'll need at least two days to hang. I'll send Daniel with the van. You will have enough, won't you? Ten at least. If possible.'

'Probably. Do you want to look at this or not?'

She stopped. 'Chickens! Um . . . not sure.'

He put the painting back against the easel with a shrug.

'Look, Henry, you don't seem very enthusiastic. Well, anyway – it's gone too far. Look, I have an eye. Trust me. All the connections.'

She was wearing a knee-length black skirt decorated with white squiggles, a low-cut white blouse and flat red shoes. Her dark hair bobbed just above shiny red-and-gold earrings. She was smart and together and it suited him to allow her to 'brisk' him along, boss him around, but he had made it quite obvious that he had no desire to hold her hand.

Then she looked at the chickens again. 'Gosh! Yes! I do see what you mean about something different. Perhaps . . . actually, I think it's OK. We'll put it in. Never know exactly what the market wants. No harm in trying. I mean, it is a good painting, Henry. Just not sure how many people want chickens on their wall. I know some people will say you're a draughts-man rather than an artist but . . .' She moved away to look at the three on the wall: one of the two mares in Lola's meadow, flies buzzing, hot flicks of the tails; another a straight-backed rider alone and stationary on a hill overlooking the valley beyond. Rather heroic.

'That's my Aunt Lola. It's nothing like her.' His laugh was a smothered grunt.

The third was of a solitary huge grey gelding standing in a stable, straw on the floor, hay in a net; a cream-and-brown painting. She nodded again. 'The frames are good too. Did you go to Holloway's? He's brilliant, I think. So helpful. A really good eye. Basically, these paintings can take clean modern frames or the fancy gilt type. Depends. But for this exhibition and the sort I've got coming – I think those plain frames are just right. Don't detract but set them off well. Well, that's all going OK, then. Any more for me to see?'

'Not really. I'm going to get the coffee. You can stay here if you want, but I'm going up.' And taking keys out of his pocket, he opened the door to the flat and disappeared up the stairs.

# Frank

Ruby stood outside the back door and shouted. 'Frank! It's Kitty on the phone.' She took a few steps towards the shed. 'Frank!'

He put down the tabletop on the bench beside Stan, and with long strides ran towards the house.

Ruby was talking when he got to the hallway where the phone hung on the wall. He took it from her.

'Hello, Kit. How are you?'

'All good, Frankie. I've got lots to tell you.' Her words were racing and breathless.

'Guess what, Frankie.'

'Go on.'

'I've got a job, Frankie, isn't it good? So soon. We were out yesterday, you know, shopping in the afternoon after Steve had finished, and in one of the main shopping parts. There's a big church near, and there was this hairdresser with a big notice in the window saying "stylist wanted".' She laughed. 'Steve made me go in 'cos actually I was a bit scared, Frankie, because there were lots of people there. But afterwards Steve said that was a good sign because it means that it's a busy place and I'm more likely to keep my job. Anyway, Frankie, I saw the boss, John, and said what I'd done, you know, and my training at evening classes and he said start on Monday. This Monday. It's for a trial week, but I'm sure it'll be OK, don't you think, Frankie?'

She sounded so happy. 'Steve says it's 'cos he fancies me. Kept looking at my legs! That I got the job!'

He could imagine her head thrown back as she laughed.

'It's not that good money Frank, just seventy quid a week, but you know I get tips and all that. Anyway, Steve is doing all right. What do you think, Frankie?'

'Sounds really good, Kit. Really good. And how's the flat? I'm making you a coffee table. I was doing it when you phoned.'

'Steve's mum and dad came up last weekend just for the Sunday and brought some kitchen bits and we've got a settee and chair from a second-hand shop. Oh, and Steve let me buy some ready-made curtains – they're pretty. He's says he'll put them up soon.'

Frank had that sickness in his stomach. 'How's his job going? Was it a good move?'

'He's busy. They're building a block of flats; it's bit of a journey out. I'll have to catch a bus too, but he says he's going to get a car on the "never-never" soon 'cos he can't be doing with the buses.' She laughed again. He could see her sitting, legs crossed, phone to her ear, smiling, eyes bright, the dark curls flashing with the movement of her head. Her long fingers tapping her knees; a habit she had.

He could hear a man's voice, shouting.

'Frank, I have to go. When will you come? It's been such ages. We're putting our names down for a council house. It's so good to have something of your own, Frankie. Be happy, Frankie.'

'I'll come with the table—'

'Oh, sorry, Frank, I forgot to say thank you. It will be really good to have a table. Come soon, then.'

'OK. Everyone is OK here, by the way. I'll say cheerio, then.'

'Bye Frankie. Take care.'

He hung the phone back on the wall. Ruby was in the kitchen fiddling over lunch. He went to her.

103

'I'll do the spuds.' He picked out some potatoes from the metal vegetable rack beside the kitchen door. 'How was church?'

'Sad. Mrs Yellon has died. The funeral's next Wednesday. And it was cold there today. Doesn't do my legs any good. I asked the vicar over coffee – he said the heating was old. Needs replacing.'

'Do they need new pipes or what, or a boiler, or . . .? You probably don't know, Ruby. Don't worry. Pity I'm not a plumber. I'd help otherwise.' She looked round at him and they both laughed.

'There is this other thing though, Frank. There's a broken bit off the end of my pew. The whole end bit, the kind of carved bit; it's just fallen off. It's rotted, I think. You couldn't do anything about that, could you, Frank? Just a thought.'

There was a stillness, rustled by breathless whispers and felted footsteps melting along the matting of the library floor. The grey sky hanging behind the narrow windows was supplemented by long strips of neon lights and Frank sat staring at a moth caught in the tubing above his head. The place smelled of baked beans.

He turned the pages of the book silently so as not to attract attention. He had already flipped through *English Church Architecture* and now hoped to find what he was looking for in *Grand Designs. A History of Victorian Architecture.* What he wanted were illustrations of wood carvings, but there was nothing in these books; they were more about the architectural designs of the churches and cathedrals, the building techniques from the crypts to the fan ceilings. He understood, for the first time, that churches were designed on the shape of the cross and, looking through the drawings, appreciated the skill of the craftsmen – the stonemasons, the carpenters – and wanted more than anything to repair the broken piece in Ruby's church. His City & Guilds training included the history of furniture-making and styles, but almost nothing about Church decorative carving. He'd been in to look at the pews' carved arms and end carvings, and found the broken end Ruby had mentioned. He made sketches in his notebook of the carved finial that he hoped to replicate. It would be something to be proud of before leaving. He could do this for her. Not for the glory of God. No way! Not like the original builders and stonemasons and carpenters, who worked for the glory of God. He was going to do it for the glory of Ruby.

Being there in the library was a new experience and something he determined to do more often now he had the confidence; made him feel less ordinary somehow.

He looked up between the pages, under his eyebrows, at the girl sitting behind the desk. There was something about her. She had a mop of frizzy red hair, short and held off her face by a blue velvet ribbon; her knees, round and neatly together, showed below the edge of her dress, mottled orange and brown, high-necked and long-sleeved. When she got up with a pile of books, he noticed the flat bronze shoes, which tapped as she walked.

It was nearly closing time and the woman who had been tidying the chairs, pushing them into place, ruffled some papers on a table and called out, 'Night, Jeanette. See you Monday.'

'Yes, see you on Monday.'

Her voice was high-pitched like a child's. Her round blue eyes matched her hairband.

He knew she'd seen him. Of course she'd seen him, but he hoped to escape while she went round the corner with another pile of books ...

He quickly replaced his books, careful to put them in exactly their right places and hurried towards the door, but she was there before he could get away, asking if she could help. 'Are you looking for anything in particular?'

'No. That's fine, thanks.'

She repeated. 'Can I help? What was it you wanted?'

'Well ... I'm interested in wood carvings. The sort you get in churches. Church carvings, I was interested to look at,' he repeated, angry that she'd stopped him, that she had asked him. 'It's not something you probably have.'

'Try me!' She smiled. 'We can order books in if what you want is not here, but you might find something helpful in the art section,' and she moved along the shelves. 'Have look here. This, for instance.' She took out a book and opened it: *Medieval Art*. There might be something here. Anyway, have a look. I'll leave you to it. Oh, and look, what about this? *Primitive Wood Carvings*.' She smiled as she passed it to him.

Frank took the books. It was gone five o'clock. 'Can I borrow them at all? I'm not a member.'

She laughed. 'That's fine, it'll only take a minute. You're allowed five books. You can have them for three weeks. After that there is a small fine.'

She moved behind the counter. 'I'll give you our leaflet so you can see all the dos and don'ts. But first let's get you joined. I'm always pleased when someone new joins. Are you new to this area, then?'

'You could say that.' He tried a small, crooked smile.

'I'm shutting shop after this,' she said.

Her head was bent over the forms. 'Could you just write down your name and address, please?' And she pushed the form across the desk.

While he filled in the details, she fetched her coat, a light blue check to match her hairband and her shoulder bag,

'Which way are you going?'

Frank nodded in the direction of home, the two books under his arm, and he turned to the door. 'Thanks for your help.'

'My name's Jeanette,' she said, 'and yours is—' She took up the form and put it in a folder. 'Frank Richardson. Are you a carpenter, then?'

She was a pale, petite little thing. 'I'll look out some more books for you in the week. Come later next week,' she piped. 'See what I've managed to find.'

She was walking beside him to the door

'Right! Well, thanks. Thanks a lot. We didn't cover church carving in City and Guilds.' Why on earth did he say that?

She closed and locked the door and he was unsure whether to wait or not, but to his relief she said, 'Well, cheerio! I go over there to the bus stop.'

There was a pride in having the books, taking them home, to have been to a library in the first place, and wanting to get back to read them. To study. Study! And he would repair Ruby's pew end one way or the other. He'd make a tracing from one of the others. It was a good feeling to know he had the skills and he had already decided that he would go back for more books; the more he could learn, the better.

He had the three books she had ordered in for him in his rucksack beside him. *Medieval Carvings*, *Gothic Church Decoration* and *The History and Symbolism of Wooden Decorations from c. 1500 to c. 1850*. The other two were in his bedroom and not due back for another two weeks, which was good. He was beginning to be obsessed by these books and his feeling of ownership. He already knew that he would never be able to return them.

He had deliberately left it until almost closing time and decided to ask her out for cup of something. He had said to himself, 'It's only a cup of tea, for Christ's sake.' And the thing was, she didn't look at him like Julie did. For although Julie was always laughing and pretending, he could see her eyes asking him. Pleading with him. Silently. She wanted more; he could sense it. This Jeanette was different. Seemed genuinely interested in his work and wanting to be helpful. He was pleased with the books she had found for him, and he had divulged to her his original reason for wanting them was to repair a broken pew end in his – he had hesitated – 'foster mother, Ruby's church'. But it wasn't just that; he was being commissioned by Tanner himself to design and then make one-offs for wealthy individuals. Currently he was working on a double wardrobe for a pretty grand house near Winchester; he'd gone with Tanner to measure up. They wanted the furniture to reflect the antique Georgian, 'In a modern sort of way,' the woman had said vaguely, so these books he could see would be invaluable in giving him ideas. The wardrobe he 'modernised' by making it in quarter-sawn light oak, which produces a distinctive grain but, of course, is lighter, more modern than the traditional mahogany. In fact, the wardrobe was entered as part of his final exam.

'I'd like to see some of your work,' Jeanette had said. 'Perhaps the pew end when it's done. When will it be? Do you think?'

Today it was an orange velvet band pulling the curls from her forehead and a green dress, again round-necked and short, to the knees; she had on the same bronze pumps.

'Fancy a cup of tea?'

Her blue eyes were open wide, like a doll's, and her complexion pale, smooth. It could be china. There was something about her, but not the sort you fantasised about. When he was rubbing himself and spewing sperm into the toilet paper he kept hidden in the bottom drawer, he thought about Julie and her mottled breasts and large nipples, which he had made out once behind a tight t-shirt. He imagined them large and brown. He could feel her fleshy thighs and fat buttocks.

'It's nice to have cup and saucers for a change – real china, I mean,' Jeanette was saying. 'I don't know about you, but I get a bit fed up with thick mugs and plastic this and plastic that.'

'I'd really like to see it,' she had said.

Now she had stopped talking about the cups and was drinking. He noticed how white her hands were. She was elfin, he decided.

'OK. Perhaps I'll show you sometime, like the piece in the church. But I've got a bit of news. My boss Tallinn is putting me forward for some kind of restoration work up Darlington way.'

'Darlington?' She put down her cup and leaned her elbows on the table. 'Darlington? 'she repeated.

'He's got a friend up there; they did their apprenticeship together years ago. Anyhow, this friend has asked Doug for a cabinetmaker who can work on this seventeenth-century place, Bishop's Lodge, it's called, which the council want renovating. I think they're planning it as an English Heritage place for tourists, well, and just people, to visit. This bloke, Doug's friend, works for English Heritage, I think. Not absolutely sure, But Doug said English Heritage are involved. Anyway, I said yes without a second's thought, because my sister Kitty lives up that way. In Doncaster. I can get to her quicker. See her more often. She's been gone since 1981.'

'So you said yes, then?'

Was she disappointed? She took a brown sugar lump and crunched it. 'Sounds really interesting.' And then put her hand across her lips 'Sorry.' She swallowed the sugar down with the remains of her tea, 'What sort of things will you be doing, then?'

He shook his head, raised his eyebrows. She was someone he could look at directly. 'Not sure, but banisters and finials, if you know what they are.'

She nodded, her elbows still on the table, her face held between her hands as she stared at him

'Oak panelling was mentioned, and shutters.' He tapped his bag. 'These books will come in really useful.'

'You can only have them for three weeks,' she half whispered. 'You'll have to bring them back before you go. But don't worry, I'll make sure the Darlington Library gets them in for you. I will certainly do that.'

She deserved a smile. 'That's kind, Jeanette. Thanks for your trouble. And don't worry, I'll get them back before I go.'

'If it's soon, you know, that you're going, will you let me see what you've done in St Margaret's?'

That evening over supper Frank said, 'Doug Tallinn called me in today.'

Stan looked up from his mash. 'Oh yes. And?'

'There may be a job going. Darlington way. One of his mates phoned from there and asked if he knew a skilled chippy who could do some restoration stuff. He said did I want to go.'

'And? Do you? Want to go?' Stan took another mouthful. 'Good money, is it? After all your work. And you've been there – what is it, seven bloody years? Though you've done good, lad. I'll say that. All those bloody exams. Blimey, I thought they'd never end.'

Ruby laughed at him. 'You loved it, Stan! Don't say you didn't. Out there, the two of you. Chewing the fat over this and that; I never saw you 'cept to eat.'

'We had to work things out, that's all. He did well, anyhow. Manager of the furniture workshop. I should bloody well think so. Of course, he'd ask you, the silly bugger. I reckon you go, Frank, if he can do without you. You're twenty-five, aren't you? A man. Get out there, lad. What do you think, Ruby?'

He saw her eyes moisten and redden, and he was like the little boy who first came crying at their door, looking at the ant in the cracked lino. He wanted to put his arms round her.

She had shuffled in her slippers to the sink, stood with her back to him. Was she crying? But she turned, red-eyed only. 'Go on, Frankie, whatever is best. We'll be here anyway. We won't be going far, will us, Stan?

But Stan had gone into the sitting room. Frank heard the telly blasting. He picked up the plates and took them to the sink.

'Go on,' he said. 'I'll do these. Go and sit down – I'll bring you your tea. It's not for three months yet, Ruby. You'll have me hanging around until then, at least.' How else could he say all he wanted to say, for Christ's sake?

'Darlington way?' Ruby looked at him. 'Where is that, exactly? Is it far? Is it a long way away, Frankie?'

'Is it a bit, Ruby, but I'll be able to keep my eye on Kitty. It's not so far from Doncaster. I'll stop off on my way up to see her, tell her where I'll be for the next year or two. You know, it's nearly two years since I last went up there.' Almost to himself, 'Too long. I need to keep an eye.' He went to her, put a hand on her shoulder. 'And I will come home to see you, I promise, and I will phone every week.'

He walked into the living room. 'It'll be good money, Stan. I'll be able to help out even more. You can count on that.'

1985–1986

# Alice

'All roads lead to Darlington,' Da said as he dragged her suitcase off the back seat.

'What's the time?' she asked. 'Are we OK for time, Da?' But he was busy scanning the board to see which platform.

'Number five,' he said. 'It's always number five. I don't know why I'm looking.'

They crossed over the bridge.

'Are you sure this is right, Da? Shall I just check?'

'You'll do as you'll do, no doubt, but this is right.'

'There's loads of people. Shall I get a seat, do you think?' The ticket was in her mac pocket, ready. She checked it was still there; took it out and looked at it. 'Carriage H,' she said. 'It's carriage H, Da.'

They walked further down the platform and he put down the case. They stood looking at each other. 'All right for money?' he asked.

'I've got money.' She tossed her head. 'I'm a working girl now!' She tapped the bag. 'Money galore.'

'That's all right, then.' He looked at her sideways, shook hair out of his eyes, then fished out a £5 note from his pocket. He passed it to her. 'There's a bit extra,' he said.

'I know I'm an art teacher and all that, but I don't feel as grown-up as I should, I don't think. I'm twenty-three, Da. I know girls of my age who are married.'

'You? Grown up? You'll never be grown-up. Not for my money, any road. You don't want to go thinking of marrying yet. Plenty of time.'

She laughed. She liked that. 'I don't know if I want to, anyway,' she said. 'I do and I don't.'

'Well, there's a surprise!' And he winked.

'I do want to see Jo – I miss her being away – and I'm sure it will be fun; we're going to an art exhibition – it's a friend of hers, I think. I'm looking forward to that, but' – she looked at him – 'I'm a bit scared at the same time. I don't know why. But I'm nervous, as if something is going to happen.'

Was that his impatient frown? she wondered.

'Why have you got that mac on? You've got a mac on, lass.'

She shrugged. 'Easier than squeezing it into my case, that's all.'

'You're only going for the weekend. Why so much? Your ma's the same. Everything but the kitchen sink.'

'I know. I know, Da.' She put her arm through his. 'I'm so happy at home, so happy with everything. I love teaching the kids, wish I could do full time, but actually I do enjoy helping out in the shop too. It's different and quite fun, and if we're not busy he lets me sit in the back and I can prepare my lessons and think up ideas. It all works out really well, one way and the other. And I see friends in Darlington, too. I enjoy Darlington. Like looking at the shops and stuff.'

Once she was settled in her seat, the suitcase carefully stashed away, she watched as clusters of houses and farms, breaking into the fields, and hills rushed past her, and wished she hadn't said any of that. Da would only worry. It was childish and selfish. She would ring them tonight. She would sound happy, no matter what. But going to London! She didn't know what to think and simply could not stop fidgeting in her seat. She thought the woman opposite was looking at her and wanted to explain that she was going to London for the first time. Perhaps the woman would laugh in surprise.

# Henry

He was renting it from the council, this Victorian chapel standing in the middle of a disused graveyard, and they had turned it into a very attractive space: brick walls painted white, floors covered with green haircord matting, spotlights that could be positioned to highlight the paintings. A square entrance lobby had two old-fashioned wooden coat stands and a long table for leaflets, catalogues and the essential visitors' book. This evening Jill, a friend of Phoebe's, had been instructed to stand with the book and to give the welcome smile in front of the large poster of Henry in his frock coat, paintbrush in hand, standing beside his *Mounting Jockeys*.

Now he looked incongruous, a pink rose hanging crookedly from his tweed jacket. Phoebe had insisted, but he was hot with anxiety and the rose was already wilting. He stood grumpily in the midst of the heave and swirl of guests who, holding high their glasses of champagne, wove in and out of the cigarette smoke, talking and laughing loudly. This is just a party, he thought as see observed the layered frilly skirts beneath tight black tops and the girl in the bright pink tight-fitting number, held up by one shoulder strap. Completely over the top, he thought, yet flattered that guests had taken the trouble to dress up for his exhibition. He imagined them saying, 'I went to Henry Bancroft's opening exhibition, you know. Yes! Right at the beginning, believe me, it was so obvious where he was going. Been following him ever since. Incredible work. Such talent!' He was grumpily aware of the gay chatter, and he convinced himself that no one was, actually, the slightest bit interested in the paintings. It was just an occasion to see and be seen. He was angry, thinking everyone stupid, and so drank heavily, taking glasses from the tin trays being handed round by dressed-up art students, and filled his mouth with the passing canapés. Then he noticed his mother for the first time as she extricated herself from a gaggle of laughing women and wandered alone towards his painting of two racing jockeys, where he joined her, suddenly needing her. Needing her approval.

'It's quite hot in here, isn't? I suppose the windows are impossible to open,' she said. They looked up at the oval and barred windows set up high above them.

'I'll get Jill to open the front doors,' he said, 'to get a bit of a draught, perhaps. Stay there.' He was grateful for any excuse to do something. But she was more taken by the heat than his work!

As he was approaching Jill, the main doors opened and three girls, followed by his friend Johnnie Munch, came into the lobby. Johnny, overexcited as usual, banged Henry on the shoulder and shouted, 'Well! The artist himself. Here to greet us, no less!' He pointed to the girls, 'Henry, this is my friend and silversmith Jo Wilkinson, and her friend Lucy and' – he turned to the third girl, still only halfway through the door – 'and . . .' He hesitated.

'Alice? Of course. This is Alice.' He held open the door for her to go in front. 'She's down from County Durham, apparently. Just to see your exhibition, I'm sure!'

Jo took Alice by the arm. 'For goodness' sake, Johnnie. Do stop going on. She's down to see me. Go on in. Standing here like lemons.' She turned to Henry. 'He's mad.' And then, in case he hadn't remembered, 'I'm Jo Wilkinson. Is it OK to be here? We do want to see your paintings. I know about you anyway because I know Phoebe through Lizzy. Lizzy Selby,

119

who works in the Whitechapel Gallery. Look, she's over there with her boss.'

Henry shook his head; he wasn't sure: he'd met so many different people through Phoebe. 'Have a drink,' he said, 'I must go and find my mother.'

They were in a knot at the bottom of the stairs; his father had a hand on the banisters, leaning towards Phoebe with that look of amused interest, his head shiny under the spotlight and the remaining curls caught in his collar; Phoebe in her tight little green skirt, the close-fitting sleeveless top, the red rose pertly pinned into position and the red shoes to match. All very carefully thought out! And Mother in her linen trouser suit, creased and careless and tired. He knew she wouldn't want to stay long. He understood that and wasn't hurt this time because she was showing genuine amazement and a kind of pride. She'd never seriously looked at his paintings before; this evening she gave him one of her amazing smiles. He would hold on to that as long as he could.

'We've booked a table for eight-thirty,' Max called to Henry. 'The car's just around the corner. I've booked for five of us. Anyone else you want to include?

'Sorry, Rob's not here. Sends his love. Something to do with work . . .'She sounded weary.'

Max took another glass of wine from the passing tray. 'Well, let's go up, shall we? Coming, Fee?' Henry was unsure whether to go with them or not. The whole thing was awkward. 'I'm very impressed, Henry. Really good stuff. Lola is furious to miss it, especially as she has deemed herself your first patron. I particularly like the one by the railings. Stood there often enough. I've bought that one. Didn't you see the red dot! Be lots more by the end. What's up here, then?'

Phoebe moved to the first step, her hand close to his on the banisters. 'Oh, you know – not racehorses. Come on.'

She led the way to the loft room where there were three paintings: the chickens, five hunting hounds surging up and over a thicket and Lola's grey mare in her field: the painting he had started while waiting for his A-level results nine years ago. He was sorry Lola could not be here. He could imagine her rushing in in her mucky jodhpurs, boots and flamboyant scarf. But, he thought, if she had worn the strapless dress, older though she was, she would have stolen the show. She always stole the show, but never consciously, just because she was what she was. Thoroughly unselfconscious. Natural. What a gift!

Phoebe excused herself and, he noted with irritation, tripped efficiently back down the stairs in her red shoes, her dark bob bouncing in rhythm.

'She knows what she's doing. It's a good contact for you, Henry.' Max raised his glass and tipped the edge of Henry's. 'I've got a lot to tell you about Italy, haven't I?' He turned to Fiona. 'Mum thinks I'm mad as usual.' She shrugged her shoulders and turned away shyly. 'She doesn't mind really. She's been over. You like the house, Fee, don't you? '

She raised her eyebrows.

'She loves it, Henry. She loves it. Tell him!'

She turned with raised eyebrows as Max leaned towards her with a kiss and a laugh.

'Of course I do. It's very lovely, Henry. Right by the lake. Huge gardens. Goodness knows how we'll manage it all.'

'Get gardeners. How else? Don't keep worrying about things; it's beautiful. We'll all get a lot of fun out of it.'

'Come on, Mother.' Henry took her arm and moved her back down the stairs.

She handed him her empty glass and took out a tissue from a pocket to blow her nose.

'Got a cold again?'

She shook her head 'Hay fever of some sort.' She gave him a wry smile. 'Allergic to crowds! Do you mind if we go now? See you at the restaurant? Get Dad for me. We'll be here all night otherwise.'

*

121

Alice stood alone, staring up at the painting: Lola in her hunting gear, straight-backed, on her bay mare, standing on the crest of a hill overlooking the tumbling Cotswolds, spread out under a grey sky broken by streaks of apricot and purple edges, the distance hazy in the morning mist. It had a red dot on it because Henry wanted Lola to have it. Phoebe grumbled about the thousands he would lose, but he chose this time to ignore he. He'd say in his head, 'Bossy!'

Now he moved around, pretending to socialise but all the time he was eyeing the willowy figure of the girl with the barley-coloured hair and long brown skirt. She even swayed slightly like a willow, he thought. She was alone and appeared engrossed. Sod all these people, he thought, and went over to her.

'It's got a red dot,' she said, turning. 'I'm not surprised.' She turned back to the painting and laughed. 'It makes me laugh to see this.' she said. 'It's so beautiful. I just can't imagine how you get, well, the perfection. No matter how hard I tried, I could never do that. Like a photograph, only so much more . . . if you see what I mean. I specially love the sky. I don't suppose I should say that.' She was looking at him and laughing, not a loud laugh but gentle, like a ripple. She laughed again. 'You should see my daubs and splodges and messing about.' As she was waving her hands around as if painting a large canvas, she lost her balance and he took her arm to steady her. She wasn't drunk. Perhaps it was just her getting a bit excited, animated?

'Sorry,' she said, 'I've got a bit of a . . .'

She turned to him, looked directly at him, obviously changing the subject, and he wondered why. 'You know Jo who I came with? She has horses and she taught me to ride a bit. I mean, not good at all. But I loved it. You seem to like horses a lot, if these paintings are anything to go by! I think they are beautiful animals, too.'

It was the simple joy, her impish smile, her lips turned up at the corners. She was speaking quickly, and he suspected that

122

she may be a bit nervous or shy or something. But whatever. It had never happened before, but he thought she was very lovely . . . and natural like Lola, but without the red lips. She didn't appear to be wearing any make-up.

'You paint too, then?' he asked.

'No, not really. Well, yes, I do . . . but it's completely different sort of painting from yours. I mean, I'm not really a painter. Not like you. I don't know why I mentioned it. But I can do enough to teach kids. That's what I do, teach art and other art stuff, you know crafty things, collages with materials, that sort of thing. That's what I do.'

He was already imagining her in the classroom, wafting between the tables, hands moving, lips smiling and the eyes of the kids, but she broke his dreaming with, 'Oh! look! Someone's waving at you. You'd better go.'

Later he asked, 'Would you like to come out for supper – with us. With my family and Phoebe, my agent, and so . . .?' His voice disappeared as he listened to himself.

She looked astonished. 'What now, you mean?' She was looking round for Jo and the others. He felt ridiculous. She said, 'Well, only if we all come, if you see what I mean?'

He said 'Yes, well, it's probably best if we leave it for tonight, on second thoughts.' And felt a complete fool.

# Max and Fiona

His cream jacket swung on a hook behind him; her coat was in a crumpled heap on the back seat. The evening was still warm and he had the roof open. He drove much too fast and hair whipped across her eyes.

'Good evening?' She felt his hand on her knee. He sometimes did that when he was driving.

She tried to think if it had been a good evening. 'It was, I'm sure. Yes, I think it all went very well.'

She knew he'd turned to look at her. 'Don't sound too enthusiastic!'

'Well – you know I'm not very good at those kinds of things.'

'But your son! Aren't you proud of him? Your good-for-nothing son!'

'I'm not sure exactly what I think.'

'And that Phoebe has it all wrapped up. Best thing that's happened to Henry. He needs someone like her, don't you think, Fee? He'll end up marrying her. You'll see!'

'Oh! God.' She sank back further into car seat and shut her eyes.

'All I need is someone bossy and efficient in the family.' She shuddered. Eyes still closed to shut it out. 'Henry won't stand it for long, I shouldn't think. Except—' She hesitated. 'He's so idle. You know how idle he is. Just be easier to go along with it, I suppose. So, you're right; she'll probably stick around. God help us.' And she wondered, was there just a suggestion of a frisson between them? Could it be that there was an attraction between Max and that girl? It would be understandable. She shuddered again.

'Fee! You're not jealous, are you?' He tapped her knee again and grinned.

'Jealous? Why? Because she's attractive and intelligent and efficient and jolly. Good heavens no. Whatever made you think that?' Now she turned to him. 'You're not being serious are you, Max? Please don't be serious. Oh God! The thought of a bossy, in-your-face daughter-in-law.'

He laughed at her helplessness. 'Well, she's got her eye on him and she's the sort that will get her way, I should imagine.' He laughed at her downcast look. 'Don't worry, darling, you will always be queen of the nest. You know how I fell in love with your outgoing, chatty, flirtatious manners, your house-wifely capabilities, your mothering instincts!'

'Oh don't!' She put her hands to her face.

'But seriously, what did you think of the exhibition? He does paint extraordinarily well, doesn't he? Sending him to Milan was worth it. Gabriel did wonders. Encouraged what he was good at, instead of all that "let's stand in a ring and close our eyes" stuff he got at Newcastle. Absolute modern rubbish. Can just imagine Henry's exasperation.'

She laughed her brief staccato laugh. 'Oh! I knew he would never last there. He's got all my bad genes.'

'That's why I married you, Fee, because of all your bad genes. How's the latest book going, anyway?'

'My heroine has just called her mum a stupid cow.'

'Really!'

'Which reminds me I must go to see Mother tomorrow.'

There was a moment's hesitation and then they both laughed.

'Shall I come with you? I should come sometimes.'

She shook her head. 'She won't know you've been the minute you leave. But it's hard work. Thinking of things to say. Talking about the weather has its limitations and she knows nothing but that precise minute. Last time, for something to say, I told her I was writing another book. She said, "Oh that's nice. I didn't know you wrote books." Then she says, "I think Daddy's coming in today." She doesn't mean you; she means Father. I say – I don't know whether I should, "Dad's dead, Mum." She looks so surprised that I have to go through it all again: when he died, what the matter was, et cetera. Then she says, "How long have I been here? I can't remember where I was before." And she can't ask me about Henry and Rob, because she's forgotten they exist.'

'Yes, I know,' he said. 'Well, look, I'll come tomorrow. Barns can drive us if you like. We can tell her about the exhibition. Take the catalogue. You have got one, by the way? He's good, don't you think, Fee? Aren't you proud of him? Come on, admit you are.'

'What I like about Henry,' she said, 'is how he is with underdogs, if you see what I mean. You know he's really good with Mum, for instance, much better than Rob, who never goes anyway. Henry goes and, well, just sits with her. He seems quite at ease there. Different from how he is other times. I like that about him.' And then, as an afterthought. 'It's rather like he is with animals. You know, I'd never thought of that before.'

'No competition, Fee. That's the thing. Don't want to be unkind to our very talented son, but there's something not quite right. Needs to feel good about himself. Animals. Your mum. See what I mean? He's in control. No threat. Nothing to make him feel bad about himself. Oh, it's complicated.'

She was staring, listening, a worried frown and then—

'Blast it!' he said suddenly, 'Look at that damned lorry. It'll be slow now –unless he turns off at Woodstock.'

# Frank

He didn't recognise her immediately. She was ash-blonde again, and her hair so short. Like a man's. No sign of the curls. They were waiting at the far end of the platform; she was holding a Littlewoods' bag and looking at Steve with that sullen look; he was heeling the stub of a cigarette. Frank stopped to adjust his rucksack and then she saw him, dropped her shopping at Steve's feet and came charging towards him. The coat he had bought her replaced by some fur thing and the bag she had loved so much gone too. On her shoulder swung a red crocodile bucket. It kept slipping off. But she was running, arms out towards him, and he thought, Oh Kitty, Kitty – what has happened to you? But she had her arms around him before he could put down his case.

'Frankie!' She was breathless.

He dropped his case and held her. When she looked up at him, he noticed her right cheek was blue with bruising, which she had tried to hide behind thick make-up.

'What's happened to your face?'

'She slipped at work, silly cow.' Steve laughed as he moved up to them and nudged her with his elbow before holding out a hand to Frank. 'You all right?'

Kitty, ignoring them, talking too much, had opened the Littlewoods bag and was pulling out a dress to show him.

'Looks nice.'

They drove through the backstreets in Steve's Ford Escort, avoiding the city centre, but every now and again Frank saw the square turrets of Doncaster cathedral. He peered through the windows. 'What's it like?' he asked. 'The cathedral.'

Kitty leaned over from the back, 'Oi! You're not going all holy, are you? He's going all holy on us, Stevie. Oh my God!'

'We only know the pubs, don't we, chuck?' And they both laughed.

'And the shops. We know them all right. Oh!' she whined, suddenly disappointed. 'Frank won't see where I work, going home this way. It's right in the centre, Frankie. With all the posh shops and things. We get lots of posh people.'

'Next time,' he said. 'I'll see it next time.' He only had a few hours before catching the train to Darlington and he was more interested in seeing how she was living – and how his table looked after a year's wear.

Steve pulled into a slipway opposite a shabby parade of shops.

She jumped out and opened his door. 'Leave everything, Frankie. Come on!' But he couldn't; the knapsack had all the books he'd stolen from the library.

There was a narrow passage alongside the bookmaker's and at the back an iron fire escape that led up to the front door. 'No. 36B' in wrought iron was pinned in the middle and a wrought-iron letterbox had some leaflets sticking out of it.

Steve took the rucksack and went up first. 'Bloody hell, this is heavy.' Balancing it on the top step, he took out a bunch of keys from his jeans pocket.

The door opened directly into a tiny kitchen area. Frank went in last with his case and shut the door behind him.

Kitty switched on the light. 'It gets a bit dark sometimes,' she said. 'Come on Frank. What do you think?'

There was only room for one at a time in the kitchen with its a sink under the window, a bit of vinyl worktop, a wall cupboard and at the end a fridge.

128

'It's OK, Kitty. Everything's fine.'

She squeezed past him into the small sitting room. 'Come and look at the curtains I told you about.'

The television was already blaring, and Steve slumped on the sofa with his feet up on the table, watching football.

'Steve! That's Frank's table. Don't do that,' she laughed.

Frank noticed the dirty mugs, the ashtray filled with dog ends and the cigarette burn.

'Have a beer, mate. Fetch us a beer, chuck.' And Steve slapped her hard on the buttocks. He saw her disguise the wince into a jolly little skip. Her giggle choked and he noted the deadening expression in her eyes as she fetched the beer from the fridge, watched her zip the can open, take something from the cupboard, which she tossed into her mouth and swilled down with a gulp of the beer.

Steve was leaning forward, his feet on the ground as if ready to spring. 'Look, I'm going down the pub. I can't fucking wait all day You coming, Frank?' And then, 'Stupid question. My brother-in-law doesn't drink, does he. Or have you changed your ways?' He picked up his beaten leather jacket and left, slamming the door shut, leaving behind an awkward stillness.

'How about a cuppa?' Her back was turned from him. He thought she was shaking.

'What's going on, Kitty?'

She turned with that surprised look she could arrange so well. 'What's going on? Nothing. Nothing's going on. I don't know what you mean. Look, I'm making a cup of tea. That's what's going on, OK? Come on, Frankie. Let's sit down, aye?'

She came in with two mugs of tea and looked about for something to put them on. 'I'm sorry the table's a bit of a mess. I do love it, though. Really love it. We should take more care, shouldn't we. Never mind, it's still OK.'

He took the mugs from her while she picked up an old newspaper from the floor and put in down for the mugs to stand on. Sitting in the armchair opposite him, she took a cigarette from the packet on the table and struck a match. She sank back and blew the smoke out of the side of her mouth, her face momentarily distorted and the swelling enlarged.

'What happened at work, then? Your face looks painful.'

'The floor was wet. I wasn't looking. It was my fault. I hit myself on the edge of a basin. Lucky I didn't knock my teeth out.' She did that laugh again and leaned forward to flick ash off the tip of the cigarette. 'Don't look like that, Frank. Don't start, please, not your first visit. I was so excited.' Her voice broke. He thought for moment she was going to cry.

'You are taking pills?'

'Yes, Frank. I took a bloody pill. It was for the swelling. The doctor gave me them. OK? Come on, Frankie, for Christ's sake. Don't look so worried. Come on now, tell me about you, about this new job. Let's have a chat before Steve comes back, aye? Just like before. He'll be back to take you, don't worry. He gets a bit – well ... you know, a bit uptight at the weekends. It's his job – it's really hard. It does him good to go down the pub. I don't mind. In fact, I quite enjoy being on my own, although I do go with him sometimes, and that's quite fun.' She was gabbling, gabbling on. 'You know, for a change. Anyway, what about you? Where you going to stay? What sort of place? Won't you miss' – she hesitated – 'home. Miss dear old Stan and Rube. I miss them. I miss you, Frankie – I wish we was nearer. That's the only thing – just a bit nearer. Know what I mean?'

The train to Darlington left at 8.15. It was dark and the city was alive with lights and a square of the cathedral, carefully lit, stood solid in the night sky. He watched them leaving, and he felt the loneliness of separation and shut his eyes.

# Frank

As soon as he entered the carriage, he noticed her. She was sitting alone, a notepad on the table in front of her, her brown shoulder bag on the seat beside her. He put his case in the stowaway before taking his seat diagonally across from her. He thought she might be looking at him, a newly arrived passenger, but he concentrated on taking out a couple of books from his rucksack; his intention was to read through the chapter on wood graining, staining and polishing. He was pleased to have the space to himself, most people having alighted at Doncaster.

She was sitting quite upright and tapping the window lightly with her fingers. She wore a light summer mac and he could see she had on jeans. Long legs, he noticed. Then she started to fiddle with a ring, silver with a purple stone, turning it into the light and twisting it round so that it sat straight on her finger. He thought that once or twice she glanced his way, so he tried to concentrate on his reading. At one point she turned to face the window, although it was dark. Perhaps she was picking out the lights from houses as they passed; it was difficult to see much else as they travelled through stretches of countryside. Her face and long fair hair were reflected in the window and he wondered if she could see a reflection of him, so he kept his head down. Perhaps it was her long fair hair, but he thought there was a gentle lightness about her.

Tall, slim, nineteen, twenty. Difficult to tell. Younger than him, anyway. He was curious about what she was drawing, for from time to time, as if suddenly taken with an idea, she withdrew a pencil from inside the pad, leaned over the table and began scribbling. It was difficult to take his eyes off her.

# Alice

S he was enjoying her journey home; all the anxiety gone
and looking forward to telling all the news. Jo had seen
her off from King's Cross with a huge bear hug, calling her
Pixie and saying how lovely it had all been and how her flat
had never looked so tidy! So she had to come again!

She rested her arm on the window ledge and watched the
grime of London give way to small towns and countryside.
It was late afternoon and the trees and hedges were etched by
the evening sun. She had taken out her sketchpad and pencil
and was wondering how she could catch the speed, the flashing sunlight and shade, which were constantly changing. She
could only scribble some kind of collage. Henry Bancroft
would have no such difficulty, she decided. He managed to
capture the speed of racing horses, the rushing of barking
hounds, the jerky pecking of chickens. A photograph could
never quite do it; a painting gave away something more. He
had said that he preferred animals to humans; it was supposed
to be a joke, but she suspected that there might be some truth
in it. She liked him: his permanent little frown, his serious
uncertainty. She still couldn't get over the fact that he had
asked her out for supper that night of the exhibition. She
squirmed in her seat. What had he done that for? Did he like
her or something? She didn't tell Jo.

After the exhibition she and Jo had gone with friends to

a pub near Jo's flat and had pasta and a glass of wine. There was a lot of talk about a Siegfried Fraser, who Jo said was the most fantastic jeweller and a member of the Goldsmiths Guild; she had been incredibly lucky to have been awarded an apprenticeship with him and now a job in his workshop. 'You might meet him tomorrow; he's often in the worship on Sundays and in any case, we're going, because I've made something for you.'

Now Alice put her hand on the table to admire the silver ring with its hammered pattern and a single amethyst set up high; it had an Elizabethan look, she thought. She held her hand to the light and then twisted the ring so that it was central on her finger.

She was distracted by the tall man who entered at Doncaster, choosing a seat diagonally across the aisle from her. He had a large suitcase, which he stowed away, and a rucksack, heavy with books, two of which he took out before hurling the rucksack up onto the rack.

As the train left, he waved to someone and then sat staring out of the window as if looking for something. The city lights were coming on and Alice saw, from her side, the lights high up in the sky, like stars: the pinnacles of a church. Perhaps that is what he was looking for. Then he rested his head against the window, folded his arms and closed his eyes; his body swaying slightly with the movement of the train. He seemed very tired, she thought. Yet there was something strong and reliable about him. She was drawn to him.

She leaned back for a moment, eyeing him cautiously until he roused himself and turned his attention to one of his books. He appeared totally engrossed as he leaned forward with arms across the table So different from Henry Bancroft, whose dark hair fell about his eyes and ears untidily. This man was very neat with his dark brown hair cut short with a straight fringe. When she looked out of the window at the moving lights and darkening countryside, she could catch his refection as he glanced across at her. Once she turned and gave a small smile before going back to her sketchbook.

As they approached Darlington, he took down his rucksack and put on a cream anorak before moving to wait by the stowed cases. Alice followed and when the train had come to a stop reached for her case, but he turned and lifted her case off the shelf before opening the carriage door.

'I'll do it,' he said and, after putting his case on to the platform, lifted hers down for her. He had gone before she could say anything, and she watched as he passed Da, who was waiting for her at the end of the platform

# Frank

It had taken him twenty minutes by bus from Crook to a stop nearly opposite Bishop's Lodge. He had seen the lodge intermittently, through the trees, set well back from the road. The bus driver gave him the nod when they arrived, and he jumped out and into the rain. A grey, breezy June morning.

The entrance to the place was guarded on either side by worn stone pillars; the gates had gone. The drive, which wound a couple of hundred metres to the lodge, was no more than a worn stony track cutting through fields of rough grass broken by clumps of trees. Now, suddenly, he was nervous as he crunched his way up the driveway. He was early; there appeared to be no one about and so he sheltered under a great yew tree, which grew near the cobbled yard to the side of the lodge.

From under the dripping tree Frank studied the house, which, so far, he had only seen from photographs. Built of the sandstone hewn centuries before into great blocks and cemented together, the place was sturdy but dilapidated. Worn stone steps led up to a thick double oak door, damaged by cracks running from top to bottom. He could see inside the fine mullioned windows, shutters, like wooden doors, some hanging crookedly – one appeared to be missing altogether – and outside many of the sills had stone missing and looked as if they had been pecked by birds over the years. Plenty to do here, then. He was looking forward to seeing the interior, for his first job was to work on the stairs and banisters.

He'd arrived late last night, having taken a taxi from Darlington. The taxi driver chatted amiably in his Geordie accent, forcing Frank into telling him why he was 'up from the sooth', and where he was going to be 'working, like.'

'Aye. I know the lodge well enough. You'll have a job on there, man. It's falling to bits. Falling to ruin. Staying in Crook toon, are you then? Crook's all right. About twenty or so minutes from Coundon, by bus that is. The land of the pit-yackers. You know. From the pits. Real good country round abouts.'

He dropped Frank outside the house, the end of a terrace, a long curving row of identical houses; tall, narrow, Edwardian. Mrs Mackie was there to greet him. A small fussy woman who quivered and bustled and talked non-stop. She'd left a plate of sandwiches in his room and offered him a cup of tea. 'I do breakfast for seven-thirty,' she said, 'and supper at seven. Now I'll let you settle in. Goodnight, then. '

The bus ride here this morning gave him his first sight of the Dales. And he was emptied, like a long sigh had escaped from him, emptied of the heaviness he hadn't known he had. So much space and green and calm. Air. He'd never smelled freshness like this before. The peace. Only his dreadful worry over Kitty. He couldn't, even with this wonderful free space all around, rid himself of this nagging anxiety, which seeped in and around him. Constantly haunting him, this vague unease he could not properly explain. And yet today he was hopeful and expectant like a child, like the kid opening the Christmas present. Somehow he would make it all come right.

Then he heard it before he saw it; the stillness broken by a white van coming round the bend, passing him and stopping in front of the stables. The doors clattered open and the driver, grabbing a bunch of keys off the dashboard, jumped out, followed by his three passengers. The guy with keys opened up the stable doors to let the others in before crossing the yard and disappearing behind the house.

'Fucking weather,' he shouted, and pulled his cap down over his ears. Later Frank learned that he'd gone to open up the back doors, for work was already beginning in the house itself. He was glad they hadn't seen him; he didn't want them to know that he'd been early, so now he strolled across the cobbles to the open doors as if he had just arrived.

It was a long space divided into two parts; the first was fitted with workstations, which ran along the walls. Each with tools and architects' drawings pinned to boards hanging on the wall behind the benches. Each bench had hooks to the side for the men's coats. The end of the barn-like space was partially separated by plasterboard walls to dull the noise and the dust when the heavy machinery was used. They called this space the machine shop.

The men were in a huddle, chatting. One was smoking despite the 'No Smoking' sign at the entrance. Bit risky in a place full of wood and sawdust. Good God! What was the bloke thinking? When he saw him, he pressed the fag end into a bucket of sand.

He had to admit they gave him a friendly greeting, each of them coming over with grin and a handshake.

'Barney. Welcome, mate.'

'George. How're y' doing?'

'Hi there! I'm Johnnie.'

He shook each hand in turn. 'Frank Richardson.'

'Mac'll be here any minute. Just gone to open the place up. He's the boss for us lot. But there's a crowd of others.'

'You could say that, man. For fuck's sake! Do they get in our way and all!' And they laughed.

'Plasterers are the worst, mind. Always in the wrong place at the wrong time, far as we go. The roofers, not so bad.'

'Cos they're on the roof!' More laughter.

138

The man with the keys returned and hung them on a hook on the inside of the door before turning to him.

'Frank Richardson? Good! Yer found us then, man?' He held out a hand, 'Mac.'

'Good to meet you.'

'You and Barney are going to work on the stair treads, and the balusters. And' – he called over to Barney – 'one of those newel posts needs replacing as well. You'll see it's been marked, same as usual.' He turned back to Frank. 'Decide between you what you begin with, aye? Barney, show him round and talk him through, will yo? OK, fellas, let's go.'

Barney left his station and came over. 'This is your bench, OK? Hook here, et cetera.'

Frank took off his jacket and hung it up. Together they looked at drawings pinned up on the wall and Barney unpinned the drawing of a baluster and handed it to him. 'This is the one for now.' And Frank studied the detailed drawings of the sizes, shapes, turns and decorations.

'I've made a start on one of the balusters, but there's three more to replace. I'll show you where the wood is'.

He followed Barney to the far end of the machine shop where lay, in careful order, various lengths and thicknesses of woods, and indicating, 'There's the oak, sycamore over there, and we've got a bit of walnut and beech as needs. Here's the yew.'

Frank nodded. But he was already looking at the two lathes and thinking of Stan.

'The balustrade and the balusters are in sycamore. Treads in oak, as you would expect.'

Frank turned back and nodded again.

'Ever worked with sycamore?' And Barney picked up a small piece lying to the side and handed it to him. 'Hard as nails,' he said, 'but fine grain.'

They returned to the benches. The others had disappeared. Barney picked up the baluster he was working on and handed it to Frank for his inspection. He looked up at the drawing. 'Yep,' he said with a suggestion of a grin. 'Not at all bad!' It was the sort of thing Stan would have said.

Barney clapped him on the shoulder. 'OK, then. Pick your wood. I'm back to the lathe.'

He was in the machine shop sizing his wood on the thicknesser when Mac came in, shouting above the noise of the machines. 'Come over to the house. See for yourself.'

They went in through the front entrance, into the square hall, which was tiled with blue-and-white floral tiles. 'From Portugal.' Mac pointed. 'All those cracked have to be relaced. The makers got a job on their hands. They's the original.'

The balustrade rose in three sharp bends on the right to a landing overlooking the hallway, along which ran identical balusters like a row of finely shaped vases.

'I'll leave you to look round. You'll notice we've marked the parts needing repairing. One or two stair treads. Take a look round. Get yourself familiar.'

By the time he returned to the barns, all the others were taking a break and eating sandwiches and drinking from thermos flasks. He hadn't thought about lunch and, feeling a bit out of it, returned to his bench, when the bloke called George called over, 'I forgot mine the first time. Come over here, mate, my wife always gives me too much.'

'Of what?' someone said, and they all jeered.

He wasn't going to accept but then changed his mind. He should try to be friendly. And they did seem easy enough.

Barney was saying he'd decided to travel in on his motorbike rather than have to rely on 'the old banger of a van!' and Frank thought it was a good idea, an entirely new idea for him, and suddenly wanted a motorbike, and remembered how he had loved the cycle dad had given him, and Carl smashing it up. He'd not let anyone smash up his motorbike, if he ever got one.

'You come by bus?' Barney was asking him.' I'm in Crook too,' he said. 'Happy to give you a lift. Could pick you up at the bus stop around seven -thirty.' He pushed a cheese sandwich wrapped in grease proof paper towards him.

'Thanks. That'll be handy 'til I get my own. But thanks. Seven -thirty, then. I'll be there.'

At supper that night, he asked Mrs Mackie if she could make him some sandwiches for his lunch and had she a thermos; he was, of course, happy to pay, and explaining he had to be at the bus stop by 7.30, asked if he could have his breakfast a 7 a.m. She wiggled a finger at him, shaking her head with a smile. 'I will,' she said, 'just for you. But not the weekends, mind.'

Before getting into bed, he took out his books, still in the rucksack, and flipped through them. He'd enjoyed his day: the men were friendly enough, quite decent blokes; the work was exciting because it was challenging. He'd never seen a house like that before, except in drawings and photographs. He was proud to be part of its restoration. And pride in himself was something he was unaccustomed to, tried to keep hidden even from himself. It was almost as difficult to bear as the anxiety. Hopefully the one would one day overcome the other.

'Architectural joiner and cabinetmaker' was what Mac had said. Dad would be proud. But Stan and Ruby? He owed them so much. He'd phone them tomorrow. He tried not to think about Kitty, but if he could get some kind of motorbike, he could visit her often. Doncaster wasn't that far away, was it?

# Alice

The smell of warm baked bread and cinnamon always reminded her of the man who came out through the shop door that day. She had just said goodbye to Da outside the bakery and turned the corner into Streatfield Road. It was busy with lunchtimers, but she noticed him immediately, coming out of the shop. He was carrying one of their brown-paper bags and walked away from her down the street towards Market Square. She recognised him from somewhere. It was the short dark hair. The jacket. The jacket was the same and the way it hung from his shoulders. Deep in thought. She could tell even from this distance and she wanted to run after him.

There were no customers and Mr Lubbock was half-hidden behind the counter, bent double putting things away in one of the long drawers. He stood up when he heard the shop bell and goggled at her as she stood puffing against the door

'Good Lord! What's up with you?'

'Who was that man? The one that's just gone out?'

He leaned towards her, over the counter, looking faintly amused. 'Never seen him before. What's so interesting?'

Alice shook off her coat. 'I thought I knew him, that's all. From somewhere. Can't think where, though. That's all. Just curious. Nothing more.'

He had returned to the drawers behind him and the boxes

of oil paints. 'I've never seen him before. I asked him. He's up here for some job over at Coundon; doing some renovation work on Bishop's Lodge. Sounds interesting. He bought the usual vinegar, burnt Sienna and Umbria stains. I thought he'd want wire wool, but he said he was all right for that and sandpaper, all the usual. Had plenty. And then – that's right – he took linseed and some shellac. He's got to make new wood match the old, he said when I asked. Interesting project.'

'I thought I knew him,' she repeated. 'That's all. Seemed to recognise him from somewhere. Don't know where.' Almost talking to herself.

She lifted the counter and walked through. 'Da sends his best, by the way, and are you going to the meeting tonight? Ma's smiling all the time.'

She hung her coat and shoulder bag in the back room. He followed, sniffing the air behind her. 'You carry the smell of gingerbread.'

'A couple of months ago. On the train!' she said suddenly. 'Coming back to Darlington. On the train. Got on at Doncaster. Now, why should I remember that? '

'You tell me! Seems to have made an impression, any road.' Mr Lubbock followed her back into the shop. 'There was someone else here, though. Asking for you. He's coming back later. Didn't know him either. Not that tall; hair all over the place. He looked worried all the time.'

She was agitated all afternoon, knowing it must be Henry from the description. She was both excited and nervous. It was the way he had looked at her when he asked her out for supper that night of the exhibition. And why now did she keep looking in the mirror to check her hair? But when he came in, hands in his pockets, slow, relaxed, hair falling over his eyes with that small, worried frown, she felt easier.

He was up to see university friends in Newcastle. Thought he'd look her up. Jo had told him where to find her. Said she worked in this shop. 'How often?' he asked. She told him

Mondays and Fridays. The other days she was at the school down the road from home. 'Art classes, you know, in a primary school. Not your kind of art.'

'Jo says your paintings are beautiful. Something to do with pebbles. Intriguing! You will show me sometime, won't you? After all, you've seen mine.'

The mention of the word 'pebbles' diminished her. The idea that they had talked about her. She would never show him her paintings – of pebbles and light on water and all that stuff. Never!

He had looked at his watch. He was meeting a friend but he'd like to take her out for supper that evening. Would she like to come out? He'd looked up a nice restaurant –Italian, in Crook. He could pick her up; he had come up in Phoebe's car. He could pick her up at her house. 'About seven p.m.?'

'How do you know where I live, Henry?' God! she thought, What's happening?

'Oh! Jo again.' And his face melted with a smile that transformed his puzzled, slightly worried expression into a humorous warmth. He appeared a very kind man when he smiled.

'You're not going out like that, surely,' Ma said. 'Why don't you wear your new skirt?'

'She's all right,' Da said. 'They all wear jeans. Nobody dresses up these days. You're all right, Alice. She's fussing.'

She studied the car out of her bedroom window. Looked spotlessly clean. Bit small for Henry, though. Not that he was a big man but, in her mind, he suited a sports car more, something a bit different. This was just a smart Mini.

Alistair opened the door to him. She heard all the voices in the hall. Alistair, home from York, where he was doing his MSc in maths, sounding perfectly relaxed, slightly cocky. Ma a bit overexcited. Saying she'd heard all about him. Alice thought, Don't say that.

'Hi!' he said when she walked in, and then went on talking to Da, looking at the photos of bikes on the wall. 'Might get one myself,' he said. 'Really good for getting around London.'

She wondered what he thought of their bungalow, knowing his family home was posh. You just knew from his parents, for a start. You just could tell. Not that they weren't friendly and easy, but you could just tell, and she would be angry if he thought their place, her home, was dull and ordinary. But to be fair, if he did, he most certainly didn't show it. Anyway, as far she was concerned, nothing was ordinary and dull with Da. Da treated everyone in the same easy manner, whether king or tramp; that was his way; that was one of his gifts.

Alistair said cheerio and went back to his room, so she picked up her cardigan, pulled her bag over her shoulder and they left. Ma waved from the doo, but Da had already disappeared.

She walked to the car, trying hard to disguise any sign of her limp, which, despite the operation, was still there at times. Just a bit.

Henry opened the door for her in a casual sort of way, with a certain indifference, as if his mind was somewhere else. As if nothing was really that important. She was rather comforted by that. She would have hated it if had fussed over her. Tried to charm her. He didn't. But she was charmed, nonetheless. Stunned, though, that someone like Henry would want to take her out. She'd only had one boyfriend: Craig, who was doing graphic design at the same college. He was handsome: more handsome than Henry. Tall, with smoothed-back blond hair. Full of confidence. Too much so. They went to the pictures a few times, but he was all over her and she hated that. It scared her, his wanting to kiss her, touch her all the time. It scared her, so she told him she couldn't go out with him any more. It had taken her too long, as it was, to find the courage to break it off. Henry was quite the opposite. She wasn't scared at all.

'I've booked at Maurizio's,' he said.

Her family had never been to Maurizio's because everyone said how expensive it was. Good food but expensive, so they'd avoided it, but she tried to behave as if she had been there before, as if it was nothing unusual.

It was busy, but Henry had booked a table by the window and there it was, waiting for them. The waiters fussed around in their white shirts and bow ties, taking her cardigan as it were some precious mink coat and pulling back a chair for her. She wanted to laugh.

Henry ordered red wine and chose veal. She had their speciality spaghetti bolognaise because it was familiar, although a mistake, because she had forgotten how difficult it was to eat without making a mess. Impossible, she thought, to be appealing when sucking up strings of pasta. Henry didn't seem to notice.

He spoke about the house his father was buying in Italy and how foolish his mother thought it was, but he, Henry had been over with his father, Max, to see it, and had to admit the house, just across from the lake, was actually very nice indeed. And the village itself, unassuming, quiet, but what he described as a genuine sort of place. He thought he could work well there. 'The light is good,' he mumbled. Sometimes he seemed almost grumpy. 'Perhaps you would like to go over and stay a few days. The sun would do you good.'

'Ooh! Not sure about that.'

He changed the subject. 'I'm not going back 'til Monday, so, as I have the car, would you like to go out somewhere tomorrow? Do you have a special place you would like to show me?'

She knew at once where she wanted to go. 'There's a seaside place we always went to for days out. We've not been for ages. I'd love to go there. I love it there. In all weather.' And she laughed, recalling the rain and wind and rattling grasses; her joy at it all.

'Fine by me,' he said. 'Just tell me where, exactly.'

'Da will tell you everything. I'm really hopeless at directions.'

'I'm not great myself,' he said and smiled at her. She liked his smile a lot; the small gap between his front teeth gave him an unexpectedly impish look.

He picked her up at twelve and it took an hour to the coast. Da had written out directions and shown Henry the map as well. She read out the instructions and miraculously they got to the cove without a single mistake. Her place, her beach, her stones. There was sun today, but the wind still there sharply whipping through the seagrasses.

They parked on the sandy drive above the grasses and scrambled down to the sand, Henry putting out his hand for her. The sand was untouched just there, smooth as icing, and they made footprints as they walked down to the edge of the water.

'The tide's coming in,' she said. 'You can always tell by looking at that jetty.' She pointed. 'It's great there. Stones collect all around. They jangle. I could stand and listen and watch for ever. Drove my parents mad.'

'Was that the beginning of your fascination with pebbles in water, then?'

This was a subject she badly wanted to avoid. So abruptly she said, 'I was only a child, but probably.' Then, to change the subject, 'If you look beyond, you can see the harbour and the boats moored.'

'Well,' he said. 'We can certainly walk over and see, but not 'til we've had a bite. Don't know about you, but I'm hungry. It'll all be here when we get back.' And again, he took her hand. Took care of her. She wanted to throw her arms round him but didn't, of course. Not this time.

# Frank

Her hands shook and the cup rattled in its saucer and the tea spilled over as she put it down in front of him. She was a little mosquito of a woman: pinched face, buzzing constantly, her head shaking excitably. 'Don't forget it's my evening off,' she'd rasped, clipped and breathless. 'Just to remind you.'

'Ta. That's alreet.' He tried imitating the locals for fun. 'It's doon the pub for mae then? Reet?'

She gave an asthmatic giggle and shook her little hands at him.

The other lodger, a silent, older man 'in retail', who travelled to Newcastle every day, had already gone; his place at the table cleared away She'd nodded towards the empty chair. 'You're a pair if ever there was one. Never saying a word to each other. Never a word.'

The dining room was filled with heavy, ornately carved furniture, the carvings blackened in the creases where dirt and polish had collected over the years. He took an interest in styles of furniture and their woods now. And he'd noticed this area was littered with antique and second-hand shops. Up the dale, in the most out-of-the-way hamlet, he'd noticed a little shop with furniture and gilt-framed pictures stuck outside on the pavement. When he could get around, he wanted to explore these shops. See what he could find. He fancied something for himself, liked the idea of some well-made piece, 'with real quality', as Stan would say. Craftsmanship. This furniture was oak, Edwardian in style and locally made, he reckoned. He ran his hand along the edge of the sideboard. The carving was part machine, part hand. Bit clumsy.

Since that first visit to the library at home and his repair of the church pew, he had become interested in restoration work. He fancied he could detect the genuine from the copy now by the patina of the wood and the type of joints and dowels. And the inside of drawers was a useful guide, as were handles, if there were any. He'd brought the books he'd stolen from the library with him.

What he wanted was some kind of bike to get about; he couldn't afford a car, but he had saved enough for a bike. The idea pleased him; he could explore the area. The Dales. And get to the sea. More than anything he wanted to visit the coast. Unbelievably, he'd never seen the sea. He was fairly certain Kitty hadn't either.

He'd asked Mrs Mackie, 'Whereabouts is Wear Farm? Is it round here at all?' He picked up the *Weardale News* and pointed to the advertisement. Held it up for her to see better, pointed to the spot. 'Look there! They've got a motorbike for sale.'

Mr Wilkinson had apologised for it not being cleaned up for when he wheeled it out of the barn. It was dusty, with spikes of straw caught in the wheels. 'No use to us any more,' he had said. 'Not now my daughter's flown the nest. It was hers when she was at college, doing her silversmithing. Used to ride to Darlington every day. She's in London now, trying to make a living with her jewellery. Bit different from Wear Farm life, I should say. Well, is it any good to you? Without waiting for a reply, he went back into the barn, returning with a can. He unscrewed the cap and funnelled in some petrol. 'Ever ridden one?'

''Fraid not.' He'd saved hard for this; wanted so much to

ride out into the Dales that he'd only seen from bus and from the Bishop's Lodge windows.

'Have a go round the yard,' he had said. 'Take your time. I shan't stand and watch.' He showed Frank how to start up, the gears, the accelerator on the handle. The brake on the other.

Frank had waited until he had disappeared and then started up the bike. Practising the revving and braking. Sat on it. Adjusted his position. Got a feel for the handles; rubbed his hands round and back, round and back, getting the feel, imagining racing along, the wind whipping in his face. He sat and looked around again, making sure no one was watching. Then, finally starting up, he pressed in the clutch, put it into gear, took his foot off the ground and accelerated. It lurched forward, the front wheel turning in a small circle. He had to push down hard with his foot to stop the bike from toppling over. He sat rigid in the silence. Waited. Then he tried again. This time, wobbling a bit, he managed to circle round the yard until the engine cut out. He could smell the exhaust fumes. The stink of petrol. Finally, he did several turns, controlling the speed, steering uncertainly. He wished it wasn't so noisy. Mr Wilkinson appeared from somewhere and stood, arms folded. 'Be a lot easier on the open road. Do you want it, then? You'll have to do your Part One test. In meantime I've got her L-plate somewhere. Hang on a bit. Can't be on the open road without the L-plate. Do it proper, now.'

And here he was, his boots sinking into the wet sand, leaving deep footprints. Like a child, he made for the very edge of the sea, stood while the foam spread out like long fingers over the tips of his boots. He screwed his eyes into the horizon, misty and merging into the grey drizzle. He was alone on this great flat stretch of sand and he made his mark and watched the imprints fill with seawater. Swell after swell, he watched the heave and roll of the sea; listened to the rhythmic swish and swish and the clatter of pebbles as they rolled in with the water. Seagulls circled in the wind and screamed. He was transported, his spirits freed, and he smiled to himself, wanting to run with the wind, like a child. Made him think of the kid. The kid would love this. He liked the kid; he wished he could be here now. He remembered his expression when he saw the garage he had made for his cars. How he'd played with it over and over, talking to himself, zooming up and down the ramps, in and out of the exits and entrances. Frank had watched. Yes, he really did like that kid. And Julie. She was a decent girl; the kid would be all right with her: she was a good mother; not a mother who would let her kid down. But he couldn't go on with it. He'd been like a tight string, holding his breath, frightened. He couldn't give her what he thought she wanted from him. But she hadn't fussed, got angry, blamed him. Just looked sad when he told her he was going away. He felt rotten about that.

He turned suddenly and walked with purposeful, long strides beside the incoming water, towards a wooden jetty, half rotting and smothered in barnacles. Pebbles had collected along the bottom of the wooden posts and lay green and blue. He moved them with the toe of his boot and they rolled clean and smooth. He toed them repeatedly, somehow fascinated, and then, splashing his hand into the water, picked up a handful. French-polished, glistening as they lay in the palm of his hand. But they belonged to the sea and so he took them, one at a time, and hurled them as far as he could out into the oncoming waves. He wondered if they would somehow return to this spot, whether in some way he had disturbed them.

He'd write the kid a card. With a picture of the sea. Say hello to him. Say hello to his Mum. Say goodbye.

There was urgency to the sea along the edges of the jetty, and the bottoms of his trousers were suddenly soaked by an extra surge of water, which ran over his boots. He should go now. Perhaps it was time to go; it was getting dark and he'd only had the bike since Wednesday.

He followed the shadow of his footprints back to the sand dunes, where long seagrasses bent and creaked in the heavy air. The bike was waiting for him, propped against a sandbank. He sat down, hidden from the world, wet socks and trousers; hair damp and dripping down his forehead. He waited until the sea had disappeared into the darkening sky and he was left with just the rhythmic tumbling and swishing.

# Fiona

*A year later*

She stood staring, hypnotised by the slow swaying of the poplars: the silver shimmering in the evening sun. She heard below their voices and a door slam. Someone had put on music – Max most likely. This was it, then. Soon to have two married sons: Robert, now living in London, having got his law degree, was working in the legal department of Shell, a big job that took him abroad often, as he was in a team working with governments on the sale of land for the purpose of oil and gas refineries. It was all very complicated, it seemed to her. Last year he married Anne, equally clever but a plain little thing who did something with research and statistics. She was a civil servant of some sort; confident, considered and polite. She had been very carefully nurtured. Not like the boys, who had had to find their own ways in most things: Fiona always too absorbed with her stories and Max away and busy. Had theirs been a happy home? She wasn't sure. It was a divided home: Max and Robert cheerful and energetic; she and Henry uncomfortable and awkward. But he did appear less morose these days, since he had found this Alice girl.

Fiona pressed her fingers across her forehead. Anne's father had been a consultant somewhere and her mother played a good hand of bridge was all she knew. Probably that wasn't good enough; she should try to show more interest. Unlike her daughter, the mother-in-law, Jenny, was loud with her own attractiveness, sexy. Perhaps, for all her precise and careful ways, Anne was sexy. Must be. He could have had any number of beautiful, lively girls. There was one she had quite liked. What was her name? Rosemary? Anita? Anyway, she was very sexy. Perhaps Anne was stunning with sex. Perhaps she changed from the neat, careful girl into a raving sex goddess. Fiona shrugged. What did she know? She remembered wondering once what it must be like to be really sexy. She wondered for the millionth time if she had been a dreadful disappointment to Max. Henry would be like her, she feared, a bit of a dead loss when it came to passion, with his lank hair and a body unstructured and sickish, like hers. No grit. She shook herself.

Good God! And now Henry and a wedding next weekend. He was marrying this nymph, this will o' the wisp kind of girl – could almost be in one of her stories! Alice, with her soft Durham accent and her shifting temperament. She was like the poplars, tall and frail, shifting in the light, as it were, between uncertainty and wilfulness. She had that slight limp, which she obviously tried so hard to disguise. Henry must feel protective towards her, a kind of pity, as if she were a wounded animal. She really thought he felt a tenderness for her, was uncommonly at ease as he was with animals. And Alice? Well, no threat with that limp. Theirs was a cautious coming together. But she'd never seen Henry so – well – self-assured, even a bit cocky! Even his voice was louder! She laughed. She had to go down. This was their last family gathering before the wedding next weekend. Perhaps after that it would be very occasional, since it had been agreed that Henry and Alice would move to the Italian house. Henry was pleased with the idea, was sure he could work well there and travel just as easily from there as he could from London. Of course, she thought, good for you Henry, but what about Alice? With her mother so far gone now with dementia and Lawrence having to cope on his own. She had said she would be sad to leave her ma and da. Fiona just prayed he might turn out to be a decent husband like his father, and think about Alice and not himself all the time.

And the house! Yes, it was all very lovely, the house by the lake: the garden, the sweet and dry smells of fruit and fir; the balmy air, though it did rain quite often, being near mountains. Of course, it was quite beautiful, but she preferred to be here in her room with Max around somewhere. Over there he went berserk with this and that. Excited like a child; totally over the top, fiddling about with his camera or with the old car, which he kept there in the purpose-built garage, one of his many projects. Extending bits of the house; sorting a studio for Henry, chatting up the locals, exploring all the eating places and tasting all the local wines. They had only had the house a couple of years and he seemed to know everyone. Oh God, and the endless suppers in the garden, where she had to spend the whole time swatting mosquitoes. At least she had persuaded Max to have Lilly and Barns over for some of the time. That way she could get on with her writing. She didn't have to spend all her time thinking about the next al fresco supper. She shuddered. But it was lovely and Max was happy. Now she must go down and be jolly.

# Alice

If it had been up to Henry, it would have been in a register office with as few people as possible, but Ma was so disappointed, so wanted her to be married 'properly', as she put it, in their local church. 'It's such a pretty one, Alice. That little old building.' And there was no way Da wouldn't do whatever made her happy, things being as they were. Though she did hear him mutter about the fact that none of them went there except to be buried.

Of course, Henry agreed, and she was surprised how enthusiastic Max was. She called him Max now, and already gathered that he was enthusiastic over most things; he was just that kind of man. Henry couldn't have been more different.

She was so nervously excited, so kind of overcome by it all, that she just floated into the wedding. It would be simple. Just the immediate families and a few friends. She was absolutely happy about that. And her dress would be simple too. So she drew out a design based on a pre-Raphaelite painting. Ma swore by the local dressmaker, Mrs Cousins, who bought the material wholesale. Ivory-coloured shot silk, a scoop neck, not too low, long sleeves, gently shaped and the length just below her ankles; no train, no veil, just a little coronet of flowers. Flat shoes, so she could walk without a limp. No bridesmaids, not even Jo. 'You can be "best woman",' she had told her. 'You can sit with Henry and me at the meal.'

'The meal' nearly became a matter of dispute because Da was insisting on paying for everything, including the refreshments afterwards in the church hall. 'Let them know we're not on the breadline.'

But Max was equally insistent that he contribute, wanting to take over a restaurant he'd discovered near Durham. Discovering places to eat was one of his great hobbies, she later discovered.

In the end Da agreed when Alistair pointed out that it would all be far less stressful for them, especially Ma.

What happened in the church service was left entirely to Alice. who discussed it with Henry, who said he had no idea what was best, and so in the end the Reverend Charles chose the music and hymns.

Because it was a small church, having very few guests didn't matter at all. The men wore grey suits because Da had said he wasn't going to dress up like a penguin, not for anyone.

She was especially happy when Alistair said her dress was lovely and suited her well and, holding Da's arm, she walked up to Henry without any sign of a limp. True, they had practised a lot!

Cars took them to the restaurant afterwards, although Da teased her, saying she should go on one of his bikes! That seemed such fun, and she was reminded of that happy, smiling girl in the poster on Da's wall. But she really couldn't.

The entire restaurant had been taken over and Da said it must have cost a fortune and then shrugged. The tables were arranged in an oblong. White tablecloths, flowers, wine glasses. She, Henry, Da, Ma and Jo, as promised, sat one end and Max and Fiona, with Lola, Robert and Anne sat at the other. The rest down either side. Phoebe was sitting commandingly upright between Alistair and Paul, a university friend of Henry's whom Alice had not met before.

Da made a toast and said he would rather give her away than one of his bikes. And then why on earth they wanted to live in a big house by a lake in sunny Italy when they could enjoy the bracing air of the Dales, he would never understand. Everyone laughed and Ma took her chin off her hands and smiled at him.

Max made a toast joking that he was unaccustomed to public speaking and had been taught never to speak with a full mouth and that now he had his heart in his mouth he ought to shut up and sit down. A few hoorays and clinking of glasses. He said something about Henry having to leave the country and then how his son had managed to get such a beautiful, delightful girl to become his wife, he would never know. But, more seriously, she and all her family were their family now and how happy they were to have her as a daughter-in-law.

To her surprise, after thanking everyone for coming, Henry said their new home in Italy was open to anyone who wanted to visit. She thought she didn't remember discussing that.

Ma had to wipe her tears away, so Alice nudged Henry, who concluded by saying they would be coming home often; it was, after all only a two-hour flight away.

Afterwards, Alistair and Anne drove them to the hotel just outside Durham because it was on their way home anyway.

That first, proper night as a married couple was pretty much a disaster. She felt sick and Henry just said something like, 'We don't have to if you don't feel like it.' But she didn't feel guilty or a failure or anything like that, because before, on that first weekend away, she had felt really on for it, forgetting her terror until afterwards, when she became so anxious, terrified until her period started. She was taking the pill, but the doctor had said in answer to her question, 'Well, nothing is a hundred per cent safe, Alice. If you're that worried, get your husband to use a condom as well.'

But she hadn't yet had the courage to bring up the subject, afraid he would feel differently about her, not want her any more. She was a coward. But how could she make anyone understand about the grotesque noises she had heard that night in the hospital; the woman screaming as she gave birth. Alice knew she could never bear that kind of pain. The idea terrified her. She still had nightmares about it sometimes. What could she say to Henry?

Theirs was not a passionate kind of relationship in a sexual sort of way, she had decided, so she didn't feel guilty when she made excuses of one sort or another; her leg was paining or her back, because of her hip problems, of course, and he had always shown concern over that. Over her. She felt protected by him. She wasn't sure about their sex life. She would talk to him – she would. She would try to explain, say how careful they had to be. About what the doctor had said about being doubly sure, but she'd wait until they were together in Italy. Just the two of them.

They flew from Newcastle to Verona and were met by Max's 'man', Manuel, who was almost a friend and spoke good English. Henry could speak Italian but was lazy and never did so unless he had to. I will try to learn, she promised herself.

From the airport, Manuel drove past the Roman amphitheatre, where he said they could go to the opera, and Henry had asked her if she would like that, and then excitedly pointed out the house with Juliet's balcony. The anxiety had gone, she felt well; it was all so wonderful and she threw her arms around him, saying, 'Oh, I love it all. I love it.' And he kissed her.

'Thought you would.'

The drive to the house took about an hour, and all the time Alice was staring out of the car window, absorbed by the little communities, the countryside, the light. The everything. Leaving Manuel and Henry to chat away. She just kept looking as the sun, sliding behind the hills, cast pink lights on the lake.

Eventually Manuel turned into a narrow road beside the lake, stopping a few houses up. And there it was: long and pink, standing back from the road. Five long windows on the ground floor, all shuttered but for one, mirrored by smaller windows upstairs. A sharp-pointed orangey-red tiled roof. A wrought-iron gate opened onto a stony path, which led through the garden to the wooden front door, behind an iron grille.

She was stiff and Henry helped her from the car. With the engine stopped, she could hear the lap, lap of the water. Turning round and round she tried to absorb the house, the garden, the lake. This was to be their home for as long as they wanted, and she burst into tears.

'I wish Ma and Da were here.'

Henry opened the gate and she felt his arm around her. 'They will be soon. We'll try to get them over as soon as we can. Come, Alice. Stop the drama and let's get you inside.'

She stood in the hall waiting while Henry and Manuel brought in endless cases and the packages with Henry's painting equipment.

It was all so spacious. Stone walls painted white, cream shutters at all the windows, and on the floors cream marble tiles decorated with figures of eight in pale grey. The staircase ran up from the right and she looked up to where it divided at the top as the wrought-iron railings curled round. She felt homesick, a stranger in unfamiliar surroundings. And her hip ached from the journey and she didn't think she could cope with Max and co. coming over so soon, just three days' time. Fiona had protested, but Max argued that they needed to get there to help them settle down, 'show them the ropes'. But everyone knew he would find any excuse to be there, despite Fiona's reluctance.

Gabriella, who looked after the house, came in daily to clean and cook and generally do what she could to help Alice unpack, and the house became more familiar and Alice less homesick. She was beginning to enjoy the space, the light, the views from the windows and their bedroom with its own bathroom. Apart from the disastrous wedding night, she had never stayed in a posh hotel, but she thought, This house is nicer than any posh hotel.

Henry spent all his time setting up his studio which, formerly the dining room, looked over the back garden. North-east light was good, apparently. The sitting room was the other side of the hall: large sofas and armchairs, rugs and lamps and two of Henry's paintings, one of chickens and the other the horses in Lola's field.

Beyond this, at the very end of the house, was a self-contained unit: a bedsitting room and bathroom, which Max had built for Lilly and Barns, or visitors. It could only be accessed from an outside door at the side. Lilly and Barns, when they came over, used the family kitchen, as Lilly cooked for them all, and if the family did go out without them, she and Barns cooked for themselves. Max insisted, 'They're part of the family, as far as I'm concerned. It's their holiday too.'

Alice was happiest in the kitchen, which was huge, running the entire depth of the house. It had large windows overlooking the front garden and two smaller windows either side of the long, red kitchen range with its tiled shelf, like a mantelpiece, above, now dotted with odd bits: a box of matches, some keys, a vase with a dried twig in it and an old wooden clock, another of Max's finds. Max had also come across, on one of his 'adventures', the long pine table with an assortment of chairs. Alice loved it in there, with its cupboards and shelves and the breeze through the side door, which led into the garden. The sun came round in the early afternoon and then she would close the shutters, for she had already learned that closed windows and shutters helped to keep a room cooler during the hot summer, and she discovered the pleasure of walking barefoot on the cold floor tiles. She rested after lunch in the darkened bedroom. It was so peaceful she could hear the lap of the water against the lakeside wall.

On the third morning before the 'invasion', Henry asked Gabriella to take her shopping before it was too hot. She had not yet explored the village, thinking there would be plenty of time for that and in any case, she was nervous to go alone, as she spoke no Italian. Henry assured her most people spoke English of some sort and it would all be much easier than she expected. But to go out with Gabriella was a perfect idea.

The house was only a few minutes' walk, along the lakeside to the church square and the shops.

Gabriella took her firstly to the small supermarket, where they bought cheeses, olives, some cold meats and pasta. The smells from the baker's, from where they bought a loaf and some rolls, was sweeter than the smells from the bakery at home. At the end of the row of shops, the flower shop, where Gabriella took her last, wafted lavender perfumes. Alice insisted on buying lilies and large daisies; she didn't know their proper names. The owner a pretty young woman who obviously knew Gabriella well, chatted with her as she put together Alice's bouquet of flowers, which she tied with lengths of straw. She gave Alice the bouquet and then, taking her by the shoulders, kissed her on each cheek. 'Be happy! Happy!'

They arrived early evening and the peace was shattered, Max's boisterous voice greeting them as he got out of the car. Manuel had fetched them from the airport, but Max had his beloved Alfa Romeo waiting for him in one of the garages at the end of the long drive beside the house. 'When in Rome do as Rome does,' was his answer to Fiona's complaint about the extravagance, and he and Barns went immediately to inspect it before Barns was instructed to back it out to the end of the drive. Max needed to be sure all was in working order. No flat battery. 'We'll take her for a spin later,' he called to Barns as he and Lilly, with their one case, went into their 'quarters'.

Henry helped with the other cases and Alice, halfway down the path, waited to greet them. A huge bear hug from Max and two tired, hot cheeks offered awkwardly by Fiona, who made for the kitchen, flopping down on one of the chairs.

162

Henry seemed neither pleased nor displeased to see them She watched him as he acknowledged his father's slap on the back and the quick kiss on his mother's cheek. There was no need for Alice to be anxious about being a good hostess, for Max, in the most generous kind of way, took it all over.

'Good journey? Would you like a cup of tea?' Because that's what Ma would have wanted.

'Cup of tea?' Max shouted. 'Surely, Henry, you've put wine and beer in the fridge.'

'Dad! What else would I do, knowing you were coming to stay?'

Alice was about to say that Gabriella had left food in the fridge but, no, they were all going out and Barns would drive to some restaurant that Max especially liked. 'No need to book on a Wednesday. Do you like oysters, Alice?'

Luckily, he didn't wait for an answer, as he and Fiona were halfway up the stairs: 'For a clean-up and a bit of a rest for Fee.'

Alice was anxious again. She had never had oysters and knew she would hate them.

Henry was fiddling about with bottles in the fridge. 'Henry, I don't want oysters. Da says they can give you food poisoning. You know how easily I get sick.' She was leaning over one of the chairs, watching him. She liked him a lot. She took for granted that that was love. But anyway, she liked him very much; he was peculiar in an artist's sort of way, busy in his own mind, absent from her. But never unkind. Yet if she went into his studio because she was bored or feeling lonely, he would hardly speak but just continue with his painting. 'Later, Alice, OK? Bit busy at the moment.'

Funny, she thought, because he spoke for ages with Phoebe on the phone. At their wedding, she noticed how Phoebe took ownership of Henry. 'Oh, he doesn't like this,' or, 'He never goes there,' and so on. Fiona never said much about her, but Alice knew she thought Phoebe was a bossy so-and-so. It was odd, though, how Henry, who never got cross with Alice, seemed very irritated by Phoebe at times. He even raised his voice on the phone. She'd heard him. 'For goodness' sake, Phoebe, will you stop going on, stop pressuring me. I'll do it all in my good time. How many times . . .?' And, 'Yes, yes, Phoebe, I will be back in London when it suits me, and not before – all right?'

'Where will you stay when you go back to London?' Alice had asked. 'Now your Dad has taken over your flat.' But he never really answered.

They had several outings during that week, Barns driving while Lilly mostly stayed at home and Alice enjoyed seeing more of the places round the lake: the hillside villages, all with their churches. It was astonishing to her how they were drenched in shining gilt, like gold, everywhere, so ornate: carvings, statues and paintings. Henry did take some interest too, which was unusual for him.

One of the trips Max insisted upon was a visit to an old mill, a paper mill, just beyond the village, which he said was a fascinating place and being renovated by the Industrial Trust. 'Not sure if it will ever be a working mill again, but it will certainly be a tourist attraction. Bring in the visitors.'

Fiona stayed at home in the bedroom and got on with her writing, which took up most of her time. Max said it was her way of escaping the irritations of life. Alice thought that actually Henry was very like her, only he painted and she wrote. It was daunting to be part of such a talented family. She daren't get out her paints, daren't slosh about painting her pebbles in sunlit water. When Henry went to London perhaps, she would have a go.

The mill was disappointing; it was more like a building site, with men and noise everywhere. For Alice, it was impossible to imagine how it had been before or how it would look when all the work was finished. Hardly any point in staying! But Max insisted they walk up to the wreck of the mill house. Henry took her arm up the slope, for the ground was uneven.

Max was interested as he watched the men at work on the roof. The timbers were all in place and the tilers were crawling up and down, laying the local brownish-red tiles. He called up to one in Italian, 'You're doing a good job there. When will it all be finished'?

'His Italian is abysmal,' Henry muttered, and she tried not to laugh.

On the way back to the car Max pointed out the row of motorbikes lined up outside the prefabricated buildings, 'That's what I ought to get,' he said.

'I think not, Dad. Drop that one unless you want a divorce.'

Max threw his head back and laughed. 'Well, Lawrence has bikes, hasn't he, Alice?'

'Da loves his bikes, loves the . . .' and she just managed to withhold the tears.

It was very quiet once they'd gone home and she, feeling lonely again, phoned Da.

'Can't you possibly come over, Da?'

# Alice

E ven after seven months, because of the excitement, the childish anticipation of another day, she woke early, lying on her back, her side close to Henry, comforted by the solidity and warmth of his body.

It was still dark outside, and the heat of summer had given way to changeable weather: balmy, still dampness, cold-wind chill or what she thought of as bright-blue sunshine.

She put on her dressing gown and went downstairs to prepare breakfast. Her only must-do task of the day, for all the other meals were prepared by Gabriella.

This morning she had to put on the lights, for even with the shutters open it was still dim in the kitchen, yet she could see, looking out towards the lake, a rising, spreading glow in the sky and guessed it would be a fine day.

Henry would have egg and toast today. He alternated between that and warm rolls with jam or the marmalade he'd brought back from one of his frequent trips to London. He always had coffee; she had tea.

Mealtimes were the opportunity to get his attention and so she especially enjoyed them. His being so attentive towards her had been one of the things that had attracted her to him. She was happy, but things were not as she had expected. He was concerned solely with his paintings, which she understood and accepted; she had to make her own entertainment. And as it was early days with plenty to explore and do, she filled her time reasonably well.

'I'm going shopping with Gabriella this morning, remember? Is there anything you want?'

He shook his head and drank some coffee.

'I think it's going to be a fine day, don't you? Look!' And she pointed to the streaks of fire-glow light.

He looked and nodded. 'You might be right.'

'Henry, would you have time to drive me to that garden centre we were talking about? I do want to buy two big pots for outside the door, you know. Could we go later this afternoon? I know you're busy finishing, but I want to plant some Christmas roses. Any chance?'

He took his second cup of coffee with him into the studio as usual and she cleared up before going back upstairs to shower and dress. She was happy, wasn't she? She was lucky. He had to work, for goodness' sake. She was proud of him. And he had to go back to London, of course he did. She couldn't help but wonder about Phoebe. She asked him once, when she really didn't mean to, if he ever stayed with her, and he had given such a grumpy reply: 'Only if I have to.' Anyway, she was going shopping now and he had promised to take her out this afternoon. She was really looking forward to that.

Gabriella was already preparing something when she returned to the kitchen. Alice had grown fond of her and usually greeted her with a peck on both cheeks. It was so great to have her company. and because everybody seemed to know and like Gabriella, they were very friendly towards her, too. She felt included. Not so alone. Not so homesick.

Before going out together, Alice took in another coffee for Henry, making space on the table on which he kept his brushes and paints. She had already learned to expect nothing more than a grunt for thanks. She'd also learned quickly not to disturb him when he was working: he did not take kindly to it. Fair enough, she thought. She supposed that it was normal for married people to be ... well ... to kind of take things for granted. What had she expected? That she would be his first consideration? That taking care of her would be the most important thing for him? It had appeared like that before. But he had to work. He had to travel. And she had to find ways of keeping herself busy. It was going to be more difficult during these winter months. If only she dared get back to painting! But she was too shy to paint in front of Henry, who was such a fine artist. She would be so embarrassed. But, perhaps, the next time he was away. Just when he was away. She might dare.

'Can we go to the flower shop? I'd like to, Gabriella.' She put an arm round her shoulders as they walked down the path towards the lake. 'You know ... I must find things to do, Gabriella.'

'We go to Angelina Fiori. OK? I talk to Angelina.' And Gabriella poked a finger into the side of her head with a sly glance.' I think of something for you.'

The sun that morning was warm on their backs as they walked the lakeside path to the shops, Alice halting every so often to watch the boats swaying and the light rays appearing and disappearing with the rippling water. She loved to hear the lap, lap of the water as it smoothed across small pebbly patches along the shoreline, where often boats were moored. And Gabriella laughed and tugged her by the arm to hurry.

It was the last shop they called on and this morning, as Alice was selecting flowers and foliage, she heard Angelina and Gabriella speaking quickly together. They had moved to the back of the shop and Alice observed them glancing towards her. They had been friends for a long time, so it was not entirely unusual for them to chat at length, but this morning it seemed different to her, as if, somehow, she was involved in their conversation. She had learned to speak a little Italian, but this she could not understand at all. She was a bit anxious at first, but then they were smiling and she decided whatever it was, it must not be too awful.

She was right! They came over to her just outside the shop and Gabriella pulled her to stand up. 'Angelina say you come here on Saturday to help.'

'You come to work Angelina Fiori ... no? To help? On Saturdays? You like the flowers, no?'

Both of them stood there smiling at her, waiting.

She asked Gabriella, whose English was better, 'Does she want me to help her here on Saturdays?'

And together, nodding, 'Si. Si.'

Over lunch she watched Henry's face as she told him they'd asked her to help out at the flower shop on Saturdays. He gave her one of the wide smiles she loved. 'And are you going to?'

Nothing could be better for her now. He had smiled and they were going to the garden centre to buy the pots. It was like it used to be. And she would keep occupied when he was away.

1986–1987

# Frank

'You've got two letters,' she wheezed in his ear, and waved them like flags before handing them to him and then stood waiting expectantly, watching him, her head nodding encouragingly.

'It's my birthday, that's why.' He put them on the table and continued spreading his toast.

'Oh! Well, that's why then. Someone remembered? If I'd known, I'd have baked a cake.' And she giggled like a naughty child might.

He nodded. 'Sure.'

'Happy birthday, anyway,' she panted. 'Don't forget it's Saturday – no meal tonight. Down the pub for you. You can have a drink on me.'

'I'm going up the Dales,' he said, 'on the bike.'

'That's good. Go up to St John's Chapel. We used to like that. It's the highest point up the dale. Windy. Can be. Wrap up, that's all I'd say.'

He found her later in the kitchen, still washing up from breakfast. There was something about it that reminded him of home: the vinyl top, speckled browns and greens; the lino tiles on the floor. Only the table was pine, not Formica. He stood in the doorway.

'Have you got a bucket?

She turned with a start, child-like, breathless, her little-girl short hair now grey, held back with a slide.

'I'd like to give the bike a clean. If I can have a bucket with some soapy water.'

'Are you going on one of your trips? It's bitterly cold. You'll need to wrap up.'

She pointed to the door of what had once been a large pantry. It was full of brushes and mops, a vacuum cleaner and shelves of cleaning materials, a bag of dusters and a dustpan and brush. A yellow bucket was hanging from a nail. He took it down and then rummaged in the bag for a piece of cloth.

'You gave me a fright,' she said as he approached the sink. She waited as he filled the bucket and squeezed in liquid soap. 'I'll come and inspect when you've done,' and poked him in the side.

She let him keep the bike down the side, leaning against a concrete coal bunker. He wheeled it round the back to the slabs outside the kitchen door.

He washed down the bike, rubbed up the chrome and polished the saddle and handles. The letters were still waiting to be opened.

Before leaving, he decided to open his cards. He recognised the handwriting. Kitty's half printed; he could tell she'd tried hard to be neat. Ruby's was full of curves, slanting and faint. He opened them sitting on the bed, already dressed in his waterproofs. Kitty's card was 'To My Brother. Happy Birthday!' in gold lettering with two glasses of bubbly underneath. Inside she had written: *To dear Frankie. Happy birthday with all our love Kitty and Steve.* At the bottom she'd printed: *We are fine and still working at the same place. Hope you are well.*

Ruby's card was of an old steam engine leaving a station. Frank choked as he read: *To Frank. Many happy returns of your birthday. Love from Ruby and Stan.* On the other page she'd added: *My legs are no better. Stan says how's the job going?*

He put the cards on the chest of drawers and turned away towards the door.

He'd ring them later.


The town was busy; it was market day. Cars were parked either side of Hope Street and he had to manoeuvre the bike carefully before turning into West Road, which rose steeply to the top of the town. From the top there was the view of the church tower and the surrounding hills. It was becoming familiar; he was beginning to feel at home.

Once out of the town, the roads cleared and he increased his speed towards Wolsingham, the first town up the dale. Now the landscape widened; the moors swept by, undulating green, the sky expanded and the horizon was always distant. He felt jubilant and light; breathed in the space, the emptiness. He stopped to listen in the stillness: the wind through the grasses, the movement of sheep. There were clusters of trees, now bare, along the river's side and dry-stone walls crossed the landscape. Mrs Mackie was right – it was cold and windy, but the light was clean and the colours soft.

It was in the village of Stanhope, further up the dale, that he saw the shop with bits and pieces piled up outside; a terraced house, the front altered to create a shop window. Outside were a couple of chairs and a small bookshelf. Some garden tools, tied together, were standing in a wooden barrel. There were picture frames, some wooden, others painted gold, leaning against the wall. He parked his bike alongside a side door off the road. He had noticed shops like this from the bus on his way to Coundon and dreamed of finding some rare piece hidden away in a dark corner, but now he was rather uncertain about going inside. He stood looking at the frames, some with pictures of local scenes, he guessed. He knew nothing about paintings. Nothing.

Suddenly, the shop door opened and a small man wearing slippers looked at him through wire-framed glasses. He was slurping tea from a mug.

'What you looking for?' he asked. 'Anything in particular – or just looking? I've not seen you before. Where are you from, then? You can just have a look round. It's all right with me.' He straightened one of the chairs and then moved back inside the shop. 'Come on,' he shouted. 'You can come and nose around like the others. It's all the same to me.'

Frank went in.

'Shut the door behind you, then. It's cold enough.' He was wearing mittens; his fingers, red and rough, poked through grey holes. Frank took off his helmet and put it down by the door. The man was sitting behind a small table, the mug of tea beside him. A door behind was slightly ajar and Frank thought he heard someone on the telephone.

'Interested in pictures? I saw you looking at them outside. Go on! Have a nose about. I'll leave you for a moment. Not to worry – you'll not get far on that bike with anything worth having.' And he disappeared through the door.

It was like someone's attic, this tiny room. Someone's life stacked up in piles. A life made up of bits and pieces. Pictures covered the walls; shelves were filled, untidily, with books, china ornaments. There was a basket of lace bits, an old mangle, fishing rods and a box of old postcards. Inside he smiled, for everything he owned could be packed into his case and rucksack.

It was the green vase that caught his eye. Something about it reminded him of home, of Mum. He had money in his pocket now; it was for her only, he wanted to buy it; the longing was shocking. She would be sitting on the sofa, smiling, 'Oh! It's lovely Frankie. Put it on the mantelpiece,' she would say. She would be there still, laughing, sitting on the sofa, thanking him for his presents. She would be there now if he hadn't left her, if he hadn't panicked and run next door with Kitty. If he had stayed that night, Mum would be there still. But there was something about that vase: he knew that Mum would love it, so he took it off the shelf. The price tag round its neck said *50p*. It was only a tiny vase. It would fit perfectly in his waterproof pocket. The little green vase for Mum. He'd wait for the right moment.

'I had a pair of them. Sold the other some time ago. Nice young couple. He was an artist of some sort. She wanted it, so he bought it for her. Local lass.'

Frank turned quickly to the box of cards, remembering he had meant to send the kid a card, and so he began rummaging through the box. Old-fashioned pictures in sepia of churches and market squares; a country house with people playing croquet. There were other cards, in coloured wash, of hills and sheep. Sheep-dog trials. Haymaking. Then he found a seaside scene. Bridlington. The sea in a blue wash, stretches of sand and two children building sandcastles, a woman, face shaded by a hat, watching from a deckchair. Frank was not sure – which one would the kid like best? He searched through some at the bottom of the box.

'There's more here.' The man had returned now, wearing a grey woollen cardigan. He pointed to a box under a small table. Frank lifted it up.

'You looking for anything special? They're all collectable. I have folk and dealers who come just for the postcards.'

'How much?'

'Depends'

He looked through the second box, but it was the seascape he wanted for the kid. He returned to it and held it up.

'Oh, that one! You've got a sharp eye. That's worth having, that is. The artist, Rowland Wells, is collectable. You've got a real eye.'

'It's for a kid I know.'

'For a kid? He won't appreciate it.'

'How much, though?'

The man opened a book on the table and ran his finger down the page of pencilled items. 'You can have it for one pound fifty.'

It was a lot for a postcard but he had money and it was for the kid. 'OK,' he said. 'That's OK.'

'What about for you? You could take something small on the back of that bike.'

'I'll come back another day now I know you're here.'

'Right ho!' He fumbled the money into a tin and found a paper bag for the postcard. 'Hope your kid likes it, then.' He handed Frank the bag. 'Up here for work, are you? Or is it a holiday? You're from down south, is my guess.'

He picked up his helmet. 'From Hampshire.'

'Near London, is it?'

'Not really.' And he thought, all these years and we never went to London, not for a day out. He could have taken Kitty. She would have loved that.

'What brings you up this way, then?

'I'm a chippy. Working at Bishop's Lodge at Coundon.'

'Oh, aye, I know it. It's been in the papers, that has. Costing millions. Been boarded up for years. Waste of money, if you ask me, which you won't. English Heritage got something to do with it. Got their hands on it.'

'Yep. But it's worth doing up, shame to let it rot away.'

'And a job for you!' He laughed. 'Course you like the idea.'

'It'll bring in money ... you know, locally, when it's done. Bishop Auckland council are going to open it up for visitors, I think, and have things going on there. I don't know, but things like conferences and such. Anyway, you'll see. Maybe change your mind.'

'Doubt that! But then you never know.'

He could feel the stolen vase in his pocket; he wanted to go. 'It's got a seventeenth-century staircase with turned balustrades and some original shutters that need renovating.'

'You'll be busy then.'

'If I don't mess up. Could be a year or more.' He thought about Ruby and Stan and the money he sent them every month.

'Ah well!' The man fingered his empty mug and then stared at him through his glasses. 'Why they couldn't find a local chippy . . . no disrespect. Seems daft to me.'

He shrugged. 'That's OK. Most are from round this way.'

He opened the door. It was raining now.

'Take care on those wet roads.'

'I'll come back.'

Maybe it was the vase made him phone. Thinking of Mum. Thinking of how things were then. With them all.

The hall was dimly lit, no lights on anywhere else and he wondered where Mrs Mackie went on Saturdays. After he had phoned, he would go down to the pub for his supper. Barney was sure to be there with Di, his 'missus' as he called her. Nice woman.

He didn't think Kitty would be in on a Saturday night, but he'd try anyway.

The phone was on the hall table, which stood beside one of the dining-room chairs upholstered in a floral material now faded and colourless. He sat down without taking off his coat, unsure as he often was with Kitty and glad there was no one around to listen.

At once he knew there was something was wrong, for he had to repeat 'Hello! Are you there, Kitty? What's up?' And then, to help her, 'I phoned to thank you for my card.'

He heard the child-like voice, the half-stifled sob.

'Kitty?' The terror was never far away.

Then she spoke after a shallow laugh and a voice brittle-bright. 'Sorry, Frankie. Oh! It's nothing really.' She broke off for a second. 'Thing I— God, you're not going to believe this – it's so stupid – you won't believe how stupid, Frank. Me falling down these steps. What a right idiot! Anyway, I did, and I broke my left arm.' Then loudly. 'Did you hear? I broke my bloody arm, OK? And no, I wasn't drunk so don't even begin—'

'I'm coming down.'

'No!' It was almost a scream. Then, he could hear the effort, her voice lower and cold, 'No, Frank. Don't come down. I don't want you to.'

He should never have gone, should never have taken a taxi from the station to surprise her alone in the flat, but had guessed right that Steve would be down the pub.

She looked puffy-eyed and pale, her hair shaggy over her eyes. Her left arm was in plaster, partly covered by a loose, fluffy cardigan. He knew she was lying, lying hopelessly. He asked, sitting in the mess of the room, the air clogged with cigarette smoke and the smell of alcohol, his table marked and stained with cigarette burns and rings left by mugs and beer cans, 'Was it the drink or was it Steve?' He asked her but she wasn't having any. She'd told him to piss off. She'd said not to come, hadn't she? Not to interfere like he always did. Like an old woman. Why did he think she'd left in the first place? To get away from him. He just didn't get it, did he? Never had. How she hated him fussing all over her, all the time; it wasn't normal; like he wasn't normal sometimes. He should go before Steve got back, before Steve had a go at him. She was with Steve now; couldn't he get that into his thick head? With Steve.

He didn't remember the journey home, just several buses, some going the wrong way; the rain and the cold.

It was still there, the little green vase, standing there on the chest of drawers. He took a swipe at it and it circled to the floor. Smashing into pieces. He put his foot onto the pile of broken glass and crushed it to smithereens. Then he lay on the bed, relieving himself. Self-abuse?

But it was only a momentary comfort, a temporary relief. Unsatisfactory satisfaction. And then the shame, the disgust that Kitty had for him.

*

Yet the worry, the obsession, wouldn't go away. He could think of nothing else and he couldn't stay away. In a kind of madness, he was drawn there. Three times he took the train to Doncaster. Then buses. Once to the centre to see her at work. To look, like he used to, through the steamy windows, at the girls in their platform heels and tight-fitting tops over miniskirts. He never saw her.

Another time, he stood in the shadows across the road from the bookmaker's and stared at the flat window, the window to the living room. Watched water drip off the end of the gutter. Like him on the edge of the playground that morning at his new school.

The curtains were partly drawn. Crookedly hung pinkish curtains, through which he saw moving shadows. His heart was shaking with agitation as Steve came down the steps, his leather jacket slung over one shoulder, a fag between his fingers, which he crushed before unlocking the car door. She was alone then. The pavements and road were dimly lit from the shop lights, but even in the darkness of the doorway she might see him and if she saw him, if she recognised him standing there ... He didn't dare go up the steps, didn't dare knock on the door. A gang of teenagers passed, one eyeing him standing there in the shadows, turned back to look and muttered something, and someone laughed.

One time, to save money, he biked it down; it took hours and all the time he wondered what it was that possessed him, what force had taken hold that he should behave like this and be unable to stop. It took him two hours to get there, and for what? To stand alone and cold in the dark outside the flat and then to bike it all the way back. It had to stop.

So, when he heard the guys at work talking something about the Heritage Trust and a nineteenth-century mill in Italy somewhere, he asked the boss what was going on.

'Funny you should ask,' he said. 'I was thinking of you. No ties ... well, as far as I know. So, thought you might consider this job in Italy. There's a group of them from the Heritage Trust looking for real craftsmen. It's a big renovation job. Anywise, you can meet them day after tomorrow. Find out more.'

They were standing in the hall of the lodge, Frank finishing the balustrades, layering wax over the staining to match the others.

'Can't let you go 'til we're finished here, though. Could be another six months to a year's work here still. Anywise, talk to the guys tomorrow. Make sure there'll still be work for you in Italy, if that's what you want.'

He trembled at the thought of leaving her behind. Leaving. But he couldn't go on with this behaviour – almost madness. He had to get away. If they would have him, he'd go. He would do it without thinking, without thinking about the leaving. And he hoped it would be sooner rather than later.

# Frank

*Eight months later*

He couldn't go to Italy without seeing them, without saying goodbye.

When the train pulled into the station, so familiar, he had a childish sense of pride, a sense of ownership. This was home. His home.

The station, situated in the backstreets, was neglected and dirty, with litter trapped in corners and under the benches; the shops nearby jumbled, colourless squares behind dirty windows.

He walked through a shortcut towards the park, passing the library and the bus stop to school, the ironmonger's where he went with Stan to buy bits and pieces: tools, linseed oil, turps and varnish, where he had stolen bags of screws and nails. Nothing much had changed except the pub, which had given over to meals and looked bright and brash. He disliked the changes, made him uneasy, but the hairdresser's and the launderette were there, already busy this Saturday morning. This was his place; he belonged, not the strangers he saw through the open doors.

There were children on the swings and two mothers with prams. The green benches had been freshly painted and one or two of the concrete paths patched with lighter concrete.

He sat on his usual seat looking across at the launderette and suddenly wanting to see Julie come out and cross the park to sit next to him. And the kid. Then he remembered the kid would be a schoolboy now. Different. He wondered about the garage he'd made for him, if it'd been dumped now he was older.

Hopelessly stupid, he wandered across to the launderette. She wasn't there, of course, and now he felt a stranger in this, his own special place. In any case, for all he knew she could have moved away, got married. Anything. He'd only sent the one postcard.

He crossed to the other side, to the church, unlatched the iron gates that guarded the path to the church door from the outside world. The church stood stubbornly dull and cold as before. The oak door at the side opened and he went into the dimness. A yellowish light seeping through stained glass hung about the place. Dust motes floated through the light like larvae in a rank pool.

He found the pew, his carved end still solid. He ran his hand round it and over it. He could have done a better job. No doubt about that. He sat in the pew, holding aimlessly in his mind the hanging Christ on the wooden cross, which stood in the middle of the altar. He, the man on the cross, hadn't done much for them: for Kitty. For Mum. But Stan and Ruby? They are the ones who have done things. Perhaps the Big Bang was actually God exploding into all the stuff that got into creation and into people. Like Ruby and Stan. Little bits of God in them, that's what he thought, anyway. Not Him hanging there. He felt the rage surging. If he could pray. If God could answer prayers, he knew with all his being what he would pray for. Who he would pray for. 'Kitty. Take care of Kitty.' He twisted awkwardly in the pew; he could do nothing for her now. Nothing. Nothing for Kitty. It was to have been his life's work to keep her safe and happy, to stop things from ever happening again. But he could do nothing but leave her to the beatings and the drink and the pills, just like Mum. Oh, Mum.

'You bloody God,' he hissed. And the groan from his heart vibrated through the yellow light.

The Saturday shoppers were out, the park dotted with children, the benches occupied by chatting mums and men reading newspapers. He crossed the cracked path to the other side in silence, turned up the road away from the launderette and the hairdresser's, and left into the council estate. He'd phoned a couple days ago to say he was coming and heard the excitement in Ruby's voice as she called back to Stan, 'It's Frank. It's Frankie, Stan. He's coming this Saturday. This Saturday,' she repeated. 'Can you stay, Frankie? Just one night. Just one. Your room is still here.' And she laughed at the idea of the room disappearing. 'We could all go out for our fish and chips. Frankie?'

It was Stan who opened the back door. The old lino had gone, replaced with mottled cream-vinyl tiles. And the table with the Formica top. Gone. In its place a sturdy pine job made by Stan. That was different, but Ruby was Ruby standing there balancing on her walking frame, her swollen ankles bulging over her slippers. He'd forgotten how tiny she was. A little round dormouse, bright-eyed with expectation. He bent to kiss her and she clutched at him round his neck as he bent almost double.

Stan put on the kettle; the hissing lost in Ruby's chatter.

After the mug of tea and the elevenses biscuit to dunk in, he asked Stan if he could go to the shed. See what he was doing.

Stan took his cap from the hook on the back door. 'Not doing much. Not these days. She takes up time. Pushing her shopping and all that. Church on Sundays. I don't go in … all that palaver.'

The shed was unusually tidy, the floor swept clean of shavings, but the smell of varnish and the flecks of sawdust on the windows were reassuring.

They stood together just inside the wide-open door, stood side by side. He couldn't speak, but only remember that night he and Kitty had run there away from the terror, had hidden and waited.

'You doing all right then, lad?'

He smiled. It was a long time since he had been called lad. 'You taught me well,' was all he said. He wanted to say, 'I love you.' He wanted to call him Dad, but he just mumbled, 'I've got you to thank. You taught me everything,'

Stan turned to face him. 'And what's all this Italy lark, then? Is work so bad here you have to go to the other side of the world?'

'It's not that. It's the heritage people again. They asked me. They were pleased with the work on the lodge. And I enjoyed it, Stan. Takes my mind off things, like you used to say.'

'Too true!' And he rasped a chuckle. 'So, what is it now then, Frank – in Italy,' he sniffed.

'Bigger job altogether. It's a nineteenth-century water mill. Mill house and all. The mill wheel is rotted and the wooden sleepers and rails running up and down the hillside. It was a paper mill when it was working. Lot of local wood, trees, you know. But I guess new methods put it out of business. Anyroad, it's pretty derelict now. Everything needs doing over. I've seen pictures. It's quite mountainous, with grassy slopes, from what I could see. I've seen the architects. Me and others. There's three of us going over. It'll be a long job. Lots of work, Stan. I'll be there some time. Course, the site managers will be local, so that should be interesting – language-wise.'

He moved into the light outside, couldn't look directly at Stan.

'Well, if it's what you want. Anyroad!' And he elbowed him with a grin. 'Anyroad! My arse! And what about that sister of yours? She worries, you know.' And he waved towards the house. 'Worries all the time. About that Kit.'

'She'll know where to find me.' He took hold of the door, ready to close it, waiting for Stan to come out into the light.

'We don't get to hear much, and she worries,' Stan repeated.

'If she needs me, she'll know where I am,' he repeated almost to himself.

They were at the back door when Stan touched his arm. 'The money's handy,' he said, 'but no need to go on, Frank. We can manage.'

'I get good money.' He wanted to say Dad. 'I get good money, Dad.'

Stan went to the station with him, panting slightly; it was too much for Ruby despite the fact that the station was not far from the green. She cried a little when, for the first time, he hugged her.

They didn't speak, he and Stan, as they crossed the green and continued in silence until they reached the station platform when, without turning his head, Stan said, 'You're going a long way away, son.'

He'd never said 'son' before.

'When you come home, you should start your own business. You know, your own workshop and like. I've always said, haven't I now, be your own boss. You don't want no bloody employer breathing down your neck all the time. Take it from me.'

'Maybe! You never know, Stan. But for the while this will do me. Like I said, it's real money and I can help out like before. And Kit too.'

'And I've told you, no need.'

'Yep! OK, but just treat yourself, man. Get that shed of yours sorted out. Buy some new tools. I don't know, anything. Treat Ruby . . . I'll . . .'

The train pulled in and he slung on his backpack, as Stan – he was old now – struggled to open the carriage door for him.

'Leave it, Stan! Leave it!'

He loved Stan, though when he thought of his dad, tall, strong with that blond hair, handsome with a great grin, no wonder Mum went for him. He had loved him, despite everything. Now he just didn't know. Just wished things had been different.

Stan clapped him on the shoulder. 'Get in there! Get a seat.'

'I'll ring as soon as I get there ... with the number. I'll phone every week or more. Anyroad.' And he grinned at Stan.

'Anyroad? For God's sake!'' Stan sniffed and turned away.

'I can be home in two hours. Do you hear me?'

But Stan was walking away and didn't see his waving hand.

Kitty had sounded especially pleased to hear his voice. Excited, even. She had something to tell him. And he wondered if it was a new job, perhaps? Or new curtains? Something like that. He explained, rather briefly, because she rarely concentrated on details, about the job in Italy, and said he just wanted to pop in to say cheerio. And, of course, if she had something special to tell him, then all the more reason. She had given a little scream when he said Italy, but aside of that she didn't seem unduly sad, for which he was thankful, as he didn't want her to be sad. He was the sad one, running away to Italy to escape a kind of grief.

The last time he'd visited her, he'd been standing in the shadows across the road, with that uncontrollable panic; his anxiety, which drove him to see her, to check on her. He would never do that again. Italy was his escape from ... a kind of grief?

He took a taxi to save time; she'd sounded so happy and excited, to see him.

'Frankie!' She flung her arms around him. 'Oh, Frankie!'

'Hello, Kit.' And saw at once what it was she wanted to tell him.

'He's not here,' she said, laughing. 'Thank God! Oh, I don't mean it like that, it's just, well ...'

The place was tidier than he had ever seen it and the teak

table he had so carefully made for her had been painted green, he supposed to hide the damage, but it was already scratched in places, the green paint chipping off, revealing the wood underneath.

'Guess what, Frankie?'

'What?'

'Look! Look!' She burst out laughing as she patted her stomach.

'Yes! And?'

'For God's sake, Frank Richardson. For God's sake, look at me.' She twirled around in front of him. 'Who's going to be an uncle, then? Uncle Frankie, Uncle Frankie.' And she twirled again. He hadn't seen her so happy for a long time. The short blonde hair had gone and there she was with her long dark hair swinging and her long legs jigging around. Beautiful Kit.

'We'll be a real family, won't we?' she was saying. 'Won't we, Frankie?'

'If you say so ...' was all he could manage. And then, 'It's great news, Kit. If you're happy, I'm happy. That's all.'

'And guess what?

'Go on.'

'Guess what I'm going to call them. Daisy for a girl, 'cos of all those daisy chains I made for Mum. And Donnie if it's a boy.'

'Donnie? Is that a boy's name?'

''Tis if you want it to be. What do you think, then? Good?' She took hold of his arm. 'Aren't you pleased, Frankie? Pleased for us ... well, for me, then?'

'Steve is pleased, too, isn't he?'

She let go of his arm and moved to the other side of the coffee table. Shrugged. Laughed. He knew that laugh.

'Bit pissed off to start with. Y' know, he doesn't want his life to change that much. But don't worry, Frankie, he'll come round to it. He'll love it when he sees it. Same for most men.' She laughed again. 'He's into the races, see. Goes to the races

189

every Saturday. Takes me out to the pub after, if he's won. Everyone goes there. They all know him. Most night he pops in after work.'

He turned to look out of the window. At the late shoppers. The small Co-op.

'He does the betting shop, too,' she said.

It was Saturday, so he'd be at the races. 'What time does he come back?'

'Depends.'

'You're not on stuff, are you, Kitty? Not again, girl.'

Then she shouted, 'No, Frank! Look at me.' She patted her stomach. 'I knew you'd carry on, bring all that up again. For Christ's sake, I'm pregnant. No pills. No drink. Not even a fag. I only care about the baby. I want to be a really good mum, not like ours was. No way.'

'Please, don't say that, Kit. It's not right.'

Two lads, overweight, with beer cans, came out of the betting shop and he thought, Drugs. Drink. Violence. He knew Steve had beaten her up goodness knows how many times. He knew, though, she'd never admit it to him. To him. It was her pride. How could she know that she'd chosen a man like Dad? No, worse than Dad. He could never love a man like Steve, but he loved Dad. 'Don't talk about Mum like that,' he repeated.

There was a cheap kind of caff over the road. Breakfast all day.

'Are you hungry?' He had to get out. 'What's that caff like, over there?'

She came to the window and took his arm again. Put her head on his shoulder. 'Oh, it's good. And I'm starving as well. But I've got no dosh, though.'

'I've got money. Come on. Put your coat on or something.'

She gave him a slight slap on his back. 'For God's sake, Frankie, we're only going across the road, not to the bloody Arctic! '

*

Over their sausage, eggs and chips he told her about Italy and the mill and the chance he had to do really well and make money. 'You must never worry about cash,' he said.

She'd stopped eating, a chip held on a fork near her mouth, he thought she was going to cry, so he went on talking. 'Tomorrow I want you to go to your nearest bank and get them to help you open a bank account.' He opened his rucksack, which was on the floor beside him, and took out a brown envelope. 'Here. There's two hundred pounds. Put in it the bank. And do not tell Steve, OK? It's just for you . . . just in case . . .'

'Frankie!' Now she did burst into tears. Head in her hands, shoulders shaking.

'You're being a drama queen, Kit,' he joked as best he could. Then she started her giggle. The other customers were staring and he wished they would stop.

He began to whisper. Leaned forward. 'Just listen for once, will you, it's important. When you have opened your bank account you will have a cheque book with all the details on it. You can give me those over the phone and every week I'll put in a bit for you and the . . . well, the kid, whatever it is. He keeps you short, doesn't he? Well, I know he does. So this is just for you, just a safety net, a kind of protection.' He didn't mean to use the word 'protection' – he should have said insurance. But she wouldn't have understood anyway.

'But you won't be here. You won't be here, you know, when the baby comes.' And the crying started all over again.

'Kitty! Listen, I'll be only a couple of hours away, not much further than now. Seems far because it's Italy, but it's not. So, I'll be here for sure. Which reminds me.' He took out a note pad and a biro from his pocket as Kitty was mouthing and smiling at a woman on another table. 'Kitty! Stop messing about and concentrate.' She adopted her mock-serious expression, which he ignored. 'Here are my new telephone numbers. Look. One is my lodging place and this my work.

191

Don't lose this. Write them down somewhere safe. Kit! Are you listening? 'He looked across to the other table. 'Who is that anyway? A friend or what?'

'Yvonne! Von,' she called across, 'this is my brother, Frank. He's off to Italy.'

The woman, Yvonne, with a man and two kids, got up, grinning. She was plump and cheerful-looking, a bit like Julie.

'She's my best. You're my best, aren't you, Von?'

'If you say so!' She patted Kitty on the shoulder and then held out a hand towards him and he wasn't sure whether to stand up or not.

'We have some good times,' Yvonne was saying. 'She comes round of an evening when Steve's out or I go to her – that's if Dave's there to watch the kids, which, to be fair, he usually is. But what do you think of the news then?'

He couldn't say that he was worried stupid, scared for the baby, child, kid, whatever. Angry. How much he hated Steve. 'It's great news. Yeah, really good news.'

Kitty squealed, 'You haven't even asked when it's going to arrive yet. So I'll tell you. Right. Not quite your birthday, Frankie, but near . . . November the fourteenth.'

Perhaps Yvonne could see what Kitty didn't want to see, for she turned to him. 'I'll make sure she's all right. So don't worry. Tell you what! Got anything to write on? I'll give you our telephone number. How about that? Better safe than sorry, aye?' She laughed and gave Kitty a peck on the cheek before returning to her table.

# Frank

They'd sent a large van to collect them from the airport. Three of them. Frank and Barney and Ryan from Essex, who was new to them, but he seemed an all-right bloke. Single, apparently, but a good carpenter by the sound of the jobs he'd done. He been working on repairing the roof of a seventeenth-century church somewhere in Sussex. He said he was quite used to living away from home. He was older than them. Must be in his late forties. Not too chatty. Unlike Barney, who was already on about his missus not happy about him being away. 'But happy about the money, though. The thought of her own place. You know, no more renting. I'll have to watch myself with the girls, though,' he joked.

The driver of the van, who smoked continuously, kept punching out bits of Italian at them, his head half turned and the fag in his mouth. 'Non understand,' Barney repeated endlessly. 'Mate! *Signore*. Me non understand. OK?

'Ask him his name.'

'What your NAME. YOUR NAME?'

'Why are you shouting? He's not deaf.'

The driver obviously did understand some English but, preferring not to be bothered, reluctantly mumbled, then shouted, 'Mauro!' He threw the fag end out of the van window, muttering.

It was just about an hour before the van pulled up outside

the flower shop. Without a word Mauro opened the back doors of the van and let down the ramp.

'This must be me,' Frank called back as he hurried to help the driver with his bike. His precious motorbike! No way was he going to Italy without his bike, despite the cargo expense. It was only later that he realised he could have bought a good bike here in Italy.

Mauro climbed into the back and heaved the bike up and Frank, catching the back end, steadied it as together they wheeled it down and onto the road. Mario threw his arms in the air and shook his head, pointing at the bike. *'Avresti potuto comprato prenderne uno migliore.'*

Frank shook his head to show he didn't understand. Mauro pointed to the bike, 'Bikes good here. Italian.'

While he stood there holding it upright, Mauro fetched his case and rucksack and carried them across the paved yard to the closed door of the shop, avoiding metal containers like milk churns, some with flowers in.

They'd agreed that he could bring his bike but now he stood rather nervously, wondering what he was supposed to do with it.

*'Mettilo lì.'* Mauro was pointing to the wall beyond the shop window. He jabbed his finger towards an iron ring cemented into the wall *'Senti, lega la tua moto lì.'* He was obviously getting irritated.

A woman opened the door.

*'Ciao Angelina. State già cenando?'*

*'Sì, Mauro.'* She looked across at Frank, who assumed she must be the owner, for he knew the owner's name was Angelina.

Mario gestured towards the bike, lifting his hands and shaking his head in what appeared to be some disapproval.

The woman laughed as she touched him on the shoulder and then, stepping out of the door, she beckoned to Frank and then pointed to the iron ring. *'Non è un problema la sera.'*

It was obvious that he didn't understand. She tried again. '*Bene* – good for the night. NO good in day. Many, many *fiori*.' She made a wide sweep with her arms. 'All flowers.'

He nodded, very relieved that she spoke at least some English, and wheeled the bike to the side of the shop and leaned it against the wall. She was nodding and smiling. 'Good! Good – *è al sicuro lì*.'

Mauro waved at her and turned back to the van, grumbling, and Frank guessed he was in a hurry to get home, as he pointed to Barney and Ryan, who were stretching their legs outside the van and having a smoke. He was pleased to have Barney here, Di having agreed the money was too good to miss, but making him promise to fly home every other week if he could. It was true; the wages were excellent.

'*Li sto portando al mulino*.' Mauro pointed up towards the hills, beyond the village. He knew the mill was *il mulino*. Mauro must have been explaining he was going to the mill with the other two. '

She started rattling off and clapped him on the arm as they both laughed loudly before he opened the doors for Barney and Ryan and, waving Angelina goodbye, got back into the van. All this Italian was intimidating, and he questioned whether he was going to be able to cope, be able to do his work.

'See you tomorrow, mun,' Barney shouted through the open window.

They stood side by side watching the van drive away before Angelina disappeared inside the house and he was very unsure what to do next, but she reappeared quickly with keys and indicated that he should follow her.

She held out her hand. 'You? Frank Richardson, *si*?' Her voice rose and fell like a song. '*Buonasera*, welcome to Angelina Fiori!' She pointed to the sign above the shop. He already understood the *fiori* meant 'flowers'.

Behind her, in the back room, he saw the meal on the table

and a man hidden behind a paper. Either side sat two young kids, slurping up something and eyeing him at the same time.

'*Tardi*? You late.' She tapped her watch. 'We eat. For the bambini!' And she held out her hands with a shrug. 'Come!' And he, with his stuff, followed her round the side of the shop to a back door, which she unlocked. The space inside was a chaos of containers, vases, some glass, some metal, heaped and tumbling over the stone floor and around the wooden bench, which with strewn with paper, secateurs, scissors and covered now with leftover stems and twigs. The air was heavy with perfumes he'd never smelled before. Later he would stand there and just inhale this new world.

'*Qui è dove lavoriamo, come si dice* ... Home for flowers. *Very, very disordinato.*'

'Your storeroom? Work room?'

He spoke slowly, but she shook her head and laughed. 'My English very, very little.' Her accent was almost guttural, heavy and her voice rose and fell like a preacher, he thought.

He smiled. She was doing her best and he liked her.

She unlocked a door to the left, revealing a rough wooden staircase that led up to the space above the shop. He had decided to rent instead of living in a cabin provided by the company up by the mill; he could always change if things didn't work out. But to have his own private space, no matter how small! It felt good. He understood Kitty now, how she had been so desperate to have a place of her own. Too desperate. Too impatient. And it should never have been Steve. Never.

At the top of the stairs a roughly put-together pine door opened into a narrow galley kitchenette, which led directly into the only room, lit by a large window. He walked over and looked out as she chatted on.

From the window he saw the lake and a lakeside road running away into the distance. To the left a paved square and the church with a bell tower. Perhaps I'll never want to leave here, he thought.

Angelina was opening a door into a shower room. '*Non è molto bella ma ...*' And she turned a knob, and after a second or two and some juddering, water sprayed from the shower head. 'See' water!' She was obviously relieved and they both laughed.

'Good!' he said. 'That's fine.'

It was when she pointed to some towels and bedding piled on the table by the window that he realised there was no bed.

'Bed? Bed?' he asked rather stupidly

She put her hands to her head. 'Awh! *Letto*! *Si*, the bed!' and tugged at a lever on the wall, which pulled down, magically, a double bed with a mattress. She laughed again at his amazement and relief.

'And finish.' And she began to push the bed back into its place.

'That's OK.' He stopped her. 'That's fine.'

'Fine?' she repeated. 'OK for you?'

'*Grazie*, thank you. I like it very much.'

She handed him the keys. Then, indicating eating with her hands and mouth, and looking from the window, pointed to the left. '*Vai là, in paese é il posto migliore per un pizza.*'

She must be indicating where he could find somewhere to eat. '*Si. Grazie.*'

'*Oh, parli Italiano*?' And repeating in English, 'You speak Italian?'

'No. 'Fraid not.'

She shrugged.

'But I'll learn.'

She nodded. '*Bene, bene.*'

She gave him the keys. '*Buonanotte.*' And returned through the kitchen and to the stairs leading back to the shop. And then he remembered that he hadn't asked her about using her phone. He must do that tomorrow. But anyway, tomorrow he could phone from work, he was sure. They would be wondering back home, and he had promised to keep in touch. He was

197

almost ashamed to have abandoned them, for that was how it felt sometimes. Abandoning them. Financially he could do right by them. But was that the same?

He returned to the window and the view. Couldn't believe any of it. There was the lake, many colours in the sunset sky; the church, in the shade now, its great double doors shut; he could see greenish bells hanging in the squat bell tower above the clock. It was nine twenty and he was hungry, and abroad. Abroad! He could never have guessed such a thing. He dumped the linen across the bed and lifted his case onto the table and the rucksack, heavy with books, onto one of the canvas chairs placed at each end of the table. He would unpack later. There was a small freestanding wardrobe and a chest with two drawers above cupboard doors. It was all just fine and he would make it home. He checked for his wallet, put his passport into a pocket in his rucksack, picked up the keys she had given him and left for his first Italian supper. He wasn't afraid.

He knew how to get there; he was going to bike it. Straight through the village until he reached a bridge over the river and then immediately to the left where the signpost, white with a black arrow, indicated 'Il Mulino'. He turned up the rough track bordered by vans, lorries, stacks of wood and piles of bricks. Diggers clawed out great lumps of earth and rock, beginning the landscaping, no doubt, and the preparation for a properly laid road. Felled trees were being hauled onto lorries. A building site, which was heaving already: brickies, chippies, their shouts echoing across. And it was only seven o'clock and already very warm.

He got off the bike and began wheeling it up the slope in the direction of some temporary buildings, assuming the offices would be there, when he saw motorbikes, mopeds and bicycles parked outside the Portakabins, and so he left his there too. For some extraordinary reason, he wasn't experiencing his normal anxiety, but was hopeful, excited even, and being surrounded by the other men didn't faze him as it used to do.

He looked across at the men stripping part of the mill roof to expose a skeleton of huge beams, many of which would need replacing, but he wouldn't be working on the roof. He was pretty chuffed to be tasked with renovating the mill wheel. They'd already sent him photos and draughtman's drawings, which he had studied for hours before leaving home. Even before sleeping last night he had felt the need to go over them again. He had them with him now, in his rucksack.

Just for a moment he wished he could find Barney, but he was nowhere to be seen. He wondered what it was like in the cabins and felt liberated to be renting above the flower shop. Angelina Fiori. He must call it by its proper name, not just the flower shop.

The office was next to the men's housing and beyond that a series of enormous tents, marquees, clearly workshops of some kind. The location, the language. So unfamiliar. It was amusing, really.

A couple of men in jeans and sweatshirts came out of the nearest hangar and went into the office and this encouraged him to do the same. Two managers sat behind a makeshift wooden desk scattered with papers and behind them, pinned on wooden boards, were lists, photos, maps and architectural drawings. The two who had entered before him gabbled away and then left each going in different directions. He moved to the front of the tables and waited while the managers, ignoring him, spoke together. He was momentarily uncomfortable; it felt like being at school. And then he remembered Andy and his 'Franko, boyo' stuff, which lifted his spirits – God knows why. Andy was doing something in politics somewhere in London; they hadn't kept in touch. He was sorry about that.

'Name?'

'Frank Richardson.'

They found his name and ticked it off one of the lists.

'Marco!' And the stocky guy with a shaven head leaned across the table, holding out his hand. '*Buongiorno!*'

Then the other, Viktor, leaner, younger, wearing a baseball cap, shook his hand. Frank nodded then waited, as they spoke again. Suddenly Viktor got up and, pointing the way out, said,' You come, please,' and Frank followed him to the next hangar.

On the way they were halted by a brickie, his shorts spattered with cement and a trowel in his hand. He obviously asked him a question, for Viktor shook his head and pointed down the slope towards the parked lorries.

The hangar, built with wooden slats, had a clear, tent-like roof for light, which waved slightly in response to the cooling air from the fans whirring around the structure. The place was fitted with benches on which drawings and plans were piled beside tools lying haphazardly, ready for some kind of organisation. He followed to a bench.

'OK?' Viktor eyed him hopefully.

'OK.'

'Machines in there,' and Viktor pointed in the direction of the next hangar. But he had already noted the throbbing of drills and the whining of saws.

'You work on the . . .' He indicated the round wheel with his arms and Frank nodded.

'*Un lavora complicato!*' And he laughed, muttering in Italian. '*Ora guardiamo la* . . . the . . .'

'Wheel?' Frank helped him out.

'*Si*, is wheel, *la ruota*, wheel.' And touching his head with his finger, laughed again.

A man shouldering a long plank emerged from the third and last hangar.

'Wood there, *si*?'

'*Si*.'

As they strolled towards *il mulino* Frank said, 'I came at seven. Was I late?' He pointed to his watch. 'late?'

'*Tardi?*'

'What time to start work?'

'Oh! *Si, si, alle sei o allesette*, six or seven. But twelve o'clock' – he moved his hands back and forth, as if smoothing something – 'all stop. Stop! It very hot. Siesta!'

The fans kept the hangars cooler, but it was still hot work and he frequently wiped sweat off his forehead. His hair was damp with the heat. It didn't worry him, only he smiled inside himself at the contrast between here and County Durham!

Both Barney and Ryan had stations in the hangar, along with three locals. Barney, a first-class cabinetmaker, was working with him on the wheel, but his task was to make the outer ring using cypress wood, while Frank had the challenging task of shaping the paddles in oak, the hardest and most water resistant of the woods. Ryan was making new window frames following drawings of the original mill. He watched him once or twice, noticed his concentration, his obvious attention to detail. He would be slow but he would be perfect. It was good that they were in the same hangar.

The midday break was announced by the sounds of motor-bikes firing up and car doors banging as some men went home for the two-hour break. But most went to the makeshift canteen, where a cold meal was provided for those who wanted it. The three of them sat together for this lunch of bread, cheeses, cold meats and pastry squares filled with some vegetable mixture he had never had before. There were a few workers who brought their own lunches and bottles of beer and found shady places to eat and rest.

Each morning in the office, men signed up if they wanted lunch or and supper. He signed for lunch only, as the idea of getting back to his own place pleased him so much, he couldn't express it. And tonight, he would go back to Federico's and have another pizza. But at the weekend he would shop and fend for himself in his own kitchen. Learning to cook would be an interesting exercise.

At the end of the shift, they had no choice but to pack up, for the mangers came round to turn off the fans, close the doors and lock up.

Barney and Ryan were staying in their cabins, saying tomorrow they would catch the bus into town.

'I can always give one of you a lift.'

'Get a sidecar, Richie, then you can take us both.'

'Oh yeah! Don't mean to be rude, but you, Barney, might have difficulty squeezing into a sidecar. A tank's more likely.'

On his way home he noticed the girls. Quite a few, sort of hanging around. Short skirts, tight jeans, black boots, dangling earrings, bright lips. One got onto the back of a motorbike. There were two waiting at the bus stop; they were different. One he noticed in particular: long legs in jeans and wavy dark hair hanging down her back. Made him think of Kitty.

When he got back to his place, before going to Federico's, he phoned her from the shop, making quite sure she had his numbers, home and work.

'You phone any time,' he said.

# Alice

It was a far cry from the little red dot who skipped and hopped on the beach to find pebbles, defying the wind and the drizzle. She had been so bored and depressed. Listless in her loose blue cotton kaftan. Hair in a knot on top to help keep her neck cooler. Gabriella gone for the day and no one to talk to. She remembered how excited she had been every morning when she woke up with Henry beside her. It must be the heat, she had told herself, that made her feel this way. And often, as she wandered through the house seeking somewhere cool, she had longed to be back home. She remembered that. I'm going home for Christmas. Why not? But she was married now! She thought, It's not as if he's unkind, exactly, just, well ... and she spoke out loud to herself in the garden, 'Doesn't seem like a marriage to me. More like just living with a friend.' And then whispering, '... only really interested in his painting.' But he wasn't unkind. Got irritable and sulky when she grumbled, when she wandered around aimlessly, flipping and flopping about from shade to shade. He got fed up with her then. 'Must be fair,' another whisper. 'Did have the swing hung in the shadiest part and the hammock between the trees.'

She supposed he did his best, considering. Anything to keep her happy. 'Out of the way!' She kept herself as busy as she could, still going shopping with Gabriella and helping in the shop on Saturdays, which she loved. But in this heat?

And Henry away more and more. He must have sensed it, because he arranged for her to meet their neighbours, whom he already knew, since Max and Fiona had continually entertained them in the garden.

It was early one Saturday evening when a woman appeared on their doorstep. It was the neighbour from next door, Maria, come to introduce herself. Alice was surprised how petite she was, very slim, with neck-length hair tucked behind her ears; her face half hidden behind dark glasses. She smiled as she held out her hand, '*Buona serata*! I'm Maria. Are you Alice?' Her English was excellent.

Alice was certain it must be Henry she had come to see.

'No! No! That's OK. Don't disturb him. But we would like you both to come to us this evening for something in the garden. It would be good to get to know each other.'

Alice already knew that most people entertained in their back gardens, which surprised her, for she much preferred to be in the front: long gardens facing south and the lake, filled with trees of all sorts – olives, apricots, figs, orange and walnut – so there was plenty of filtered light and shade. She much preferred the front.

'Come at eight,' Maria said. 'Come and meet the rest of the family. The girls are with us this weekend.'

It amused Alice, thinking of Da and his tea at six. 'Antipasti at eight! Rubbish, if you ask me. But it takes all sorts,' she could hear him say.

It was the long, straight, gypsy-type skirt, browns and creams, with the sleeveless white top she chose to wear. Hair down to her shoulders. She hadn't decided whether to disguise her limp or not. She'd see about that. Depending. Henry had, at the beginning, been very attentive when she limped. She had felt cared for, 'looked after'. But now? Recently it appeared to irritate him. She irritated him. It was not at all what she had expected when she agreed to marry him, but perhaps she had expected too much. She did wonder increasingly about what was going on in London. But was positive, no matter what was going on, he would never leave her for Phoebe. 'Perhaps I'll leave him,' she joked to herself.

She waited in the kitchen for Henry to appear; he was always late.

'You haven't told me anything about them, Henry.'

So he explained that they were both doctors: Maria a paediatrician and Alfredo a gynaecologist working in the same hospital in Verona, where the girls went to school. They owned a flat there, where they lived during the week, but most but weekends and holidays they came here, to the house.

She had decided not to disguise her limp and held onto Henry's arm as they approached in the garden. 'Alice! Walk properly.'

'The ground is uneven, Henry,' she whispered back, but he let go of her arm anyway.

In the end, none of it mattered; she needn't have felt intimidated, for they were easy and friendly and, noticing her slight limp, had taken an interest in her medical history, which boosted her morale. Everyone at home took little notice when she moaned about her disability, telling her to stop being self-pitying, so it was a change to be the centre of attention for once.

They drank wine and ate olives and cheese and small sausages and various meats with bread dipped in oil and vinegar, which the girls handed round before leaving them on the table.

There was, as always, a great deal of discussion directed towards Henry and his paintings and his very exciting forthcoming trip to Morocco.

'I shall take photos and make sketches there,' he explained. 'They want four initially: three for the advertising and one commission by the owner of a stud who wants a painting of his favourite Barb stallion. A bay, I believe. I had always thought of Barb stallions as being black or white, but actually that's not the case. They come in all colours. More interesting actually, from a painting point of view.'

She noted that, as usual, the only time he ever really engaged in conversation was when it was about his painting and him, of course.

'Are you going, Alice?'

'Oh no – too hot for me! Anyway, he can get on better on his own. Can't you, Henry?'

She didn't give away that he'd never ever suggested she accompany him on any of his trips. Even to London, which, now she thought about it, was really absurd.

But she enjoyed the evening, and Henry, giving her a parental pat and a smile, seemed relieved if she had made some friends.

The days started earlier in the warm season and Gabriella, in her calf-length black skirt, high-necked blouse and flat shoes arrived daily at around nine in the morning. Her husband had died of cancer a few years earlier and she had to keep their two sons at home while they finished their apprenticeships; one in building, the other in plumbing. Someone had told Max about her when he was looking around for a housekeeper of sorts. She prepared their meals, did the shopping, washing and ironing. Well, anything that needed doing in the house, except her sister, Sophia, did come in twice a week to concentrate on the housework, so all Alice had to do was prepare breakfast. Not much work there. And after she had cleared away, there was nothing left to do except arrange the flowers she bought and lay the table for their meals, if Gabriella hadn't already done it.

'Get her to teach you to cook. Learn some Italian dishes.' Henry always sounded mildly exasperated.

What she really looked forward to and what made all the difference was helping out at the shop on Saturdays. She helped customers choose their flowers and Angelina taught her how properly to arrange them before tying them with the raffia.

And, of course, she was familiar with shop work, having worked at Mr Lubbock in Darlington, so she got the hang of things easily. Her Italian was improving and she often found herself acting as translator for the English, which helped Angelina. She enjoyed meeting English tourists. Once a couple from Newcastle came in and it had been such fun chatting about home.

But starting the flower paintings? Well, that came out of the blue. She still hadn't dared to paint. The pebbles were in a jar on the mantelpiece over the kitchen range and her paints and brushes hidden away in a drawer. Henry kept urging her to paint, even bought her paints back from one of his trips to London, but she couldn't bring herself. Not with his fantastic canvases in the studio. On the walls of this house. 'My stuff! You'd have to be joking!'

But something so unexpected happened.

Angelina always had a wonderful assortment of flowers, grasses and leaves, all shades of greens and bluey greens, and Alice had chosen a wild-looking mixture of lavender with white geraniums and rosemary.

When she got home, she put them in the usual glass tumbler, sat down, arms folded across the table, chin on her arms and thought how lovely they were, just shoved in like that, with the stalks misty and shifting in the light and shade, and out of nowhere came this overwhelming desire to get out her paints. And the thing was: Henry was away. She could paint alone and then chuck it all away without anyone knowing. Anyone laughing.

She took out her sketchpad, paints, brushes and mixing tray, which she had hidden in the drawer under old teacloths, and found an odd glass for the water. And then, now excited, all boredom gone, she went into Henry's studio and helped herself to three sticks of charcoal.

So now, the stick of charcoal between her fingers, she allowed her hand to move in its own way, almost without thinking, loosely flowing, feeling the stems, the petals, the little rosemary spikes. And now! Water having drenched the paper, images appeared and wavered in the coloured washes as the green mixes from the tray, daubed on, ran down into leaves and then into bluish rosemary stems, shifting in the glass of water. And the petals, uneven, half broken, waited for their shadows and the brightness of their red stamens.

At that moment she didn't know if it was good or not. It really didn't matter, because she was happy for the first time since ... She couldn't remember. She could be happy now; happy when he was away. His being away, being remote, not really being there, didn't matter at all any more. Not at all. And the boredom had gone.

She couldn't remember why, perhaps there was no special reason, but the following Saturday she took the finished painting to show Angelina who, when she saw it, clapped her hands, kissed her on both cheeks and immediately held up the painting above an urn of flowers that stood on the counter. 'More! More!' she said. 'I tell you. See ... the flowers, a bunch ... and then ...' She waved her arm as if with a magic wand. 'Look! look!' And Alice saw how the flowers and the painting complemented each other. She'd not actually thought of that, intended that. But it was true: the one enhanced the other.

And so every week she took paintings for Angelina, who began pinning them, all unframed, of course, to the white wall behind the counter, and she purposely arranged flowers in the vases and urns to reflect the paintings.

When a painting actually sold, they hugged each other and, laughing so much with astonishment and excitement, Alice nearly lost her balance and had to be steadied.

'You drink! You drink, I believe.'

She had waited days after he'd come home from his last trip. Waited. At first she just said she was trying out colours, not painting anything, just cleaning the palettes and sorting out her paints and brushes. She wasn't really, actually, painting anything, so there was nothing to show him. But she couldn't go on like that; it was stupid to go like that. He had to see them at some point.

She chose the two she would next be taking to the shop.

When he had stopped for lunch, when he was sitting down in the kitchen, she put them on the table for him to see. 'You don't have to say anything, Henry, but the thing is, Angelina likes them and she's been putting one or two up in the shop and I probably wouldn't be showing you now, but actually, I know it must seem ridiculous to you, but one sold last Saturday.'

She was gabbling, as he picked up one, looked at it, looked at her.

'Very good, Alice. I couldn't do that. I like it.' And he picked up the second one. And she sank onto her chair, put her arms on the table and sobbed.

# Frank

The rain was a surprise to him, although seeing it was a lake district, it shouldn't have been. It was October and just lately it had rained a lot; it was still warm, but the days were shorter and the hours at work less. He still arrived at seven with the others and worked 'til six, but the light was more difficult despite the electric lighting shining from every conceivable hanging point outside and inside the hangars. There was mud! The unmade track had been laid with grit for the time being and there were tarpaulins draped and hanging all over the place.

The waterwheel was nearly finished. Barney was now working on window frames with Ryan, leaving Frank to complete the job. The eight paddles had been shaped and now he had only to fix the elm spokes into place and shape the oak central arm on which the wheel would hang and turn. Then he would have the satisfaction of seeing it put into place and have the slight anxiety, when the sluice was opened to let the water run, to see if it all worked. I had taken nearly eight months so far.

It was torrential rain as he left work and even with his waterproofs, he expected to be soaked by the time he got home.

The rain so heavy and clouds so low he had to put on his headlights. And there she was, at the bus stop crouching beneath a light blue umbrella and with the collar of her raincoat pulled up over her ears. There were no other girls tonight. He drove past her a little way before stopping. When he turned, she was running towards him, rain cascading off the sides of her umbrella.

'*Dove vuoi andare?* Where to?'

'You English? *Al negozio di fiori. Lo conosci?* You understand?'

He nodded as she swung her leg over the back of the bike.

'Angelina Fiori. You know it?' And, putting her arms around him, she hid her head against his back.

He concentrated on his driving but was only too conscious of the arms around him.

He stopped outside the shop with the engine running, steadying the bike with his foot on the ground. He turned his head slightly. '*Vuoi andare da* Angelina Fiori? Where exactly? I'll take you.'

'*Vuoi andare da.* Just up there.' And she pointed over his shoulder to the little road that ran up from the side of the shop towards the hills.

'The third block,' she shouted as he revved up.

The small houses, each with stone balconies with hanging flowers and washing lines, were in groups of three; each group divided by an arched alleyway through which there were signs of gardens and patios. Her place was the ninth house up the road and beside an archway; the front door, like the others, opened directly onto the street.

He drove slowly up the road. 'Yes, here,' she shouted, and he stopped, turned off the engine and waited for her to get to her door and go inside. But she stood inside the doorway, shaking off the rain, laughing. She shouted, 'Thank you very much,' and he nodded.

As he was turning his bike round, she shouted in English, 'Please come for a coffee.'

In a way he was dreading this. Having noticed her on so

211

many occasions and wondered about her, he now wanted to flee.

She must have noticed his uncertainty because, defying the rain, she ran out and pulled at his arm, nodding towards her door.

He leaned his bike against the inside wall of the alley and, ducking the dripping gutters, reached her doorway, where she was waiting. She pulled him in, laughing again at their dripping clothes and hair. 'I'm Greta. Give to me and I'll dry in there.' She took his waterproofs into the kitchen and hung them over some kind of rack.

'Frank Richardson,' he called after her.

'Sit,' she shouted. 'Sit. I'll make coffee.' And then, appearing in the doorway of the front room, 'Or a glass of red wine?'

She wasn't a girl. She was a young woman. It was the long legs in jeans that he had first noticed, but she was a good bit shorter than him and the long legs an illusion. Perhaps the shape of the jeans made them appear long and slim. Anyway, none of that mattered. She was rather un-Italian, he thought, with her reddish-brown hair and green eyes. He'd never noticed anyone with green eyes before. She was just natural-looking, he thought, and wearing no make-up.

She came in with a bottle and two glasses. He couldn't say no. Just could not. 'This is your home?' It was such a stupid question. 'I live above Angelina Fiori,' he added quickly.

'My home and my office.' She swirled round, waving her arms.

'Office?'

'I'm an architect. My office.' She pointed behind her. 'In the back. Come and see.'

Although this evening because of the cloud and rain it was shadowy, he understood that normally the light would be good. There was a large knee-hole desk facing the doors, which opened onto the patio and small back garden. She had

212

rows of shelves for books and files and a rather fine wooden filing cabinet. 'That's nice.' And he pointed to it.

'My father's. This was his business originally. He's stopped now. How do you say ...?'

'Retired?'

'Yes. Retired. He's in Verona now, since my mother died. But I see him often. He still is good. He helps me, often.'

'Very nice room,' he said. He was following back to the front room. 'Are those drawings you are working on? On your desk. I noticed.'

She poured him a glass of wine and he thought. She doesn't know I'm a chippy. She doesn't know I work from drawings like that. And he was curious why she was so often at the bus stop. Just standing there.

'Why at the bus stop?' he asked, and she laughed. 'Driving lessons.' And she rocked with her hands to indicate the driving wheel. 'My instructor, Giorgio, picks me up from here but drops me off at the bus stop afterwards, so he can get to his next student quickly.'

'But in the pouring rain?'

She pulled as face. 'I know, but I did agree, so ... I take my test next week.' And she questioned him with her eyebrows. 'We'll celebrate if I pass. Yes? Oh – and then I can give *you* a lift if it's raining.'

He couldn't help smiling.

'I have a Fiat already.'

The slight tension, awkwardness seeped away. If it was the wine, he should drink more often! And she was so at ease with herself. That helped too.

'I have thought of learning to drive myself,' he said. 'When I get home, I shall have my own business. I'll need a van of some sort.'

'Giorgio will teach you. He's good.' She went back through the sliding doors and he heard a drawer open and shut, the rustle of paper.

'Here's his number.' She poured another glass of wine and asked how long he had been working at the mill and what exactly did he do. 'You are expert?'

He shrugged his shoulders. 'You speak very good English.'

She said she had to be good at English because she had English clients; recently she had drawn up plans for an extension to a lakeside house for an English lawyer, 'Max Bancroft. Very nice man.'

'I'm a cabinetmaker.' And as he explained his work and the wheel, the shape of the spokes, the types of wood, the wheel itself, he was conscious of his own enthusiasm, that he was talking a lot. 'You can see why I was interested in your drawings. I work from architect and draughtsman drawings all the time. And, if I'm designing, I make my own. So ...' He must stop talking. 'I think there'll be at least another two years' work there. Hope so.'

'There is no problem for work,' she said. 'I always have need for you, if you want. Lots of clients want things, extensions, cupboards, many kinds of things. When you are finished at *il mulino*. But you have to drive. Get a van?'

'I'll think about it.' And she laughed, shaking her head.

'I think you think a lot. No? A very careful man, I think.'

'Guess so!' He had the paper with the number on in his hand. She touched it as he was putting it into his pocket. 'You think about it,' she teased and he nodded, knowing she was right. Then he couldn't help a wry smile in her direction. Perhaps he was too careful. Perhaps he thought too much.

As he was leaving, she pressured: 'We celebrate, yes ... if I pass?'

There was nothing he could do but nod with, 'OK then.'

He cooked for himself that evening. Fish. Angelina had given him some sort of local fish and tried to explain how to cook it. He had come to know her as a generous-hearted woman. Some people might just think of her as plump and jolly, but he didn't; he thought of her as what Stan would 'the salt of the earth'. Several times she had given him food, saying it was too much for them and twice he had been invited to share their supper. He might even call them friends.

He sat at the table with his plate of fried fish and beans and some of yesterday's bread, looking out at the lake, which was dark beneath the heavy clouds. It was certain to rain some more. He thought about Greta; thought it was lucky he had stopped to pick her up. If she could give him work, he could stay on for as long as there was work, knowing he had already saved enough for that house he was going to buy back home. One day. He fetched the paper from his pocket and stared at the number. He knew he had to phone sometime, but not tonight. And he would buy a boat, a cheap one that he could work on. Everything could be good if only Kitty was nearby, and Stan and Ruby too. That was the one thing that troubled him. And only another month before she had the baby. With her own kid she really wouldn't have any time for him.

A week later the white Fiat was parked just beyond the bus stop and honked as he passed. He pulled into the side. She was waving her arm through the open window. At least it wasn't raining. He was pleased for her, happy for her happiness. He walked, his long strides, to the side of the car. Bent down, his head to the open window. 'Congratulations!' He touched the bonnet of her car. 'Nice one!'

'What?'

'Nice car.'

'I am, very, very happy. So happy! Tomorrow we celebrate. OK?'

He thought quickly. Tomorrow was Saturday. He couldn't think of an excuse. 'OK then. Yes, OK.'

'You trust my driving?' She fooled around with her hands and arms as if swerving to avoid goodness what. 'I'm very, very safe.' And winked.

'I should hope so!'

Why did she always repeat 'very' very'? It was he thought an Italian thing.

She went on, speaking quickly, her accent intensifying, 'I'm outside the shop seven-thirty. There is a place, very, very good, in the next town.' She pointed behind her. 'I hope you like oysters.'

'Never had them.' He wasn't in awe of her any more.

'You have to try, I tell you.'

'If you say so.'

'Or are you going to think about it?' She laughed loudly, doubling up rather like Kitty, and he knew he was smiling too.

She started up the engine. 'Seven-thirty? I see you then.' She closed the window and pulled away without a jolt, he noticed, and gave a little fluttering wave. Frank raised his hand as she disappeared. He would give her time; no way did he want to look as if he was following her. No way.

He showered, put on a shirt instead of his usual t-shirt, his best jeans, and shoes rather than trainers. He'd got beyond wondering what on earth she could see in him. And had decided that whatever it was, he didn't care and was unusually relaxed about his outfit. It was supper out, that's all. She, he had concluded, was an intelligent, relaxed, cup-half-full young woman and easy to like. He guessed she was in her late twenties, perhaps early thirties. Difficult to tell. Either way, he would be thirty-four this November, so a good bit older.

He was just collecting his wallet when he heard the quick honk of the car horn.

She was wearing a dress. Sea-green with sleeves and a V-neck. Not too low. Flat green pumps. No jewellery. She was attractive, but not overdone or cheap-looking.

She tried to persuade him to have oysters, but he chose antipasti instead. The oysters arrived in a huge metal tin filled with ice and the oysters. Frank was quite absorbed, watching

216

the performance. She took out an oyster shell, prised it open with a special knife provided, loosened the flesh from the shell and then tossed it into the back of her throat as if she were swallowing a tablet. This was not her first time, he thought.

She saw him watching her and so, giving him a cheeky grin, prepared an oyster as usual and then, raising her eyebrows, knifed it towards him. 'You let it slide down.' She held her head back.' You don't chew ... just swallow.'

The oyster dangling on the end of the fork touched his lips as if tempting a sick child to eat. He was terrified he would choke or it would end up on his shirt or something, but because of her now pleading gaze, he opened his mouth, held back his head as she almost threw the flesh into his throat. It slid down. He didn't know what was so funny, but she couldn't stop laughing and, in the end, he was laughing too. But with relief more than anything!

She told him about her family in Verona: her mother had been a fashion designer but gave it up to look after the family and was especially happy when her eldest daughter, Greta's sister, followed in her footsteps. 'She's now an established fashion designer working in Milan. My other sister teaches in Turin and my brother Stefano is in London. He's an architect too. So, big family! I'm very, very happy for that.'

It was all perfectly normal to her and she chatted quite naturally without a hint of vanity or flirtatiousness. He couldn't understand what she could possibly see in him, if she did see anything, of course. He was a working-class boy; she was posh. Didn't flaunt it, but was posh. He told her about Kitty, married, having a baby due next month, and about Ruby and Stan. 'They fostered us,' he admitted. 'We were fostered kids. Doesn't matter why.' And she didn't ask. He told her about Stan's shed and tools and how he had inspired and taught him in the early days. How proud they were of each other. He'd never opened up like that before.

But he went on explaining that becoming a cabinetmaker, which took five years altogether, meant he had learned how to understand technical drawings; about different kinds of buildings and structures, such as *il mulino*; about churches and ancient buildings; about materials: different woods and their properties. 'There's was a lot to learn. I enjoyed that. You never stop learning,' he added. And he thought about the library books he'd stolen 'Anyway, I keep in work, that's the main thing.' He was talking and talking. And now he did care what she thought of him. The wine again?

When the bill arrived, he took it off the dish and his wallet from his pocket. She protested. He insisted. The bottle of wine stood empty on the table.

'We have coffee at my place?' she questioned as they got into the car.

What he needed was fresh air and a walk along the lake to clear his head. He knew he had had too much to drink. God help him if he was to turn out drunk like his father.

But he went in anyway. That was the mistake. They stood close together in the hallway, she looking up at him, then her arms around his neck. She was very lovely that night and he kissed her. It was a light kiss, he thought, but she kissed more and he didn't pull away then. He could feel the hard-on and she laughed and put her hand on the zip of his jeans, all the time looking with a sweet expression into his face. She felt for his penis beneath his jeans.

'We go upstairs?'

He just followed, all sense gone; he was aroused and she was a lovely woman. He watched her undress and stand before him naked. It was when she came to undress him that the memories overcame him. Carl's white buttocks thumping up and down, groaning, and Mum's legs in the air.

'Sorry,' he said. 'Sorry. Not your fault.'

He wanted to disappear, to throw himself into the lake and disappear for the shame. He couldn't face the shame.

Face her. Then the anger, the rage as he hissed, 'Call yourself a fucking man?'

On Monday, when he got back from the mill, he found an envelope had been pushed under his door at the top of the stairs. Angelina, obviously. But no – the note was from Greta, in English.

> Dear Frank,
>> Thank you very, very much for supper. I enjoyed.
>> We are still friends?
>> There will be work, if you want.
>>> Greta

# Alice

Because Henry was going to be in Morocco for ten days, she had decided to go home to see Da and Ma. It was winter now and sometimes quite cold, certainly rainy, and the days were short, so going back would not be such a weather shock. And she'd been meaning to go for ages. She should have gone before, but now she was so busy with her paintings and happy even when Henry was away, she'd preferred to stay. Selfish? But now there really were no excuses and Da was sounding so worried and tired. Not like himself at all. Last phone call he'd told her that he and Alistair had gone to inspect Greenfield Home to see what it was like, because Da said he couldn't give Ma all she needed any more. He couldn't do it 24/7.

Manuel had taken her to the airport near Verona and she took a flight to Newcastle and then a cab all the way home; it was still home. More home than the house in Italy. It was a little bit of snug familiarity, like being wrapped in a blanket on a cold day; like being by the fire with the wind outside; like tea at six.

But she burst into tears when Da opened the door to her. Afterwards she thought he didn't need that. He didn't need more misery. But it had been the sight of him: those dear creases down his face deeper, longer and his sharp eyes dull with tiredness, with worry.

Immediately, he said, 'She might not know you, Alice. She gets confused. But just act normal. Take off your coat, anyroad.'

Ma was smiling, but not at her. She was surrounded by her beloved books; seemed they were her only comfort, her books. She looked up at Alice.

'Hello, Ma.'

'Just sit down, lass. Just sit there. Tell her about your journey, you know, your painting, your house over there, your friends, You know, Alice, she likes to hear chat. You chat and I'll make us tea.'

Ma smiled and, nodding, picked up a book and gazed at it, turning pages randomly before putting it down. And then suddenly, 'I like your hair. You always had lovely hair. I remember.'

It was only when Da was putting the mug of tea on the table beside her that she said, 'Alice! Is Alice having any?' and then she started humming to herself.

She was not brave; she was no support or help. She was too miserable.

But nevertheless, she was sure Da was pleased to have her there. Surely he was.

Da never cried. But he was changed. And she sobbed that first night when she was in her own bed. Alone in her own room. Hers.

The next day Alistair came over from York, where he was living and teaching, and sat with Ma so that she and Da. could go out together.

'Too cold for a motorbike ride, Alice. Anyway, I've not had the time just of late to keep them all up to scratch, so it's the car, lass.'

It was a short trip to Crook, where they stopped for tea and a toasted teacake. It was so crowded; she'd forgotten how busy places could get. And the shoppers were grey and huddled and hurrying. So different from Italy!

Over tea they had time to chat more, and she tried to describe their life, her life, and Da made an effort, but she could tell that his mind was elsewhere. She didn't tell him that Henry was probably having an affair with Phoebe and that she didn't think she cared that much. But his eyes brightened just that bit and he looked at her with that twisted grin when she told him about her paintings and the flower shop and her selling some.

'That's the best I've heard for a long time,' he said, adding in his gruff tone, 'and not before time, if I may say so.' Da was back for that moment and she laughed at him as he shook his head as he had so often done when, as a child, she perplexed him.

She didn't want to go to see Greenfield Home; her heart sank at the thought of it, making the excuse that if he and Alistair thought it was OK, then it must be. And it was so near to home, too, so Da could get there anytime he wanted to. She wanted to be encouraging. 'And Da, at least you and Ma have loved each other so much, all this time, all these years. She would do the same for you.'

Now she was back in Italy and waiting for Henry, who was returning today, after a stopover in London. Had to see Phoebe, of course. Despite that, for some strange reason, she was excited about his coming home. She thought she must have missed him more than she realised. Perhaps it was because of Da being so changed, things being so sad at home.

When she heard the car, she hurried towards the gate as fast as she could, opening the gate as he got out. When he saw her standing there he smiled and gave a flick of a hello wave before taking his case from Manuel. He seemed pleased to see her and she flung her arms round him. 'I missed you.'

'Missed you too, Alice.' And he'd never admitted that before. Had he changed? He appeared different, and all thoughts of London and Phoebe deserted her.

And she couldn't stop talking, asking questions, wanting to see photos, and he didn't seem to mind. Didn't rush into his studio, away from her.

He told her about the lavish hotel where he met Rafeek Alami, the minister for travel, and his entourage. And he showed her photos of the beach, the desert, to scrubland and mountains.

'What's this horse? It's gorgeous. What colour is it called?'

'That's Dahab – means "golden" in Arabic – and he's a brass colour, isn't he? Unusual bay, beautiful with the white mane and tail. He's the Barb stallion owned by Zouina Cheval. He's the guy who's commissioned me to paint Dahab. He wants him standing on a rocky outcrop against a blue sky. He liked the sketch I did. I'll show you later.' He was unusually chatty.

While he was unpacking and showering, she looked through his photos again. There was one photo of a grey horse with red trappings and a man dressed in a yellow kaftan sort of thing with a white head-and-face covering, so you could only see his eyes. He was holding a long pole, which looked, from the photo, to be carved and sharp at the end. Looked menacing. 'Like Lawrence of Arabia.'

'This one is a bit scary. Didn't you think it was a bit scary, Henry? With that pole thing.'

'It's called a locked pole. And you're right, they are sharp.'

He was sitting beside her at the kitchen table. 'I have to paint him for the tourist office.'

'Not sure that would tempt me to go. So threatening-looking,'

He actually smiled, that wide smile.

'What else? What else have you to paint?'

'These as well.' And he picked out two riders galloping through the sea, and another photo of a trail of tourists riding an assorted colour of horses across the desert at twilight.

'Did you like it over there? Did you think it was beautiful?'

But he was fishing in his attaché case, which was on the table.

'Didn't have much spare time but thought you might like these. Saw them in the market.' He handed her a roughly wrapped small bag of something and left the room as she opened it.

Inside the cheap paper was a selection of polished stones of all shapes and colours.

'Oh my God! Henry!'

Then he returned and stood behind her as she rattled the stones in her cupped palms. 'What stones are they?'

'They're semi-precious, that's all I know, but I think that is turquoise and that amber, do you think? To be honest, I don't know what they all are, but they had basketfuls in the market. You bought them by the handful, but I tried to pick nice ones.'

She twisted round to look at him. 'I absolutely love them to bits.'

'Good! You like them, then.' And it was the gruff voice again as he walked out and into his studio. But she wasn't upset. It was his way. Then shouted, 'Don't bother with supper – I booked a table at the oyster place. Early. Six-thirty.'

She really wanted to look nice for him. It was like a date and she wanted to look sexy. She didn't really do sexy, not with a limp, never tried to be sexy before, because she wasn't sexy, was she? Not like other women. But anyway, she didn't care and found a matching pair of black panties and bra.

She wasn't going to look tarty; if she tarted up, she would look just a fright, and she was sure Henry would hate it, so she wore her best fawn velvet jeans and a long tunic-length brown-and-green shirt, finishing off with her beige leather belt, which hung loose around her hips. She had boots and a warm coat and was sure she'd be warm enough in the restaurant. Her hair was ... well ... her hair: long, straight to her shoulders. Nothing ever changed there. She was still corn at the moment but kept an eye out for the grey. She was, after all, nearly thirty. Finally she tried the lipstick, but rubbed it off.

Henry had gone downstairs ages before and she supposed

he was in his studio but no, he was sitting at the kitchen table drinking a glass of red wine.

'You're not going to get drunk, are you?' He'd started drinking a lot, she'd noticed. She put on her coat. 'I shan't have oysters, you know. You know that. I'll probably have the veal; it's always nice.'

'Alice – why don't you wait to look at the menu first before deciding? Come on!'

She never knew if the black panties had anything to do with it, but he was really turned on. And so was she. Best ever!

'You should go to Morocco more often.'

'Probably!' And they both laughed.

# Frank

It was November and dark, although it was only six o'clock; a sharp wind was blowing down from the hills and the lake water was ruffling noisily. He had been working on the heavy oak arm of the wheel, shaping it on his lathe with soundless concentration. He was tired and had left the mill earlier than usual, deciding he needed fresh air and a walk.

Now he was striding back from the lakeside hotel, which stood a couple of miles from the village, and beyond the lakeside houses. Someone had told him about it and that the owners kept a boatyard nearby. It was the boatyard he was interested in, for he had decided to buy a boat, one that needed doing up that he could work on at the weekends.

Beyond the lakeside houses, hills sloped down to the lake and there were places where the path wound up the slopes of the hills away from the lake and then back down again. But it was a good excuse for a walk; somewhere definite to aim for. To keep his loneliness at bay.

He saw the hotel some time before he reached it, for it was brightly lit and there were coloured lights around the decking that hung over the lake. The hotel was popular with Germans, apparently, as well as English; he had noticed tourists wandering around the village from time to time.

It was cold and he walked quickly down from the hillside, back onto the path, past the lakeside houses, church square and across to Angelina Fiori, anxious now to get inside. But as he approached, he heard the shop phone ringing and knew it must be for him, for the phone was always for him after shop hours.

He had been waiting for this call. It was 15 November and the baby was overdue. And he was right. It was Yvonne. She must have heard the tension in his voice.

'She's fine.' She was laughing. 'Typical Kitty! Can't do anything by halves. It was all so quick. Baby girl. Seven and half pounds. She's called Daisy, of course. All's well. Gorgeous little soul. You should see them both. Kitty's so happy, Frank.' And she was laughing again.

Kitty so happy. He could see her eyes wide and bright. Laughing. They'd left a note for Steve as they hadn't been able to get hold of him. Didn't know where he was. She'd gone with Kitty in the ambulance and stayed, but Kitty had hardly time to get off her clothes when out the baby popped. Yvonne was leaving the hospital now but would go in again tomorrow, 'To see what's what.' She stopped and he could hear hospital noises in the background.

'When will she be home?' He was excited now.

And Yvonne gabbled again. Not sure, but likely in a couple of days. She would make sure all was OK and if needs be, Kitty could stay with them 'til everything, like home support and so on, was in place. But when could he come over? Kitty was so excited to see him. To show him the baby. So when could he make it, so she could tell Kitty when she saw her tomorrow.

'I'll be over by Monday,' he said. 'I'll let you know exactly. I've got your home number. I'll ring tomorrow when I know exactly.'

He wanted to be silent. To be alone. Mum would be so happy. He was proud to be an uncle; he wanted to take care of them, for he didn't trust Steve to do the right thing. That was his deepest fear, his ongoing fear. And where the hell was Steve in all this? The rage was seeping in again.

Phoning Stan and Ruby calmed him, hearing their voices, Ruby's scream of delight and Stan's, 'As long as the two of them is well, that's the main thing to me. But what sort of name is Daisy?' But he could see the grin, the raised eyebrows; he felt their warmth. And the rage dissipated. He stood for a moment planning, in his head, what he had to do about his travel, about taking time off work, when the phone chimed again.

'What's happened now, for Christ's sake?'

But he needn't have worried. It was Kitty.

'Guess what, Frankie? Guess what? Guess what?'

'Go on.'

'She's arrived! My little Daisy. Frankie! She's a fat little thing and guess what? She popped out ever so quick. She's impatient, like me.'

'Well done, Kit.' He wanted to be with her. His wished the kid was his. 'Where are you now? How can you phone?'

'Oh, I had to phone you Frankie. And they've let me use the hospital phone, but I have to be quick. Anyway, Frankie I'll be home tomorrow; I think I want to be home with her. When are you coming? I can't wait for you to see her. She's like a doll – perfect little thing.'

'Must be like her mother, then!' That made her laugh and he was happy. 'I'll be over on Monday.'

More laughter. 'Got to go. Can't wait to see you. Love you, Frankie.' And he heard the quick 'kiss kiss' down the phone before it clicked silent. She'd never mentioned Steve.

It was just after three in the afternoon when he took the taxi from Manchester Airport. And it was dark already. He'd forgotten how early it got dark back home. All the car lights were on and the windscreen wipers, for the rain was heavy. He noticed the difference. In Italy, even by the lake, even if it was raining and windy like the other night, there was a softer, balmier air. And cleaner. Here he smelled the car fumes, the

228

smoky, choking air and noticed the litter, blowing into gutters and street corners. Rough sleepers already curled up in their sleeping bags in doorways, under bridges.

He knew Kitty was at home. Yvonne had phoned again and said Steve was picking her up. Frank didn't ask, but she said Steve seemed quite chuffed with the baby.

And how long will that last? spat into his head. And he realised that up 'til now he'd been almost scared of Steve. It went far back, to when Steve was his boss. His jokes were cruel and his comments about women dirty, yet he'd seemed popular with the other men. Frank supposed he would be called 'a man's man', whatever that was, but he had never liked him and the idea of Kit being with him . . . he couldn't express it. Being with Steve. He drank and gambled and was sometimes violent. And she, of all people, knew about that. They both did. He didn't know anything about prayer, but sitting in the taxi he prayed or thought, said in his head, 'Please let him change.'

One thing, though: he wasn't afraid of him any more.

Steve opened the door to him with, 'Hi mate. Good to see you. Come on in.'

Kitty gave out a whispered scream. 'Frankie!'

She was on the sofa in her dressing gown; the baby in a pram-come-carry cot beside her and he guessed, hoped, it was his money that had paid for it. He stepped over a couple of beer glasses and an ashtray and looked into the pram. Kitty, he knew, was silently exploding to know what he thought. She had one hand to her mouth, her eyes wide, waiting for him to say something.

'I've seen worse,' he said, and bent to kiss her congratulations, but she was hitting him on the arm with a giggle.

'Well done, Kit! And' – he had to turn to Steve, who was standing with his hands on his hips by the kitchen door – 'Steve! Congratulations.' He put his hand on Kitty's shoulder. 'She's a bonny baby, Kit. Really she is.' And he thought, She's my flesh and blood too. And Mum and Dad? Where was Dad, anyway? Somewhere the kid had a grandfather. How wild Mum would have been! His heart was broken about it all, but he didn't say because he didn't want to upset Kitty at all. Not at all.

He looked properly at the kid. Eyes tight shut, tiny nose, lips slightly quivering, blonde fluff on her head. She was going to be blonde, like Steve ... and like Dad. He'd never really looked at a baby before. Avoiding next door's, always. Not like Kitty, who had liked to rock the pram. He was shocked to see how tiny she was, how vulnerable. How did parents forget all that? They had been tiny and vulnerable once, but it hadn't stopped the violence, the drugs, the drink, the ...

'How are you feeling, anyway? It's early days, I know. But, how are you?'

She was bending over the pram and pulling with the pink blanket down so that he could see better.

'She'll need a haircut soon!' he said.

She laughed. 'Well, I'm the right person for that. Don't be silly, Frankie. Do you want to hold her? You have to bond, you know. You're her Uncle Frank. You're her flesh and blood.'

He nodded and Kitty lifted the baby into his arms. 'Hello, lass,' he whispered in her ear.

1988–1990

# Frank

It was so unlike him to be impetuous, but this morning he had been just that. How very childish! Kitty had her Daisy, so he would have his boat and wait no longer. He could have taken his time looking, waiting, deciding, and as Greta may have teased, 'Why don't you just think about it, Frank? Don't do anything rash!' But he had been rash and he didn't care.

He saw the wooden dinghy at the boatyard by the hotel. It had oars and could be fitted with rudder and outboard motor so he could row across the lake or in time, when ready, could motor round. And it needed work, which is what he wanted, something to occupy him at the weekends. He could take his time; there was no rush; he was as pleased as it was possible to be. And what clinched the whole thing was the guy had a mooring near to the church he was willing to rent out. And he threw in a tarpaulin. That was it! He didn't even wait to calculate costs, he was going to have this boat that for so long he had been thinking about.

It was lunchtime, and quiet as he hung around the church square waiting for the boat to be delivered. The church was usually empty at midday; he'd noticed that and had once been in to look around. Now he decided he would kill a few minutes by going in again. It was more than the architecture that drew him to churches, but he had no idea what it was, not really.

This square, solid little church was so different from

Ruby's. Her church, built in the early twentieth century – the stonework, in a cheap-looking mock-Gothic style, shaped by machines – was dull and plain, though he would have never said so. This church was also in the dark now, but a darkness broken by the golden lights spinning off the gilt adornments. The altar was smothered in richly embroidered cloths and there were lit candles flickering in alcoves.

He was surprised to see someone there; an older woman in black, sitting near the front, her rosary running through her fingers.

He sat at the back and watched her. He couldn't help thinking it was like some magical spell, a witch-doctor kind of thing, to believe that beads could do anything.

There was so much he thought was unbelievable about it all. How could any sect or whatever have a man hanging on a cross, crucified, bleeding, suffering that kind of torture, as an emblem, the badge if you like, of anything good? He just didn't get it. It was disgusting. People had crucifixes hanging above their beds, for God's sake. Was it any better than the symbols of the Ku Klux Klan or the Nazi swastika? He thought this Christ hanging on a cross was sending the worst possible message. Well, it was to him, anyway. And then there was the Virgin Mary! Endless statues of the so-called pure maiden draped in scarlet or white or, more often, blue, her head modestly, humbly lowered, a gentle accepting smile on her perfect lips. Why, he thought, are they so dishonest?

He knew the Christmas story, of course, because they had a nativity play every Christmas at school and one year, his last year in junior school, when he was just twelve, he'd been chosen to be one of the three kings, because they said he was tall and held himself straight. He had a cardboard crown sprayed in gold on his head, a red sort of cape that tied round his neck, which he wore over his school uniform. He was the king who offered gold and he had been pleased about that, because he couldn't relate to frankincense or myrrh at all. On his knees he had to offer the gold-painted box to Mary. He found that extremely difficult. Of course, he knew Jade had been chosen because she was pretty but actually, she was a cow. A real cow: spiteful and a bully with her gang of friends. Really unkind to other girls and boys alike. She'd never dared to trouble him, though! But here she was as Mary! What a bloody joke! And the idea of kneeling down to her was an anathema to him.

Anyway, if you thought about it, the real Mary was just the mistress of a carpenter, not that pure, then and they'd made this long journey to Bethlehem so she would have been smelly and unwashed; her clothes were probably made of roughly woven brown or grey wool, not blue or scarlet robes, and she may well have been short and plump. Who knows? Her hair most likely was badly in need of a wash and she might have had spots on her chin like Julie. Who knows? He didn't think she was a bad person. Not at all. But please get it a bit right. He considered who he might choose to be a Mary and decided the best person he knew so far was definitely Julie. Julie with her kid. He never saw any wrong in her. Julie had had sex; Mary had had sex, but he didn't think that, in that instance, that she had been violated by the carpenter, Joseph. He supposed that meant that not all sex was a kind of violation. It could sometimes be OK. He supposed.

He liked to think of Joseph as a kind man, goodness knows why. What was most unbelievable was that it had never occurred to him that he was a carpenter, too. He was a carpenter like Joseph. Was he a kind man? Could he have sex without it ever being a kind of violation?

He looked at his watch and realised he'd been in the church for far longer than he'd intended and hurried out, praying he hadn't missed the guy with his boat.

As he passed out into the light he wondered if he, like Joseph, would, could ever meet his Mary.

He was crossing the church square towards the lakeside and his boat when he saw her again, the tall young woman, slim, with the corn-coloured hair. He had noticed her in the shop most Saturdays, helping out, when he was first at the mill, and then she stopped coming. And he had missed seeing her, for she reminded him of someone, but he didn't know why or who. Just that feeling he had seen her somewhere before. Now that he was no longer working permanently at the mill, only called in if there was something tricky they needed help with, he saw her more often, mostly Tuesdays. She was shopping with a friend and he'd seen her buying flowers on a Tuesday. And then again on Saturdays, when she was clearly helping out. She was on his mind quite a bit. Perhaps when he got back this evening he would ask Angelina about her.

They'd rated him at the mill. The wheel had first turned smoothly and, once the sluice was opened, the paddles he and Barney had worked on pushed the water forcefully down to the river. That had been a good day, that first time. He'd been anxious, no hiding from that, especially as the men had crowded round to watch. It had gone silent as they waited for the sluice to open and for the released water to rush down towards the wheel. They all waited. And then, slowly, slowly the wheel began to turn and then faster, faster, and the men in the grinding rooms at the top of the house, shouted that the millstones were turning. Then the men cheered and he grinned as they clapped him on his back. He wished Stan could have been there, or Dad, even. But he was proud. And relieved! And the men respected him; that was something he was now able to accept. Quietly, though, for he knew life could change, just like that. From good to bad.

After the wheel he was able to use all his cabinet-making skills as he worked in the house, building replica furniture for the old-style kitchen, which included a large pine dresser. Now the interior designers had filled the shelves with rows of assorted china appropriate for its age. He made and fitted skirtings and doors, as well as the wooden staircase that wound up to the working area at the top, housing the huge grinding stones, which, powered by the waterwheel, crushed wood into fine chips, ready to be shipped off to the paper-making factories. He'd learned a lot, had worked long, hard days and been well rewarded with regular bonuses. So now he was able to pay more into Stan's and Kitty's accounts.

They had asked him to stay on, but he needed a break, wanted to buy that boat, spend time just absorbing whatever it was that needed absorbing about himself, about his life. Being alone meant you could be yourself. And here in Italy, mostly alone, the constant unease, the unconscious threat, left him, and he needed to consolidate that. To understand it all. And his confidence, ease of mind, was secured by knowing there was always work at the mill if he wanted; it secured this growing sense of well-being and it was handy still having contact with the mill, for many reasons. Firstly, he could go up and use any of their big machines if he needed to. Secondly, there was a plentiful supply still of wood and he could buy it very cheaply from them. He had stolen a slide rule and a chisel, but he knew that was the last time. He didn't need to steal any more.

All the men who had lived in the Portakabins had left, including his two mates, and the area was now in the process of being turned into a visitors' complex with café, shop, toilets. The road had been laid and the area to the right was now a car park.

He hadn't wasted his free time, though. He'd passed his test and bought a Fiat van, the inside of which he had prepared to take his tools. All he needed now was to rent a lock-up place for his van and to get some private work. Not too much, for he had his wooden boat to restore. He was lucky to have this mooring pitch so close to the shop, just along the lakeside path. He so enjoyed working on it and again there was much to learn, so he was frequent visitor to the boatyard for advice.

237

At the moment he was replacing damaged and rotted planks with oak lengths he had bought from the mill stock and shaped in the tool shop. The sun was hot, but he was OK with the heat, only stopping for a drink of cola or to watch other boats, some speed, some yachts, moving across the lake. In those moments of rest he again wondered if he dared to approach Greta about potential work. He still felt ashamed about that evening, although whenever they had bumped into one another since, she had appeared perfectly relaxed and friendly. Still, he couldn't make up his mind what to do, whether he had the nerve. She could help, he was sure; he just had to bottle his shame, pride, whatever it was, and go to see her. He would ring; he had the number. If it was the wrong move, well, far worse had happened in his life.

When he returned home, Angelina was shutting the shop, carrying urns inside. She saw him coming and waved and called out, and he helped her in with a couple of urns. Inside the shop they stood together, the door still open onto the yard and the back doors open into the storeroom, through which he went reach his own 'front door'. She pushed an urn to one side and then threw back her head to rid the hair falling over her eyes.

'Busy day?'

'Very, very! Phew.' She breathed out hard. 'But that's good. No?'

The shop telephone, which he used for all incoming and outgoing calls, was half hidden behind the remains of cut foliage and raffia. He didn't need to ask her permission any more, as they had come to an agreement that provided he was careful to lock the outer doors, she would leave this middle and dividing door open so that he could access the telephone any time. At the end of each month the cost of his calls was added to his rent. Frankly, it couldn't have been easier; she had been helpful all along. In return he offered more in rent, which he could easily afford.

She was now carrying empty urns and scraps of rubbish into the workshop, chaotic as ever, and he went in with her and tried to tidy a little. She laughed at him.

Then he asked, 'You have help sometimes? The lady with fair hair? Every Saturday? Today?'

She brushed some clinging pine needles off her dress. And then, as if suddenly understanding, 'Oh, *si, si*. Alice. The English lady. She helps me. And with English too! I like her very, very much.'

'I thought she was English. But she stopped coming for quite a long time and now she's back.'

Angelina leaned against the door, her expression solemn. '*Si*. She was ill.' And she pointed to her head. 'In the head, a little, I believe.'

Why did this upset him? Why this concern?

'*Lei ha abortito*. You understand *abortito*.

He nodded.

'Two years now. She *era malata*' – and pointing to her head – 'here. In the head, *malata*, sick,' she repeated.

She must have seen his expression, his head hanging, his sloping shoulders, so he shifted himself, stood straight in order to face her.

'It's OK,' she whispered as some sort of comfort. 'She OK, OK now. She is good. Completely good. Look, Frank. *Guardali*.' And she passed through into the shop and pointed at the wall behind the counter. Pointed towards three watercolours of flowers.

'Alice.' She looked at him. 'She paints.' And she pointed again. 'They are very very *bene*, no? *Vendiamo i quadri*. We sell. To many people.' And she laughed.

He thought, Fragile-looking. Yes, that was the word he had been searching for. Fragile-looking. Her paintings free-flowing, light, like her hair. Fragile. And he had lifted her case for her when they both got off the train at Darlington. He remembered now.

'No frames,' he said. 'They need frames.' He turned towards her. 'I'd like to make some frames.' He ran a pointed finger round a painting and then repeated the shape with his hands. 'Can I take a measurement? Measure,' he repeated and, walking behind the counter, looked more closely. 'I'll measure later. OK? I'd very much like to make frames for them.'

'How much we pay?'

'God, Angelina! Nothing. Absolutely nothing. *Di nulla*! My pleasure.'

Later he came down from his place, through the workroom and into the shop, where he measured up for the frames. All the paintings were the same size, so just one set of measurements, which he scribbled down in his notebook. Then he phoned Greta, for knowing he would be making frames for Alice's paintings had rid him of any misgivings he had about ringing. He didn't care if she gave him the cold shoulder.

# Henry

He was irritable. He had already snapped over breakfast when she asked him a second time if he was sure that he didn't want another coffee, saying something like, 'If I say no, Alice, I mean no. Why do you keep on?' He was irritable and taking it out on her when actually it wasn't her; he was thoroughly annoyed that he was allowing Phoebe to visit. He had successfully prevented her from visiting them in Italy for three years, so why now? The pressure! Of course, it was her pressure all the time. Going on and on. On the other hand, he couldn't think of any good reason why she shouldn't visit. She did everything for him apart from actually painting. Arranged exhibitions, maintained the contacts in Morocco: booked his tickets. She even kept all the accounts; he had to ask her how much money he had. So she had the right, he supposed, to come over to see his latest work for the Moroccan tourist board. After all, it was all through her in the first place. And that annoyed him too.

She was arriving today and he was angry, depressed. He was caught between needing, yet not wanting her. It didn't make him feel good about himself, so he was – well, there was no other word for it – irritable.

Now, unable to work, he gazed out of the long windows that opened out onto the back garden. It was always a surprise, the little square swimming pool, the unnaturally blue water smudged with shadow and set stubbornly in the middle of glaring white marble. The back garden sloped up from the house towards the hills behind and was formally laid out with stony paths and clipped hedges. All kept in order by a gardener Father had found. Some tall trees poked up into the sky and grey-leafed olive trees with tangled, brittle branches clustered in groups, their gnarled, misshapen trunks bent and twisted, the remains of earlier groves that grew on the hills before the lakeside houses were built. It was a dry space, shadowed by the house, and then suddenly up by the windows the light reflecting off the marble and the blue of the pool. Temporarily, he was mesmerised by a glistening black beetle, first crawling along the water's edge and then stumbling over onto its crackly back, its legs wriggling frantically. Helplessly. He stood and watched. Perhaps he should paint beetles!

The painting was almost complete. As they always requested, a silky black Barb stallion, standing, head high, neck arched, on a sandy hillock overlooking the sea. The other commission, a small herd of wild-eyed horses, with power-fully muscled hind quarters galloping through patchy, desert scrubland, nostrils flaring, was finished and propped against the wall, covered by an old sheet.

It could have been daunting, going over there the first time, but the good old public-school 'how to conduct yourself' sort of thing, the social etiquette stuff, all came in handy, making him appear more confident than he was. He trusted that he had succeeded in behaving in a well ... as 'a man about town' sort of person. He thought he did. In any case, they liked his work and paid very well. He was making more than his lawyer brother, Robert, and the family would never get over that! Precious, handsome, clever, amiable Robert, beaten financially – and famously, as well, come to think of it –by his not-very-interesting brother. What a laugh! The whole thing gave him immense satisfaction. More than satisfaction. He was bloody delighted. Of course, it lamely flickered through his mind that Phoebe expected to be rewarded for his growing success; she wanted to monopolise him, have him in every way, for him to be hers. Already said that she wanted their child. No way that was going to happen! If Alice wasn't going to have one, she most certainly wasn't either. In any case, they'd both make hopeless parents. She was too bossy and he, well, he just wouldn't have the time. Like his mother. She never had the time. But at least she had never cheated. Never cheated on Father. But he'd cheated: he'd cheated at school, more than once and now, well, he was cheating on Alice. She must have guessed but had never made any kind of scene. She even seemed happy at last, now that she had started painting again, but she only had the kitchen table. That's why he was going to spend a lot of money having a studio built for her in the attic, to make it up to her if he could, so he didn't need to feel guilty any more, especially as he was going to be away for longer periods at a time. He needed to encourage her to be busy and creative. That way he could get on with his life, his cheating.

In the beginning, he had wanted very much to look after her, her disability making him feel strong and needed, but that had been a mistake. And he hadn't understood how wilful she was. She went her own way; she didn't need him; didn't even appear to be worried or jealous. And he wanted her to be jealous. Yes, still lovely to look at, he thought, still frail, in a way. Though not as much as she liked to appear sometimes. She put it on if it suited her.

Basically, it all came down to the baby thing and he was heartily sick of it, had been anyway. Anyone would have been. It just went on and on. What the hell was he supposed to do? Always so tense, so terrified of having a baby. She was haunted by something she had heard when she was in hospital having her hip operation. He actually couldn't remember exactly what it was. Perhaps he'd been a bit too indifferent, not taken it seriously enough, not really bothered to listen. But then, to be fair, he was busy with his painting, building a reputation. Making them a living, after all. He just didn't have time for all the hysteria. Anyway, what could he have said or done that would have made the slightest difference? Nothing. So he had to give up. Anyone would have done in his position.

She'd been adamant that she couldn't have a baby. Could not bear the pain. He had to use a wretched condom even though she was taking the pill. He was fed up about that. But there were enough times when, satisfied it had been safe, she curled her arms around him and melted. That had been enough for him at the time. It was enough. And then it would begin. The hysteria. She would be silent and withdrawn, sometimes trembling, so terrified that she might be pregnant, after all and moaning to him, 'But Henry, nothing is a hundred per cent safe. My doctor told me.' Christ! It had just been that one time, after he got back from his first Moroccan trip and she had been so pleased to see him, and he her, if it came to that. After that night ... Fuck it! He just hadn't had time for the condom. And of course, she had to get bloody well pregnant. And then basically went mad. No exaggeration. Her panic, her terror was beyond reason. She went mad. Mad. She went berserk. She had to get rid of it. Now. Now. Thank God for the Talianis next door. Signed to say her mental health warranted an abortion. So that was it. The abortion. And if he was disappointed, the relief that it would be over was greater than any regrets.

They'd all assumed that everything would be OK after that. And sure, at first, she was calmer, almost back to normal, and then the nightmares began. It was the last straw. No one could have stood it. She would wake screaming and sobbing, saying she'd killed this little boy. Charlie. She'd killed Charlie. She knew it was Charlie with the dark curls and blue eyes. Dark hair like his; blue eyes like hers. She'd killed Charlie with her pebbles. He'd come to her in the garden with the jar of pebbles and she'd licked one pebble to show him the bright colours. And he'd been thrilled, happy and trotted off with the jar. It was all absolutely clear, real. Then she would scream, 'And when I went back to the house, this actual house, down the actual path, like it is, he was lying there, dead, with the pebble stuck in his throat.' And she would hold herself across her stomach, doubling up, rocking backwards and forwards. Nothing he did, nor anything Gabriella tried to do, or even the Talianis could help her. Nothing. No one. She had killed her baby, her child, her boy. He remembered a doctor telling him that some women did have bad reactions after an abortion, suffering from guilt. Whatever it was, she stopped painting, stayed in her room, didn't go to the flower shop and for months refused to sit in the garden that she loved. Hell! It was hell. Too stressful for words. Exhausting. Thank God for the therapist in Verona, arranged by next door and gradually, whatever it was, she began to get better. The nightmares ceased, she started going to the shops with Gabriella, and even sat in the garden again. He remembered that afternoon well. He'd gone into the kitchen to fetch a beer and saw her through the window sitting in the rocker. The relief! Almost a kind of joy. He had stood there looking, not making a sound, afraid that he might break some spell and everything would go wrong again. He remembered that, all right. He also remembered that he drank a lot that night. Drink was a must-have, anyway.

And then one time, while he was away, she started painting again. The flowers. 'Well, I had to get away,' he mumbled to himself as he stared out into the garden, 'had to escape.' At least Phoebe wanted what was best for him. All the time. Made him feel OK, less of a failure. Alice had made him angry and he couldn't deal with it. Alice! Alice! Alice! It had all been about Alice. It affected his painting and he had to think about himself. His life. What was good for him. And Phoebe agreed. 'Just come to me,' she would say and so, for sanity's sake, he'd been spending more time away in London.

And he felt perfectly justified. It must have become obvious to everyone he was now with Phoebe, having an affair. Or whatever. She wanted their child. But not a chance. No way! If Alice wasn't having a kid, then neither was she. In any case they'd make hopeless parents: she was too bossy and he, well he just wouldn't have the time. Like his mother. She never had the time. But at least she'd never cheated. Never cheated on Dad. He'd cheated at school, more than once, as it happens, and now, well, he was cheating on Alice. Either way, he was dreading having Phoebe here, having her visit.

It was typical of Phoebe to catch an early flight, so Manuel brought her to the door just after two in the afternoon. Alice was resting, as usual, and he suspected she would keep out of the way as long as possible. He didn't blame her. They'd met at the wedding, of course, where Phoebe vied for his attention, took a kind of ownership. Rather obviously. Alice never spoke of her after the wedding, had seldom mentioned her since. Once, he remembered she did ask if he ever stayed with her when he was in London, to which he had carefully replied, 'Only if I'm desperate,' which seemed to satisfy her. He knew Alice didn't like her and he perfectly understood, was just slightly annoyed that she didn't appear at all jealous. She had every reason to be, after all. He sighed heavily. 'Fuck it! I could do without all this. And I've done no work.'

Already Phoebe was clipping about the place, inspecting and commenting. But where was his studio? She wanted to see his latest work, how he was getting on with the Barb stallions? 'Making progress,' she chirped.

Alice must be lying there, hearing it all. Listening. So he tried to sound as matter-of -fact as possible as he ushered Phoebe into his studio. Alice wouldn't be able to hear anything from there; the shrill, bossy voice would not disturb her. Or the sexual innuendos.

'Yes, Henry, I approve,' she said, standing there in her short multi-floral skirt, neat-collared shirt and flashy sandals; the well-cut bob, now flicked out at the sides, swung around her face as she moved. Actually, there was something about her. It was her confidence, her utter self-assurance that defeated him, and yet he needed her. But he kept control in his own way, over sex. When he withheld it, made her wait another day, another night, making any excuse he liked, he took control and the result was staggeringly successful. Now she was quiet, less confident, more compliant. Gave him the power. She was the needy one now. It worked a treat.

'You're right, Henry, the light in here is excellent,' she was saying. 'But that doesn't stop me from . . .' She hesitated. 'Well, you know how I feel, what I think about you being here. You know it's better for you to be in London, don't you? Don't you, Henry?'

'Or better for you?'

She moved across to the windows and stood looking out at the garden and pool.

'You're such an idiot. Getting married.'

'Cut it out, Phoebe. Come on, and I'll show you to your room.' He grinned secretly because Alice had insisted Phoebe had the bedroom at the other end of the house, as far away from them as possible! Alice usually had her own way.

They met her going up the stairs as she was coming down. She had a long strand of hair hanging down the side of her face. 'Hello Phoebe,' she said as they all stood looking at each other. 'Did you have a good flight?'

'Excellent, thanks. Rubbish food, of course.'

'Can I get you anything, then?' And Alice squeezed past them.

'Cup of tea would be great. Thanks. We'll just dump my things.'

Henry gave Phoebe a small shrove up the stairs, thinking, She said 'we'll' on purpose. She really is a cow at times.

He dumped her case on a chair. She threw herself on the bed, skirt up to her thighs and kicked off her sandals, which went flying across the room. He'd seen it all before. 'No chance, I suppose. While I'm here? Have to wait 'til you're at my place, I suppose.' Hands behind her head, she wriggled her legs up and down on the edge of the bed.

He left the room without speaking.

Thank God it was only three days. He'd done practically no painting. Alice did precious little to help, saying her leg was playing up. He'd taken Phoebe out to see the mill, as he couldn't think of anything else to do, and her last night out for supper, Alice preferring to stay at home. That was no surprise. He couldn't blame her. She was always pleasant, but cool. There was a knowing quietness. She wasn't giving anything away, especially not to Phoebe.

# Alice

*A month later*

The walk down the garden path towards the wrought-iron gate pleased her as she, moving through them, interrupted the streams of light and the shadows. And the reflections off the lake, tantalisingly, appeared and disappeared between the trees. There was that wonderful wafting smell of ripening lemons meandering into streams of coolness. She drew in her breath, for the perfumes were calming and it was already hot, and so she had, for coolness' sake, bundled her hair up inside her navy straw hat, bit battered but a favourite.

It was Saturday and the day she most looked forward to; she had her routine, for first, before going to the shop to help Angelina, she liked to stop off at the market, which was held in the church square every Saturday where, all on her own, without the advice of Gabriella, she could make her own choices of fruit, vegetables and cheese. She was perfectly confident now, her Italian being quite sufficient and anyway, she had watched the Italian women, how they shopped, picking out what they wanted, smelling, looking, and buying only after being completely satisfied. It was never a question of, for example, six apples please and leave it to the stallholder to pick out and bag up the apples. Oh no, the Italian women picked out their own. Very carefully. Now she did the same.

It was only a few hundred yards from the house, and today she felt no need to take her stick. In any case, she always had the low lake wall to lean on if necessary. The bells were striking now across the valley and up to the hillsides behind, and she didn't plan to take too long shopping, for the shop was busy every Saturday; flowers bought for the church; flowers for presents and birthdays; flowers to decorate vases on tables and windowsills. She so enjoyed picking out the blooms from the tall metal urns as they were chosen, sometimes suggesting an addition of colour or texture, often imagining that it would make a good painting. and then wrapping them, as usual, in the brown paper tied with pale raffia. For her trouble Gabriella gave her a great bunch to take home with her.

Then she saw him and stopped where she was.

The wooden dinghy was upturned on the lake shore. The newly varnished planks gleamed like polished wood in the morning sunlight. He was bent over, sawing a plank that was balanced on two oil drums: rounded shoulders, head down, dark, cropped hair. The tall, lean body, slightly hunched. She had seen that concentration before, the bent shoulders under short dark hair. Somewhere. Somewhere. That self-absorption. She had seen it and been attracted by it. Yet unnerved. Like a magnet, drawn in then and pushed away.

She didn't know why she was nervous and intended to hurry past, but he stood up and spoke to her, as if he had seen her coming. 'Hi! Good morning.'

'Oh! You're English!'

'Indeed I am. Are you off to the shop?'

It was the directness. The way he looked at her as if he knew her. She didn't like it. She was afraid of what she felt. But she stopped anyway. Stopped by the lake wall that separated her from the pebbly beach, her basket scraping against the rough stone as she swayed slightly. He had returned to his work sawing the plank. His brown hands and long fingers. Then he stood up. Suddenly. And before she could move on, 'I've been renting above Angelina Fiori for three years, so I've seen you there. Alice Bancroft, isn't it?'

She was utterly confused, couldn't read his expression at all, thought he was well ... a bit odd, but she couldn't be rude. He was obliging her to talk.

Normally she could be jokey, laughing, but now she was a fool, stuttering, saying banal things like some inept child. She wanted to get away to the shop. And he, with one hand on the boat, which crunched on the gravel below as it rocked, was smiling at her.

Why? What had she done that was so funny? 'You know a lot,' she said. 'Who are you, then?'

'Frank Richardson. I've been working at *il mulino* for the past three years. Ever been there?

He wasn't looking at her now as he toed the pebbles. But he was waiting for her answer.

'I went once, at the beginning when it was just, well, a bit of a mess.'

'You should go again now. It's quite a place. How long have you lived here?'

She didn't like the questions. She wanted to get to the shop. Away from this man who seemed so familiar. The attraction was frightening; she wanted to leave and get to the shop.

She picked up her basket and began to move away. 'We've been living here for three years. My husband's a painter.' She wasn't sure why she said that. Henry being a painter seemed to make her reason for being there all right. And protected her.

'If I'm right,' he said, 'I'm coming to see you around five today. About your studio? I'm a chippy, you see.'

This man was coming into her life whether she liked it or not. Something was happening she was unable to control, but she wasn't going to show any interest. 'Oh! OK! That's a coincidence. But I don't know anything about any arrangements.

It's all down to my husband. Nothing to do with me. And I must get going.'

'I like your flower paintings.' His voice was almost gruff. 'You'll need a studio.'

She thought, Oh God, don't say it was him who made those frames! Of course it was, but she wasn't going to say anything more. She didn't want any more conversation.

'Must be off. Thanks, anyway.'

'See you at five, then.'

Was he watching her walk away? She mustn't turn round. Then she heard him call after her. 'We've met before, you know.' And then louder, 'On the train to Darlington.'

She kept on walking along the lakeside wall. Pretending not to hear. But she already knew.

# Henry

He heard her come in, back from the shop, and go into the kitchen as she usually did. Heard the water splashing, he assumed into her usual jug, where he guessed she would be arranging the flowers she always brought home on a Saturday. What was unusual was that she hadn't called out. Normally she came into his studio to find him, to start her chat about the day. She was always happy and chatty after her day at the shop. But this evening there was silence from the kitchen. He put his brush into the jar of turps and wiped his hands, 'Alice!' he called. 'Alice.'

She was sitting at the end of the table in her usual seat, elbows on the table, the flowers in front of her. 'What's up? Is there something wrong?'

'Sorry,' she said. 'I meant to say hi. How are you? Did you get lots done?'

'You seem very quiet. Has something happened?'

She stood up, pushed the vase of flowers into the middle of the table before going to the sink, where she began to clear away the cut stems.

Something was wrong. 'You know we've got the guy coming about your studio this evening. I did tell you. Frank . . . something or other.'

'Richardson. He's called Frank Richardson. I met him this morning on the way to the market. He's got a boat.'

She wasn't smiling and had that stubborn look. He couldn't understand why and was becoming increasingly impatient.

'So? So? Alice! Is there a problem? There seems to be a problem. Whatever it is, we'd better sort it before he comes. About five.' He thought, It doesn't seem to matter what, there's always some sort of problem, and he was bloody fed up. All this studio business was for her. Personally, he could do without all the work that would go on. He couldn't concentrate with bloody building stuff and people traipsing in and out, but it was for her, to give her somewhere she could paint and ... it made him less guilty, going to London so frequently. Staying longer. He would just have to go more often to London, anyway, while it was all going on. Perfectly reasonable excuse.

'There's no problem,' she was saying. 'No problem But, if you don't mind, Henry, I'll just keep out of the way. I am a bit tired anyway, so I'll just keep in my room, out of the way.'

He shut the kitchen door behind him as if someone might be listening. He thought, She's having another of her turns. I'm not standing for it. Fuck it! 'Now is not the time, Alice.'

'Time? What do you mean?'

She had returned to her seat and he moved to the other end of the table, thinking it might be a commanding position. He was trying to control his temper.

'Alice! This studio is for you, for God's sake. Greta has specially recommended this Frank whatever-his-name-is ... And Dad always relied on her for all the other work she's planned and organised for him here. She's completely reliable. If she recommends this whatever-his-name-is, Frank something or other, believe me, he will be good. So show some interest and enthusiasm for once.'

'Richardson.'

'... and he will most definitely want to discuss what you want. I mean, it's rude and thoughtless of you for you not to be around. What the hell has got into you? I know you can be bloody selfish at times, with your thises and that's, but this won't do, I'm afraid. You will bloody well be here to see him.'

He waited, thinking she was going to cry. 'Did anything happen this morning, or what?'

He went to the fridge, pulled out a bottle of opened wine and poured himself a drink. No wonder he drank so much. There always seemed to be one drama after another. Oh, and now? Not tears exactly, but that pathetic, helpless look.

Her head was down; she would not look at him. Then, 'I don't know how to explain,' she said, 'but you know someone is framing my paintings. Well, I'm pretty sure it's him, almost positive. He didn't say exactly, but I'm certain; he kept saying how much he liked my paintings, so I just got this feeling.' Now she was looking at him. 'I just feel awkward about it, that's all.'

'He fetched another glass from the shelf. 'Do you want some? Might do you good.'

She shook her head. 'I just wonder why he would bother, Henry. It's a bit weird, don't you see?'

He put a half-full glass of wine in front of her, anyway. 'Not really, Alice. The guy rents above the shop, been there years, and he will know everything going on there. He'll have seen your paintings and probably asked Angelina if she wanted frames for them. Nothing weird about that, is there? Why didn't you ask him anyway? I'll ask him when I see him, if that will help.'

She was shaking her head and staring at him. 'Please don't say anything, Henry.'

He refilled his glass, needing to escape the emotion, get away, back to his studio. Being angry sapped his energy and he now didn't feel up to dealing with this Frank bloke. Fuck Alice.

Alice called after him, 'You know a lot! Why didn't you

tell me about this carpenter bloke who Greta thinks is so marvellous? If I'd known, I might not have been so unprepared when I saw him this morning, that's all.'

He pretended not hear her.

It was obvious that she expected him to open the door, which annoyed him.

The man was tall, much taller than him, and slim, but muscly and strong-looking. So tanned: must work outside a lot. He was carrying a folder, probably with the plans. Henry noticed his eyes, deep brown and slightly narrowed in the light. Serious, almost stern-looking, as he waited. He wanted to appear relaxed, welcoming almost, and held out his hand. 'Henry Bancroft.'

He wasn't responding. 'Frank Richardson.' Very detached.

He needed a bit of help here and so quickly led him across the hall to the kitchen, where Alice was waiting at the end of the table, and was thankful that she managed some sort of smile. The sulky look gone, at least for the moment, as the guy nodded, his expression softening somewhat.

Not sure what to do next, he did his saunter to the other side of the table and leaned across it. He noticed Frank Richardson's hands: long fingers. He was unsure, but knew he must ask him questions. It was the thing to do. 'You've been working on the old mill, Greta tells me.'

He nodded, with a brief, 'Correct,' and glanced at Alice, who was looking down at her hands and thought, Let's get this over with ASAP.

'I haven't been up to see it, but I understand it's going to be a great tourist attraction when it's finished.' He was drawing on what he wryly described as his 'Moroccan confidence'.

Alice interrupted with, 'We did go up, Henry, with Max at the beginning, when work had just started.' She looked at Frank, 'But, as I ... you know, we haven't been since. To see it.'

Her interruptions were annoying Henry. He needed to regain control here. So he asked, 'What did you do exactly?'

'Because I'm a qualified cabinetmaker, I get to do more specialised stuff. Up there I repaired the waterwheel and then worked on making replica furniture for the mill house. From plans,' he added. 'We had architects' drawings to follow, like these,' and he held up the folder, 'so there's no problem.'

This Frank Richardson seemed as though he would do a good job. That was a relief; he didn't want problems, didn't want to have to, well, do anything much. If this guy was as good as he appeared to be, then he could leave him to it. He wouldn't need to stay around, could still go to London. In fact, being away when the work was going on would be essential. Anyone could understand that. So, let's get on with it, and he was about to take him upstairs to show him the attic space when the guy pointed to something on the mantelpiece and said, 'That's nice. That green vase there.'

Very odd! Especially as Alice, who had been almost mute so far, started explaining how it was the first present he had bought her. And how there had been two but she had only wanted the one. It was a little junk shop up the Dales near her home. He wished she would stop going on, sure that this Frank Richardson wouldn't be the slightest bit interested, and he wanted to just dismiss the whole thing and move on and get on, for God's sake. What was all this?

'We might as well go on up, then? I'll just fetch my plans. There're one of two changes we want to make. I'll talk to you about that when we're up there. Get your opinion.'

As he moved towards the stairs, he heard the guy asking Alice if she wanted to come as well. As it was for her. Why did he do that? A bit out of order! Bloody cheek, actually. Anyway, she couldn't, because the ladder steps were impossible for her. 'Do you want to come?' he had said. Something about 'dodgy hip', she replied.

But that wasn't all. 'Well then! The first thing we need to do is to build the staircase, don't you think? Seems sensible to me.'

Was he speaking to him or to Alice? Either way, the man seemed to be taking control. There was a certainty about this Frank Richardson. Perhaps that was all for the good, in the circumstances.

Up there in the semi-light the two of them stood, and Henry started to explain about Alice, but the bloke put up his hand, saying he had heard. He was very sorry. He hoped this studio would be a good thing for her. He clearly didn't want to hear any more, which disappointed him. He needed people to understand, but Frank Richardson turned away and, opening his folder, he took out the plans, opened them up, and studied them for a moment. 'Well, we'd better get on with this. What were the changes you wanted to make?'

# Frank

He was caught by surprise, for the door opened suddenly without any warning sounds. The man stood there – he guessed he must be her husband – barefoot, grey shorts, creased shirt with rolled-up sleeves. He noticed the splodges of paint.

'Henry Bancroft,' he said, holding out his hand.

He was friendly enough. 'Frank Richardson.'

'Come on in.' He turned away across the tiled hall. 'We're in the kitchen.'

He had thought of nothing else, wondering if she remembered their being on the same train to Darlington, and was unsettled about seeing her again, but reminding himself that she was married strengthened his resolve to just concentrate on the work. It was just a job, after all.

The hallway had been shadowy but there was brightness in the kitchen as the evening sun gushed through two long windows and the open back door, and she was there, sitting at the end of a long pine table. He noticed how the evening sun lit up the side of her face, strands of her hair. It was inevitable, all of it.

'Hi!' he said, to keep it simple.

She didn't get up but twisted slightly to acknowledge him and smiled. And that was quite OK She didn't need to say anything, this woman he had so often noticed and wondered

259

about. It was his secret, another secret, and his fingers tightened around his folder, like folding his arms tightly, as he so often did. It had been his way of holding on.

Bancroft crossed to the other side and leaned, with both hands outspread, on the table, his back to the stove, above which was a mantelpiece with an assortment of photos and small china jugs, and that's when he saw the green vase. Hit in the guts, punched! 'Hell!' He couldn't help himself. 'Sorry! That's nice, that little green vase.' And heard her voice telling how and where they bought it. So, it was them the old man had referred to all that time back. God in Heaven, it was Mum's little green vase.

Henry Bancroft turned round to look at it. 'Just one of many treasures I have given Alice!' And he gave a snorted laugh.

'It was the colour. The light through the glass.'

He stopped listening, remembering the shattered pieces under his feet. On the bedroom floor. Mum's green vase that he had stolen for her.

'There was a pair,' she was going on, 'but I only wanted one. One made it more special in a way, if you see what I mean?'

If Henry Bancroft hadn't stopped him by asking questions about his work at the mill, he would have walked away: left the house, left the job, left her. But Bancroft did ask him questions and the moment moved.

He was easy enough to talk about himself now – if it was to do with work, that is. 'No matter how simple,' Stan told him, 'you can feel pride in good work.'

Henry swung his arm towards the open kitchen door. 'Well, let's go and have a look, shall we? There are some changes we need to discuss.'

He thought, why is he excluding her from all this? It's going to be her studio. He needed to know what she wanted, to hear what she had to say. It was her, this Alice, and he wanted to please. Very much. So, he asked if she would go with them, but she couldn't climb the attic ladder because of her hip. He had noticed her limping more than once and that made him determined to get on with it, to build her a staircase up to the attic space she could climb. Climb easily. He would watch her walking up the stairs so he could build exactly the right step for her: the length, the depth.

'Greta will have spoken to you about what we want, of course, and you have her plans, so shall we go?' And again, he followed him, this time across the hall and up the curving, marbled stairs. On the top landing, which was wide and long, there was a loft ladder in place, leading up to the blackness of roof space.

'There's plenty of head room, so you needn't worry. Even your height. We've got electric light up there. I'll go first and switch it on.' He was shorter and stockier than him. Kept flicking his hair out of his eyes with a flip of the head. No way he could work with hair flopping over his eyes like that. His had to be tamed with the crew cut.

He followed him up the ladder and into the space, which was hot and airless, beams and floorboards criss-crossing with shadows from the electric lights.

It was a good space. 'Good space.' And with a surge of enthusiasm, he unfolded the plans and pulled out a pencil from his t-shirt pocket. 'Right,' he said, and waited.

He realised that this man, owner, husband, successful painter, was not as confident as he might at first appear.

Henry turned suddenly to look at him. 'She's been very ill, you know. She ... she well, she lost a baby. Made her ill.'

Frank concentrated on the plans, not wanting to hear him speak about her like that, especially to him, a stranger, and a man. He didn't like that at all. He's looking for sympathy, he thought, and already disliked him. Bancroft was disloyal to speak like that. Made him even more determined to get on so that he could build her a studio as quickly as possible. And make her happy. It was going to be a great deal of work; he'd be here for quite some time. She'd be here, too.

Frank pointed to the back of the house. 'Is that north? She'll want lots of light. She'd like the morning sun as well, I should think.'

He wanted to make it the best possible place. See that smile. And he, turning round slowly absorbing every detail, thought about a skylight and central fan to keep her cool in the heat, for it would get hot up here in the summer and yes, he was sure she would appreciate a window seat. None were in the plans, but that didn't matter, if that's what she would like.

'A space like this you can have windows all round – and a skylight. A circular skylight. Like a church apse.' He was talking to himself. Moving about carefully over the joists, he took out his measure and ran it up and down.

Henry Bancroft looked helpless, standing there, watching him. 'She'll need shutters, of course, and a fan in the middle, but that's a detail, isn't it? She had a breakdown, you know.'

Frank thought, Of course I know! Everyone knows.

But Bancroft was going on. 'Yes, well . . . Do you want to measure up some more? Then, when we get back down, you can tell her some of your ideas. See what she says.'

They were standing there in the semi-light among the beams and joists of the attic, he waiting as Henry muttered on, as if to himself. And he had to just stand there and listen and wait and be still. There was a great deal he kept to himself.

# Alice

*Five months later*

It was dark and cool after the garden and smelled of lemons and pine, the tiles soothingly cold under her bare feet. She glanced up the stairs, tempted to go directly to her studio at the top, to continue the painting, but knew she must first make the phone call.

The garishly red phone sat incongruously on the kitchen table among the stripes of sunlight filtering through the wooden shutters, while the plastered walls wavered with the blues and greens from the garden. She didn't know if she could bear to leave this place, especially since she was so happy now. But it hadn't always been like this, had it? She had to remind herself that it had not always been like this.

She dialled the number and sat on the cushioned chair, waiting.

She had to phone Da, to tell him everything. Would it cheer him up a bit? She needed his grounded, hidden tones to steady her.

And there it was, but the changed voice, changed since Ma went into care; there was a deadness, flatness. He went every day. Every day. Kept saying. 'She's happy enough, though. I'm sure she's happy enough.'

'It's me, Da.'

'So, it is! Well, there's a nice surprise! How are you, lass?'

'Sorry if it's been a bit long, Da, but so much has been going on. And every day I've meant to phone you.' Then she told him she was feeling herself again, how much she loved the studio.'

'I'm so excited about it all. Honestly, you would say I'm like a child!' Would this help to make him happy? Would it cheer him up?

'That's grand, girl. Your ma would be telling everyone. I'll tell her this afternoon.'

'Honestly Da, it's fantastic. You would think so. Tell her it's almost finished. He built the staircase first; it's wooden, oak – or is it elm? Can't remember, anyway, not tiles like the other, which I prefer actually, and he kind of measured it specially to be good for me, you know, my hip, my steps, sort of thing. It's gorgeous, with rails both sides. He's so thoughtful. We didn't have to ask, he just did it. And windows, shaped like in churches, rounded at the top, so kind of soft-looking, and a domed skylight, which gets light all round. I just can't tell you! And now he's finishing off the window seat I wanted. There's just some bits and pieces still to do, like shelves and cupboards, things like that, but it's practically there. Da, you will love it when you see it. Tell Ma. To me it's wonderful.'

'Really grand,' he was saying. 'Your ma would be smiling all over. We're happy for you, Pixie. And Alistair will be too, when I tell him. Just you getting back to yourself again. That's all we want.'

She was spread across the kitchen table, the phone against her ear, the other hand holding back hair that had fallen across her face. Her forehead was moist with the heat, for it was close and airless. She shouldn't be so happy, sound so happy. It was cruel of her. Was it thoughtless? But she had to tell him this. 'And Da! I've started a real painting up there. You know, not my flowers, but guess what . . .'

'Go on, then.'

264

'Pebbles!' And the astonished pause on the other end, made her burst out laughing. 'I thought you'd be surprised. I wish you could come over, Da. To see it all.'

'No chance, lass. You know that. Not now.'

'How is Ma?'

There was a moment's pause and she could hear he had turned away from the phone to cough.

'She looks well. She sleeps a lot now. Reg came with me yesterday. You remember Reg, from the allotments.'

'Of course, I remember him; I loved Reg; he was soft with me, wasn't he, Da?'

'True enough! You played him like fish on a line, if you ask me. Of course, Ma didn't know him, and he was shocked, hadn't realised, but anyway, she smiled at him all the time. Still, he was upset. And she will have all her books around her.' Alice could hear the tenderness. It was always special when it came from Da. 'She knows if any book is in a different place. Goes mad then.' Now he laughed. 'Funny, some things! But she's happy enough. Still knows me! And I should bloody well think so, after all these years.'

She was too choked to speak.

'Now tell me, that guy Frank is doing a really good job, is he?'

It was the way he asked. Out of the blue. She was familiar with Da and his questions. Always something behind them. She didn't care if he knew.

'Da, he's marvellous. Really. His work is fantastic. And ...' She wasn't sure if this was right. 'And he's so nice, Da. So thoughtful, I told you. He's such a nice person. I'm stupid, I know, but you know, Da, I'll miss him when it's all finished. I like having him around.'

She'd never said that out loud before. Not to anyone, not Gabriella nor Angelina. No one.

Da was asking, 'Henry still away a lot, is he? Don't know what's going on there, Alice.'

She told him yes, and that he was travelling abroad, to Morocco, and back and forth to London for exhibitions and stuff. She didn't mention Phoebe.

'What's going on, Alice? Doesn't sound much of a marriage to me. You're on your own so much. I suppose it's that agent of his. What's her name?'

'Phoebe.'

She heard him sniff; it was his annoyed, irritable sniff.

'It's OK, Da. He's away at the moment, but honestly, I don't mind. Not at all. So, it's OK. I'm happy.'

'It's not that Frank man, is it?'

Now she laughed; the naughty girl with the kitten.

'Oh, I see,' was all he said.

She told him because she trusted him entirely. 'It's not Henry's fault, Da. He is a nice man – don't think he's not – and he tries, but Frank, well, he looks after me in little ways. Like, for instance, I know Henry bought me those semi-precious stones from Morocco, which I do like very much but . . . who do you think found me pebbles, I mean pebbles, Da? From the lake side? Just plain, ordinary pebbles, like from the seaside. He knew I'd thrown my own ones – you know, from Seaham – away. He knows why. I told him, Da. So, I think it was a brave, an amazing thing to think of. To do for me. That's why I've started the painting, to kind of show my appreciation.'

There was silence the other end, so she rather gabbled on now, not knowing what she was saying, just filling the silence. With Da, silences always meant something.

'He's a bit like you, Da, you know, a no-nonsense sort of person. Doesn't speak unless there's something worth saying sort of thing. He knew about the pebbles and my illness, but he said it was time to move on and start painting them again and not to be afraid any more. Da! Are you there? You don't have to say anything, I'm just telling you. I'm trying to paint pebbles and water again. That's all, really. The thing is, I don't really want the studio to ever be finished.'

'Don't be daft! You always were a daft lass. Anyroad, what-ever makes you happy is good enough for Ma and me. Just try, just for once, Alice, try to keep your feet on the ground. Just for once, aye?'

She'd invited Frank for supper, but there was still time to go back to the attic, to the painting. He'd want to see what she'd done so far. She knew it, although he never said. Very often they just knew things without saying.

How peculiar that Henry's architect had recommended Frank: that his idea for her to have a studio of her own had brought the man on the train to her. Really strange! It was a kind of circle.

She watched him working and thought he brought a kind of intensity to it. He was entirely absorbed, self-contained, didn't need anyone. It was a bit like Henry when he was paint-ing. She could stand there and he appeared not to notice her at all. Sometimes he did. With a nod. Yes, he did.

The wide stairs wound round and then again up to the studio, although she referred to it as the attic. One hand on the rail, her presence hazy in the mist of sun motes revolving before the dirty landing windows. She mounted the stairs, impatient, frightened the moment would pass, nervous of seeing her beginnings.

The windows and skylight faced north, and so the attic was flooded with clean, blue light. Light. In the heat of the summer there was a fan. Now it was revolving, slowly, heavily, with a regular creak and a low hum. Papers flickered in the draft. She leaned in the doorway, panting slightly, wiped her hand across her sweaty forehead and stared at her painting and then at the pebbles strewn in a round bowl of water, their mottled smoothness, their creamy browns, flecked with blues and greenish hues. She could detect the blue and greys of the sea, the yellow creams of sand, the pinks of coral, the cool greens of the seaweed, the scales of the fish, polished, swift, all there in the pebbles. She could see from the beginning of time: their stillness, their secretiveness. Henry would have painted the pebbles, truly, perfectly, the glints of light, the surfaces cold, smooth to the touch. Tactile. She looked at her beginnings, after so long and yet –'Nothing's changed,' she whispered. 'Struggling as usual.'

Her paintings told a different story. If she had known what to say, if she could have explained – but her paintings were drawn out of her, in spite of herself they happened. Now the pebbles lay, roughly developed across her canvas, neither flat nor solid, but revolving in the ebb and flow of the water. Hidden sides in light, rolling and still, patterns. She lifted the paintbrush out of the pot and wiped the tip onto the rag that she had stuffed into her pocket.

Obsessed by how the lights were transformed by the swirling water, she forgot the time and was shocked to hear Frank's steps up the path. When she hurried into the kitchen, he was waiting by the open kitchen door. 'How's you?'

'Fine! How're you doing?'

'Good!' It was their usual greeting. He stepped inside and she noticed the bottle of yellow-coloured wine.

She indicated the bottle. 'Good choice! 'Cos I am doing fish.'

He nodded, a slight satisfaction. 'Shall I open?' Without a word he went to the drawer in the dresser and pulled out the corkscrew.

She put the glasses on the table. 'I've laid outside.'

He sat down at the table and watched her preparing the fish. 'I've started, Frank. Do you want to see? It's only just started, though.'

'It's all right. You can show me later.'

'I don't know how to thank you, Frank. Nobody else would have dared,' she repeated. 'I wouldn't have dared myself. Even look at pebbles again since, you know, my illness.' She had to be careful now. Not to cry. Didn't think he liked crying much. She turned back to the fish. 'Did I ever tell you the first time I tried to paint pebbles? I was six years old. I'll tell you sometime.'

'You might have. I knew pebbles were special to you, that's all. Anyway . . .'

She passed him the plates and picked up the bowl of salad. 'Everything else is out there. Just this and the wine.'

He took the bowl and handed the stick to her. 'Go on. I'll bring it out. Go and sit down.'

It was dark in the garden by the time they had finished the fish, but there was enough light from the house for them to see. Moths fluttered in and out of the lights and she flipped one away from his face, watching as he cleared away the plates.

'There's peaches in the bowl. Cream's in the fridge.' And then, without knowing she was going to, 'I phoned Da earlier. Do you think, although I don't really want to, but do you think I should go home? I feel a bit guilty staying out here where it's all so lovely, with him and Ma not well. Am I being selfish?' But he didn't appear to hear her and was walking back with the peaches. She was so familiar with that slow walk of his, almost deliberate, his shoulders swaying from side to side. He toed some gravel from off the parched grass back onto the path. What was it about Frank?

It was breathless and still, as if the garden was waiting for a storm. The air was heavy with the scents of pine and sweet-gum, orange and night-scented stock, seeds Da sent her every year. Cicadas clipped away in the darkness. The light from the house caught him as he returned. 'There's a storm coming.'

'I love thunderstorms.' She didn't want to talk about going home any more.

'You'll miss this weather.' He put down the bowl of peaches. 'Bit different in County Durham.' He put a peach on a plate and passed it to her.

She tried to laugh. 'Yes, I know. Same for you, too. When

you go back to visit Kitty, don't you feel the cold? Will you ever go back to live, do you think?'

He didn't often grin. 'Sometime, probably. But not just yet'.

The joy of the evening faded for her. 'When, then? And where? Where will you go? Well, I suppose it'll depend on work, won't it. Has done so far.' She was trying desperately to sound normal, look normal, but the thought of being without him . . .

'Oh, I'll stay up North. Darlington way, no doubt, when the time comes.' And he looked at her with a grin, adding, 'Weather or no weather!'

She clapped her hands on the table: joy had returned. 'We might end up being neighbours! Be within a stone's throw if each other. Can you imagine that?'

He was concentrating on his peach. 'Eat your peach.'

'But Frank' – she couldn't let it go – 'we were so near before, and never knowing it.'

Now he leaned forward, elbows on the table, 'Bishop's Lodge out at Coundon way and you'd never even heard of it!'

'I wish I had, though. But I know where Coundon is. It used to be all coal mining; I think. Anyway, for sure I shall visit next time I'm back and see all your work. You're so clever, Frank. Amazing! You're so clever.'

He shrugged.

'Look at my attic.' She wanted to reach out and touch him, but . . .

'Yep. Glad you're pleased.'

'But how did you get into it all, Frank? You never really say.'

'Long story.'

'So?'

'Let's go up and look at your painting. Have you finished?' He pointed to the peaches left in the bowl.

She nodded, feeling silly for going on, asking him questions. She'd noticed before that he didn't like questions very much.

'You go on,' he said. 'I'll bring these.'

270

Now it had come to it, she dreaded him seeing the painting. Frank was so precise, so perfect in his work. He would think her rubbish. But he'd never say. He would just think it. Actually, he would much prefer Henry's work. Everybody rated Henry. Now she wished beyond everything that he would go away and never see it. But he was already coming up the stairs behind her. Then she heard the first tremors of thunder.

The house now was mellow-lit in comparison with the dark outside, and the wooden stairs glowed bronzy in the lights. She could hear the creak, creak, creak of the fan as she approached the top of the stairs.

She avoided the painting and went to sit on the cushioned window seat Frank had decided to build for her but not quite completed to his satisfaction. Edging or something. The painting was facing away from the door. He wouldn't see it immediately. She heard his footsteps stop on the stairs, knew what he was doing and laughed, calling, 'I know! It came down this morning when I drew the curtains. Don't worry, now Frank.' The longer he kept her waiting, the more anxious she became.

'Can't do it now. Where's the screw gone? It needs another screw. Have to fix it tomorrow.' She heard the footsteps resume.

He waited in the doorway as he always did. Looked at her. Looked at the fan. She laughed again. He would never accept a creaking fan!

He walked round to face the painting. She had learned there were times when it was better not to speak, but the silence was very difficult for her. She pretended to look out of the window. Rolls of thunder were drawing nearer and that was a welcome distraction. Why didn't he say anything?

He concentrated for a moment on the pebbles in the bowl of water and then looked at her. 'I like the colours. What's good? You've started again. That's the most important thing.'

'Yes, but do you like it or what? I mean – I know it's probably not your thing. Henry's would be more your thing. It's just a beginning, so can you say? What do you think?'

'I said, I like the colours. I can't say any more until it is finished, can I? What I think is not important, in any case. It's what it means to you. Nobody else matters. Only you. A guy called Stan taught me that. Sometime I'll tell you about him. But I am sure for lots of reasons I'll like it very much.'

She wanted to say, 'That's why I can't do without you.' Instead she said, 'Oh! Thank you.'

He walked back to the door. 'What's all this about going home?' He was leaning against the door frame, hands in pockets.

She rubbed her hand up and down the gingham cushion. 'I don't know. I just think I should, that's all, really.' She looked at him, wondering if she was hurting his feelings, if he cared at all. She wanted to add, 'But I don't want to leave you.' Didn't, of course. That, she was sure, would not have pleased him.

He nodded. She waited. He stood there. The trees in the garden rustled and twisted in the oncoming storm.

He half turned in the doorway and spread out his legs, folding his arms. Neither of them spoke but listened to the wind and rumbles of thunder.

'Come on,' he said as he turned away from her. 'I'd better get the cushions in. Take your time.' She listened to his long strides, two at a time, down the stairs, and the rain on the windows.

# Frank

S he had found one of Henry's rain jackets, and although it
was too short for Frank, he held it round his shoulders with
the hood flapping over his head. It was something to keep off
the battering rain.

He was just crossing the church square when he saw someone under an umbrella running in his direction. It didn't occur
to him that the person, running in this rain, was coming to
find him. Why would he? But it was Angelina, panting, and
he was frightened.

'*Grazie al cielo ti ho trovata.* Oh!' She pulled at his arm. '*Presto
vieni.* Come quick. The phone.'

Now he was running ahead of her, the jacket over his arm,
his hair plastered with the rain. It had to be Kitty.

'Shop open,' he heard her shout.

She'd scribbled down a number; it wasn't Kitty.

Now he was blank with foreboding; didn't know how to
phone the number. He dialled wrongly the first time, his
fingers wet, and he was rushing. The second time it rang and
Yvonne began rushing speech. In his panic he had difficulty
understanding her. She was shouting; he could hear crying;
someone, he thought it was Kitty, calling out. They must be
quiet. He couldn't take it in with all this noise. Please! Then a
man's voice. Dave. Steady, quiet. 'Don't worry. They're with
us. But been a bit of trouble. We're not sure exactly what

happened but Daisy's got a broken arm and he went for Kitty. We'll keep them here 'til you come, Frank, but we don't know what to do for the best.'

'OK! OK!' He had to swallow the absurd laughter of relief. 'Keep them with you, please. I'll be over tomorrow.' Oh my God. He'd thought they were going to tell him Kitty was dead.

'Yvonne took Daisy to outpatients and her arm is bandaged, not in plaster. She's quite proud of it!' And Dave gave a reassuring chuckle. And then, in a low tone, 'There's no way they can go back. In my book, that is.'

'I'll catch the first plane I can. What's your house number again?' He was taut and in control, the fear replaced by murderous rage. 'I'm catching the first plane. Just keep them safe.'

He asked the taxi driver to stop outside Yvonne's house and waited until he had driven away, then rang the bell, heard some kind of yell and a shush and then footsteps. 'Who is it?' A man's voice.

'Frank.'

The door opened just enough for him to recognise Dave, who took off the chain, and the door opened properly. 'Come in, mate. Dump it there.' Then he locked and chained the door again.

First it was Yvonne and then, behind her, looking almost sheepish, Kitty. But once she saw him, she burst past Yvonne, throwing herself at him, her arms around his neck, moaning as she cried.

He felt nothing. 'Stop it, Kit. That's enough.' He pulled away her arms and held her hands. All this emotion was getting in the way. Muddling things up. 'Stop this now, Kitty. We've got things to do.'

Dave paced in and out of the front room. Yvonne led Kitty back to the settee who, holding her side, lowered herself with an 'ouch!'

'Where's the kid?'

Yvonne whispered, 'Still asleep. She's all right though, Frank, so don't be too worried. The arm. It will mend in no time, they say.'

He had to get on, to do what had to be done, but first, 'Kit. Just tell me what happened.'

'Can't you sit down for a minute, Frankie?'

'What happened, Kit? You need to tell me.'

She didn't look well; her face puffy, eyes red. He'd noticed her wincing as she moved. He knew she didn't want him to know. 'Come on! It's OK. Just tell me.'

She put her face in her hands and was shaking her head. 'It was all over nothing. Honestly, Frankie, she was just playing with her cars and other stuff. I know it was untidy, a bit untidy, but still . . . he came home earlier than most. Drunk.'

He was so angry with her, so angry that she had got herself into this mess and she was crying again.

'She keeps saying she's sorry for being naughty. But she didn't do nothing, Frank.' She buried her head in a cushion so he could barely hear her. 'He trips over something, God knows, and next thing he's swearing, picks her up and chucks her across the room. I tried to stop it, stop him, Frankie. I tried but he started on me. Then he went. Daisy never did a thing. She loves him.'

Kids always think it's their fault, he thought, and questioned how he could still, in spite of everything, think he still loved his Dad. 'Yes, I know, Kit. It's just complicated,' he said out loud.

'What are we going to do, Frankie? I don't know what to do for the best. Frankie, I didn't do anything wrong. You do believe me?'

Despite his fury, he wanted to take her into his arms. She was like a child herself. A foolish, stubborn kid. Instead, he held her hands in his, just for a moment. 'You don't deserve this, Kit. There's nothing you could do to deserve this.'

But his frustration with her remained. 'Anyway . . . you do nothing but stay here. I'm going round there. Collect some of your things.'

He could see into the kitchen where the two boys in their school uniforms were half eating, half eyeing each other, the one with his back to him turning his head quickly, secretly, to catch a glance at what was going on. Dave, muttering something, tapped one on the head. He came into the sitting room. 'OK then. Just taking them in the car this morning. Won't be long. OK?'

Yvonne went to the window to watch them off. Kitty was leaning back with her eyes closed, holding her stomach. 'Have you eaten?' she asked.

'Had breakfast on the plane. Look, Kit, sit up for a minute. The keys? Have you got them?'

She pointed into the kitchen. 'Von? Where did you put the keys?'

He could see she was shaking and heard the voice quiet and frightened. 'What are you going to do, Frankie?'

'Not sure. Do you think he's there? And you've got to stop this crying. It's not helping anything.'

She shrugged mumbling 'Don't know – probably not. Don't know.'

Yvonne handed the keys to him.

'OK. Look Kitty, we need to get some of your stuff. Yes? Some of Daisy's things. Your stuff. You're leaving. You must know that. For the kid's sake. Think of the kid, Kitty. And no, Kit, the tears will not change anything. Where are your suitcases? Where's most of the stuff you need? Kitty?'

He waited while she wiped away tears on the arm of her jumper.

'Under the bed. In the drawers. I don't care. Get her toys or something if you can. Oh, for Christ's sake, any bloody thing. I don't care.' She was shouting. 'I don't bloody care anymore.'

The face at the bottom of the stairs stopped her. The kid,

solemn faced, walking importantly towards him, held up her bandaged arm towards him, proudly. Watching his face. And, trying not to smile bent down and gave her a hug. 'Hi Daisy.' She took his hand as he stood up. Ashamed eyes looking down. 'I didn't mean it. To be naughty.'

'You weren't naughty.'

She let go of his hand and ran to Kitty, who pulled her onto her knees, cuddling her. 'I've told you, darlin'. You weren't naughty. We all love you. Don't we Uncle Frank? Von? We love you so much, Daisy.'

The kid, her head against Kitty's chest whispered, 'Dad doesn't.'

'I'm going round there now, OK? Get some of your stuff. When I get back, we'll have to phone the police.' He was expecting the yell.

'Oh! Please no. No, Frank. Please no, Frank.'

As he closed the door behind him, Kitty was still shouting, 'No police, Frank. Don't call the police.'

The flat was empty. Dishes in the sink, the smell of cannabis, nicotine, alcohol. The sitting room in disarray, TV on its side, and a chair. For a moment he was afraid Steve might be asleep in the bedroom, but the door was open wide enough for him to see the unmade but empty bed.

He must be quick. He pulled two suitcases from under the bed and placed them on top of the crumpled sheets, unzipped them and pushed back the lids. Beginning with any drawers and any hanging spaces he could see, he pushed whatever he could into the first case. He would buy them whatever they needed, in any case. He rolled off a dressing table all her cosmetics, and odd bits of cheap jewellery. Then he went into the kid's room which, in contrast, was strangely tidy, the bed made up neatly, the soft toys in a heap against the pillows and small play pushchair with dolls in a corner. He bundled up all the soft toys, a couple of books from off the cupboard, putting them in a pile on the bed while he fetched the second suitcase. There was a small, pink, cheap-looking cupboard with shelves and some hanging space and he, with no idea about kids' stuff, pushed all he could into the case, squashing soft toys and some books on top.

He was just wondering whether he could find a carrier bag for more bits and pieces when he heard the clank of the metal steps, the door open and then bang shut. He heard the fridge door shut, the clip of a tin ripped open, the click of a lighter. Steve, almost certainly leaning against the sink with beer in hand and a fag in his mouth.

He wasn't scared – his loathing, hatred so great – and this bastard wasn't going to stop him from protecting Kitty.

Steve sounded unsteady on his feet and he imagined he was lurching from one thing to another, propping himself against the walls.

And it was pointless hiding like this, so he moved to the open doorway of the kid's room. 'Hello, Steve.'

Silence, just some heavy breathing. Steve was trying to get it together. Trying to focus.

'I'm taking some of their belongings, Steve. And just to let you know, they'll not be coming back. Ever.'

The laugh turned into a choking cough he couldn't control. And between the spasms, 'She isn't going the fuck anywhere, the fucking bitch. Nowhere.' Ripping more of the can open, he staggered towards him, brandishing the jagged tin. 'You fucking get out, you fucking waster. You're taking nothing.'

He had moved in front of the table, the cigarette ash spilling on the carpet as he tossed the butt away towards the settee, where it smouldered itself out, leaving a brown hole. It was just that one moment, when Steve glanced at the butt end, when Frank lunged at him, punching him so hard in the stomach and chest that he fell backwards across the table and, thrashing to save himself, the beer can caught his face and neck and he lay on the floor, blood flowing. He held his neck, groaning, the blood oozing between his fingers. And Frank stood there.

'Don't leave me like this, mate.' It was a whimper now.

Frank returned to the bedrooms, zipped shut the cases and, stepping over him, walked out of the flat back to Kitty and the kid. He didn't know whether to call an ambulance or not; if he did, the police were bound to be involved. And then?

What he wanted was to leave him to die, wanted him erased from their lives for ever. With the police? He could be done for GBH or manslaughter, even, depending. Like father, like son. Would he end up in prison too?

He stood at the corner of the road, put down the cases, took out his phone, dialled 999 and asked for an ambulance. It was urgent. A man had cut himself and was bleeding badly.

Only after they heard the ambulance hoot, the police cars whine and Dave had come back asking why the area was being cordoned off, that there were police everywhere, did Frank say in answer to his question, 'There was an accident and I called for an ambulance.'

Kitty was upstairs with the kid, quite excitedly, he thought, unpacking the suitcases. Certainly, Daisy's high-pitched delight filled the upstairs landing, especially when she saw her little pushchair, which he had managed to carry back on his shoulder, like a shoulder bag.

Yvonne had sat down on the settee with her hands over her mouth and Dave stood facing him. 'What sort of accident?'

No one was surprised when the police, a man and a woman, stood outside the door, introducing themselves like friendly neighbours; the male, PC Duncan, the woman, PC Talbert, asking Dave if they could come in, if he was the man who called the ambulance.

Kitty and Daisy were upstairs, Yvonne rigid on the settee and Dave flustered, his face red and damp.

Frank pushed his way between Dave and the police saying, 'It was me who made the call.'

'Frank Richardson?'

'Yes.'

'Frank Richardson,' said PC Talbert, 'we would like you to accompany us to the station to answer some questions and to help us with our enquires into Mr Steve Cook's accident. He gave us your name. Is that all right, sir?'

They were so polite. But he knew it was just a trap; they had already made up their minds to charge him with GBH or murder or manslaughter if Steve died. They didn't say and so he asked, 'Is he OK?' to which they replied that he'd been taken to hospital, but they had no further information at the moment.

'He battered his wife and child. You might like to know that. They came here last night. For safety from him. She's all bruised and the child's arm is broken. Perhaps you'd like to know that too.' Yvonne stood in the doorway, all nerves seemingly gone, and she was angry.

The police glanced briefly at each other; it was obvious that this was news to them.

The woman said, 'We're sending other officers round for you to talk to. Please stay here, all of you, for the time being, until we get someone round. Just until we've taken your statements. We'll get in touch with someone straight away. PC Duncan will make the call now.' And with that, Duncan went outside and Frank saw him on his phone.

The woman said to him. 'If you could get your coat, then, sir. None of this should take too long.' But she didn't fool him, not for one moment. He was going to be like Dad. In prison. He could see it as clear a day.

At least he wasn't handcuffed, but gently guided into the back of the waiting police car. He thought, as they drove on, if they don't get me for this, they'll get me for something . . . stealing the library books, the green vase, the men's-only mags from the top shelves he was too ashamed to buy openly. I'm a thief. There was a criminal gene in his family. No escaping, however hard he tried.

No one spoke, and he was back in the shed that night, helpless as his bike was smashed to pieces.

When the police told him that they would need at least another week to complete their enquiries and would need to know where to get hold of them, he decided, with Kitty, to go and stay with Ruby and Stan, if they could. The police were satisfied with that, taking the address, telephone number and his passport, instructing him to report to the Doncaster police station the following Monday.

He was going to try to make it seem like a holiday for all of them. Kitty had not visited since Daisy was born and Ruby yelled with delight when he asked her if they could bring Daisy to meet them. And Daisy was excited too.

They looked older. Stan had shrunk a bit, which made his nose seem even longer, and his knuckles were swollen with arthritis, but this didn't keep him away from his beloved shed. He was still making or mending for neighbours when he could.

Ruby cried. She was so overjoyed to see them and it was only minutes before Daisy was on her lap eating chocolate biscuits! Some things never change. But she was swollen more than ever, and breathless, needed a Zimmer frame around the house. If they went out, to church or the shops, Stan or a neighbour pushed her in her wheelchair, which had been provided by social services. On the whole, Frank had nothing good to feel about social services – too many memories, that dreadful Sonia, who he'd hated so much – but he had to admit they seemed to be taking good care of Ruby and Stan. A one-bedroomed flat had been reserved for them in a new residential home, which was not yet quite completed. Still waiting for fixtures and fittings apparently, but they could visit anyway and this afternoon they were going to go, all of them. He would push Ruby. Stan would stumble along independently as usual, and Kitty would walk beside him. Daisy, he guessed, would skip beside Ruby's wheelchair, holding her hand. She loved Ruby.

But it was more difficult than he had anticipated, hard to keep the truth from them, hard to hide stuff. He hadn't enjoyed persuading Daisy to tell a porky – Kitty's word – about her accident. 'We don't want to worry them and spoil our holiday, do we? So just say you tripped over a toy.' She was a good kid and did just that when, naturally, Ruby asked, 'How did you hurt yourself, pet?' But each time he had to turn away, ashamed of the lie.

They'd done all they could to treat them, bringing home meals – even Kitty did some cooking – took them to the park, to the shops, but there were limits to what they could do. And Kitty was a problem, often in her room, where he knew she was crying. They were bound to notice and wonder. He was constantly anxious.

He decided he had to get out on his own, said he needed a bit of fresh air and a stroll around. He wandered round some of his old haunts; the hairdresser was still there, bringing back memories. And the pub, as garish as before, the newsagent's, where he had stolen stuff, and the library. He daren't go in; Jeanette could still work there; she might ask him about the books. He couldn't resist going into the church to inspect the pew-end again; the last time was when he had come to say goodbye before going to Italy. Over three years! It was still in place and looking pretty good. It hadn't been a bad job, considering. In rhythmic movements, he rubbed his hand over the smooth, glossy piece he had carved so carefully, in a kind of unacknowledged ritualistic prayer that everything would be all right. A prayer to Ruby.

He'd been angry the last time he'd been here. This time he was frightened as well as angry. Yet in Italy, his hurt and anger

282

had, as it were, been absorbed, dissipated by the warmth and the peace he experienced there. Even more so since he had been building the studio for Alice. One day he would take her out in his boat.

He wandered onto the green and sat down. It was the same bench and, across the road, the launderette; the blue plastic baskets changed to pink. Made him think about Julie. She was an OK girl. Perhaps she would have been all right. He didn't know. He didn't know anything much about that. And the kid, Kevin? He'd be almost ready to leave school, if he hadn't already. He wondered what he'd end up doing and, stupidly, if he still had the garage he'd made for all his Dinky cars. And Julie, she was all right.

The green was unkept as ever but for the new swings and a slide, where now some teenagers were messing about, and the bandstand had been painted green. But the grass was still thin and patchy, and the concrete paths cracked and uneven.

He was trying to keep calm, trying to be strong beneath the unthinkable: that he might, after all, end up in prison.

The whole police thing could have been interesting if it had involved someone else. As it was, it was shaming. They'd written up their statements, taken photographs of Kitty's bruising and Daisy's arm. Verified facts from the hospital. One thing, though, Dave, and particularly Yvonne, had vouched for Steve's violent behaviour. He kept reassuring himself, as he was thinking it all through again, that forensics had determined that Steve had cut himself in falling and that only his fingerprints were on the can, it had been accepted, so far, that Frank was defending himself from a 'vicious attack' – their words. He remembered quite clearly. In any case, the blood tests they took showed Steve was full of drugs and alcohol. So he should be in the clear and they could never know that he might well have killed him. How easy it would have been? Wanted to kill him as much as he'd wanted to kill Carl. But it was the waiting. Waiting.

He leaned forward and, folding his arms, pushed clenched fists under his armpits. He must have looked as if he were in pain or something. Now he released his arms and, straightening himself, checked round to see if the teenagers were looking at him and thinking him odd.

He'd been right to take a stroll; it had refreshed him, lessened the anxiety, and now he was in control of himself and ready to go back to them.

# Frank

*A few days later*

He needed a drink! He needed something. For the relief ... the relief. He had had all his documents returned by the police. He was free.

Kitty had cried when they said goodbye to Yvonne, who insisted they let her know their new address and telephone number. 'We'll still keep in touch, Kit. You can come and stay. Or I to you. Give me a break from the rest.' And then they both laughed.

They had told Stan and Ruby as little as possible: only that Kitty was leaving Steve because of his drinking and gambling and that she and Daisy would be living with Frank. Ruby looked worried at first, but Stan had muttered to him that he'd never trusted Steve anyway. Something about his eyes. 'Better off with you, by far. You'll take good care, lad. No doubts in my mind.' And now, having left them down south, they were on their way from Doncaster to Darlington.

There was something calming about the rhythmic throbbing of the train. He couldn't get three seats together, so Kitty and the girl were the other side of the aisle just behind him. He turned round to check on them. Both asleep, the kid's head rocking on her arm. He was going back to Darlington to find somewhere for them all to live. A rented house? Although he could afford to buy, he needed to find something as quickly as possible, so renting, for the time being, seemed the sensible option. And he hadn't forgotten his promise to Alice to return to finish the studio as soon as he could. He guessed she would be waiting to hear from him, but for the moment the right thing to do was to concentrate on getting them settled; give them security, away from that bastard, that awful life. He hoped it would be exciting for them, would cheer Kitty up, give her something positive to think about, for she was depressed and crying a lot. It had been his dream for so long to make sure she would be safe and happy, and now the thought of it – well, perhaps he shouldn't be, but he was. He was happy. He tried to remember other times when he'd been happy. When his new bike arrived? When he passed his City & Guilds and could work properly for good wages? When he mended the church pew for Ruby? And, of course, building the studio for Alice. Having her around. But he was careful, and prepared he thought, for happiness to be shattered like a broken vase. And he'd more or less accepted that it would always be like that.

Maybe now there was just a chance, a little chance! They could be like a proper family, the three of them.

He looked behind him; they were both still asleep.

Yesterday morning, early, he had phoned as requested and heard them confirm there were no charges to answer. He was free to go and would he come and pick up his passport.

It was too late for them to travel straight on to Darlington, much as he wanted to get away from Doncaster, and so he'd booked two rooms in a Travelodge, just off the town centre, and they'd enjoyed going for fish and chips, had a laugh.

He'd left them just after eight, Kitty putting the kid and herself to bed. Both were exhausted, but the excitement, for him at least, was feeding in. He said to not open the door at all and he was going out for a bit a fresh air. He'd look in before going to bed, just to check on them. He wasn't going to be late.

He couldn't find the words to explain his relief. He was overcome. He wanted so much to share with someone who would understand. Perhaps Alice? Celebrate with Alice over a bottle of wine. He'd already allowed himself to share a little with her. Slowly. Carefully.

Doncaster city was dominated by its well-lit cathedral tower, whose long, heavily carved pinnacles pointed sharp fingers up into the evening skyline. It would be interesting to look inside, that was all. Just a brief look.

The door was still open, and a few people emerged from, he assumed, some evening service, like they had in Italy. He sat at the back and listened to the softly recorded organ music, which permeated all around.

Perhaps it was his unexpected joy that broke him, but his shoulders shuddered as he bent over. Just the music and his shaking.

1990–1991

# Frank

They took a taxi to his old digs. Mrs Mackie had agreed to have them 'for old time's sake', although she had, she said, given up lodgers. But to help them out and if the child was no trouble. Just for a short stay, then. The breathy giggle was still there.

He had the same room and stared for a second at the thread-bare patch of carpet where he had smashed the vase. Kitty and Daisy had to share a bed in the other room. 'It won't be long, Kit,' he told her at breakfast. 'I'm off today to find us something.'

First he took them the short walk to the shops and the park, where there was a well-kitted-out play area for kids. Not like the poor swings and slides at home. Funny he should still think of it as home. This play area was brightly coloured, looked new, with slides and roundabout, swings – double and single – and a climbing frame. The whole area was surrounded by benches for the adults, grandparents, mostly. There was a lot of screaming and laughing and warning shouts as adult hands reached and stretched, holding and guiding the small children. Daisy was excited and Kitty cheered up too. He gave her money for lunch out and told her to get back to the house not too late. They could watch TV in the sitting room. He was going to the estate agents and the bike-hire place so he could get around quickly and independently. He'd find them somewhere good, if not today, then by tomorrow, for sure. 'Cheer up, Kit. It'll all turn out right.'

Afterwards, he thought how extraordinary it was, how things sometimes just turn up, and how, if someone told you, you'd suspect they were making it up. He could hear Alice's laughing, 'I don't believe it, Frank. It's unbelievable.'

He was motoring on the hired motorbike towards Glynton Estate Agent, papers stuffed in his jacket pocket: a terraced house, just two bedrooms, not ideal, but for rent immediately, so he was going to view.

The area was familiar, but he couldn't remember why. When had he ever been here before? It was a country road with scattered houses either side and, beyond, grassy meadows, fringed by hills, smudged with heather and sheep. It was the house on his left, and the entrance he remembered. He stopped, got off the bike and went over to the gate. The house, double-fronted and in the grey stone of the Dales, and the courtyard with barns to the side. Bloody hell! This is where he'd bought his bike! Learned to ride it round the courtyard! He smiled wryly to himself. The memory of the sudden independence, the freedom.

'Hi there! Can I help?'

She was a plump young woman with short black hair dyed with red streaks, great dangly earrings, bright-red lipstick and a wide smile. She'd come out of the house and was walking his way with manly strides, broken by an odd hop.

He jumped back from the gate. 'Sorry, No, it's OK.'

Now she was leaning on the gate towards him, her hands smothered in rings. Every finger. Still smiling.

'Sorry, no ... it's just, I was passing and, well ... this is where I bought a motorbike. Long time ago, though!'

She laughed and gave and another odd skip on the spot. 'My bike. Good God! That was my bike. Not that one.' And she flapped a hand towards his hired Honda. 'I'm Jo. Daughter to them indoors!' She thumbed back to the house.

And he remembered.

'I thought you'd moved to London. Jewellery?' And he pointed to the rings.

She laughed again and put her hands behind her back in mock shame.

'True.' she nodded. 'It's still true. Just home to see Mam and Dad. Keep my beady eye on what they're up to, you know. What brings you this way? No more bikes here now!' she joked.

He left out most of it, but explained he was going to see a house to let in the village. He took the details out of his pocket and opened them. 'Do you know where it is, exactly? Not far from here, I think. Bit nearer the village?'

She took the details from him. 'Crikey! Yes, we all know that one!'

'Not good, then?'

She shook her head. 'Landlord's a bit of a bastard ... over repairs and things. Got a bit of a reputation.'

She handed him back the paper. 'But hey! Hang on a minute. Hang on, will you?' She turned back to the house calling, 'Da! Dad!' and, as she reached the front door, the man appeared. He was older, walked with a limp now, but he recognised Mr Wilkinson. Still a big man, tousled hair and bearded. She was gabbling excitedly as she held his arm, telling him, 'He bought my bike, Dad. You sold him my bike!' and she did that odd skip and laughed. He felt foolish, standing there, the other side of the gate, like something on show. He couldn't understand what was going on. What she was so excited about?

Mr Wilkinson opened the gate and held out his hand. 'It's some years, but I remember you. Green behind the ears when it came to the bike. But you picked it up quick enough. Don't suppose the old thing is still on the road. Is this the replacement?' He didn't seem impressed and Frank explained that he'd hired it so he could get around to . . .

'What's your name again?'

'He's looking to rent a place, Da. God, he's going to look at Bert's. Look!' She took the details from him and poked a finger at them. 'You know what I'm thinking?' And they gave each other knowing looks before she asked, 'What do you think?'

He felt left out of this conversation and time was going on; he had to be on his way, or he would be late for his appointment. He stretched his arm out of his jacket to look at his watch.

'Sorry! What did you say your name was?

'Frank Richardson.'

'Aye, that's it. Well, Frank Richardson, you bought a bike from us, so how about looking at our cottage? Stranger things, as they say.'

'I'll take you.' Her voice was loud with excitement. 'It's only just a few hundred yards. Key in the usual place, Da?'

'Look, mind,' he explained, 'it's only a farm cottage, which we've let as a holiday place for years, but we're getting too old for all the changeover work and, well, we just want rid of it now, rent permanently, or sell, even. We've not yet decided either way, but you're more than welcome to take a look. Take him over, then, lass.'

Jo, was already through the gate and marching onwards along the road, waving him on to follow her.

'Don't go badgering him now. He's got a mind of his own.' Tom Wilkinson shouted from the gate.

The place stood directly onto the road and beside a narrow drive leading to a gate that opened onto fields behind the cottage. The front door was on the side, which Jo opened with the key hidden on a beam inside the overhanging porch. It all needed work. He could see that at once and wondered what state the interior would be in.

She was still talking as she opened the door. 'It's all furnished. Not great, but it's all here for the moment. If you're in a hurry. I think you said you were in a kind of hurry.'

He was used to taking things in: a fireplace on the facing wall; on the left a glass door leading into the kitchen; a sofa covered in a sort of brown corduroy; baggy armchairs, odd lamps, one with a brown stain. The place was carpeted and there was a long-tasselled rust-coloured rug in front of the fireplace. The kitchen had a table in the middle, four 1930's chairs, solid wood; he could work with those. Pots and pans hung around and there was brown-and-white pottery. She opened a drawer to show some mixed-up cutlery. Again, old fashioned and in need of a good shine-up. There was a door from the kitchen into a small garden that was separated from the meadows beyond by a drystone wall.

'There's a brook where those trees are.' She was pointing out of the kitchen window.

He immediately thought of the kid when he saw the horses, a chestnut and a grey, munching the grass. He knew nothing about horses, but was sure Daisy, even Kitty, would like them a lot. This place was growing on him.

'Two of ours,' she was saying. 'We still do livery, but have given up the riding school. Can't get the help and it's too much for them, but we have up to six livery, and fantastic Laura to take care of them, but she needs help sometimes and the parents are scared stiff she'll leave. It's so difficult to get people these days; everyone wants to go into the city, if you see what I mean. Like Durham or Darlington, even.'

He followed her upstairs. The largest bedroom overlooked the road. The other two, one not much more than a box room, had windows on to back garden. The bathroom and toilet, all in one, was in the middle of the landing between the bedrooms. It was pretty rough-looking.

'Not ideal,' she was saying, 'but I think there's lots that could be done. Thing is, we haven't done anything much for years. Just holiday lets if and when.' She was looking at him. 'What do you think, then? Is it any good for you, for the moment, at least? I think we'd love to have you here.'

He didn't understand why she should say that. He could be anyone. 'Let me talk to your father. Just one or two things.'

They were in the sitting room watching some cartoon thing, Daisy sitting cross-legged on the floor in front of the small TV, Kitty curled up in a corner of the sofa. She had obviously been crying again.

Why the bloody hell couldn't she make a bit more effort? It was disappointing and he was sick of it. 'I've got somewhere,' he announced. 'Somewhere I can rent for the moment. But if you like it, Kit, I can buy it.' He sat on one of the hard chairs and put his head in his hands.

'Things turn up,' he muttered.

'What?'

'I said, things turn up.' And he told her about the cottage and also about a barn Tom Wilkinson had offered him to rent as a workshop, so he could begin to build up his own business. 'He's been very kind, actually. Very helpful. Not sure why, but anyway . . . and, Kit, the village, which is just up the road, has nice little shops, a pub, a church.' He hesitated and tried a grin. 'And, Kit, there's a primary school, next village down. With a school bus collects all the kids, apparently. Couldn't be better, I don't think. Couldn't be better, for my money. We'll go tomorrow, all of us. See what you think. What do you think?' He bent down to Daisy, 'Guess what? As your Mam would say.'

She looked at him and then scrabbled up onto the sofa. 'What?'

'There's horses outside the back. In a field outside. At the back.'

'Horses,' she screamed and pulled at Kitty's arm, 'Horses! Dad likes horses, doesn't he, Mam? He loves them.' She grinned up at Frank and curled an arm round Kitty's neck. 'Don't be sad, Mam. We're going to see horses.'

'We'll all go tomorrow,' he repeated, ignoring Kitty. Why the hell couldn't she, just for once, put on a brave face for the kid ... and, well, for all of them. Everyone, in their own way, had to put on brave faces. That was fucking life. It made him angry because today had been magic, really. Something was looking out for them. Later he would phone Alice and let her know what was happening. She would have to wait a few more weeks while they settled in before he returned to finish the studio for her. But talking to her would be a good end to a good day.

Jo came over, as she had done over the last weeks, to see how they were settling in. She hugged Kitty like an old friend and lifted Daisy high above her head with a whoop, Daisy kicking and laughing.

'We're doing fine,' he replied.

'Yes! It's really OK. We like it a lot.' Kitty was for once making an effort, but she looked pale and tired. 'We got all new bed stuff like you said, didn't we, Frank? Daisy! Why don't you take Jo up and show her? It's all balloons,' she added and managed a smile. 'The patterns on her bed stuff. We're going to get curtains to match.'

Jo followed Daisy, who was already running up the stairs.

Kitty followed him into the kitchen, where he was filling the kettle. He knew what she was going to say. 'I'll only be gone the one night, Frankie. Can't you see I need to see him? I'm sorry, Frankie, but I've phoned Von about staying with her. She'll be OK about that.'

He wanted to shake her. He wanted to slap her. 'Do you know what, Kitty? You're a bloody fool. Anyway, I've said all I'm going to say. Just think about your kid, Just for once. She's not safe with him. I'm not sure I care about you any more, Kitty, if he beats you up, if that's what you want, but Daisy's not going back if I have to go to court over it. But have your own way again, like you always do. Go to Doncaster. Stay with Yvonne and may it do you good. Now, shut up about it. I've had enough.'

He slammed down the kettle and walked out of the back door into the overgrown garden. Kicking at the long grass.

He was out there some time, leaning over the wall at the bottom, watching the horses. He could hear the splash of water from the beck across the field. He would take Daisy to explore sometime. Look for tiddlers. But for now, he was trying to calm his rage. Surely she wouldn't go back to him. He was running his hand across his head, thinking, when he heard them, Daisy dragging Jo by the hand, talking non-stop.

'OK if I take her home to see the horses?' Jo was saying. 'Are you coming to work in the barn today? Dad enjoys having you around.'

'Later,' he said. 'You two go on. Does she need a coat?' he added. It wasn't the first time that he realised how little he knew about kids. He'd learn. The way things were going, he might be a single parent.

'Oh, by the way,' Jo called back, 'Kitty looks as if she needs cheering up, so I said I'd take her to the pub this evening. That OK? We'll not be late.'

He'd done with worrying. No more energy and Jo was pretty sensible, he thought, and they were grown-us, after all, and Kitty had to have a life. She wasn't his prisoner.

He walked slowly back to the house, wanting to be back in Italy, in his boat on the lake, in the warmth, free and at peace. Alice nearby.

Kitty was on the phone, standing by the front window with her back to him. Everything was silent. She wasn't speaking, just standing there with the phone halfway to her ear, her dark hair pushed back. Suddenly, she turned and with a howl cast the phone across the room. It landed at his feet.

'Don't come near me,' her voice dark and threatening. 'Don't come near me.'

Then she sank onto the floor and he stood there waiting. Saying nothing.

She looked up at him, staring straight into his eyes, defiant. 'Well done! You fucking win. You fucking win. HA, HA, HA, and hoo-bloody-ray for you.'

Still he said nothing.

'I'm not going.' He'd not heard her voice like that before. 'Von says he's not there any more.' There was a pause. Then the shouting. 'He's fucking moved in with some bloody old whore.' Now she was yelling. 'It didn't take him long to find someone else to shag.' She threw a cushion across the floor. 'And I tell you what? I'm bloody fucking well having a night out.'

'Fine!' he said. 'Jo told me.' He didn't say he was sorry for her, because he knew well the response he would get. And it wouldn't be true. He was not sorry. He was bloody relieved and, frankly, delighted. At last . . . after all these years.

That evening, after they'd had gone down the road to the village pub and Daisy was in bed – he actually managed a story – he phoned Alice. She had laughed and reminded him of the time difference, saying she was ready for bed. He pretended not to hear the pleasure in her voice and concentrated on filling her in on the barest details, saying he would tell more another time but was sorry he couldn't be over just yet, as he wanted Kitty and Daisy to settle down in their new home before he left them. But, as soon as ever, he'd be over to finish off the work in the studio and, while he was there, he'd have to pack up as much of his stuff as he could, ready to be transported back home, or he'd try to sell some of the tools. Anyway, he'd decide all that, when he was over there. And how was she? How were the paintings coming along.?

'Are you're leaving us for good, then, Frank?'

The tone of her voice was flat but, pretending not to notice, he carried on, 'Can't leave them, you see. Have to stay and try to build a business here.' He kept talking to avoid the sadness in her voice. He just couldn't do anything about that. He told her about the offer of the barn as a workshop.

'What about your precious boat, then? It's done up so well.'

'Yep. Well, have to sell it, of course. But I can get another. We're close enough to the sea here.'

'Oh Frank. Isn't it strange you're so close to Da and the beach we always went to? I'll have to go home to see Da soon, anyway. Maybe we could meet up.'

Her voice was picking up. He wanted her to be happy, but she was married and not his responsibility.

'How are things at home? Your ma? How is he coping these days?'

She told him that Ma didn't really know Da sometimes, but he still went to see her every day. Alistair went once a month and Da knew he could always rely on him; otherwise, stubborn and independent, he didn't ask for any help. Old friends were company when he saw them on the allotments. He enjoyed that. And his motorbikes, when he had time.

Frank heard the crack in her voice. 'I'm selfish,' she said. 'I love it here in the warmth . . . for my . . . condition, you know. I don't go back as much as I should.'

'Well, you can change all that, if you want to, Alice, if you feel you should. Perhaps you should . . . go back a bit more. Up to you.' He had enough to think about just now.

'But now you're there, Frank . . . well, perhaps.' She didn't finish. 'Henry has been several times since you've been away, and I think Max and co. may be descending again next week and they're bringing his Aunt Lola. She's a character. I like her a lot. So does Henry. Even you'd be at ease with Lola. It will be chaotic and I get tired. But I'm painting.'

'The pebbles?'

'Trying, but ...' There was a hesitation. 'I'm just long-ing ... well, you know, Frank. I don't have to say.'

'I'll ring again,' he said. 'I'll come over as soon as I can.'

Watching, from the kitchen window, the rain spitting off the stone wall was calming. Alice had seemed happy to hear him; he should have phoned her sooner.

He hadn't waited up for Kitty as he knew that she would be so annoyed, but he had lain awake waiting. He heard the door and their voices, quite soft; he didn't think she was drunk. He hoped going out would have put her in a better frame of mind after the scene earlier.

He was rinsing some plates, the drying-up cloth over his shoulder, when he heard Daisy go into the bathroom. She didn't shut the door and so he heard the trickles into the pan, then her feet across the little space to Kitty. The kid was talking and then laughing. There was a shout. Frank put the cereal and milk on the table ready. Coco Pops. There was another shout, sort of angry, and then a whine. She wanted something.

Standing with his hands on the back of a chair, he waited and listened, then called, 'Daisy!' Then at the bottom of the stairs. 'Daisy! Let Mum sleep. Your breakfast's ready.'

There was another shout in temper, frustration, and Daisy came stomping down the stairs, jumping off the bottom step as usual.

'Mam won't wake up, Fwank.'

'She's just tired. Come on, have your Coco Pops. She'll be down in a minute.'

She sat on her chair, legs swinging, 'But she won't wake up. She's all funny.'

'Funny?' He was pouring the cereal into a brown bowl, 'You're funny.' And he touched the top of her head. 'Let's go and see anyway if she wants a cup of tea.'

He tapped on the open door before going in. 'Kitty! Kit!?'

And there he was, the ten-year-old boy staring at the closed eyes, the spittle in the corner of the mouth, the arms splayed out, the hanging hand.

While Daisy was finishing her Coco Pops, he phoned for Jo to come quick. Then 999.

He didn't think the kid would have understood anything, yet she started towards the stairs. He grabbed her. 'Mum's not well. You stay here.' And she began to cry.

He tried to keep still by folding his arms tightly and pushing his clenched fists into his armpits, then pushed his hands into his pockets. Fidgeting. Bending over, he held his head in his hands. And again. Finally, he got up and walked up and down the corridor. And again. A repeated ritual. The mind was blank, the shivering uncontrolled, treading water.

What goes round comes round. And he'd tried so hard to break the circle. Pretty, laughing Mum, snakes curling round Carl's arms, and Kitty. Helpless. Dad. The smashed bike. Dad's bike. Smashed. And the smell of linseed oil in the shed. The ant on the lino. The biscuit tin.

He stretched his arms behind his head, folded his arms in preparation, his hands in his pockets, and another walk, and nurses and doctors passing him but not the right ones. He couldn't remember the door she had been taken through. To find her. He had to find her. He wanted to bang on the doors. He had to be there.

He searched for Ruby's God. For Ruby, then for Stan. There must be someone.

He was counting his long strides down the corridor when someone called his name. 'Mr Richardson?' and all he could do was just stand there and wait for them to tell him.

A hand touched his shoulder. 'Mr Richardson?'

'Yes.'

'Everything's under control. Fortunately, she didn't take enough . . . she'll be fine.' The doctor went on about draining and clearing out and transfusion and sleep. But he was leaning against the wall pushing his fists into his eyes.

'When you're ready, Mr Richardson.' A hand touched his shoulder.' You can see her for a minute or two, but she's very sleepy.'

'Five minutes,' he said and, turning his back, walked away down the corridor towards the exit.

Outside, in the shadows he blew his nose and scrubbed his eyes dry, frustrated that they had seen him like that. He didn't let people see things like that. Not ever. Never. He pushed back his hair, smoothed his fringe, put the handkerchief away and concentrated on his long strides, straight back, focused eyes that preserved him so well.

There were two doctors talking, secretively. They nodded and one led him to a door at the end of the corridor.

The doctor opened the door and then left him, but a nurse was there fiddling with a tube.

Kitty was watching, her eyes closing every so often. He stood by the bed. When she turned and saw him, her eyes streamed as she whispered, 'I'm sorry, Frankie. Please, Frankie, I'm so, so sorry.'

His voice was gruff. The nurse looked at him in surprise. 'Don't talk. Get some sleep. I'll see you tomorrow.'

Although he had closed the kitchen door, he could hear their voices: the two mental health nurses and Kitty. They had visited every day since she came home and he could tell that she looked forward to seeing them. He could hear her voice, quite strong, quite cheery at times. Sometimes they allowed Daisy to be with them as they chatted. He wasn't good at chatting.

He realised that although she suspected Steve was cheating on her, the shock of learning that he had actually shacked up with someone else was the last straw for Kitty. He understood that. Yet he was angry with her. He'd asked about the tablets, where did she get them. She'd had them all the time, from the flat, hidden away. She tried to explain, 'I just wanted to escape my feelings, Frank. I just wanted a long sleep to get away from the feelings.' And then kept repeating how sorry she was. How she would never be such a silly cow again.

'It's not a matter of just being a silly cow, Kitty. It's much more than that. It's selfish, Kitty, very selfish. Did you stop for one second to think about Daisy?' Fearing that somehow he was to blame, if he had given her the support she needed. He would try harder to understand the person she was, try to accept she had her own life to live. She did not belong to him.

In the meantime, they had prescribed mild antidepressants, which he had to keep for her, giving her one every morning. He kept them in his pockets all the time, just in case.

Then a lady, Susan Radcliffe, some kind of child therapist, came to visit Daisy. They drew pictures together and the woman showed Daisy drawings and then asked questions. Once he heard her ask, 'Would you like to write a letter to your dad? I can write it down for you if you want to, or you can draw him a picture. Your dad loves you very much because you're a lovely person, but your dad isn't very well and can't look after you any more, or your mum. But he loves you.'

Daisy chose to draw a picture. He watched through the slightly opened kitchen door, intrigued and thinking that they didn't do things like this when he and Kitty were kids. There were no Susan Radcliffe's for them, and he wondered if it would have made any difference.

'It's the horse,' and she pointed towards the kitchen and the garden, 'out there in the field.' Then, deeply concentrating, 'Some trees.' Her head was bent over the paper as she scribbled with the crayons. 'And lots of blue sky.'

'Blue sky?' the lady had said. 'That's good, it must be sunny then.'

Daisy held up the drawing for the lady to admire. 'It's very sunny,' she said.

And that was it! He had decided that, when the mental

health team agreed, he was going to take them with him to Italy. Kit badly needed a break. Get some colour into her face. And the kid deserved some fun. Escape from all the drama. He had his place to go to and, he was sure – hoped, anyway – that Alice would let Kitty and Daisy stay with her while he finished off the work on her studio. Then he would have to pack up his stuff ready for returning home. It would take a few weeks and he was looking forward to them all being together. To hear some laughter. To see Alice smile. And remembered the time he first met her, when she walked towards him beside the lake wall, wearing her floppy straw hat. She was as fair-haired as Kitty was dark.

He would be sorry to say goodbye but comforted himself with the knowledge that he could always go come back for holidays. Perhaps he wouldn't sell his boat.

But he was here now and must get up to the barn to finish the workbench. It was going to be a busy day one way and another.


The wood had been delivered, planks of oak, ready cut for his bench top. He had the legs, tongue and grooved, prepared and knew he would get it completed by the end of the afternoon, leaving him time to look for a suitable van; he'd sell the one in Italy. Tom Wilkinson had recommended someone he knew. So now he must get on and it occurred to him as he was working that, up until now, benches had always been provided for him. Now, making one especially for himself, to his specification, exactly as he wanted, was giving him unexpected pleasure. Here he was, independent after nearly twenty years, and recalled Stan's, 'Be your own boss, lad, and you'll never go short. You don't want any bloody bosses breathing down your neck, take it from me,' and, grinning inside himself, breathed out. 'What a great little man.'

He was placing the planks in position on the floor ready to fix the legs when Tom appeared between the open doors.

'Everything all right, Frank? I see you got the wood.' And he walked over to examine the work, nodding with a grin. 'You've managed with what tools I had, then?'

He was glad Tom had appeared, because there was something he wanted to talk to him about.

'The tools are good, thanks. And thanks for the loan. I'll have my own once I get them back from Italy, but 'til then, well, these are fine. But now you're here, I wanted to ask you, Tom – any chance I could put in a couple of windows? All my expense, of course. The light's not that good. Any chance?'

He watched as Tom studied up and down, arms folded. Thinking.

'I'm happy to pay more rent.' He was desperate for windows. So he persisted.

'I think a window there,' and he pointed towards the side behind the bench and then turning round, 'and over there, opposite. I reckon about six by five at least, to make it worthwhile.'

Tom began strolling around; it wasn't a big barn, more like a very large shed, all wooden with a slate roof. There was one bare bulb hanging in the middle.

'Structure take it, you think?'

'No problem. It's sound enough. I've had a good look at it all. May have to replace the odd beam eventually, but it's fine at the moment.'

And he waited. In his mind he had it all planned out: where the machine tools would go, where any spare wood. He would build a platform with a pulley to store wood up in the roof. But he must have more light. Yes, he had it planned. At night, he'd been thinking of nothing else. It was going to be quite a different thing, working for himself. He had to make a success of it.

'You know, never thought of it before – suppose we had no need. But now you mention it, I think it would be a grand improvement. Very good idea. I'm quite relaxed about it. If you're sure then about the structure. Anyway, I'll take your word for it.'

'I'll pay you more rent,' he repeated.

Tom was looking from side to side, probably imagining the windows. 'We can talk about that another time,' he said.

A car pulled into the yard; it was Laura, come for her daily routine working with the horses. 'Can't get here until after nine,' she'd told Frank. 'I always drop the boys off first,' adding, 'it's the school bus drops them off here after school, you will have noticed. Your Daisy seems to enjoy "the big boys", as she calls them. She's cute, that kid. We'll have to have her round for tea sometime. And Kitty. You're welcome, of course.' That offer was definitely an afterthought, he reckoned.

'She enjoys having your sister around,' Tom was saying. 'Company for her. And help. She's getting quite handy with those horses. How is she, by the way?'

All this was difficult for him, talking about Kitty. 'She's getting well settled, thanks.' He didn't add 'I think'. He didn't say, 'Well, you can never be sure with Kitty,' but went on as positively as he could, 'and it's good for her to make friends. She's missing friends, so being here with Laura, they seem to be getting on well. I'll let you know in good time, but I'm thinking of taking them with me to Italy when I go back. Got a job to finish there. Give them a bit of a holiday. Get some Italian sun in their cheeks. They'll be up later. I hope you don't mind the kid around, but she loves it up here.'

'That's all right, Frank, that Daisy's no trouble to us and the dog gets lots of exercise, that's for sure!' And he was laughing as he turned to go. 'So I'll let you get on – just ask if there's anything I can do. I'll go and say good morning to Laura now.'

'Will only be this summer,' he called after him, 'because she starts school in September. We went to the open day last week to show her around and meet the teachers.'

At that school, a different sort of pride, special, when he

307

walked into the classroom with Kitty and Daisy, wanting everyone to think he was her father. But Kit was quick enough to always say, 'And this is her uncle Frank, my brother. We're staying with him for the time being.' Staying, not living with, he noticed. Once she added, 'Until we get our own place.'

For the Dales it was a warm afternoon and flies scattered in the roof beams. He could hear Kitty and Laura as they worked in the yard and the clink of hooves on the paving and Daisy, who had been playing with the cats, was now skipping round the yard with the retriever on his lead, which the Wilkinsons kindly supplied for her, although the dog had no need of it at all. It made Frank want to laugh. The kid always became hyper waiting for Laura's boys to arrive; they were older but were tolerant enough and if at all impatient, Daisy did not notice. She had a lot of her mother in her.

Now she came hurrying into his place with the dog. Stood for a moment before pointing up to cobwebs in the roof. 'Guess what's over there, Fwank? What are those things?'

'Cobwebs! You know that. Spiders make them for catching flies.'

But she had skipped out into the light, calling, 'When will the bus be here?'

Later that afternoon he set off on his hired motorbike, money drawn from the bank in two envelopes inside his leather jacket. If you had cash you got a better deal; he understood that.

He knew Crook well, of course, and enjoyed the ride through the Dales, remembering the freedom he experienced those years ago when he bought his first bike. Mrs Mackie had been good to allow him to leave it down her side alley as she did. Had he appeared grateful? He couldn't remember.

The garage was two miles outside Crook, a jumble of sheds, random cars outside and a couple of petrol pumps. It didn't look very promising.

A man wearing a blue overall and rolling a tyre in front

of him appeared from an open shed door. He stopped when he saw Frank, propped the tyre against the door and nodded. 'How do?' He looked at the bike. 'We don't do bikes, mun,' and then, 'Oh! You Tom's man, are you? I should've known. Looking for a van, I hear.'

'Correct.'

'You a carpenter, I hear.' He gave a shout of laughter and pointed to the sheds. 'These could do with a shake-up, don't you think?'

'Just a bit.'

The man laughed again and called behind him. 'Gary! Get out here, mun. Tell him about that van you repaired for Jimmy.' Then he turned back to Frank. 'Jimmy's van is a good one and we did it up fine for him and then, silly bugger, he went and had a stroke. Can't drive any more. So, van's for sale.'

'When can I see it?'

The man looked at Gary and raised his eyebrows. 'You could run it over tonight, couldn't you? To the Wilkinsons', so he can take a look. Or tomorrow?'

Frank studied the younger man's face. For a moment he looked reluctant, but then nodded. 'OK then. I'll be there about six this evening. OK?'

Kitty and Daisy were more excited about him buying a van than he was, insisting they had an early supper so that they could all go back to the farm in time for the van to arrive.

But it was already there, waiting. You couldn't miss it — sky blue, black upholstery, room enough for three and two doors at the back. A Ford Transit. He didn't mind the colour and was already imagining the lettering on either side. In black? In a darker blue? He wasn't sure, but it would be Frank Richardson, Cabinetmaker. He wondered if he could put an address – Wear Farm, or perhaps his home phone number. But it was impossible to think now, as the chap Gary was waiting to talk to him, and Daisy and Kitty were disturbing everyone with their chatter and excitement, already sitting in the front, fiddling with windows and compartments. Tom came out to inspect, shook Gary's hand and asked after the man, Jimmy, who had had the stroke. 'Sorry to hear about that. Quite a shock.'

'Can we have a drive?' Kitty was calling through the window; they'd made themselves comfortable already. Of course, he'd have to have it. He knew that.

'Is it OK to take it out for a short run?' he asked.

'Key's still in the ignition,' Gary replied. 'It's only done thirty-three thousand. Goes well. But just a quick one.'

'If you want it,' Tom was saying, 'you can park it here 'til you've got the insurance sorted.'

He got into the driving seat and drove them a mile down the road and back. When they moaned and pleaded for a longer go in it, he said, 'Can't do more now, but a long ride tomorrow, when I've got the insurance sorted. I shouldn't really be doing this but . . .'

'Promise?

'Promise a good long tour around tomorrow.'

'I love it, Frankie, and it goes like a bomb,' Kitty yelled, her hand waving back and forth out of the open window.

'Yes, 'he said, 'it goes like a bomb so I think we'll have it, shall we?'

'Yeeeeeees,' they screamed in chorus and he laughed with them.

1991–1992

# Alice

The studio was not completely finished: there were still the cupboard and shelves for her painting materials to build; the window seat had to be edged, he said, although as far as she was concerned, it was fine as it was. And there was some adjustment to the skylight window; she wasn't sure what. She bent over with a laugh to herself. He was so particular. Everything had to be perfect. Anyway, she could paint up there and felt close to him.

Now she was working on another painting for the shop: orange lilies mixed with sprigs of rosemary, just dumped, as she always did, into white pottery jug. She was getting quite a name! She shook her head as she thought about it. Unbelievable! And Angelina's friend, Sophia, who had a flower shop in Milan, had asked if Alice would paint some flowers for her to sell. In Verona! She was getting a reputation, as Henry would say, in the art world. She shook her head. Crazy! Even the other day a woman called, asking if she would paint a bowl of pink roses she wanted for a present for her sister, who loved roses.

'I'm actually making money, Da. Making money,' she had announced when she last spoke to him. And then after the call said to herself, 'Perhaps that wonderful, capable Phoebe would like to organise an exhibition for me!'

How she wanted Frank to be here to make frames for her.

He made such lovely frames: differently grained and coloured woods to complement her paintings. The frames Angelina was buying from some wholesaler at the moment were cheap-looking, Alice thought.

One painting, which she now looked at with distaste, would never deserve a frame. Her attempt at oils. White sails on a blue lake. It was laboured and ordinary and she loathed it. Oils didn't work for her. It had to be watercolours. She had been so busy keeping up with the flower paintings that she had hardly had time to work on Frank's pebble painting. She thought of it as his painting.

He'd been gone away for months and she knew so little. Surely he wouldn't let her down. Surely he would keep his promise and return and finish the work.

Henry was coming home again next week. He had to finish the black stallion commissioned by the board of governors for a retiring president. It seemed a very expensive gift to her, for Henry's work was selling for tens of thousands. This black stallion galloping along a beach, for instance. She had gone in earlier and stood looking at it, and although it was unfinished, she still marvelled at Henry's technique. There must be more to it than just draughtman's skills, of course, yet she had never given that any thought before, and so she studied the painting: the horse's footprints in the wet sand, the splashes of water as the hooves pounded through the edge of the cold sea. How did she know it was cold? And the drops running off the gleaming haunches; the tail and mane whipping up in wet streams. 'I love this,' she whispered and with some discomfort realised that she'd never actually thought about Henry before, not really. She knew she liked him a lot, loved that rare wide smile, which transformed him. If only he could smile more! But they did have a certain quietness between them. Now she wondered if his paintings revealed things about him that he kept hidden. Were they his escape from loneliness, the discomfort she had noticed when he was around a certain kind of person? Animals were no threat to him. She noticed how tension simply eased away from him when he was painting. And, out loud to herself, 'I don't think anyone really understands you. Certainly not that Phoebe.'

For the first time then, standing in front of the black stallion, she was shocked to suspect that his secret self went into the paintings. Secrets from her? Oh yes! The paintings were much more than mere technique. She'd been shallow in her response to his work. And it came into her head that she never really thought about anyone else. Not deeply. Not caring about what made them tick or what they felt or they needed to hide. Was that true? Was she so self-absorbed? Pushing her unkempt hair off her face, she tossed these thoughts aside. They annoyed her. And like a spoiled child, she wanted to chuck her stick across the room. 'Anyway, I feel something different about, Frank,' she said aloud. 'I know that.'

She moved from the window seat to the chair in front of her easel; she always sat down, unlike Henry, and her paintings were small in comparison – this one was twelve by eight inches. Beside the chair was a low stool on which she put her paints, water in a jam jar and a selection of small brushes and pieces of charcoal. She outlined, sketched, in faint, loose movements with the charcoal before she began to paint. She kind of just let it all flow, nothing exact – how could flowers, leaves, whatever, be exact? She just let her hand, arm, glide the charcoal, as if feeling rather than seeing. Anyway, for good or bad that's how it was for her. She never painted hard lines, and she allowed the colours to melt into each other, which created shadows and depths.

The yellow of the lilies was not just yellow. She squinted at them, eyes half closed, and she could see pale lemon and orange, even suggestions of green. They were so much more than yellow. The white jug would remain unpainted; just the white paper, dappled and shaded by the bluish grey washes which ran and soaked into the paper.

First it would be the jug, then the flowers, and finally a smudgy background and darker shadows beneath the vase. Sometimes she painted the edge of a table with a cloth hanging loosely and crookedly. It just depended. But now, after the first wash of water and bluish shadows to give the jug solidity, she had to stop, for the light was fading, the evening sun moving round and away to the side of the house.

Gabriella had left her supper ready: spinach, cheese and ham pie with salad was waiting under a plate at the end of the table. There was the usual bowl of fruit – grapes, apples apricots – and she knew there were two small strawberry tarts in the fridge.

Sometimes she carried her supper into the garden, if her leg allowed her to walk carrying a tray, but tonight she was unsteady coming down the stairs. She would eat in the kitchen. And then the phone rang.

When she heard his voice, it was as if she was skipping again, skipping and hopping along the sand in the wind and the spits of rain, picking up those precious pebbles and running back to Da and Ma, who were laughing with her as they waited in the long, shaking grasses on the edge of the beach.

'It's been so long, Frank.'

'Yes, Sorry . . . a lot's been happening.'

'But are you OK, Frank? It's been such ages.'

She listened to him; the calm voice, but unnaturally deep and steady; something was up.

'Kitty's not been well. No, it's OK, she's better, but . . .'

And then she had to put her hand over her mouth as he asked if they could come over for a couple of weeks, perhaps more. Could she cope with his sister and the kid? He, of course, would stay in his flat above the shop. He wanted to finish off the work in her studio. That was important. But he couldn't leave Kitty and Daisy behind just at the moment. 'Explain when I see you.' And he had to pack up all his stuff, arrange for his tools, as many as possible, to be transported home.

Home! He said 'home'.

'Are you really not going to stay here any more, Frank?' How quickly the skipping came to a halt.

He told her about the cottage he was renting, would perhaps buy. How he was going to set up his business there. He had already bought a van, and the owner of the farm, Mr Wilkinson, was leasing him one of the barns for his workshop.

'Mr Wilkinson?' With a slight scream. 'You've got to be joking, Frank. No! You're joking! I can't believe it, Frank. Not Tom Wilkinson. You don't mean Tom Wilkinson of Wear Farm? It's not possible.'

'Why isn't possible, Alice? Is there a problem or what?'

'Oh my God. Oh my God! It's just that ... You've got to sit down! Tom Wilkinson and Maggie are my friends, Frank. Their daughter, Jo, and I went to school together and that's where I often went after school to ride a pony or ... and I got my kitten from them. I can't believe this.' Suddenly she was cross and resentful; he would be leaving her to go back to her life, her place, her people.

'I met your friend Jo,' he was saying.

Suddenly unreasonable, she was jealous.

'Nice woman. Lots of jewellery ... and she skips quite a bit. She's gone back to London now, but she was kind to Kitty when she was around. But now,' he told her, 'Kitty is friends with Laura' who looks after the horses.'

'Don't know her.' Could he detect her sulky tone? 'Do you realise how close you are to Da, to my home there? Just a few miles.'

No, he hadn't realised, hadn't had much time to think, but yes, it was a strange coincidence and yes, he would certainly go and introduce himself sometime and they could talk motorbikes! 'But about our coming over and them staying with you. Is it too much for you?'

It was unsettling. She was depressed that he showed no signs of regret in leaving. 'I'd really love it, Frank. It's no trouble. When? When, Frank, can you come?'

He told her he would try to get tickets for the end of next week. He'd let her know at once the exact day and time.

'Manuel will pick you up. 'And then she remembered. 'Henry may be here. But that won't make any difference. I'm looking forward to seeing you, Frank.'

# Epilogue

They were all sitting round the table, apart from Alice, who was still in the garden. Henry was particularly affable, with the occasional smile lighting his puzzled expression as he looked at the kid's painting that Kitty held up for him to admire. Kitty was looking well; she seemed happy, and Daisy had little freckles on her nose from the unusually warm sun. Gabbling in her high-pitched voice, she held up one painting after another that she had done with Alice in the studio. It was clear to him that Henry had taken to the kid. Now he was pushing back his chair and offering a hand to her. 'Come and see,' he said. 'Just for a minute?' He looked at Kitty.

'Come with me,' he repeated and waited as she jumped off her chair. 'See what you think of my paintings,' he was saying as he led her to his studio. 'They're not as good fun as yours, as . . .'and his voice disappeared behind the shut door.

'He's nice, isn't he, Frank? Nice to Daisy.'

'Very nice. Why don't you go and see his paintings?'

He'd finished the work here and had been busy selling his van and packing up what tools he could, ready to be transported back home. Tools were expensive to replace and he had to watch the money situation, for his busines was not yet established and he couldn't take anything for granted. He had his responsibilities.

Gabriella was fussing at the stove, going to the open kitchen door to see if Alice was coming. She was sighing and flustered as she began putting the supper on the table. Bolognaise, pasta, salad, cheeses and bread with a fruit bowl of apples, grapes and apricots. Ice cream and strawberry tarts were waiting in the fridge.

She hurried into the hallway, calling, 'Are you having supper or not?' and waited until the door opened and Kitty and Henry, followed by Daisy, who ran past them, returned to the kitchen and their places at the table.

'Can I start?'

'We should wait for Alice. I'll go and call her,' Frank said.

He began to crunch down the gravel path towards the wicker chair, where he could see Alice was sitting, her arms hanging loosely by her side. He called, 'Alice! Alice. Supper's ready.'

She sat forward slowly and looked up at him. He put out his hand to help her up. 'Supper's ready. Everyone's waiting.'

Tears were bubbling down her nose and she was licking them off her lips.

'What's wrong? Is your leg hurting?' He picked up her stick, which was leaning against the table, and offered her his arm.

She stood where she was, staring into the distance. 'I fell asleep.' And looking up at him, 'He came to me again with the pebbles, just like before, and I licked one to show him how shiny it became, and the colours, and he said, just like before, "They're my treasures." He didn't want a swing . . .' She put her hand across her eyes. 'You came just in time, Frank. You broke it, the dream.' She dropped her head onto his shoulder, sobbing. 'You broke it, stopped it. I won't be ill again, will I? I've been so happy with you here.'

He put his arm round her shoulders, felt her head against him. 'No, Alice. You're not going to be ill again. Things are so different now. Look at all your lovely paintings. You're getting to be famous, almost.' And he nudged her shoulder and was pleased to hear that familiar giggle.

They began walking back to the house. The kitchen lights were on now and Daisy's voice pealed out through the open windows and Alice squeezed his arm, 'I love her,' she said.

'So it seems. That's good.'

'But I did wonder ... do you think that just having a child here brought it all to the surface? Bringing that dream back? I don't want to go on about it, but just with you I can ask.'

He stopped for a moment outside the kitchen door and whispered in her ear. 'We all have our demons, Alice. Nothing's straightforward in this life. But you'll be fine. And you can be a real good auntie to that kid. I'll bring her over for holidays with you ... when she's older. You'll be just fine.'

'Will I? But you're going back soon.'

He couldn't look at her but prodded the ground with her stick to distract, distract from what he suspected was to follow. Yet he was prepared; he had his responsibilities for now. It was too soon and he too uncertain to tell her he loved her.

'Frank! I don't think I can manage without you. Sorry to say that when ...'

'There's an answer to that, you know.'

'What?'

'Well, spend some time with your Da. I'm sure he needs you, Alice. And one day you can buy a house near the beach in that seaside place you love – Seaham, you said.'

He rejoiced in her laughing. 'Did I tell you how, when I was little, I used to beg Da to buy a house there so I could run on the beach every day and look for pebbles?'

'Well, there you are, then. Nice dreams can come true. And this place will always be here for you. You've got it made, girl! And Henry will make sure you're OK.'

He felt her stiffen and wanted to change the subject. She'd never mentioned the word 'divorce'. 'And I'm going to get another boat, sometime, back home. I've got the bug. Moor it near that house you're going to buy. How about that!'

'Two boats, Frank? But you are keeping yours here, then?' The prospect of that made everything different. She could still be happy just knowing his boat was there.

'I told you, Alice. Come on! After all my work on it. We'll all go out in it, tomorrow. What do you think?'

She'd moved away and was leaning against the outside wall. 'Oh! Frank, that would be great. I think it would be great. But with life jackets?'

'Oh yes! Life jackets. I haven't forgotten. We all need life jackets, for sure. Life jackets!'

He put an arm around her shoulder and tapped gently.

'Trouble is, Alice, Henry needs a mother and you' – he nudged her shoulder – 'well, you're a child who needs another father!' He tried to joke and nudged her again, smiling.

'And you, Frank? You're like mother and father to everyone. So, what do you need, then?'

'No idea what you're on about.'

'Perhaps ... well, you know ... perhaps because of ... well ...'

'I have nothing to complain about, Alice, if that's what you're thinking.'

He didn't mean to shut her out. 'Come on, they're waiting. Tell you one thing, though. Make you smile. I visited your beach, Seaham. Just after I got my bike. First long bike ride. Picked up some pebbles there too!' Laughing. 'Chucked them back, though!'

Daisy yelled, 'Now can we have our food?' as Alice took her place at the end of the kitchen table opposite Henry, and he went to his chair opposite that Kit, who, with her long, dark curls, could be Italian. And Daisy. Well, Daisy was as blonde as sunlight. And Alice? Blonde as sunlight. They could be mother and daughter!

Gabriella said she was going now, and they all called thank you for a lovely supper, except for Daisy, who had her mouth full.

'After supper we're all going to speak to Ruby and Stan. Give them our news. See how they are. What do you think?'

'I want to speak. I love them.' Her mouth was still full.

He looked up at the little green vase, Mum's vase, and then round the table, all there together, and remembered how lonely and isolated he'd felt when standing on the edge of the playground in that new school, and how different it was now. This was family.

# Acknowledgements

I would like to thank several people: the late Piers Plowright, writer and broadcaster, for his friendship and encouragement; for all things carpentry Master Cabinet Maker Paul Crudge, Maurizia Trowel for help with Italian and Pinner police for advice. Last but by no means least for her meticulous care and great support my editor Kate Quarry and Muswell Press Directors Sarah and Kate Beal for their belief in this novel, their professionalism and help.

# A Note on the Author

Sylvia Colley taught English at the Purcell School. She has published two books of poetry *Juliet* and *It's Not What I Wanted Though*; and two acclaimed novels, *Lights on Bright Water* and *Ask Me to Dance*. Her poetry and documentary, *The Tale of Three Daughters*, have been broadcast on BBC Radio 4. She lives in Pinner, North London